A Pawn for a King
Ada de Warenne 1123-1178

A Novel

A Pawn for a King
Ada de Warenne 1123-1178

A Novel

Sarah Hinze

Three Orchard Productions

A Pawn for a King: Ada de Warenne 1123 – 1178

© 2019 by Sarah Hinze

ISBN: 978-1-7334242-0-2

Published by:
Three Orchard Productions
4435 E. Broadway Road #6
Mesa, AZ 85206

Cover photo: © fotolit / 123RF Stock Photo
Cover design: © Roger Fowkes, MiraLinx, LLC
www.Miralinx.com
Celtic Knot design: © Rachael Fowkes

Author: Sarah Hinze
Sarahhinze.hinze@gmail.com
www.sarahhinze.com

Printed in the United States of America

Dedicated with a prayer for the
advancement of human rights
throughout the world.

Some characters and historical events
have been altered for dramatic effect.

Who can find a virtuous woman?
for her price is far above rubies.
The heart of her husband
doth safely trust in her.
She stretches out her hand to the poor;
yea, she reaches forth her hands to the needy.
her husband is known in the gates,
when he sits among the elders of the land.
She opens her mouth with wisdom;
and in her tongue is the law of kindness.
her children arise up, and call her blessed;
her husband also, and he praises her.
A woman that fears the Lord,
she shall be praised.

from Proverbs, Chapter 31

THE ROYAL SCOTTISH SUCCESSION

(PERTAINING TO THIS BOOK)

10TH-13TH CENTURIES

Malcolm II 980-1034 (reign 1005-1034)

Bethóc m: Crínán of Dunkeld, Mormaer of Atholl

Duncan I 1001-1040 (reign 1034-1040)

Malcolm III Canmore 1031-1093 (reign 1058-1093) —— married *Ingibiorg Finnsdottir* (1st wife)

Margaret of Wessex 1045-1093

Edward 1068-1093	*Edmund* 1070-1097	*Ethelred* 1072-1093	*Edgar* 1074-1107 (reign 1097-1107)	*Alexander* 1078-1124 (reign 1107-1124)

Matilda 1080-1118 m *Henry* 1068-1135 King of England 1100-1135

Matilda 1102-1167 Empress of Germany m *Henry V* Emperor of Germany

m 2nd *Geoffrey de Anjou*

Henry Plantagenet 1133-1189 King of England 1154-1189

Geoffrey II 1134-1158

William 1136-1164

Mary 1082-1116 m *Eustace* Count of Boulogne

Matilda 1105-1152 of Boulogne, Queen of England m *Steven* de Blois King of England 1135-1154 (grandson of William the Conqueror)

Eustace 1127-1153

William 1135-1159

Marie 1136-1182

David 1084-1153 m *Maud* (reign 1124-1153)

Henry 1114-1152 Prince of Scots, Earl of Huntingdon and Northumbria m *Ada de Warenne* 1123-1178 (daughter of William de Warenne, II Earl of Surrey Elizabeth de Vermandie, who was the granddaughter of Henry I of France)

Malcolm IV 1142-1165 Malcolm the Chaste, King of Scots (reign 1153-1165)

William 1143-1214 m Ermengarde de Beaumont William the Lion, King of Scots (reign 1165-1214)

Ada 1144-1206 m Floris III, Count of Holland

David 1146-1219 m Matilda of Chester (ancestor to *Robert the Bruce*)

Margaret 1149-1201 m Conan IV, Duke of Brittany

Matilda 1152-1152

Duncan 1060-1094 (reign 1094)

Domnall 1062-1085

Foreword

When Sarah Hinze invited me to read early manuscripts of *A Pawn for a King*, I understood why this story would be a special one to tell. Ada de Warenne was an important British noblewoman, the mother of Scottish kings, and an ancestress to Sarah. What I found, however, as I read Sarah's treatment of her life story, was that Ada de Warenne became special and important to me, as well.

Ada de Warenne is one of the truly great and inspiring figures of medieval Britain. She was born in about the year 1123, daughter of William de Warenne, the second Earl of Surrey, and Isabel de Vermandois, granddaughter of King Henry I of France. Ada would marry Henry, Earl of Huntingdon and Prince of Scots, the son of the great King David I. Their marriage would produce two kings, Malcolm IV and William, "the Lion." The descendants of their third son, David, would eventually inherit the throne, beginning with the famous Scottish hero, Robert the Bruce.

Ada's marriage to Henry is what inspired the title of this book, *A Pawn for a King*. Much like innumerous other royal (and non-royal) marital unions throughout history, their marriage is often said to have been orchestrated as a peace deal (the Second Treaty of Durham) between King Stephen of England and King David of Scotland to help mend the rifts between the two peoples. Although Ada was only sixteen years old at the time and is often seen as merely a "pawn" in these proceedings, Sarah aptly illustrates how strong and independent she truly was and how her marriage to Henry was founded on attraction, love, and loyalty to each other.

Henry of Scotland was greatly beloved by his people and known for being not only physically handsome but also kind and virtuous. He was a good husband to Ada and, although he was often traveling on royal business, he was a good father to his children. There is evidence that his marriage to Ada was not entirely out of political convenience, but that she had truly captured his heart before their union was announced.

Orderic Vitalis was an English chronicler and monk, the author of *The Ecclesiastical History of England and Normandy*, and a contemporary of Ada and Henry. His view of Henry's feelings towards Ada was that "as Henry was much attached to Adeline, daughter of William, Earl of Surrey, he demanded her in marriage" (*Historia Ecclesiastica*, Vol. IV). So, although the marriage clearly served a political, diplomatic purpose, Ada and Henry's story was surely also one of true attraction, romance, and deep, lasting love.

Sarah also expertly depicts Ada de Warenne as the powerful, capable, and assertive woman that she was. As the Scottish Queen Mother when her sons were on the throne, Ada actively exercised her influence, rights, and powers for the benefit of her family and her people. In recent times, scholars have begun to recognize a movement in medieval Scotland that involved noblewomen exercising the right to adopt charters granting land and property to religious groups and other entities. This was a significant step in the history of women's rights and political influence in the region. Historian Matthew H. Hammond stated that "Without a doubt, the story of women's charters in Scotland north of Forth can be said to have begun with one individual — Countess Ada of Northumbria." Ada's charters included donations involving the abbey in Dunfermline, the priory of St Andrews, and other gifts in Crail and additional towns in the Scottish Kingdom of Fife.

When I learned of the magnanimity and kindness of Lady Ada and of the beneficiaries of her generous grants throughout Fife, I realized that, although I am not one of her descendants, my life had also been blessed by her. Partially because I do have Scottish ancestry, I decided nearly ten years ago to pursue an advanced degree at one of Scotland's greatest educational institutions, the University of St Andrews. My family and I adored the three years that we spent living in Fife. We visited many of the places where Ada de Warenne would have visited, including the picturesque fishing village of Crail where she lived for a time. Little did I realize, until now, that some of the locations that we learned to love and cherish owed their existence to this great woman, the beloved Queen Mother of Scotland's kings.

I hope you enjoy this delightful, historical novel by Sarah Hinze as much as I have. Let yourself be immersed, through her fun and fascinating prose, in the life and times of Ada de Warenne, a figure of immense importance in the history of Scotland. You will learn to love Ada and her family, to mourn with her through her many trials and sorrows, and to rejoice with her in her passions and triumphs. You will be encouraged by her courage and gain much from her example of a life well

iii

lived. I thank Sarah for inviting me to take this journey with Ada and enrich my life by learning about hers.

—David J. Larsen, PhD

Chapter One

Anno Domini 1139
The King's Palace at Westminster, London

Clove-covered pinecones crackled in the fireplace, stirring me awake. I smiled. No doubt Henry had ordered them on hearing of my fondness. He had an uncanny knack of noting and attending to the smallest of details—to the woes of his enemies and the delight of those in his favor.

I inhaled deeply, enjoying the pleasing fragrance. Was this a dream? Had I truly wed Prince Henry of the Scots but four months past?

But it wasn't a dream. I'd not dreamed at all last night. A rare occurrence. I dream most nights—dreams of the future and sometimes the past—if there is a lesson to gain. I've learned to not share details, fearing others would think me mad of wit. I alone am aware when my dreams come true.

I reached for my husband. My hand was met with naught but an empty bed and cold linens, *again*. Did Henry never take a proper rest? For an indulgent moment, I sunk my face into his pillow. A pleasant scent greeted me—a blend of leather and pine. It was proof enough that our marriage was real and a reminder to be up and busy myself, looking to my own duties.

I sat up, rubbing the sleep from my eyes. It was still early. A grey hint of the day barely lit the finely crafted shutters, and the bells had not yet sounded for prayers at dawn.

Henry was likely off overseeing details for our departure. I had best be about my own preparations, lest I delay the company. Or worse, they depart without me.

Throwing back the coverlet, I shivered as my bare feet met the smooth stone floor of the elegant bedchamber in the king's palace. At all our holdings in England, *Maman* had ordered furs placed at every bedside, both for warmth and comfort. It felt lovely to sink one's toes into the softness. I was surprised King Stephen hadn't thought to do the same here.

Maman. I'd only been wed a few months and already I was pining for my mother and father. But they were gone. My beloved *Père* had died the year before, and my mother, the great-granddaughter of King Henry I of France, had departed for Normandy after my wedding nuptials were complete.

I worried for her. Ever since Father passed, it was as if she had one foot in this world and the other in the next. How I missed our early morning visits. Ofttimes, she'd slip into my bedchamber before responsibilities of the day weighed heavily upon us. We spoke of trivial matters; advice on my attire, news of the family, humorous blunders made by visitors, menus to be seen to. They were but commonplace exchanges, peppered with laughter and embraces.

Being here without my mother made me realize such simple, stolen moments were the stuff and substance of a happy life. When I had my own daughters someday, I would continue the tradition.

This morning, there was no one to chat with about nonsense. The exquisite chamber was as silent as a tomb. Though my heart flowed with love for my new husband, parting from my mother pulled more at my heartstrings than I had expected.

A loud knock at the door startled me.

Likely it was a servant come to help me dress. I wrapped myself in a robe and opened the door whilst tying my sash. As I lifted my eyes, heat rose to my face. Henry's cousin stood in the hallway, gazing coolly at me.

Kelton's fine clothing bespoke his position, a great knight of Scotland and a favorite of King Stephen's. Henry had privately explained to me that Kelton was born as a bastard to Henry's uncle, King Alexander, but raised with a noble family. Through Henry's compassion, he'd decided to make Kelton steward to supervise our estate in the north. Tall, with dark hair and deep-set brown eyes, the physical similarities to my husband were quite striking. From a distance, one could hardly tell them apart.

I lifted my chin. "How may I help you, Kelton?"

"Good morrow, Countess Adaline," he said formally. "I took it upon myself to inform you that we shall soon be ready to depart. I was certain you would not wish to keep the company waiting."

Interesting. Any of the servants could have done so. What was Kelton truly about? "*Merci*," I offered. "May I ask where my husband has removed to?"

Something flickered in his eyes. "Prince Henry requested that you not be disturbed." Virtually admitting defiance to my husband's order, he proffered a smile. "But, by all means, Countess, take as long as you wish." Bowing with a flourish, he turned to leave without answering my question regarding Henry's location.

I opened my mouth to censure him, then closed it again. As I watched his departing figure, I decided it would not be prudent to antagonize him. Kelton could yet prove to be an ally or at least a source of information. Henry was often so occupied it was proving difficult to keep pace with his doings.

"Excuse me, my lord," I called after Kelton sweetly.

He whirled about. "Aye, Countess?"

My good humor felt strained. Either the man didn't know I preferred to be called Ada by family, or he was deliberately seeking to annoy me. Upon my marriage to his cousin, I gained the titles of Countess of Huntingdon and Countess of Northumbria. Titles were not necessary amongst close noble families. I suspected he was at ill will with me because I carried a family title by decree of the king.

"Again, *merci* for your thoughtfulness," I said. "It's most appreciated. Have the extra reinforcements Prince Henry expected arrived?"

Kelton hesitated. "At my suggestion, a contingency of our men will meet up with the extra guardsmen. Within a day or so, we shall rejoin the company with greater forces." Again, he had not answered directly.

"*We* will rejoin the company?" I questioned.

"I shall be leading the group," he clarified, his face expressionless. "Have no fear, Countess Adaline. We shall be well fortified before we are exposed to any real danger."

That news brought me no comfort. Our forces would be further reduced over the next several days. Tensions remained high. Stephen's position as the King of England was unsecured at best while Empress Matilda, his cousin and rival, was seeking to take the throne. Enemies were everywhere. Forces worked against King Stephen in the south from Normandy.

My new father-in-law, King David of the Scots, had fought for Empress Matilda, opposing Stephen's rise to power, but a new peace treaty had been forged between them, ceasing the hostilities. Part of the agreement between the kings included my marriage to Prince Henry. I had become a pawn for the king.

To ensure compliance with the treaty, my husband, Kelton, and a few others from baronies in the north were under obligation as hostages for a year of service to King Stephen. Hence our stay at the palace in London.

It was for this reason Henry readied himself this morning to follow the king to take Ludlow Castle, near the Welsh borders. I would follow as part of the king's company. So, why would Kelton leave the company more vulnerable at such a dangerous time?

"I will be down shortly." I nodded politely. "If you could be so kind as to give orders for my mount to be saddled, I would be most grateful."

"As you wish, Countess." He touched a finger to his forehead, then strode off down the passageway.

Was Kelton friend or foe to Henry? It was hard to say. I knew so little about those surrounding Henry and who, if any, I could depend upon. There was so much to learn in my new role as a future sovereign's wife. In spite of all my mother's advice and teachings, I hardly knew where to begin. One step at a time, I supposed. I pulled the bell cord to summon the servants' aid in dressing.

A servant arrived and dressed me in a surcoat.

I held a looking glass as she fixed my hair.

"Your dark auburn hair is beautiful, my lady. And so thick."
She sectioned it into two long plaits.

How Henry loved my hair. In the privacy of our
bedchamber, he was particularly fond of loosening my braids
and running it through his fingers.

I smiled in the knowledge that Henry found my appearance
to his liking. "*Merci*. At my mother's insistence, it has never
been cut."

"It reaches nearly three-quarters to the floor." She adorned
it with ribbons and gold combs and then arranged a wimple
and circlet on top of my head. "It's thick enough that there's no
need of weaving in horsehair as some of the other fine ladies
have me do to add length or fullness."

I stood and adjusted the wimple chin strap. I nodded my
appreciation to her. "*Merci*."

Two housecarls entered the chamber to remove our trunks.

I hurried down the wide halls and stairways of Westminster
Palace to the chapel for my prayers. When done, I entered the
Great Hall and ordered bread and cheese wrapped in a cloth
to consume later.

It was in this Great Hall that I'd first met Henry the year
before. And here that I danced with my father for the last time.
I sighed.

That evening, I had stood between *Maman* and my sister,
Gundred, as *Père* introduced us to many dignitaries. Several
wore long robes—the pelisse so favored in London. Ribbons
and medals of honor hung from those robes and added to the
splendor of the occasion.

I'd worn a dark green frock with silver thread embroidered
at the hem and along the edges of trumpet sleeves that hung
low, covering my hands.

"Hold still," my mother had whispered in my ear. She pushed up my sleeve and took my hand.

"Forgive me, *Maman*." Looking around the Great Hall, I tried to stay calm. Wreaths of multi-colored flowers decorated the room. Long tables lined the walls, brimming with dishes of fine foods such as white cheese covered with fennel seeds and strawberries. My mouth watered at the chicken, venison, and fish set out on large platters. Pastries of every kind, including custards and fruit pies topped with smaller pies to represent crowns, appeared so delicious. Plates were stacked next to mugs filled with ale and wine.

Across the room, I spotted a handsome young man. Once I realized he was gazing at me, I lowered my eyes and whispered, "*Maman*, there is a young man with King Stephen who is looking directly at me."

I despised men's stares, fearing they might be evaluating me as a possible bride because of my mother's lineage and father's wealth, for it was said *Père* was the wealthiest man in all of England. The word "pawn" echoed in my mind. I knew I would be considered for marriage as a pawn for peace, a pawn for wealth, a pawn for nobility. I expected to be ordered to marry a nobleman as old as Methuselah like my mother's and sister's first husbands.

"He's most likely Prince Henry of Scotland." Mother's voice broke into my thoughts. She slipped her arm around my waist.

Father invited, "Come." Taking Mother's arm, he motioned to Gundred and me. "We must greet King Stephen."

"I entreat you, Ada," Mother pleaded. "Greet the prince in a manner befitting your station."

Since I was a child, I'd heard my parents and others speak of Prince Henry, the son of Scotland's King David and Queen Maud. Curiously, Mother's eyes always lit up at the mention of his name. But at sixteen, if I had my way—which seemed less and less likely—I was not interested in marrying for a long, long time.

"How are you this fine evening, Earl Warenne?" King Stephen greeted. He was a thin man with close-set eyes, about forty, but not yet grey.

"I fare well, my Sire." Father turned to Mother. "You know my wife, Elizabeth of Vermandois, Countess of Leicester. May I also have the pleasure of introducing my daughter, Lady Gundred? You know Gundred's husband, Roger de Beaumont, Earl of Warwick." He placed his hand on my shoulder and drew me gently forward. "And this is my youngest daughter, Lady Ada."

Mother, Gundred, and I curtsied.

"Of course." King Stephen nodded and gestured toward the young man beside him. "This is the Earl of Huntingdon, Henry Mac David, Prince of Strathclyde, an ally." He chuckled as if it was a jest. "A *conquered* ally, that is. I've gained lands for England from his father in our last battle."

The young man did not smile at the quip as he bowed to my mother and Gundred and then to me.

Our eyes met, my face warmed, and I quickly glanced away in surprise. This prince was not an old graybeard.

While King Stephen spoke with my father, Prince Henry feigned interest in their conversation whilst stealing glances at me. Dutifully, I smiled in return. A strange tingling danced around my heart. I reached to rub it away.

"*Maman*," I whispered, wishing to escape both the prince's presence and the strange feeling. "My friend, Heloise, is across the room. May I be excused to visit her?"

"Ada!" she quietly hissed. "The king has not yet excused us."

Why had I said that? My shoulders slumped briefly, then I pulled myself to stand as a lady should. Trained in the etiquette of nobility, I should find myself honored to stand alongside our divine king. I rubbed moist hands on my skirt.

Prince Henry excused himself and moved toward Mother and me. Tall and handsome, he looked at me with warm, questioning brown eyes.

"Your bread and cheese, my lady." A servant's voice pulled me from the memory.

"*Merci.*" I took the cloth-wrapped bundle and walked away, still tingling from the memory of Henry and our first meeting. I discovered later that the king knew even then that I was to be his pawn for peace with Scotland and would soon order Henry to marry me.

What no one expected was for us to fall in love.

Chapter Two

As Kelton had said, I found the men-at-arms assembling in the courtyard, nearly prepared to leave. Clattering of horse's hooves, swords, and halberds rang against the stone walls of the palace. Hundreds of men, nobles, and knights, wore tunics of many colors, bearing insignias of heraldry. Mounted on a magnificent white horse, the king was already at the head of the company, his standard bearer flying the flag of St George's cross that waved in the cool Autumn breeze.

Several quadrigas and carts loaded high with foodstuffs, tents, blacksmith tools and other supplies, awaited vans carrying servants, my chamber ladies, and others.

Prince Henry had his own company of men-at-arms, but the only retainer from my family's contingency was Alexander St Martin. A head taller than the rest, I spied his muscular body as he sat mounted beside Kelton and several other able-bodied men. He'd been loyal to my family his entire life as had his father before him.

Henry was on foot, speaking with them. His presence alone often took my breath away. He wore a dark blue tunic, which accentuated his comely face and his muscular form. Over that, a heavy sword had been strapped about his hips, ready for trouble at a moment's notice. There was something about Henry—a charisma and a quiet confidence that bespoke well of his authority. He wore the mantle of Prince of Scots without posturing or seeking to curry favor—a dangerous game which so many at court continually played.

I caught his eye and he left to come to me.

"Good morrow, love." He approached, his brown eyes bright. His thick hair and beard looked as if they'd been trimmed that morning.

I yearned to reach up and touch his strong jaw, but surely such an intimate gesture would be inappropriate in the presence of the company. I instead gave him a bright smile. "Are these the men who will depart with Kelton?"

"Do not trouble yourself with such things, Lady Ada." A nasally voice behind me caused me to cringe. "Such matters are not of your concern."

I turned.

William Peverel, his wife a cousin through my father's family, stared at me with dull eyes. "But then, are we not all subject to the wishes of our sovereign? Our holdings, who we fight, and who we wed are not of our own choosing."

In one statement, he had insulted me, my husband, our marriage, and all the lands forfeit as a result. I didn't care for his insinuation that we were merely puppets, subject to King Stephen's whims or that he was actually right. I looked to Henry, unsure how to respond.

Henry's jaw tightened, then he laughed, dispelling the awkward moment. "Though subject to the king's commands—

as surely God wills — does not each soul still bear responsibility for his own choices, Lord Peverel?"

He took my hand. "When I took vows with Lady Ada, certainly I was the victor." He kissed my fingers lightly and looked at Peverel pointedly. "Would that all in your household be as fortunate to enjoy such a joyous union."

Peverel grunted and his face grew sour. "I will have no peace until my remaining daughter has married well." His crooked smile reappeared. "I believe your cousin Kelton is in need of a wife, is he not?"

Henry looked blandly on the man's obvious grasp at power. "The marriage of my cousin is not something I'm at liberty to discuss." His jaw clenched again. "Nevertheless, we thank you for your well-wishes and shall be on our way."

He steered me to my canopied van.

Glancing around to find Kelton, I wondered if my horse had been prepared. I spotted him laughing with a huddle of guardsmen. He met my eyes, then turned away, giving no response to my questioning gaze. Mayhap, he would have no fealty to me after all.

Just as Henry opened my van door, a young knight approached, leading my chestnut mare, Cooper. He bowed respectfully. "I apologize for the delay, my lady. This animal has a mind of her own. On this fine morning, she had no wish to be saddled."

As if she knew we spoke of her, Cooper shook her long mane and pawed the ground.

Henry widened his eyes. "You would ride today?"

"If that is acceptable to you?" I smiled at him. "I'm well experienced in the saddle and wish to enjoy more time at your side."

Henry's features went blank. I'd learned his expression became guarded when he pondered a decision.

"If you wish it," he answered shortly.

My heart sank. I'd supposed Henry would be pleased for me to ride with him. My father always had been.

Putting out my hand to take the reins, I noted the emblem on the young knight's tunic. "You are from the house of Giffard?" The family was loyal to my own.

The lad straightened, his nutmeg-brown hair cropped short on top, so common of the Normans. His golden-hazel eyes offered kindness. "Aye, your Highness. I am Hugh Giffard. My eldest brother has been granted lands north of Edinburgh, and my next brother desires to enter the priesthood at Haddington." His grin displayed a chipped front tooth. It didn't seem to make him self-conscious of his smile and somehow made him more likable.

Prince Henry seemed bemused with the lad's enthusiastic response. "And what is *your* desire, Hugh of Giffard?"

Giffard took on a more serious expression that made him look older than I had first thought, mayhap just younger than Henry, about a score and one. He bowed formally. "My desire is but to serve you and your lady, sire."

Henry studied the young man for a moment then turned to me. "I've watched Giffard at practice and also his skill with a horse. Although Norman, he swears fealty to the mac Davids." Henry looked pointedly at Giffard again.

"Aye, your Highness." Giffard grinned confidently. "I do, indeed."

One of Henry's men nodded at my husband. "He's as loyal as any man you'll ever find."

With a smile, Henry said to me, "As you're probably aware, his family has connections to the Warennes. The Giffards along with your grandfather and St Martin's grandfather, all fought at the Battle of Hastings with The Conqueror. With that history and his fine skills, I've appointed him as your personal guardsman."

My shoulders slumped. Clearly Henry didn't wish for me to ride with him.

He put his arm around me. "Unfortunately, my love, at times my duties will not permit me to be with you as I would prefer. However, Giffard can remain at your side at *all* times during this journey." He raised his chin with regal authority. "Will you not, Hugh of Giffard?"

"Indeed so, your Highness," Giffard promised earnestly. "I shall protect your lady with my very life."

As if he had expected as much, he gave Giffard a curt nod, grasping both his forearms in a gesture of homage. Giffard did likewise, and Henry said something to him that I could not hear, and in all seriousness, Giffard inclined his head.

"Trust me." Henry returned to me; his voice soft. "This is for the best just now, particularly with our decreased numbers."

"As you say." I was still unsure.

"Have no fear, my lady, I shall provide you with good company," Giffard said. "I will regale you with fantastical tales of renown deeds."

I sighed inwardly. Having several brothers, I knew what manner of tales they relished the hearing of. Still, I understood what Henry was about. His time and attentions were better spent strategizing with King Stephen and his men, than indulging the self-centered whims of a dour bride. The work he was doing was important.

Surely he was the man I'd dreamt of when but a young girl—the man who would help bring God's peace to the land.

I smiled to acknowledge Giffard's offer, then curtseyed low to my husband. "Your Highness," I said formally. "Might I then have your leave to ride for a time with Sir Giffard and enjoy the fresh air?"

A look of esteem grew in Henry's eyes and he smiled approval.

In that moment, I discovered few things in this world—and naught in the next—I would not do to earn that look from him again.

His deep-brown eyes shone in playfulness. "Aye, *Your Highness*," he said with mock seriousness. "Do enjoy the *fresh air*. At least, I hope you might, once we escape the bounds of London-town."

Caught! There was no place on God's great earth viler-smelling than the crowded streets of London.

Henry moved close enough for only me to hear. "Of a truth, Ada, your support means more than I can express. Certainly, it's more than I dared hope for." He looked at me earnestly. "God Himself smiled on me when He gave you to me in marriage."

His words of praise made my face grow warm. Would that I never gave him cause to be sorry for having wed with me. So pleased was I that he felt it was God who ordained our marriage and not the king, I couldn't give answer. But I managed to grant Henry a most favorable smile.

Once settled on my horse, I waited with Giffard as the group readied to depart.

My mare danced about, anxious to be going.

"Easy, Cooper." I patted her on the neck. "We shall be on our way soon enough."

A servant led forward Henry's grey-dappled warhorse.

Henry shook his head at me before he mounted. "I cannot understand why anyone would name a horse. That's like giving a name to a cart or a sword." Winking at me, he mounted and said to Giffard, "Does *your* horse bear a name?"

The young man had barely gotten into his saddle and appeared unsettled by the question. "Well, not truly, your Highness."

Henry chuckled. "See Ada? A man of sense." Grinning, he surveyed his men. "We shall move out shortly. I'll give leave to Kelton, see to our carts one last time, and bid a final farewell to Lord Peverel. Unless you would prefer to speak with him, Countess Ada."

I smothered a laugh. "Oh, nae, I believe I will serve best by remaining here with the valiant *Monsieur* Giffard at my side." I gave a nod to Giffard, who coughed in embarrassment.

After some minutes, King Stephen signaled the trumpet to sound.

A priest offered a prayer to bless our journey, and the king's group departed with him at its head, Kelton close behind.

Other companies marched out slowly. Not ready, Henry's men-at-arms took some time before we left the palace grounds, joining at the end of the long regiment and eating the dust of those before us.

Giffard and I rode amongst a small group of guardsmen near the rear of Henry's company. Giffard sat tall in the saddle, attempting to look fierce and regal, as a royal protector should.

"Are you also of the Giffards who serve my sister Gundred and her husband at Warwick Castle?"

"Aye, I am, my lady." He smiled his chipped-tooth grin. "We are kinsmen."

I chuckled but felt a strong sense of security with this young man. His family had served mine for generations. God was favoring me with protection, I was sure.

Behind us, my empty van lurched along, pulled by its matched set of Flemish stallions, followed by a mixed assemblage of carts and servitors—some riding, others walking. Ahead of us, I occasionally spied Henry mingling amidst his men-at-arms, talking, nodding, and laughing. My heart swelled. We were indeed united in love and in purpose. I hoped the plans he and King Stephen devised would usher in peace quickly.

Past the noon hour, Giffard and I rode slowly in silence through the busy city of London. I kept a cloth to my face to deaden the stench. It didn't work.

Outside the city, we reached harvested fields of brown stubble. The other companies had marched far ahead of us, leaving the air clean and sweet. Ahead lay a massive green forest, quiet and still.

A thought continued to pester me like an errant fly buzzing about my mind. At last I could hold it in no longer. I turned to Giffard. "You answered my husband, 'not truly.'"

He gave me a perplexed look. "My lady?"

"When Prince Henry asked if your horse had a name, you didn't say him nae. You said, 'not truly.'"

Giffard swallowed. "Of a truth, your Highness, this is my older brother's mount. At times he doth call him The Black Steed. But it's not a *name* in its self, my lady. He also refers to his stately palomino as The Tan One and his dappled mare as The Spotted Lady." Giffard cleared his throat. "It's more of a title than a name, but I cared not to prattle on thusly to the prince." He looked to the ground. "Should I confess when next I see him?"

I coughed to cover my laugh. "There is not a need." I attempted a sober nod. "I would say fairly that you answered in truth."

Giffard looked much relieved. "Countess Ada, may I ask how your mount came by the name of Cooper? Did she kick a barrel? Or did her color match that of a newly-milled stave?"

I smiled, fondly remembering my father's thoughtful gift. "Neither," I told him. "My father merely *acquired* her from a cooper." I grinned at Giffard. "Mayhap I am more like your brother than not." At this, we laughed together.

As we moved closer to the forest, we chatted easily of our homes behind and our hopes ahead. After a while, Giffard revealed, "I'm thinking that in time, I might care to wed a Scot lassie myself and strengthen the bonds between our kingdoms, as you and Prince Henry have done."

"I most heartily approve," I announced.

Giffard beamed. Then his brow furrowed. "Still, I fear the fighting is far from over. There will likely be much bloodshed yet to come. But perchance your union will bring years of peace in the northern borders. One could hope, thanks to you both."

That was the wish of my heart. "*Merci, Monsieur* Giffard, for voicing such kind sentiments."

He could not know how welcome such friendly words were. I supposed that I had not only gained an ardent protector in Giffard, but perchance a true ally for Henry and myself.

As the trees came up before us, a multitude of shouts rose up along with the scraping of swords being drawn from their scabbards.

Chapter Three

"To the forest!" one of Henry's guardsmen shouted.

Giffard smacked Cooper on her rump, sending us galloping into the woods. He and a few other men on horses closed ranks around me.

My heart raced. Where was Henry? I couldn't see anything through the thick bodies of men.

We dismounted and secluded ourselves in a thick copse of brush and trees.

As we waited, I became frantic with worry over Henry and the company. They must have already been in the forest when we were not. *God, keep him safe!*

We remained hidden in silence until I could bear it no longer. I whispered, "Giffard, send a man on foot to learn what has befallen the company."

Giffard moved quietly through the trees and found someone to do my bidding.

After what felt like hours, the man finally returned, closely followed by Henry and a few of his men.

"Praise God!" Henry cried, spotting me. "We thought you'd been taken!"

"I am well." I launched myself into his arms and he lifted me off my feet. "Thanks to *Monsieur* Giffard and your men."

Henry acknowledged their service with a nod, then set me down. He cupped my face in his hands, rubbing his thumbs over my cheeks, then released me and looked me over as if to ascertain that I truly was unharmed. When he seemed satisfied, he kissed me most ardently.

My face heated. When I could take breath again, I asked, "And you, Henry? Are you well? Is the company safe?"

Henry's shoulders sagged in weariness. He took me by the hand and towed me to a fallen log, his guardsmen trailing closely behind. He sat down heavily and pulled me next to him. Rubbing a hand across his eyes, he said, "All is well enough."

I steeled myself for the worst. "What has happened?"

He looked at me. "We were betrayed, Ada. Ambushed." He sighed. "A well-coordinated attack, both from within our ranks and without. Quite convenient as to the timing, I would say, when our numbers have just been reduced."

Our eyes met. His brows furrowed. "Your van was overtaken. They ran it off, believing you to be inside."

"But Henry, who would wish to capture me? And why?"

Henry kissed my hand. "My precious, Ada." His voice was sober. "When you wed with me, *my* enemies became *your* enemies."

I blinked. Already it had begun.

"I know not who is responsible," Henry went on. "But he had his hopes thwarted this day. He lost himself a goodly number of men in a bungled attempt to capture a lady's maid."

"A lady's maid?" Whatever was Henry talking about? Had he taken a blow to the head in the skirmish?

He grinned wickedly. "When his lads opened your van door, they were met with an unexpected surprise. The prize inside was not *you*, but rather a handmaiden in fine clothing."

One of my maids had been inside? "Who?" I cried. "Is she safe?"

Henry laughed out loud. "I would suppose so. It seems St Martin is quite fond of carrying a sword beneath his skirts."

St Martin had been in the van dressed as a woman? Where had the muscled giant found a gown large enough?

I swatted at Henry for jesting when I'd been so concerned for my ladies. But what a clever man he was. He had suspected such an attack and set a man in my place.

No wonder he was so unenthused when I expressed a wish to ride at his side. All along, he'd been hatching a subterfuge and wished to move about more freely, to keep me safe.

By the grace of God and the cunning of my husband, the plot had been frustrated. But would there be no end to such traps meant to do us harm? Our life together had barely begun. Would this be the way of things now? As my heart grew heavy, my gaze drifted downward toward the side of Henry's tunic.

"Henry!" I screamed, pointing.

The guardsmen jumped to their feet, hands on their sword hilts, looking about for the danger.

Henry motioned them down and glanced at his tunic stained red with blood. "It's nothing, Ada." He shrugged. "A flesh wound. Not deep."

Was he telling the truth of the matter? "Are you quite certain?"

"I promise, my love. Another scar for you to kiss." He grinned.

I blushed at the mention of our second night of marriage when I'd counted all his scars, and he'd regaled the occasion of receiving each wound. Henry had been trained as a warrior knight since his youth and had fought in many battles.

He pressed my hand to his lips again. "I'm well enough, although I cannot say as much for those who attempted to take you. I wish I knew who was behind this deed and how they came about the knowledge of our forces being divided."

Who in our own company sought to do harm to Henry and me? Giffard and I exchanged a brief look.

He nodded slightly, as if to reassure me that he would keep an attentive eye.

The attack had come not long after Kelton separated from us. Was he behind it? Should I mention such a thought to Henry? Or would he be offended at the suggestion of possible disloyalty by the hands of his own kinsman?

For a time, I would hold my peace and wait to see what Hugh Giffard might uncover.

Chapter Four

We arrived at Ludlow Castle on a cold, blustery day and set up camp on the surrounding hills with well-furnished tents, provisions, and servitors. The fortress itself sat on a higher hill with a river to the west, a steep incline on the north, and deep rock-cut ditches to the south and east—a highly defensible position.

Two years before, after King Stephen had seized the English throne, he took Ludlow Castle from Gilbert de Lacy and gave it to Robert fitz Miles in exchange for promises of future political support. But a civil war between cousins, King Stephen and the Empress Matilda, soon erupted and de Lacy took his chance to rise up against King Stephen, acquiring Ludlow Castle again.

Wisely, King Stephen opted not to attack directly but rather lay siege to the castle. Our forces had taken the bridge over the river to the entrance of the hold and encircled the castle elsewhere.

It was hoped the peaceful assault would lead to surrender, though blood had already been spilt from those attempting to leave the castle. For the most part, however, Henry said it had been an exercise in boredom, waiting for something to happen.

A few weeks into the siege, Henry left with King Stephen to survey the castle walls under cover of darkness.

The camp at night was ever noisy with brawling, robust singing, and words not meant for a lady—keeping me awake. Hours later, I paced about the tent, cold and worried why Henry had not come. I was glad to be traveling with him, but he was seldom with me. I had yet to make friends, for no noble women traveled with us.

Suddenly, there was much movement and excited speech outside. Just as I was about to pull the tent flap, St Martin and Kelton with two other guardsmen rushed in, carrying an unconscious Henry.

I covered my mouth to stifle a scream. Tears gathered at my eyes. I hastened to Henry's side as they laid him on our pallet. "What has happened?"

St Martin placed a hand on my shoulder, his blue eyes trying to convey calm. "Apparently, the castle garrison had thrown a heavy grappling hook from the beacon tower, hoping to inflict harm at random. It came down on Henry, catching the side of his cloak. As they pulled on the hook, it pierced through his chainmail. Surely, if not for the quick action of King Stephen, it would have ripped deeper into his side and killed him."

"What did the king do?"

"He pulled his sword and slashed the rope, cutting it in two before Henry was yanked up further. As he fell with the hook, it sunk further into him, deepening the wound."

King Stephen entered the tent with another man. "This is my personal physician."

I moved aside.

The physician quickly went to work. With the help of St Martin, they removed Henry's chainmail and bloody tunic.

I winced as a cut was revealed above his left hip—deep, swollen, and red.

Kelton stood near the tent flap, pale, fists clenched.

The physician sewed the cut closed with a needle and a long strand of horse hair. "He's not bleeding freely. This is good." He covered the wound in a poultice.

They pushed Henry to sit and tightly wrapped his lower abdomen in cloth, covering the long laceration.

Pale and limp, he moaned as they laid him back down. "Ada?" He opened his eyes.

I knelt beside him and brushed his hair from his face, not knowing what to say.

Despite his pain, he smiled. "After a few days of rest, all will be well."

St Martin blew out his breath. "Did he hit his head as well?"

After everyone left, I couldn't sleep, worried as always. I spent considerable time petitioning God to protect Henry and heal him of his wound. Surely we had been watched over thus far, especially with King Stephen's miraculous action, sparing Henry's life.

When Henry developed a fever, the physician returned and placed fresh suckers above and below the wound to help draw out the bad humors.

I never left his side, caring for him personally and overseeing the physician's orders. But Henry did not regain his strength.

A few nights later, I was awakened by Henry thrashing wildly beside me. He raged against an unseen enemy, calling orders in a battle only he could see.

Supposing Henry to be suffering from a nightmare, I leaned up beside him and laid my hand gently on his shoulder to nudge him into wakefulness.

Quick as lightning, his strong arm swung up and struck me across the face and mouth, knocking me hard to the ground. The metallic taste of blood cloyed in my mouth.

Before I could recover, he rolled his body atop mine, pinning me beneath his weight.

"Help!" I yelled. "Giffard!"

Henry's hands went around my throat, as if to squeeze the life from me. I beat helplessly at his shoulders and squirmed beneath him, but his weight held me solid. I could not breathe. Blackness moved toward the center of my eyes.

Would I perish by the hands of my beloved?

Then, all of a sudden, his weight lifted off me.

I coughed and sputtered, sucking in breath.

Guardsmen poured into the tent.

Torchlight revealed a bucking Prince Henry being held down by three men.

Had the world gone completely mad? My eyes could not make sense of the scene before me.

"My lady!" Giffard stood gaping, his face pale with horror. He averted his eyes.

I blinked. What was the matter with him? I looked down. My chemise had been torn. Before I could react, a fur was tossed over me and tucked securely beneath my legs. Then strong arms lifted me from the tent into the cold darkness of the night.

Troubled voices mumbled all around the camp.

What did it all mean? My head and throat pained me greatly. My stomach felt sick. In a tent, I was set down carefully on something soft. I rolled on my side and retched, again and again, until my innards had nothing more to offer. I fell back, exhausted and weak.

Cloths dabbed at my face and lips. Women's voices whispered softly around me. It sounded like the angels in heaven singing, but I could not understand their words. Something cool was laid on my cheek and face. Then shock, pain, and weariness combined to overcome me, and all became as night.

Choked by a dark, evil force, I screamed, "Help me, Henry!"

"I'm here, my lady." But it was Giffard who answered.

I opened my eyes and my maid stepped aside to allow him closer.

As his face came into focus, I was flooded with relief. All was well. I was safe. I attempted to rise, but the throbbing pains in my head forced me down. I closed my eyes again. "Where is Prince Henry?" I whispered, my throat burning in pain.

"His Highness is, ah, *resting,* my lady." Giffard sounded troubled.

I peeked open my eyes again. I didn't recognize the tent. Sunlight streamed through the cracks in the cloth door. It must have been mid-morning at the least. So late, and Henry was *resting?* That was not his way.

Then, I remembered. It had not been a nightmare. Henry had sought to kill me. I could not deny the throbbing of my head, the aching of my throat, the pain of my swollen lips.

"I would see him," I said to Giffard.

"My lady, I am not certain—"

"I will see Prince Henry at once," I ordered in the regal tone my mother used when dealing with balky servants.

"Of course, my lady. I shall return presently."

Giffard left and quickly returned with another guardsmen. As they helped me from the tent, both at my sides, the bright light felt like an arrow shot through my brain. But it mattered not. I had to know what had become of Henry. Why had he hurt me? What was Giffard keeping from me? Was Henry dying? Or—already dead? I shuddered, stumbling.

The men tightened their hold on my arms.

When we entered my tent, they set me on a padded stool at Henry's side. His face was pale as linen, but his chest rose and fell. He was alive.

I wept.

The physician hovered nearby.

"What is wrong with him?" I whispered hoarsely.

The physician cleared his throat. "His wound has putrefied, your Highness." His voice dropped. "I fear he has contracted blood poisoning."

Nae! I'd heard of that. My brothers called it the battlefield fever. Few recovered from it. Madness came first, followed by death. My heart sank.

As if sensing my presence, Henry murmured, "Ada," without opening his eyes. "What fine falcons. Let us take luncheon."

I stared in horror and sorrow. Reaching to touch his forehead, I was shocked to feel his skin as hot as coals. At least I could take small comfort in knowing Henry had not intended to harm me. The fever made him delirious. He thought I was an enemy.

Would he die?

It had not been six months since we wed. I'd not yet found courage to tell him of my dream—and the children who would be ours. My monthly courses had recently come upon me, so no child as yet lay within my womb.

Surely, God would not take this fine man from me. Not yet.

As the day waned, Henry didn't improve. It was determined best to move him to a local inn in the morning in hopes that quiet and rest might help restore him to health. A bed was prepared in a quadriga pulled by four horses, where he was carefully laid by his men.

I sat at his side, keeping cool cloths on his head, holding his hand, and offering such encouraging words as I could manage. I had never felt so helpless.

As we lumbered along the rutted road, the jostling briefly lifted him into consciousness. He opened his eyes and looked blearily in my direction.

"Henry!" I cried out. "Can you hear me?"

"Aye, my love," he rasped. Then he faded away again.

Eventually, with the rocking rhythms of the quadriga, my eyes drooped in weariness, and I found myself in my heavenly dream once more. Henry and I walked through a beautiful garden rimmed with tall golden grass. In the middle of the garden, there stood a considerable tree with an enormous canopy of leaves with a stone wall behind it. The canopy provided shade and protection for several children beneath. Some ran about, playing games, laughing, and enjoying themselves, whilst others sang together in celestial tones. The smallest child, a dark-haired lassie, approached Henry. Then she turned to me. Her mouth didn't move, but I somehow heard her thoughts and felt her emotions. She didn't want me to be sad. When the time came for Henry to leave, she would join him so he'd not be lonely. She smiled at me with loving eyes and reached for Henry to pick her up. When he did, she threw her little arms about his neck.

The quadriga jolted, jerking me to wakefulness.

Was it a sign that Henry would die? I fell to my knees and pleaded, "O, God! I beseech Thee, do not take him from me! Not yet!" Tears coursed down my cheeks as I pleaded again and again.

But the heavens remained silent.

Eventually, my sobbing stilled. A sense of peace rose within me. After a few moments, I felt no fear. Somehow, some way, I knew in my heart my beloved would live.

For now.

Had not God brought us thus far?

Surely, our lives were safe in His capable hands.

Chapter Five

The quadriga came to rest in front of a roadhouse inn. Kelton and St Martin hurried to carry in Henry's limp body while other guardsmen herded away the onlookers and cleared out the main hall.

They laid Henry on a trestle table and, per the physician's instructions, stripped away his tunic. The wound above the hip-bone looked dark and ugly, with red streaks flaring outward from it.

The physician said, "The wound must be re-opened so the prince's humors can be restored."

Kelton nodded grimly. "Hold him down."

Guardsmen surrounded Henry, securing his arms and legs, as the healer bent over him with a knife.

How could I bear to watch? Yet, I could not look away.

"Wait!" St Martin called. "Let the knife first be run through the fire. I've heard heat helps restore the humors."

The physician nodded. St Martin took the knife to the fireplace. Then once more it was lifted above Henry.

"Not too deep!" I cried out.

Giffard and St Martin shared a look. The men closed ranks around Henry that I might not witness what was happening to him.

I clasped my hands in silent prayer and held my breath.

A deep moan displayed Henry's awareness and misery to the new wound inflicted.

His men held him fast. A stream of dark-red blood dripped onto the floor at their feet.

I swayed in lightheadedness and grabbed to the back of a nearby chair.

The physician took up a jug of strong drink. Although I couldn't see, I assumed he poured it across the wound because Henry went limp. The physician said, "The wound must be kept open for these next three days. Rinse it with ale once each day. Cover it with fresh linen cloths to keep out the maggots. That is all that can be done for him." He moved away.

Some of the men stepped aside, and I approached Henry.

He lay so pale and still. If not for the promise of God I'd experienced in the quadriga, I would have collapsed under the weight of worry and fear. But I believed Henry would live.

Kelton walked to the doorway. "Now we wait."

"And pray," I added.

Giffard came to my side. "If Prince Henry survives the night," he said gently, "he may yet have a chance, my lady."

"He will," I said with conviction. "He *must!*"

Henry was carried to a quiet bedchamber.

I followed behind.

Once settled, the only signs of life were the slight rising and falling of his chest and his steady breath.

Holding onto his hand, I continued to pray and speak words of love and encouragement. Sometimes I sang the lullabies that comforted me as a child.

Food was brought to me, but I sent it away. I had no desire to eat. Even the few sips of wine I took to appease my ladies hurt to swallow because of the squeezing my throat had endured. My stomach still felt ill from the constant throbbing of my head.

Late in the night, when the servants left us, I noted a small looking glass on a trunk at Henry's bedside. I held it up. My breath hitched. My appearance was like unto a poor child's nightmare. Deep purple marks encircled both eyes and smeared my cheeks and throat, and my lips had swollen beyond recognition.

When the prayer bell rang the next evening, it was clear Henry was growing worse. He looked paler than before, and his breathing had grown shallow. He'd not stirred even once.

On my knees at his bedside, I continued my petitions to the heavens, holding the crucifix of Queen Margaret, calling on the powers of God. Could I unite with the strength of Margaret's goodness? I recalled Henry's words when he gave me the cross on our first wedding night. "This was my grandmother's, Queen Margaret." He spoke reverently. "My mother and she were both noble queens of Scotland, as you will be someday."

The queens of Scotland. The future felt as overwhelming then as it did this night. I held up the silver cross etched in intricate design, attached to a string of silver beads. The beads draped through my fingers. "I love this Henry—such a sacred gift," I whispered to his still form. I remember holding it near my heart that night, trying to connect to those women whose station I may someday inherit.

A scuffle down the hall brought me from my sweet blur of memory. Curious at the angry voices at such an hour, I dragged myself to my feet, enduring the throbbing pain in my head brought on by movement.

Giffard stood at the side of a black-cloaked woman in the hallway. He stepped forward, explaining, "This woman is well known in the village. She comes to the forest to collect healing herbs—"

"Poisons, more likely!" Kelton railed loudly. "What *can* be done *has* been done. How dare you bring a witch into the presence of the prince. Would you curse him to hell before he dies?" Kelton held his hand on his sword, as if to strike and drive the woman away.

I looked to St Martin for guidance, but the knight inclined his head toward me, acknowledging it was my decision.

God moved in mysterious ways, did He not? At the very least, we could first hear what the woman had to offer. "Let her pass," I ordered.

Kelton shook his head in anger, but stood aside. Even he comprehended a wife held more authority than a cousin— more especially so with the enormous St Martin standing stoutly beside her.

After the woman passed, I clutched at Giffard's arm. "Do you believe she might help him?" I whispered.

"It's possible, my lady. She has a remarkable reputation. I feel we should allow her to examine him and consider what she advises."

She waited outside Henry's bedchamber, saying naught. Her cloak covered all but her eyes as if she was enclosed in a tomb. Her silence was astute.

I peered inside at the motionless body of my husband. He was barely recognizable as the strong young man he'd been but a few days earlier. In this thing, Kelton had spoken truly— it didn't appear as if Henry was going to survive.

I searched the woman's dark eyes. They weren't kind, but they were clearly intelligent.

She waited calmly for my command.

"I would seek your help," I told her. "If you bear no ill-will toward the Scots."

"All men are one on the death-bed," she answered.

That was no great assurance. Still, I knew not what else could be done for him. I had no doubt that Giffard was loyal to Henry. If he believed the woman was a trusted healer, I would extend that trust as well and seek her advice. While I kept a careful eye upon her.

I nodded for her to go in.

She entered the bedchamber. Taking off her cloak, she laid it over a chair. Her black hair flowed down her back to her waist. Lifting the linens covering Henry, she studied his wound carefully. She bent and sniffed at it. Then she hefted the jug from the side table and sniffed at its contents as well. Extending the earthen container toward me, she said, "Has this been used to cleanse his wound?"

"It has," I answered. "It's poured over the wound once each day."

"It has been tainted with poison." She held the jug beneath my nose. "Can you not smell it, your Highness?"

I knew naught of the scent of poisons, but it was pungent and did not smell as ale should. But before I could give answer, the woman flung the jug into the hearth, smashing it to pieces. The fire exploded in a blaze.

A cold chill slithered down my spine.

Someone was trying to kill Henry.

The woman turned to Giffard. "Go to the kitchens personally. Have water boiled. Clean water. And fetch a flagon of their best wine." She set her satchel open upon the trunk and pulled out pouches of herbs and small vials.

I watched in a stupor. Surely her aid would save Henry. *It had to.*

She worked tirelessly through the night. When the morning light peeked through the shutters, Henry had been washed from head to toe, the leeches removed, and his wound rinsed with wine and covered in an herb-scented poultice.

Bending over Henry, she lifted his eyelid. "It's time." She slapped his cheeks to coax him into sipping the boiled water Giffard had brought in open bowls.

A bit of color returned to his complexion. But he didn't awaken.

"I will return shortly," the woman said.

I nodded dumbly.

She left.

I brought the blanket up to Henry's chest and smoothed it over him. I took his hand.

His thumb moved slightly.

"Henry! Can you hear me?"

Grimacing, he mumbled, "must . . . rally . . . children." Then faded away again.

As I gazed upon his handsome features, I had the distinct impression I wasn't alone in the room. I glanced over my shoulder. No one was there.

After many minutes, the healer returned with a steaming mug in her hands. "He must drink this tea, every drop. It will make him sleep longer, but it's a healing sleep. Such will give him strength." She spoke as if instructing a slow-witted servant. "Remember, let him rouse on his own."

"As you say," I answered.

"When at last he wakes, feed him liver and black pudding and as much boiled water as he'll take." She handed me a small pouch. "Then steep more of this tea and let him rest again a second time."

"For how long?"

She frowned. "For as long as he needs. If the tea is allowed to work, he should be fit to travel in a sennight or so."

She placed the hot tankard into my hands and began to pack her things.

I sniffed at the cup. It smelled of garlic, lemon, and something like . . . old meat?

"Will this brew cause him pain?"

She arched her eyebrows. "Do not fear *pain*, my lady. Pain brings life. Hate is what you should fear. It's all around you. That is the true enemy which causes him harm."

What had this woman experienced in her life? I took a gold coin from my pouch and placed it in her hands. "*Merci.* I hope you've saved my husband."

A brief smile lit her eyes. She nodded and pulled a corked crock from her cloak. "Rub this on your face and neck to restore its beauty." She put on her cloak and was gone.

A short time later, footsteps approached from the hallway. Pausing at the threshold of the bedchamber door, Giffard said, "Has the herb woman left?"

"Aye. We must get Henry to drink this tea. Can you prop him up?"

Giffard called to a servant, who helped him prop Henry.

I blew on the tea to cool it. When it was lukewarm, I rubbed his cheek, praying he would rouse. "Henry, drink this. It will help you heal."

To my surprise, his lips parted slightly, and he accepted small sips of the tea. He grimaced at the taste, but still we managed to get most of the brew in.

It was not long before he again slept deeply. This time it did seem different than before. His skin was cooler, his breaths deeper, and his color had improved.

For the first time in days, Giffard smiled. "Take your rest, my lady. I'll keep watch over my lord."

"*Merci, Monsieur* Giffard." I was grateful beyond measure to this fine young man who had served so faithfully, found the herb woman, and cared for me.

Over the next few days, Henry slept well between short periods of wakefulness.

I hoped to delay him seeing my bruised and swollen features for as long as possible. I didn't want to explain that he'd caused me pain. Whenever he stirred, I spoke soothing words, but turned my face away.

Within five days of the healer's departure, Henry not only improved, but my bruised face had turned from a sickly green to its natural color.

Chapter Six

Propped up and dressed in a clean white linen tunic, Henry leaned his head against the bedstead. His hair and beard had been trimmed and washed. "Come here, Ada."

I sat next to him and smiled.

"My beloved." His tone was husky. "Can you ever find it in your heart to forgive me?"

I looked at him in surprise. "Forgive you? For what, pray tell?"

He gave me a sheepish smile. For one brief moment I imagined how he must have looked as a boy. "I've been told I hurt you on the first night of my fever." The childishness in his features departed and he looked me over carefully.

I cared little for being scrutinized so closely. My lips and face had healed but I'd been wearing the fabric of my wimple thickly across my neck to cover the bruises. His fingers grazed a still painful spot on my cheek.

I flinched.

"Look what I've done to you." He gentle kissed my sore cheek. "Know that I knew not what I did. I would never, in my right mind, hurt you."

Hearing it thus spoken brought stinging tears to my eyes. I bit on my lip.

"Sweet Ada," Henry murmured, as if calming a fretful babe. I laid my cheek on his chest.

"Your beauty has not departed, nor that which dwells in your heart. How can I thank you for caring for me day and night?"

I sat up and looked into his eyes. "There's no thanks to be given. I love you completely and could not be taken from your side by anyone. If it wasn't for answers to my prayers, I fear the weight of it all would have crushed me."

Henry gazed at me for another moment, as if considering a weighty matter. Then a mischievous twinkle grew in his eyes.

I knew that look.

"Well then, shall we see about having this dream of yours fulfilled?" he asked.

My eyes grew wide. I'd never spoken to him of my dreams.

He gave me a knowing smile. "Apparently, I'm not the only one with vivid dreams."

My face must have shown puzzlement for Henry laughed out-right. "You talk in your sleep."

My cheeks grew warm. What exactly had I said?

"I've but one question for you, love." His eyebrows arched. "In your dream, does our eldest lad bear hair of red, like unto yours?"

I narrowed my eyes. "How did you know that?"

"I'm not certain." He grew thoughtful. "But whilst I had the fever, at times it seemed as if such a lad was nearby."

Then Henry grinned. With surprising strength for one whose life had so recently hung in the balance, he pulled me to him. "What say ye? Shall we be about this business of bringing him to us?"

I laughed with him.

All would be well. I was certain of it.

Never one with much patience to lay abed, Henry grew restless and cross. It was a good sign. He was anxious to be up and about his duties.

It was April, and King Stephen had written. Henry's year of servitude was over, and he was no longer required as a "hostage." We were free to travel to our new home, Eads Hall in Northumbria.

No doubt the townspeople were sorry to see the need for their hospitality come to an end—most likely because of the coin it entailed. Still, our stay must have endeared Prince Henry to them. As we left Ludlow, they lined the road and bid our procession farewell.

Henry and I waved from the front of a covered van. Though pleased at the opportunity to enjoy his company, for his sake, I would have preferred him to feel well enough to move freely amongst our group.

With the rumor of Henry being poisoned during his illness, we had no shortage of guardsmen. At the head of our company, next to the standard bearer, St Martin rode with twenty soldiers, Kelton amongst them.

Close by my side of the van, Giffard rode upon The Black Steed with a fierce eye out for trouble.

I chuckled, but mayhap I shouldn't tease him so.

I would be forever grateful. There was no doubt in Henry's mind as well that Giffard was a true friend. It was his seeking of the healer that had saved Henry from the poison. In spite of all careful inquiries, thus far we'd been unable to determine who sought to destroy him.

Could it be Ranulf de Gernon, Earl of Chester, the man who Henry had told me felt cheated from his northern lands when King Stephen gave them to Scotland? Could he have a spy amongst us? Although Ranulf was a deceitful man, he held much power. His father-in-law was Robert, illegitimate son of the deceased King Henry, which also gave him very close ties to Robert's half-sister, Empress Matilda.

I shook my head remembering the hours spent with charts before me, showing the royal lines and all the Matilda's that came down through generations. My Henry's aunt Matilda of Scotland married King Henry of England. They were blessed with a Matilda who married the Emperor of Germany. When widowed, she returned to England still holding the title of Empress Matilda and now fought for the crown against her cousin, King Stephen.

King Stephen married yet another Matilda—of Boulogne, France—the granddaughter of King Malcolm and Margaret of Scotland, my Henry's own grandparents. Even Henry's mother was a Matilda, but thank heavens went by Maud.

Later that afternoon, I could wonder no more about Henry's enemies and broached the difficult subject with him. "If we find that Ranulf tried to poison you, will he pay for his misdeeds? Certainly, when your father learns of it, he'll be hanged, will he not?"

Henry shook his head. "Nae, he will not."

My mouth fell open. "But you are the crown prince of the Scots!"

Henry shrugged. "And Ranulf is English with ties to royal lines. Remember, we were at war but a year ago. Indeed, a great number of his fellow countrymen would rejoice had I perished."

"Surely not King Stephen."

Henry looked at me sharply. "King Stephen is simply fighting to hold his seat. He seeks to appease those favoring Empress Matilda's claim to his throne. Ada, this is the reason Stephen wanted our marriage—and granted control of Cumbria and Northumbria to us." He frowned. "Ranulf's actions would be considered as naught more than a dalliance."

I refused to acquiesce. "But if people knew how close you were to death—"

"Then they would think me weak," he replied seriously. "Nae, it's best to leave such matters in the past and look instead to the future." He shifted positions on the cushions. "The Treaty of Durham has created a significant change for Scotland. On one hand, it lends more security to our shared borders, but it also pledges Scotland's support in fighting mutual enemies and confirming existing alliances."

When Henry's father had invaded the north of England and besieged Durham, occupying Northumbria and Cumbria, he felt these lands were his right through his wife. King Stephen broke the siege, and in negotiations, King David acquired for

Henry the earldom of Huntingdon with Carlisle and Doncaster.

I nodded. "I see."

"My father is still loyal to Empress Matilda, his cousin. He spent his youth training in the courts of her father, King Henry. The war with Matilda is not over and many Scots do not want to fight for England. But the treaty binds us to that obligation."

I understood now the reality of his mindset. I gripped his hand.

He kissed my fingertips. "I fear there will always be danger in our lives."

"Name your enemies, for they are mine now too."

"Those who would seek to take the crown and scheme away the earldoms, and any descendant of the previous kings of Scotland—which seems to be many." He lightly chuckled in frustration. "Even Kelton, my steward, claims to be the illegitimate son of King Alexander. I'm committed to preserve the throne for my posterity and will fight for it if I must. That threat will become your cross to bear as well."

Why could we not live in peace? "Are you being threatened?"

"Always, my love." Worry lines creased his brow. "You're young and beautiful and have been sheltered from trouble. Forgive me for bringing strife to your life."

"I will stand by your side."

He smiled. "Scotland is a beautiful land. You'll grow to love it."

"I'm sure I will."

"It's not full of barbarians as the English like to say. My father has worked endlessly to strengthen Scotland by establishing churches and monasteries to improve education.

And most Scots have converted to Christianity, though much superstition of the past still lingers."

As the days of travel dragged on, Henry sometimes rode in the van to give his leg a rest but usually could be found at the head of the regiment with Giffard and St Martin, only the standard bearer going before them. The banner bore the new seal Henry had designated to honor the peace treaty and his recently bestowed title of Earl of Northumbria:

Sigillvm Domini Henrici
Comes Northvmbriae
Fili Regis Scocie

I glanced back at the carts loaded with food, clothing, and gifts from diplomats who had attended our wedding. These gifts included tapestries, fine cloth, hand-copied books, and various items for our new home at Eads Hall in northern England.

Now that Henry's service to King Stephen had been satisfied, many who were to be part of our household had joined us. Three carts carried families of other nobles attached to the mac David family and another included Dame St Martin and her belongings.

Several servants came with us on horseback. Maggie, my favorite lady's maid, Chadwick, her husband—Henry's equerry—and their twin toddling boys also joined us. Our retinue consisted of about sixty people. With so many, it would take many weeks to go the distance between Ludlow and the land of Northumbria.

Henry planned our trip to Northumbria not by sea but by land. With our large cargo, he reasoned that we would not find sufficient transportation at the coast to bring our supplies inland to Eads Hall.

I spent hours talking with Sybil St Martin. She had me laughing at her foibles as a new bride, her baffles as a young mother, and the peculiarities of men.

Sending scouts and messengers ahead to make arrangements, we stopped at monasteries and inns along the way. The monasteries offered quiet and privacy. The inns bustled with activity, reeked of odd stenches, and provided almost no protection. Occasionally, we found not four walls but our tents to sleep in during the nights.

As a child, I'd traveled this route with my parents on our way to other castles my father held, but at that time I didn't appreciate the beauty of the land or enjoy the beautiful lakes.

"Scotland has not had a queen for over nine years." Henry sat next to me in my van, resting his sore hip, whilst my maid Maggie and her twins—to their delight—rode his horse beside us.

I nestled closer to him. "Since your mother died."

"I hope you're not in too much of a hurry to become queen. I am praying Father will live a full life. I'm quite content to remain a mere prince."

I squeezed his arm. "I'm happy not to be ushered into the responsibilities of a queen for a good long while."

"Do not think to sit and watch. My father will want you to fulfill many of the duties as would a queen."

"But what of the Scottish people? I would assume some are displeased that an Englishwoman was chosen as your wife.

Would they not be happier if you had married a noble Gaelic lassie?" I hoped he would counter my protest.

"It will take little time to prove yourself to the Scots. If you do everything in your power to assure my success as prince, and eventually as king, they will love you." He grinned mischievously. "You can start by returning this." He kissed me and we fell silent whilst watching the green landscape.

I said a prayer, as I had every day since our wedding, that I could fulfill that foremost duty as Henry's wife—to bear children to preserve and protect the royal lineage. After all these months, I still was not with child and needed God's blessing. I headed into unknown expectations. Would the people like me? Would I be content in my new home?

One particular day, our caravan paused near a meadow of lavender. After walking a short distance to stretch my legs, I returned to the van, settled against a cushion, and began to dream. A little while later, Henry woke me.

The carts and van had rolled on, his horse walking beside us without a rider. Maggie and the boys had moved onto the cart bench by Chadwick.

I stretched to work out stiffness in my back. "I fell asleep."

"You've not slept well on this journey. It's what you needed."

I sighed. "I had my recurring dream."

"Ha." He settled closer. "Tell me about it before you forget."

I looked at him dubiously. "You promise not to laugh?" I'd told others of my dreams only to be hurt by their dismay and unbelief.

"I promise."

I rubbed my face and tried to bring every image back. I wanted Henry to experience it the way I had. "You and I stood in a beautiful garden surrounded by tall golden grass. In the middle of this garden, there was a tree with an enormous canopy of leaves."

"We were in Reigate." He smiled knowingly.

"Nae, I think not." I'd never seen such a tree at Reigate. "The canopy provided shade and protection for several children playing beneath. Some ran about laughing, whilst others sang together in heavenly tones. They sounded much like . . . like angels." When I spoke out loud about the dream, it sounded foolish.

My face warmed. I wanted Henry to believe it as reality. It felt that way to me. "The children were very happy to have the attentions of a kind man in a white robe, who played joyously with them. He had a curious bright glow about him."

Henry looked uncertain. "Are you saying it was the Christ?"

"I believe so." The realization amazed me. "But Henry, I feel the dream has symbolism."

"Aye. Then go on."

"You and I held hands, walking in the garden toward the children." I closed my eyes to try to remember the details. "The man seemed to know each child by name. As we drew closer, some of the children left the group to come to us, their expressions bright. The oldest was a tall, handsome boy."

Henry beamed. "A boy? This must be the one with red hair."

"Aye! I remember he had reddish hair and a shy smile. The children hugged and kissed us with exuberance. In my whole life, never have I felt such complete joy and love."

"So, they knew us?"

"They must have." I spoke carefully as I recalled the next part of the dream. "The smallest girl spoke to you. 'Father,' she'd said, if I remember correctly, 'I will return with you so

-50-

you'll not be lonely.' She hugged you, but then the dream ended. That is when you woke me."

Henry sat quietly for a moment. "Your dream is telling you . . ." He turned my face toward him. "Telling *us* not to worry about propagating the royal line. We will have many bairns to fill our humble castle." He kissed the tip of my nose. "Though the sobering part about my possible early demise . . ." His grimace was more of a silly grin. "I'll just have to stay away from those nasty grappling hooks."

I wasn't comforted by his humor. What the dream implied still troubled me.

Chapter Seven

On a stretch of road skirting Sherwood Forest, Henry rode horseback in his usual lead position behind the standard bearer. Maggie and her children traveled with me, and Chadwick rode the horse that pulled our van. Farther behind were more armed riders and the supply carts.

From the woods, a band of men in armor on horses charged, swords held high.

The van stopped abruptly.

My heart skipped a beat. *God, keep us safe!* Where was Henry? I quickly found him at the lead, sword drawn and ready to fight.

Metal scraped against metal as dozens of our guardsmen pulled their swords from scabbards. Dust floated up around me as they surrounded my van.

One of the soldiers immediately broke from position and galloped down the road the way we'd come.

"Where is he going?" My voice quivered.

Chadwick gave a look of great annoyance. "He was probably a spy. Coward!"

I nodded in understanding.

"Henry mac David!" the helmeted leader called out.

Henry held up his free hand toward his men. "We will not fight immediately, but be at the ready."

The invaders moved closer.

Their leader took off his helmet. His short blond hair spiked on end, and he glared at Henry and his knights with hatred. "Get off your horse, *young prince*," he spat the title. "Or I will drag you from it."

I tensed. Would there be a fight? They were far fewer than us, but still, I feared for our plight. Henry, St Martin, and many of our knights were not in armor whereas all those intruders who had just arrived were.

"I will not," Henry answered. "What is it you want with me, Gregory? did you expect me to be daft and not know you as one of Ranulf's men?"

Ranulf. The man Henry warned me about—the one who challenged his earldoms.

I perched the best I could on the front of the van to better hear the conversation.

Gregory shifted on his saddle, clearly angry at being recognized. "I will fight you here if needed."

"King Stephen has legally given me the earldom of Carlisle. I cannot relinquish it. If Ranulf has told you differently, he's a liar." Henry's voice tightened. "Tell him you're done being his fool underling."

"Stephen?" The man laughed drily. "That contemptible maggot has treated us all ruthlessly."

I gripped the edge of the van, doubting the men would come to a favorable resolution with just words. Gregory had obviously come to fight.

"You've been lied to and have lost all ability to reason. Even if you killed me, how could you possibly retain Ranulf's forfeited lands against King Stephen's army with your meager militia?"

Gregory scowled. "I will." His free hand went for a dagger. He held it as if to plunge it in Henry's heart.

I gasped and shrank back, closer to Maggie, under the canvas of the van. I prayed the knights would not let him get near their prince.

"Where's your young English bride?" Gregory sneered. "A pretty little thing, I've heard. Are you not going to introduce me?" He motioned with his dagger toward my heavily guarded van.

I shrunk closer to Maggie, hoping Gregory wouldn't make eye contact, and she rested her hand upon my shoulder.

A horse nearby shuffled about restlessly, as if wanting to charge.

Henry yelled, "Nae! Move aside. Let us be on our way."

Gregory swiftly dropped his arm that held the dagger, and his men rushed Henry.

I screamed.

Maggie pulled me further into the van, under the cover of only a canvas. I saw little through the front opening, but heard blade against blade.

The cart swayed and tilted, tumbling over.

Maggie screamed, and the children cried and clung to one another.

I fell onto my hands and then my face and chest, scraping my cheek across the canvas where it now lay on the ground. My wrists burned with pain. "Maggie!" I looked about frantically for her and the children.

Chadwick crawled to them through the rubble.

A sword cut across the canvas, bringing sunlight. One of Gregory's men jumped off his horse, grabbed me around the waist, and dragged me from the wreckage. His body reeked of soured sweat.

As he lifted me toward his saddle, I thrashed about. "Henry!"

His hold tightened as I struggled for freedom.

"Unhand me!" I cried.

Giffard, eyes as a madman, was suddenly upon us, holding the tip of his sword to the man's neck where blood oozed. "Let her go!"

If the man moved forward, he would suffer the blade.

"Free her!" Giffard demanded.

A man wearing full armor galloped up behind Giffard.

"Giffard," I screamed.

He dodged his attacker, but not quick enough to miss the blade that caught his arm.

My aggressor swung me, belly first, onto his horse and jumped up behind me.

In the confusion, Gregory's men retreated, galloping into the forest—me with them.

Henry was flung across another man's horse, unmoving.

I screamed his name.

St Martin lay on the ground.

Outdistancing our men-at-arms, we stopped, and I was yanked off the horse.

I fell to my knees. Pain shot into my hips.

Horses could be heard in close pursuit.

Gregory pulled my chin up and held his dagger to my throat. "Follow no further, or I'll kill the countess," he yelled.

St Martin, blood oozing from his head, reigned in his horse. Pine needles and dust flew into the air. He held up his hand and shouted to the others to halt.

Gregory called, "I'll kill her now if you don't stop your pursuit. Turn around and go home. Your prince and I have business to discuss." He spoke in a smooth voice one might use to dine with the king.

"If you harm Prince Henry or his bride, I will kill you personally." St Martin's tone was a low growl.

Kelton said nothing, but did look as if he'd battled—blood on his hand.

"Who are you to threaten me?" Gregory thundered. "Now go!"

To my disbelief, Henry's men turned their horses and left us behind. How could this be? I thought them loyal men who would fight to their death.

St Martin glanced over his shoulder, trying to tell me something with his eyes that I didn't understand.

Jerked to my feet, a thick lasso was settled around my waist and cinched tight and my hands tied behind my back. Where was Henry? I couldn't see him nor Gregory. "Where's my husband?"

"Be still and quiet and no one will hurt you," a stranger said, his breath as putrid as rancid meat.

Bile rose to my throat and I forced it down as a sudden strength filled my chest. "Are you willing to have two kingdoms upon your heels? Does your life mean naught to you?"

He grunted and boosted me onto his horse, getting up behind me. "If you insist on asking questions, I'll knock you senseless as I did your husband." He pushed a hood over my head.

And everything went dark.

Chapter Eight

The rough rope binding my hands dug deep into my wrists. Breathing was foul and difficult under the hood. Fighting was futile with no hope of escape. The band spurred away in a blur of muffled sound. The galloping horse almost jarred me unconscious. With the way the horse swerved to and fro, along with the occasional brush of leaves and branches passing near me, and sometimes against me, I guessed that we rode deeper into the forest.

I had no idea of Henry's fate and prayed he was only unconscious as the braggard had said.

We thundered on. The merciless ropes and straps around me burrowed deeper, the unbearable pain at last relieved by the welcome intrusion of unconsciousness.

Suddenly, I was pulled from the horse. My feet hit the ground and I collapsed, tears burning my eyes. How long had I swooned? I listened for Henry's voice, even a sigh or a moan.

"Bring them in here." Gregory's voice.

Yanked to my feet, someone half-walked, half-dragged me into a darker space that echoed like a cave and dropped me onto the damp, cold ground. A soft moan came from ahead, bringing hope that Henry was alive.

Someone bound my feet, shuffled away, and within moments all sound had gone.

"Is anyone here?"

No sound. Nothing.

I trembled so violently I could not control the spasms. My wrists burned where the cords bound. "Someone, help me." I sobbed as a baby would. "Henry, come for me, *mon amour*." I shook until I finally slept.

When I awoke, I listened closely, holding my breath. I thought I heard labored breathing close by. *God, if it be Henry, keep him alive.*

When I awoke again, sunlight penetrated my hood, but the cave was still cold. My throat ached from dryness. My arms and legs throbbed; my wrists burned. I stretched swollen fingers and tried to move, causing a sharp pain to my head. I cried out.

"Ada?" Henry's voice bounced against the rock walls. "Ada, is that you?"

"I'm here!"

"I'm bound, and something is over my head. I cannot see you. How do you fare?"

I'd never heard him sound so troubled, and I quivered.

The crunch of heavy footsteps silenced us. The steps stopped right before my face.

I tensed. He smelled of rain and leather.

He paced around us. "My men have done well," a man finally said.

"Ranulf?" Henry coughed. "What is it you want with me?"

Ranulf scoffed. "Return the earldom of Carlisle, which was my father's and now rightly mine, and I will let you go. If not, it's unlikely you'll ever be found."

"There will be no returning lands that are rightfully mine. It will never happen." Henry's voice tightened. "Your father surrendered Carlisle when the earldom of Chester was bestowed upon him."

Ranulf laughed drily. "Stephen is no king and what he's done is illegal. He's stolen my lands the way he's stolen the throne."

"As I told Gregory, even if you killed me, how could you possibly retain the lands with the ruffians you call a militia? If Stephen doesn't kill you, my father will." Henry sounded weak, but his thought process stayed sound.

"*If* they find out who killed you." He chuckled falsely. "I think we'll let the heavens decide."

What could he mean? I swallowed, but it lodged in my dry throat. I coughed, almost suffocating under the hood.

"If someone finds you here, then all will be as it should. You'll return to your lands, and I'll not be bothered by malicious rumors that can never be proven." He laughed again. "If no one finds you, perhaps your father will believe your union was cursed and return my rightful lands. The whims of royalty—as likely to bless as to destroy."

"Ranulf," Henry sounded desperate. "Free Ada. She has done naught to deserve this fate."

"Alas, she has been a witness to it. Whatever happens to you Henry, she will share in the consequences." His footsteps faded away and silence filled the cavern.

"Ranulf!" Henry shouted.

"Will he return?" I asked, afraid of the answer if it be either aye or nae.

"I know not." Henry answered hoarsely. "Tell me you are not seriously injured, my love."

"Not seriously. My wrists burn where the ropes hold me tight."

"Are your feet bound? And do you have a hood over your head?"

"Aye," my answer came out a whimper. I bit my trembling lip. Henry didn't need me to be weak. I cleared my throat. "I believe I can roll to you."

"You stay there. I'll come to you." Henry began the effort, but I could tell by his grunts he was hurting more than he had let on. Nonetheless, he battled on, inch by inch, until at last his cords bumped against my fingers. "I need to . . ." and he said no more.

"Henry?" Had he lost consciousness from the exertion, or was he injured and lost too much blood? "Henry," I yelled.

No answer.

I tried to loosen his ropes—picking and picking at them— until my swollen fingers became numb and raw, and I could feel something sticky. Blood.

Daylight faded. The ground grew so cold I could hardly bear it. How long could we survive in this cave?

"Rest now," Henry's voice was weak but tender.

"Are you awake?" I cried.

"In and out. My head hurts."

"I cannot loosen your ropes. Can you do mine?"

I felt his fingers move lightly against mine, and then he stilled. His breathing came as if in slumber.

Ignoring the pain, I abandoned the knot I'd spent much of the day working on and heaved my body forward to lay on my stomach. I heaved again and rolled to the other side. I did this until I was against the cave wall, then pushed myself to a sitting position.

It was not fully dark, but close. I cried out to God in both prayer and anger. *Call for help.* The thought came unbidden. "Help!" I yelled, my throat as dry as sawdust. I cleared it and swallowed a few times. "Help!" I screamed again, and my voice echoed from the walls.

The light was nearly gone. I hadn't heard Henry make a sound for the last couple hours.

"Help us! We are trapped in the cave. Help!" Tears flowed freely down my face.

I heard a faint sound. An owl? I couldn't make out words. Or had I invented the noise out of desperation?

"I think I heard her over here." A voice came louder.

"In here," I screamed. My throat felt as if it tore open.

A light brightened around me, and footfalls rushed in. Many footfalls.

Someone fell to my side and untied my hood, pulling it from my head.

Giffard with St Martin, holding a torch, kneeling at Henry's side.

"Is he alive?" I feared the answer.

"He breathes, my lady." St Martin looked at me with an expression of a child waiting to be scolded, his face swollen and red.

Giffard too held a look of guilt. His injured arm had been wrapped in cloth. He unbound my feet, lifted me to stand, and turned me toward the wall. As he untied my hands, I collapsed against the cool rock, crying out.

"Forgive me, Ada," he said, his voice full of compassion.

I didn't correct him in the use of my name. The ropes finally fell free. I curled and stretched my fingers but could not feel them.

Others helped St Martin untie Henry and carry him from the cave. The jostling seemed to bring him to consciousness. "Ada," he called weakly.

Giffard wrapped his uninjured arm around my waist, and I leaned heavily on him as he led me outside.

The men put Henry on his feet and balanced him against a rock wall.

"I am here." I lightly touched his hand.

His face was pale, his hair matted in blood, but his breathing was regular. His tunic had blood about the shoulders, but it was dried, not fresh.

A guard brought me a jug of water. I grasped it with swollen hands and fed it to Henry.

He drank deeply, and I knew then we would fare well.

I drank next. Water never tasted so sweet. It soothed my burning throat.

When my thirst was sated, Giffard took the jug from me and poured it on my wrists. I winced, but the coldness was a godsend.

"How did you find us?" Henry asked, his head between his swollen hands, eyes half-closed. He spoke quietly, as if a loud noise might burst his ears.

St Martin said, "We followed the horse tracks until the rain and the thickness of fallen pine needles gave no more clues. We've been combing the area since midday. If your lady hadn't called out, we might never have found you."

Henry actually smiled. "I married well . . ." His words faded.

"Have you brought a cart?" I asked.

"Aye," a guardsman said. "It be close this way."

Henry was laid in the cart, and I sat at his side. Someone covered us with blankets. As we moved through Sherwood Forest toward the setting sun, a sudden calm rested upon me. "I give all praise to You, God. I am in your debt, for You have saved my love again."

Henry's hand touched mine gently. "I promised to protect you, and I failed." Disappointment was evident in his words.

"It was not your fault." I started trembling again and could not stop.

"We shall give our foes no more chance to attack us unaware."

Chapter Nine

We lodged near Yorkshire at Conisbrough, a castle my father once held that now belonged to my brother, William, the Third Earl of Surrey. I rejoiced for the peace and safety of its walls. Here was a place I was familiar with, yet it seemed to be in a past that was no longer mine.

Henry grew stronger each day. Our wrists healed after a fortnight thanks to ointment I had left in the crock the forest healer had given me in Ludlow. I kissed the new injury on Henry's head more times than I could count, along with all his other scars. But still my monthly courses came.

I was eager to start traveling again. Impatient to arrive at my new home. King Stephen's wife had heard of our kidnapping and sent more men-at-arms to secure our escort north.

Once again, the sound of cart wheels slapping the packed earth when it was dry and horse hooves squishing through mud when it rained, seemed never-ending. As we journeyed along rutted roads en route to Northumbria, I shared stories with Henry of when I'd traveled here as a child with my parents.

The days grew warmer as we moved into June. We again stayed at one of my brother's holdings—Sandal—to give the horses a good rest.

Though grateful for the layovers, especially the safety of familiar walls at my family's estates, I was eager to have the traveling done.

One day in our van, Henry looked at me thoughtfully. "You have much work ahead."

I thought of the carts behind us, filled with wedding gifts. "I look forward to preparing our home."

"That as well," he agreed. "But I was speaking more of the people on our land."

I pondered his meaning. In the recent battles over Northumbria, atrocities had been committed on both sides. Ill feelings ran deep. Healing those wounds would be a difficult task but I'd help in whatever ways I could.

"I shall not mislead you, Ada. This is no easy situation. Those of English descent in Northumbria will be reluctant to accept me as their overlord—nor will they trust you, for having allied yourself to me. And as you are English, the Scots in the land will not trust you either. But if we are kind and faithful, doing all in our power to govern with fairness, in time they'll come to accept us. Our union will set the standard, showing that English and Scots can live together in peace." He lifted my hand and kissed it.

A few days later, it became apparent how far north we'd traveled. The roads became steep and uneven, increasing the difficulty of travel. Gone were the lovely rolling hills of home, laden with oak and willow. We'd entered a craggy land with rugged moors, open dry grasslands, and boulders covered with deep green moss.

I tried to stay cheerful but found little joy at the thought of dwelling in such a desolate land with so few trees with which the breeze could play. But wherever Henry was, that would be home for me.

I gazed at him beside me. He grew stronger each day, his head injury leaving no permanent damage. God had truly blessed us.

Giffard rode tall and straight outside our van. I imagined St Martin confident and in charge at the front of the party, as he'd been all these months. Kelton had stayed true to us, as did all those who would become our household in Northumbria. We desperately needed kinsmen, friends, the village people, and our servants—all vassals—to swear fealty to us in order to prosper and find joy and peace as God commands.

I awoke to a quiet morning, darkness just fading away, and no sounds of our company packing to move on. I stared at the tent above me. Weary of the travel and not having a true home, if it weren't for my love for Henry, I'd be miserable.

I thought back to our wedding day. What a joyous event that had been, yet seemed so far distant with its opulent festivities, silk fabrics, vibrant flowers, and delicious food. The morning had started in my chambers with Mother and Gundred helping me dress. I'd been so apprehensive that I couldn't eat my morning meal. I took to pacing the floor.

"Calm yourself, my lady. All will be well." Maggie laid out my wedding gown on the bed.

In spite of her effort, I still paced and wrung my hands.

Gundred touched the imported silk of the dress, as blue as the Reigate sky. "It's so soft, so perfect! And look, the seal of Warenne is on the overlay with its blue and gold checkered design. You'll be stunning."

I slowed my stride long enough to gaze upon the seal. "I requested it, wanting some way to honor *Père* and our heritage." I looped my arm through Mother's. "Maggie did a splendid job with the embroidery."

I peeked over at Maggie, who bustled with preparations as though she hadn't heard the compliment. She failed at her attempt to hide a pleased smile before ducking from the room.

"The emblem is not solely his," Mother said with a touch of defensiveness in her voice. "When your father and I married, he adopted my family's seal of the Vermandois Coat of Arms as his own. The blue and yellow checks became known as the Warenne chequer."

I stroked the embroidery momentarily but then resumed my pacing. Walking was the only way to relieve my nervous energy. "Then I honor both of you—the Vermandois and the Warennes on this day."

Maggie returned to the chamber and laid a pale-blue cloak beside the dress.

Mother admired the handiwork. "Oh Maggie, I'll miss you and your talents when you go with Ada to Northumbria."

Gundred looked at me with admiration. "With Henry in his ceremonial robes and crown, you and he will be a stunning couple."

I wondered how Gundred and Mother felt about me marrying a man close to my own age. Because of Mother's noble bloodline, for her first marriage, she'd been forced to marry at age eleven to a man she didn't know. He was forty years her senior. The legal age for girls to marry at that time was twelve. Her father obtained a special dispensation from the pope to accomplish the marriage. Mother bore her first husband—whom she did not love—eight children before he died. She then found true love with my father.

Gundred was assigned to marry at the age of fifteen. More compliant than I with the thought of marrying someone old, Gundred's wedding to Geoffrey de Hussey took place at Reigate Chapel. He stood tall and straight in his regal clothing but he was ancient. I stared in disbelief at his grey hair and wrinkled face. How could my parents have allowed Gundred to marry someone so aged? Had they forgotten how miserable Mother had been in her marriage to an old man?

I was blessed to marry Henry, even if it was for the same reason as Mother's and Gundred's first marriages. We were pawns—all three of us—because of our noble bloodline.

Mother again placed a gentle hand upon mine as she often did when I needed calming. "Stop fidgeting and hold still," she whispered. She pulled from a box lined with blue velvet a magnificent gold crown with delicate scrolling along the banding and rubies and diamonds set deep within dozens of *fluers de lis*. "I wore this at my wedding."

Gundred stepped closer. "Lovely!"

Later, we arrived at Westminster Palace at the appointed time and were escorted through the cheering crowds to the top of the palace steps. There we awaited the signal for the ceremony to begin.

My stomach fluttered as if butterflies were within.

Henry stood near the doors with his father. Even at a distance, his eyes were only for me and I smiled at him. He wore a purple robe bearing the Saltire of Scotland: St. Andrew's Cross and his own gold crown.

Many of my family—siblings, uncles, aunts, nieces, nephews, cousins—waited with us on the steps. The young boys wore black tunics and stockings and the girls' bright frocks with matching ribbons streaming from garlands of fresh flowers worn on their expertly coifed hair.

Accompanied by trumpeters, the magnificent doors of Westminster Palace opened and Archbishop Theobald de Bec came forward.

The crowd quieted.

The archbishop stood before me. "Countess Ada de Warenne, someday you may become the Queen of Scots. Do you promise to honor Christ and strive for His grace in all you do in your responsibilities of caring for mankind?"

"I do." The weight of my station descended upon me. *God, be with me. You are my first sovereign.*

The trumpeters played again and the throngs cheered.

The archbishop turned and led the way into the palace with my family following behind. The children before me joyously strew flower petals while ill-trying to maintain reverence.

As I neared Henry at the door he reached for my hand. When our skin connected it gave me an unusual feeling of strength. We followed the children along the path of petals through the Great Hall and into St Stephens Chapel. Passing honored guests, including King David, King Stephen and Queen Matilda, we stepped to where the archbishop awaited us.

We knelt on cushions embroidered with colorful motifs. Throughout the ceremony I couldn't control my shaking hands. Near the end I had enough presence of mind to look at Henry's handsome face. My heart thudded hard in my chest to see his expression of joy. He slipped a ring onto my finger and raised my hand to kiss the ring as a symbol of our union.

We stood, turned and bowed to our guests.

Mother's eyes overflowed with tears and Gundred's smile could have lit the darkest corner of the room. Her new and younger husband, Earl Roger de Beaumont, was next to her side.

King Stephen came to us and held up his hand toward the gathering. "Blessed be England and her sister Scotland. This day and this marriage have brought us together in peace for the good of our countries. I present to you Prince Henry and his beautiful wife Princess Ada of Scotland!"

The guests burst into cheers and applause.

After the ceremony we greeted our guests in the Great Hall as the servants brought in tables. On each, they placed fresh flowers arranged with white and purple heather from Scotland. They scattered peppermint leaves and other herbs on the floor to freshen the air. The room filled to overflowing with our countrymen.

At the end of the nuptial feast, Henry stood and addressed the group. He lifted his wine goblet. "We are grateful to all who have joined us on this magnificent day. I make a toast to our friendships, your health, and to my lovely bride."

An approving cheer went through the group.

He grasped the handle of a large meat knife and held it high. Its long, pointed silver blade glinted in the candlelight. "I am a Scot and the old Gaelic custom is for the betrothed couple to make a small cut on their arms and then press them together to signify blood union."

A hush fell over the room.

Suddenly uncomfortable, I smiled in disbelief.

Henry took my hand and pulled me to my feet.

Murmurings rippled through the crowd.

The sight of the blade caused perspiration to bead on my forehead.

"But . . . Ada and I will forego the ritual." He laid the knife on the table and gave me a teasing grin. "We'll seal our marriage with a kiss."

I let out the breath I held and laughed nervously.

Henry stirred on the pallet beside me, pulling me from my memory. He awoke with thoughts not like my own. "I'm determined to ride." It would be his first time on a horse since his head injury. "I'll go mad to travel in that canopied van one more time. I crave to see my new homeland from atop my horse."

"Would you object to me riding alongside you?"

"It would please me." His eyes shone bright with approval.

We rode through a windy morning. Having arrived in Northumbria days before, Henry's mood had changed from frustration to elation. He chatted about memories of his childhood and the customs of his people.

I enjoyed his energetic mood but somehow felt lonelier than ever. My mind kept slipping to the past. I was months from my home in Reigate and the lush hills and woodlands of Surrey. High atop the chalky ridge of my beloved countryside, I'd sit for hours and view the vast panorama of trees and knolls stretching for leagues in every direction. From that elevated position, I could see our quaint little church topped with a carved stone cross and wisps of smoke drifting up, heaven bound, from tenant's cooking fires in our village of Cherchefelle.

Reigate. How I loved that dear place. Our castle stood regally on a sandstone mound, proudly flying the blue-and-gold-checkered flag of the de Warennes. My home truly was picturesque and peaceful and perfect to my once childish eyes.

My favorite season was early spring when the blackthorn bushes bloomed, fairly bursting with fragrant white blossoms. One day, I had discovered two copper moths dancing on one of the stems, embracing one another with folded wings, sparkling in the sun. I remember wondering if my mate would make my heart dance so. It was my dearest hope and my deepest worry. I'd suspected then I would marry without love. How wrong I'd been.

Summers at Reigate had been glorious, full of flowers and green earth. The abundant trees of our grounds brought me great comfort—like friends. I often played in a shadow-latticed forest of tulip trees and weeping willows. The sweet fragrances invited me to climb their branches. I loved the largest so much I even hugged it and talked to it and fantasized it knew me. I sequestered myself beneath its sheltering arms to dream and think—my own secret garden to find peace when I was lonely or sad.

I looked out again at the barren place that was my new home. Hiding the sadness within, I smiled to Henry.

Though normally a treat to be on Cooper, today the skies clouded over, and a drizzle descended upon us. My mantle kept me dry for a time but eventually grew heavy with dampness.

Late in the day, the clouds finally parted, allowing the late rays of sunshine to color the skies in brilliant shades of orange and red. In the distance, the silhouette of a great building stood on the rise of a hill.

"Hurrah!" came cheers from the guardsmen around us.

"Henry, whose estate is that?" I stared at the massive structure.

He looked to the distant building as if he gazed upon the Promised Land. "It's Eads Hall. We're home, Ada." His smile should have cheered me.

I sat taller in the saddle for a better look. How utterly stark the grounds were. Could nothing be grown here?

We picked up the pace.

As we drew near, I could not help but notice the lack of singing birds that were so common at Reigate—warblers, partridges, doves. I supposed it was because of the lack of places to nest. "Why is there no shrubbery or trees around the manor? Is the land so harsh?" Inwardly I quailed.

Henry was not to be brought low. "It's a place of many sheep." He chuckled. "They tend to eat anything not protected with a stonewall."

Sheep. Another thing to learn. "And you spent many happy days here as a child?" I asked, seeking to bring good cheer.

He stared ahead wistfully. "In truth, I've never darkened its halls. This is the land of my mother's nativity and family seat, our inheritance denied us for many years. However, she spent her childhood here and indeed spoke of it many times."

I touched his arm. "Our children will grow here, as well."

His smile finally touched my heart.

Stonewalls could be built to keep sheep at a distance. Trees and flowers could grow. I settled into the saddle as I accepted my fate.

Kelton appeared at my side with a smirk. "Is it not wise to remember that even the sweetest roses have thorns? Shall you tell her the story of your grandfather, cousin?"

Henry held his lips taut. "I think not."

"Come now. It's best for Countess Adaline to know all the dark with the light." Kelton raised an eyebrow.

Henry said nothing.

Kelton shrugged. "Originally Ead's Hall 'twas a hunting lodge owned by his grandfather, Waltheof—the first Earl of Northumbria." It seemed Kelton was going to ignore Henry's sentiment to not speak of this particular past. "The earl met with an unfortunate demise. He was beheaded as a traitor for his part in the Revolt of the Earls against William the Conqueror."

I shuddered. No wonder Henry had not told me that part of his family's history. My grandfather had fought *with* William the Conqueror. I kept my expression neutral. "How awful," I said.

"Aye," Kelton went on. "It was said he was secretly buried in the chapter house of Crowland Abbey in Lincolnshire a few days' south. But when the chapter house burnt down and the abbot went to move Waltheof's body, he found the corpse intact with the severed head rejoined. Some thought it a miracle."

Henry's jaw clenched.

Seeing his irritation, I attempted to shift the focus of our discussion. "Who has dwelt here since his grandfather's untimely death?"

"For a time, Henry's mother Maud before her marriage."

Kelton looked as if he couldn't continue because the rest of the story was so amusing.

"And?" I asked.

Henry looked away.

Kelton scoffed. "Did you not know? Why, Ranulf lived here last."

Chapter Ten

It felt as if I'd been kicked in the stomach. I certainly had *not* known Eads Hall had belonged to Ranulf.

Kelton chortled. "Ranulf's parents built a defense wall, servants' quarters, stables and a watchtower. Mayhap why he's not well pleased over recent events."

So this was once Ranulf's? It was not a home to kill over.

Henry turned to Kelton. "Will you ride ahead and let the servants know of our arrival?"

"I suggest we leave for Edinburgh at dawn. Uncle will be anxious for our report."

Henry shook his head. "We'll leave in a few days. I want to determine that Ada has all she needs to be comfortable in her new home."

"Very well." Kelton urged his horse forward and rode off.

With a sympathetic look, Henry said to me, "I'll not be gone long. Less than a fortnight." He gave me an encouraging smile. "It will give you more time to set up the household."

My stomach hollow, I attempted to smile but failed as he left to ride ahead to confer with Giffard and St Martin.

The reality of being left behind in this austere place without trees, gardens, family, or friends weighed heavily on me. Without Henry, how could I bear it?

When Giffard broke from them and headed toward the end of the company, I tapped my heels and steered Cooper to his side.

He slowed as I came close.

"*Monsieur* Giffard, will you be staying at Eads Hall? With Prince Henry away, I would be most grateful for your assistance."

Giffard frowned. "My deepest regrets, Lady Ada. His Highness just now requested that I ride beside him to the palace and be presented to the king. But I shall return in a fortnight. Or if you'd like, I could speak to the prince and—"

"Nae," I interrupted. "I'm certain the house will be well staffed." My voice sounded empty. "Safe travels, my friend. I will fare well."

I pondered my own words. If the estate was "well-staffed," did that not mean with Ranulf's servants? Friends and family to those who attempted to capture Henry and me? I recalled the warnings of the strange herb woman who said to fear hate as it was the greatest danger. What lay ahead?

Lifting my gaze to Eads Hall the gloom of dusk darkened around us. My responsibility to Henry had brought me to a land very different from the days of my youth. How could we turn a house filled with death and hate into a safe and loving home for our future children? I didn't know. But somehow we must. "With God nothing shall be impossible," I whispered the words of Mary, mother of our Lord. Had not God planned this for me all along? I would not contend but instead comply to my fate.

I turned Cooper toward the hall. In spite of the difficulties that I may face, I felt a surge of hope for the days ahead. Thus far, God had been at my side. Would He not remain?

Up ahead, Henry had stopped to speak with a man who'd come upon us on the road. Seeing Henry perform his duties as laird gave me strength. Together, we would fulfill our destiny according to the will of God.

Henry nodded to the stranger who limped away.

As if sensing my gaze, Henry turned and rode up beside me. "I have a surprise for you."

I laughed at the elation on his face.

He dismounted and held his hands out to me.

I slipped into his arms, and he placed me on my feet. Leading our horses, we walked the short distance to the hall, my legs sore and weary from our long journey.

"It's been a long trip with more menace than we anticipated." Henry slipped an arm around my waist. "But I pray that now we can put that behind us."

"Aye." I wished to move ahead. "Yet, will there not be concern for our safety here, living amongst those who so recently have been expected to change their allegiance?"

He pulled me close. "Kelton went ahead to ascertain where the servants' and villagers' loyalties lie. Most who aligned with Ranulf have moved to Chester with him. Those remaining are local Northumbrians—simple folk for the most part. All will be well. I feel sure of it. Servants from my father's palace have also been sent from Edinburgh to assist, though I'm not certain when they'll arrive."

As Henry spoke, servants came out from the house and stables, filling the courtyard.

A large man in a plain-grey tunic pushed open the iron double-gates. Chains hung on them with an unclasped black lock dangling on the end, apparently to protect from outside dangers. Did they use the locks daily?

I shivered.

Henry's flag, with its insignia of gold, red and blue, hung over the entry, waving in the wind.

"Look behind us." Henry turned me about to see another group of people coming up the road as the sun set behind them. A few carried torches. The man with the limp that Henry had spoken to earlier was at the forefront.

Relief washed over me. Friendly faces were just what I craved.

Henry stepped onto a large boulder and addressed the gathering. "My fine countrymen, greeting and good wishes." He turned to me. "May I introduce your new princess, my beautiful and beloved bride, Lady Ada, Countess of Northumbria. Know that we plan to make our home amongst you and will make the land fertile once again. We desire peace and goodwill."

I was learning that Henry was a wise ruler who knew how to promote fealty from his vassals. I looked forward to watching the land become fertile and those who work it growing their own families. Food, land, promises of growth— all things that could bind us to each other.

Many smiled and a scattered shout of "hurrah!" went around.

My cheeks warmed. I attempted a confident smile and held up a hand in greeting.

Kelton stepped to my side.

Henry motioned to him. "This is my kinsman, Kelton, my steward, who will make his home here. God bless you for coming to greet us. Now, let *you* be introduced to us." Henry jumped from the rock. He drew close and whispered, "I hope your memory's bright."

One by one, the people came to their new liege lord. Introducing themselves and showing homage with a bow or curtsy, they demonstrated respect for us in their demeanor.

To each, Henry gave a personal introduction to me.

I tried to remember names, but feared I would not. Most were Saxon, but many Scottish names unfamiliar to me. I'd been raised with a French mother, and mostly French staff. Gaelic names had been unknown at Reigate.

I found myself especially drawn to the women who looked me in the eyes upon introduction, even if but a brief moment. I desperately wanted them to like me and to know I was now one of them, not a Norman outsider who didn't care about their needs and lives.

Along with children of all ages, we shook the hands of the chatelaine, doorkeeper, hunter, stable hands, bakers, a smithy, men-at-arms, and keepers of sheep. The kitchen staff was also substantial, led by a short French cook named Maurice.

I smiled inwardly, pleased I would have someone to speak French to and anxious to find out if he cooked the food I'd grown up with.

The bulging, white-haired Maurice's bow was more of a shuffle and a nod. I feared he'd topple if he tried a deeper bow. He grasped my hands as if I was an old friend. "*Bonjour*," he said, "for you, I *volontier cuisinière*."

I squeezed his hands. "I'll *prendre plaisir* every meal."

Maurice beamed, kissed my hands and then my cheeks.

I laughed with both gratitude and pleasure.

He left, and a young sprite fellow announced himself as the gardener.

For what garden? Ah. There was a lone grapevine growing on one wall. Hardly enough to keep a full-time gardener busy. Perchance the kitchen gardens lay elsewhere.

I overheard Kelton speaking to a yeoman. "It's our honor to have Countess Adaline here. She will bring strength with her well-breeding. From what I hear of her noble kinsmen, I assume we can expect great things. Her brother, Earl William de Warenne of Surrey, is one of the most powerful Norman nobles in England. How much of that power is from wealth or military finesse, I know not."

Startled by his remarks, I wondered if he sought to create ill will toward me amongst the assembled group and make me seem a person they couldn't become friends with—a recent enemy who'd killed their loved ones.

I moved closer to Kelton, saying quietly, "It's my blessing to be here. I pray that I may bring honor to Northumbria in every way possible."

Whatever Kelton was about to say, he decided against, clamping his mouth shut and tilting his head toward someone behind me.

I turned to see a young man wearing priest's garb.

He clasped hands with Henry.

"This is Chaplain Robert," Henry said, "the village priest. He'll lead prayers every morning and evening for you in our home. He lives with his mother in the house by the chapel."

Chaplain Robert smiled warmly and took my hand. "I'm at your service, your Highness. Call upon or send for me at any time."

Such a contrast his sincere words made to Kelton's polished speech. I sensed I'd found an ally in Chaplain Robert. I smiled at him gratefully. "I'm most pleased to be in your presence, Chaplain."

After this final introduction, Henry turned to the crowd. "We shall settle in and bring food into Eads Hall. Come in two days for a *cèilidh,* and we shall feast to celebrate our marriage and arrival to our new home."

Cheers went up from the crowd.

"Night is upon us, and we bid you to find the comfort of your own hearths. On the morrow, come to me with your service or concerns." Henry waved his farewells.

We entered our new home into a spacious entry hall that led to the great room where massive beams and joists overhead had been painted in interwoven designs of basket-weave knots. Each square of the coffered ceiling had been illustrated in a different stylistic design of a flower in blues, greens, golds, and reds. The deep browns of the paneled walls warmed the house, making me feel as if I could sink onto the settle and forget the past weeks of distressing travel.

Hands clasped, our new chatelaine, Mariam, stood at the foot of the stairs.

She would not look me in the eye. Was she one of Ranulf's spies?

"Welcome my lord, my lady." Her dark eyes remained lowered.

"Mariam," Henry said. "Lady Ada would like to clean from the long journey before we eat. Kindly show us to our chambers."

Mariam nodded. "Sire."

We followed her up a wide staircase that opened to a landing with several bedchambers. Servants carried trunks and satchels, making their way around us. A woman of few words, Mariam swept an arm toward the furthest door, indicating our chamber. Then she went on to assign others to their sleeping quarters.

Henry waited patiently in the hallway until the servants had carried in our belongings and left us alone.

Flickering firelight revealed a large, comfortable bedchamber filled with several chests, a doorway which led to a garderobe, and an inviting bedstead made of wood decorated with carved and painted ornamentation.

I ran my hand across the beds freshly laid linens.

Henry looked at me expectantly. "I hope you find this acceptable."

"It's perfectly wonderful!" And it was. With a shuttered window to invite the eastern light in the morning, a cupboard against one wall, and a grooming area with table, chair and looking glass, what more could I want?

Henry pulled me into his arms, giving me a lingering kiss. "Wash and change for supper, as I will do as well." He winked at me. "But I would see you later tonight, your Highness—hopefully in naught but that luscious hair of yours."

I heard servants shuffling about in the hall. "Hush, Henry!" I could not suppress a giggle. "What if someone has heard you?"

Henry laughed. "Let them hear. Then they will know of a certainty that I adore my beautiful wife."

Once we'd washed and changed, Henry took me by the hand. Together we descended to the dining hall where several long tables displayed a plentiful homecoming feast for our large caravan.

"A magnificent beginning, my lord," I whispered, looking over the hall.

Kelton stood at the front of the room where many women sat at the table. All the men still stood. Behind them, painted motifs covered the plastered wall and tasteful tapestries hung on the other two walls. A magnificent fire hearth claimed the fourth wall, large enough for three men to enter. Depictions of stags had been painted above. A roaring fire burned within, and the stone floor had been covered with fresh pine branches, bringing a pleasant smell. My soul cheered for the warmth of my new home.

Henry grinned widely. "Prepare yourself for a treat, my lady. The food of the Scots." He led me to the head table. "We shall enjoy mutton, swan, onions, cabbage, and apple and cherry pies, along with good old Scots' brew from Edinburgh."

Oh my! Would our French cook really prepare the food he hoped for?

An approving "Aye" rippled around the room and the men took their seats.

Our life together had finally begun.

Chapter Eleven

In the great hall, St Martin's wife, Sybil, stood at his side while their three little ones clamored at his feet. It softened the image I had of him as a proud warrior and warmed my heart to know he could come home to those who loved him.

Even with my travels concluded, I still expected evil just around the corner. If not for Henry, St Martin and Giffard, I'd have perished. They'd kept me alive, and now they were leaving for Edinburgh. How would I know who to trust in this mansion of strangers? Worse, I couldn't share these thoughts with anyone for fear that Henry's subjects would think I didn't trust them.

Henry must have enjoyed the familial scene of the St Martins, for he clasped hands with Giffard and said, "A man of your caliber should not ignore marriage too long. Mayhap my father will have something to say about that." He slipped his arm around my shoulder, squeezed, and declared with a wink, "I recommend it, my dear friend."

"As do we," Sybil added, elbowing her quiet husband to agree.

St Martin reddened and cleared his throat. "Aye."

Giffard's mouth rose in an awkward grin. "I...I'm most grateful, my lord." He ran a hand through his thick, cropped hair.

With a sheepish expression, Giffard ducked out the door. St Martin and his family followed.

Henry said to me, "In my absence Chaplain Robert will continue to come say prayers each morning and evening. Turn to him with any need. He's a trustworthy man."

"I will, *mon amour*."

Chaplain Robert had been faithful in coming, bringing with him his widowed mother. He'd already gained my confidence.

"Together, you and I will tour Northumberian holdings after you're more settled, but for now, Eads Hall and the household staff are your responsibility."

Somewhat dubiously, I glanced around my new home. "I was taught to do such things," I said with more confidence than I felt.

Henry brushed the tip of my nose. "In these few days, you've already begun lifting this dreary house into a place of order. You have my permission to do whatever you deem is necessary to remake this home to your liking."

Again, I looked around. "*Merci* for your trust. I'll do my best."

When they left, I headed for the stables to check on Cooper. I dared not ride without an escort. The thought of being alone in this wilderness gave me a shudder.

The day was warm and the summer sky cloudless. In the far distance, down a hill and across a brook, the morning light glistened off the stonewalls of the chapel of St John that served Eads Hall and the surrounding village.

As I rounded the corner of the manor house, I was surprised to find Cooper already outside the thatched stables tied to a hitching post by the well. Two large buckets and a variety of brushes occupied a bench beside her. As I grew closer, I saw that her tail and mane had been braided with blue ribbons. I hadn't seen Cooper look so stately since Reigate.

A stable boy walked by to retrieve the buckets. He couldn't have been more than ten.

"Did you do this?" I asked in disbelief.

"Nae, tweren't me," he drawled. "Da' F'ella, it were." He rushed off as though he'd been censured.

I had no idea what or who this "Day Fella" was, but I intended to thank him and followed the boy to investigate. I passed through the double doors of the stable and hurried down the long passage lined with horse-filled stalls. A gate at the end opened and out trotted a stunning white horse led by a woman dressed in a bright sky-blue dress so vivid I was taken aback. The cost of the garment made it clear she was at least of the gentry.

Not noticing my presence, she kissed the horse's nose. "You're a good traveler, dear Snowball. I brought you a treat because you're such a sweet soul." She held a carrot in her open hand, whilst stroking her horse's face from forehead to muzzle.

I was looking at a kindred spirit. She'd even named her horse. I moved forward, determined to meet her.

Almost to the ground in a grand curtsy before I was able to speak, she seemed to recognize me immediately.

"Rise," I said. "We have yet to be introduced. Have you recently arrived for a visit?"

"Nae." She kept her head down.

I was taken by her delicate nose with freckles sprinkled across. Soft light-brown curls fell over broad shoulders. A little larger than most women, she was stocky yet carried herself as a lady.

"I'm here to be of service to you, sent by King David. My name is Fenella."

"Oh, *Dame Fenella*." The stable hand's words suddenly made sense to me. "Then your husband is a knight?"

She shook her head, at last standing. "Nae, my father is a knight, but also King David's lord chamberlain, Herbert. And I'm still a maid. I was sent to assist with your staff and prepare for your arrival but was delayed by inclement weather. I was here in the spring but left a fortnight back to attend to my father's business."

"That is a shame. I could have used your help these last days."

Again, she lowered her head. "I returned late last night and did not want to wake you, my lady." She lifted her green eyes to meet mine. "But I'm here now and prepared to serve. I spoke with your husband before he rode out."

I raised a hand to pat Snowball's neck, but the powerful animal raised on its back haunches.

I stepped back.

Fenella pulled tight the reigns of the ornery mare and clucked with her tongue.

Snowball calmed.

Fenella patted her on the neck then gave me a half smile. "My apologies. She's been trained as a warhorse and can be aggressive. Is there aught I can do for you, my lady?"

I knew exactly what I wanted. "You can ride with me and show me the land." I smiled. "And I give thanks for grooming Cooper. She's never looked so fine."

She inclined her head and smiled conspiratorially, reaching for her saddle.

Within minutes we raced across an open field and all my pent-up worries disappeared.

Fenella held herself in the saddle like a man, galloping as though she and her mount were one, rivaling my own horsemanship. She led the way past a sea of grazing sheep that moved as a body to stay clear of the thundering horses.

We raced passed a wide river where straggly trees clung to dry leaves and then up a small rise where she reigned in, as did I.

The view allowed me to gaze over the entire area. I searched for a large tree, like that in my recurring dream, but saw naught like it.

We dismounted.

I was glad for a small copse of scrub oaks that dotted the landscape, assuring me the land was not quite as barren as I'd thought. I pointed to the steeple near Eads Hall. "St John's looks quaint by the river, does it not?"

She nodded. "The river is named Allen."

It curled to the west and was lost on the horizon.

Breathing the fresh air, my spirits lifted. "Reigate, where I grew up, had the river Wey, just about that size. The church sat south of the estate as though a perfect match to this one. Even the little hamlet with the cottages is remarkably similar." In the beauties of God's creations, my mind cleared, and my worry lessened. I could be happy here, couldn't I?

"That little hamlet, as you say, is Whitfield, where most of your servants come from." She sat on a boulder and smoothed her skirt. "Some of the house staff left with Ranulf's kinsmen. I was more concerned with loyalty than ability, so you may have noticed some of the servants, especially the young ones, are not yet trained for their duties. But with care and a little patience, I'll obtain a hardworking staff for you."

I bit my lip. "We've had our troubles already."

Dame Fenella got to her feet. "Has something happened?"

I explained in the broadest terms that I'd had the servants clean and rearrange the manor and how, when Henry came home, I'd led him to the kitchen for suggestions and overheard a young servant asking why the manor wasn't clean enough for a "spoiled English princess."

"Wait." She showed me her palms. "Let me guess. Henry became angry and sent her out the door."

I nodded, wondering at her familiarity with my husband's name.

"If he knew the amount of effort it took to get these good people to work at Eads Hall." Fenella huffed.

I stiffened. "Are they not loyal to the crown of Scotland?"

"Lady Ada." She stared at me as though I were a child. "Last year, many of the men from this small town were forced to fight for England *against* Scotland. A good number of them lost their lives."

I knew this, nodding at its confirmation.

"Can you imagine how it feels to have those who were your enemies now rule over you without any say in the matter?" Fenella became impassioned. "It's miraculous how supportive they've been. Although, who knows if their hearts would have turned without incentives."

"Incentives?" I asked.

"You don't think those people welcomed you on their own accord, do you?" Fenella laughed lightly.

I reared at the offense. This woman voiced her opinions openly and had also spoken to someone about our first day here. Had it been Henry? I couldn't decide if I liked her or not. "Perchance." I thought of the people at Ludlow. They had bid us farewell without encouragement, hadn't they?

"This past month, Chaplain Robert has been encouraging the village people to welcome you here." Fenella lowered her voice. "Each family willing to attend the *cèilidh* was compensated for their time with a measure of barley. Between the cost of war and the loss of many family members and sheep, they need more food."

"I've been concerned about what this might mean for the living conditions of the little maid Henry excused," I confessed.

Fenella shook her head. "I'm more worried about how it will affect the rest of the household and even the village. If they believe you and Henry are not grateful for their sacrifice, you could have an uprising. This is not Scotland. The English king is their overlord with King David having longstanding rights to the land. It will take time to win people's hearts."

"Then what shall I do?"

Fenella eased onto her saddle. "Follow me. We'll fix this, and then we'll give Henry a piece of our minds."

Shocked at her vocal disparagement of Henry, I again wondered if she were closer to the family than I'd first realized. Had she grown up with Henry? Since her father was the Lord High Chamberlain of the royal household, responsible for access to the king, it was very likely Fenella was very close to Henry.

She reigned in her horse at the first person she saw along the road—a woman with a basket on her arm.

The stranger bowed to me, and I acknowledged her by lowering my head, and wished I could remember her name.

Fenella dismounted and spoke to her quietly for a moment and then stepped on a rock and remounted her tall horse. Snowball huffed from her large nostrils, her brown eyes looking about.

"I've learned the servant that Henry dismissed is named Glenore and she lives alone with her invalid mother. Her father died in the war. They desperately need income."

We road on, nearing the outskirts of Whitfield and Fenella brought me to a small hovel made of stonewalls packed with earth and a turf roof at the end of a lane. An ancient oak, mostly dead and sparse of leaves, towered over the tiny hovel. Goats chomped on brittle grass nearby. We dismounted and tied our mounts to the bare branches of the tree.

Fenella moved stiffly. I wasn't sure if she was uncomfortable with this task or angry at Henry for creating the situation.

I cleared my throat, worried about adding emotion that may fuel the already frayed feelings. "I'd like to speak to Glenore alone."

Her eyes registered surprise. "And what will you say?"

Strange, this new friend who questioned me. "What's in my heart," I said. "I've served the poor since my childhood and carry no ill will about what she said of me."

"And if she physically attacks you?" Fenella put her hands on her hips. "You don't know what you're going into."

Looking at the fire behind Fenella's eyes, I imagined she could protect me almost as well as St Martin. "Very well, we'll go together but I'll do the talking."

"I'll stay close." She took her place behind me. "Henry would kill me if anything happened to you," she said under her breath.

I advanced toward the hovel.

The hanging sheepskin door shifted to the side and a lame, grey-haired woman stood before me, leaning on a branch for balance. "May I help ye?"

A scraggly cat shot out from behind her with a screech.

I jumped with a start.

It disappeared around the side of the house.

The old woman laughed. "Pardon. I know not what got into that creature."

Already feeling a bit nervous, the cat had my heart beating like a rabbit. I took a deep breath to calm myself, then inquired, "Are you the mother of Glenore?"

At my words, she squinted her eyes and stepped closer, scanning me from head to toe. Her face contorted, and she paused as if to discern whether it was safe to answer. Finally, she replied, "Aye." She then bellowed over her shoulder, "Glenore!"

The mother teetered a step, allowing Glenore to step from the house.

Upon seeing me, Glenore's eyes grew big with fear. She fell to her knees and clenched her hands together. "I beg of you, my lady, do not punish me!" Tears streaked down dirty cheeks.

The mother stiffened and squinted one eye. "My *lady*? Who are ye?"

Ignoring her question, I extended my hand to Glenore. "I entreat you, do not cry. I come not to punish but to speak with you." I sensed Fenella drawing closer.

Glenore remained on her knees, avoiding me with her eyes, looking confused and frightened.

I reached forward slowly so as not to alarm her and placed my hand gently on her shoulder. "Glenore, will you not stand and speak with me?"

Still avoiding eye contact, cautiously she rose. She wiped her tears and then her nose on her sleeve. At last she stammered, "For . . . forgive the disrespectful words I used, m . . . my lady."

Her mother huffed. "She certainly deserves the sackin' for her disrespect to ye, Countess."

The mother had at last figured out I was her daughter's former employer.

Despite her scolding, the frail mother tottered forward and smoothed her daughter's hair. "Be the lassie's father died last year, and me with this ailin' leg . . . we be in need o' the shillin's, m'lady. Cudna ye give her a good thrashin' and then give her another chance? I'll teach her to watch her mouth."

I nodded to the mother. "Glenore, let the two of us take a walk together."

Glenore glanced at me sideways as we went a short distance down the lane.

Fenella stayed by the mother.

When sufficiently out of their hearing, I said to Glenore, "Will you accept my apology?"

"M'lady, I was the one . . ." She again sniffled.

"I'm grateful for my good fortune of marrying Prince Henry and want to share it with you and others of this village. The prince is a good man and was protecting me by dismissing you. Kindly understand, I do believe we can get along. What do you say? Will you accept my apology?"

The tension in Glenore's face and body eased as if she sensed my sincerity. She looked into my eyes for the first time and nodded in agreement. "Aye, m'lady, nothin' would be finer."

I blinked, realizing I hadn't considered what should come next. I looked to Fenella at the other side of the yard for a clue, but she was deep in conversation with Glenore's mother and not looking my direction. Standing up straight, I said, "I'd like your services at Eads Hall."

Glenore appeared baffled. "But what 'bout Prince Henry? He be so angry at me."

I patted her hand. "You leave the prince to me. I'll figure something out." I secretly hoped Fenella had a plan, because I knew how upset Henry was. In my heart, I also knew I was doing the right thing, but that didn't make my stomach any less clenched at the thought of telling my new husband that I'd gone behind his back.

We returned to Glenore's home where her mother was surprised at my generosity. She insisted Glenore return that very morning. I'd hoped for more time to warm Henry to the idea, but the mother was so excited I couldn't disappoint her.

Glenore packed a few of her things.

Fenella, smiling broadly at the outcome of our visit, whispered to me as we walked to our mounts, "I might have had her wait a sennight before returning, but it's your call, my lady."

Fenella shared her horse with Glenore as we rode to Eads Hall. Seeing them riding pillion, it instantly reminded me of my mother's charitable heart. It had been on a drizzly morning in the autumn of my fourteenth year when Mother walked into the solar with an air of determination. "Ada, put on warm clothing and your cloak. We're going into the village."

I set aside my embroidery and looked out the window at grey, low-hanging thunderclouds. "But why, *Maman*? A storm may be upon us. With *Père* and William away, should we not stay in the safety of the castle?"

King Henry had taken to his sickbed and his earls called to his side. Father and William had gone straightway.

"Never mind the weather." She pulled on the cloak she carried. "We must visit one of our tenants. We'll take guards."

I stood and swallowed hard. *"Moi?"* I could see no reason to leave the warm fire. I wanted to finish the hem I was embroidering.

She glanced toward me before pulling up her hood. "You're no longer a child. It's time you learn to extend a kind hand to the less fortunate. It's your duty as a noblewoman."

There it was again, always the expectation, the duty that ran my life and kept me from having a girlhood. I wanted to stamp my foot and refuse to leave but I had to do as Mother said. I retrieved my cloak.

"Lowly" was what Cook and others called the tenants. They didn't learn French even though it was Frenchmen who ruled them. Here we were, nobles going off to visit peasants.

Chadwick saddled our horses and four of our housecarls mounted to ride as protection. As women, we rarely departed from our property because of the English sentiment against the French for ruling over them. Additionally, in recent months, bands of robbers—both native and foreign—roamed the land.

I mounted Cooper, whose golden mane was kept braided at my insistence. A bag had been tied to the saddle. "What are we bringing with us?"

"Provisions. We don't know what needs we may find."

Our guards rode both behind and in front of us. Moving slowly through meadow and woodland I took in nature's beauty and smells. The village of Cherchefelle with its diverse surprises was like another world from my castle life. We passed wheat fields, flocks of sheep, a mill, and in a small marketplace, vendors sold baskets, shoes, and other wares. In feudal pattern, these peasants worked one-fourth of their time on my father's estate and also worked their own land to pay their rent to him each quarter.

Mother looked the other way as we passed a one-story building with a sign over the door that read "John Kelley's Alehouse."

Months earlier, she'd tried to convince my father to shut down the alehouse because of questionable activities. Father upheld the man's rights and the pub stayed open. As we passed it, I tried with little success to keep my eyes focused ahead on the narrow dirt road.

Traveling a path through a thicket of trees, we soon arrived at a row of hovels made of stone, packed with earth. A few tent-like shelters also stood alongside the road. Stenches from sewage and garbage made my stomach turn. A dog looking hungry and weak raised his head from a doorstep, stood and stretched, then followed us.

"This is the place," Mother said to Edmund, the lead housecarl.

The dwelling she indicated appeared in much need of repair. The doorstep was only a wooden box, a tattered blanket serving as a door.

Dismounting, Mother untied the bag of provisions from my saddle. Edmund came beside her but kept a distance as she stepped toward the house. The other guards and I remained on our horses.

Neighbors came out of their dwellings, looks of confusion on their faces.

Mud squished beneath Mother's shoes as she stepped to the hovel.

I looked up and willed the clouds to not rain until we completed our task and returned to the safety of home.

I expected Mother to leave the provisions on the doorstep, but instead she called out, "Greeting! Maggie, are you here?"

The cloth parted and a young face peered out, fear and suspicion in the girl's brown eyes. She could hardly be older than I.

"Dear God! Is that you?" Mother stepped closer. "Maggie, it is I, Lady de Warenne."

I dismounted but remained at Cooper's side.

The fear in the young girl's face softened as she recognized Mother and stepped outside with a curtsy. She tugged her shawl as if trying to hide her large abdomen. Her eyes passed over me to the guards still mounted.

I'd never seen such a pregnant belly on so young a person or a more pathetic looking creature. Her tattered dress barely hung below her knees. Bruises covered her face and arms and she wore rags for shoes. "Lowly" was confirmed in my mind and I wished I hadn't come. Here I was standing in mud, breathing fetid air. I shivered from the cold.

Mother offered her the bag of food.

"Oh, Lady de Warenne, you are most kind!" Moisture filled Maggie's eyes.

My mouth fell open. The peasant spoke as gentry.

Tears trailed down Maggie's dirty cheeks. "I've prayed for help. I feel so alone here."

I felt a twinge of compassion but in my confusion, I pushed the sensation aside.

Mother put her hand on the girl's shoulder. "Word came to me of your troubles. I felt we should come to see how you're doing."

They put their heads close and spoke quietly.

I shivered and gazed longingly back down the road toward home.

Maggie stepped from Mother, staring at the ground. "Since my mother died . . ." A sob caught in her throat.

Mother surprised me by wrapping her arm around Maggie's grimy shoulders, encouraging her to continue.

The story spilled out, revealing that not more than two years previous her mother had died in childbirth along with the baby. "My father in his grief has lost our home and wealth—spending it on drink and I don't know what else. We've been living here for nigh on a year. He comes home drunk every night. One night he brought home a traveler . . . who . . . who forced himself on me. Father did not protect me." She halted to control a sob. "He curses and beats me even when he's not drunk, but it's worse, so much worse, when he's drunken."

Mother peered into the shack. "Where is your brother?"

Maggie hugged herself. "John? He disappeared. He said he wanted to be anywhere but here." She looked at Mother with pleading eyes. "I have no one except Father." Her tears seemed never-ending.

I looked away from the anguish I saw written on her face.

"Maggie, get your things—if you have any," Mother said. "You'll come with us. You must not stay here another day."

My body went rigid. What was she thinking? Where was the nobility she'd taught me?

Maggie's brown eyes grew big. "But, *Domina*! I cannot—"

"Aye, you can. I insist."

I suppressed a gasp.

Mother planted a fist on her hip. "You're going to have a baby—or babies, from the looks of you—and you need proper care. After your delivery you can work as a maidservant in my household."

My feet seemed immovable while I tried to understand. I gazed at the surprised faces of the neighbors. None moved, obviously waiting to witness what would happen next.

Mother motioned me forward. "Help Maggie collect her things."

My hand flew to my chest. "*Moi?*" The word came out as a croak. I looked to Edmund for help.

He bowed kindly and indicated the door with a gesture of his hand.

"Be quick about it!" Mother ordered.

Terrified of what filth might lay inside, I timidly followed Maggie into the dismal one-room hovel. Two cots filled opposite walls. Other than a few pots and a fire pit, the room appeared nearly empty.

Not knowing what I was supposed to help with, I stood near the door while Maggie wept softly as she pulled a few articles of clothing from a basket and put them onto the cot. After folding them carefully as though they were her only treasures, she bundled them into a wool bag. She pulled on worn slippers that looked once to have been grand.

Finally, with reverence, she knelt and slid a small box from beneath the cot and gazed at the contents momentarily. She stood and showed me a gem encrusted brooch inside.

How did she keep hidden from her father such an exquisite breastpin? "It's beautiful." I thought of the brooch on my mother's bureau that I dearly coveted. Suddenly Maggie was no longer a ragged, pregnant tenant, but a girl my own age with feelings like my own.

Maggie explained, "It was my mother's. It's all I have of hers." She took the brooch out and rubbed its gems against her dress. "I've kept it hidden so my father couldn't sell it for ale. He traded her other belongings for food and drink but I'll keep this forever."

Maggie tried to pin the piece of jewelry to her dress. Her hands trembled and she lost her grip. The brooch tumbled to the floor.

I hurried to rescue it. "Allow me to pin it on you."

She gave me a nod.

I eased the pin into the threadbare dress. "Come, Maggie." Gently I took her arm. "We'll help you through this."

She peered into my eyes. "How I appreciate you coming. You're as kind as your mother."

Now it was my turn to feel the sting of tears. Maggie had looked past my pride and had forgiven my arrogance. She'd accepted me as the noblewoman I should have been but was not. I decided then I'd become the person she thought I could be.

We exited the hovel.

Mother took the bag of food brought for Maggie and handed it to another needy soul surrounded by several hungry looking waifs. The dumbfounded woman proffered a curtsy of gratitude and uttered something ending in "m'lady."

Mother smiled and nodded back.

Edmund helped Maggie onto Cooper. She road pillion to Reigate with me.

I smiled at the memory of Mother's kindness so many years before. As we passed through Whitfield, young children pointed in our direction. Some ran into their homes. I assumed to tell their mothers of Glenore's return to the manor on a fine white horse. Hopefully, word would spread about my generosity quickly. Fenella was right, this act would create goodwill. If I could get Henry to understand.

Apprehension shone in the girl's eyes as she entered the kitchen to resume her duties.

Maurice welcomed her kindly, then followed me a few steps from the kitchen and gave me one of his awkward bows. "Lady Ada, that was kindly of *vois*." He gave me a toothy smile.

As Maurice returned to the kitchen, Fenella moved to my side. "Have you decided how you're going to break the news to Henry yet?"

Trying my hardest to sound confident, I said, "I'm sure something will come to me."

Chapter Twelve

A sennight later, I was disheartened when a missive arrived at Eads Hall indicating Henry had extended his time away for another sennight. King David had made him king-designate of Scotland and his father considered moving a contingency to Carlisle and wanted his son to assess the situation.

Fenella and I decided to treat the time as a holiday.

We rode over the hills of the countryside, meeting the local yeomen, craftsmen, and tradesmen. We went to St John's to assist bringing bread to the poor. We took a midday meal to a field, spreading it on a blanket before us, the French food Maurice packed unsurprisingly tasty.

Throughout those days, I was impressed by Fenella's uncanny ability to treat both royals and commoners with the same respect.

When I asked her on it, she told me her father had worked generously with serf, servant, merchant, and noble in the Scottish court. "He taught me to value every station. He judges all crimes committed within the burgh and he also sets the fees of the workmen and the prices of provisions."

"I've heard royal chamberlains are great officers of state. But I didn't realize your father would have such monumental responsibilities. I can't imagine a calling any more trustworthy."

"Aye. He's a good man and has four sons following in his stead." Fenella laughed. "Growing up at court with four knighted brothers, I was often enlisted to be a sparring partner with the weakest candidates."

I blinked. "As a child, you wielded a sword?"

"Aye." She smiled proudly. "But the battle axe is my weapon of choice. One good smack and it's all over."

I shuddered.

On another day late in the week, we rode near the Allen River. Fenella dismounted near a rocky bank next to a group of men in threadbare clothing, fishing with nets.

"Have you ever fished?" Fenella asked.

My stomach roiled. "Nae."

Fenella left to talk to the fishermen and returned with two nets. She set out climbing over the rocks and bid me follow.

With my first step, I slipped on the slick slime of a rock but then righted myself.

Fenella had no such incidents and continued her climb with sure footing well past the others who fished.

My wimple became lost to the water, my gown soaked, and my hair loose of its braid, but the afternoon had been one of the most exhilarating in recent memory.

Late in the day, we caught up with the fishermen. They wrapped the four large salmon Fenella and I had netted single-handedly to take back for our supper.

Upon arriving home, I handed our catch to Maurice. I was heading to my chamber to clean when I heard the front door open.

Giffard stepped into the hall with a clank of weaponry and armor, looking as harried as I felt. "Prince Henry will be arriving in the next hour."

"What's wrong?" I asked, assuming the cause for such a change of plans would be bad fortune.

"He fares well. We accompanied Kelton down from Edinburgh. At Hexham, Prince Henry's horse stumbled. It was a two-day journey to our next destination but only half a day here. The prince is concerned that if his mount is not cared for, it will go lame."

Fenella stepped forward. "Is the hoof cracked? Is the leg swelling?"

Giffard tried to keep his expression serious, but he couldn't stop the sudden smile. "I'm most sorry, my lady. I didn't get a close look at the animal."

"Then what good are you?" She put her hands on her hips and glared. "There's naught to do but prepare for the worst." Fenella turned my way. "Lady Ada, I will take my leave to the stables to await the injured grey."

"Aye, go," I said, then turned to Giffard. "And why don't you go help her?"

I'd never seen Giffard so happy to follow a command.

Though I wanted nothing more than to retire to my dressing room to clean up, I hurried to the kitchen to inform Maurice. "We shall have guests for supper. I don't know their number, but Prince Henry is returning with Kelton and his guards."

Maurice held a cleaver in his hand before one of the large salmons. "Well, if it weren't for the company, we'd be eating fish for a sennight. Be assured, we'll be ready." He laid the clever down. "I'll give orders to the remainder of the staff."

Glenore looked at me with sheer terror in her eyes. "M'lady, what shall I do?" Her voice squeaked like a mouse. "Will he be cross I'm here?"

I placed my hands on her shoulders. "It's very important he doesn't see you until I speak to him first. After we sit to eat, I'll broach the subject. Watch from the doorway, and when you see the prince agreeable, then make your entrance."

Apprehension shone in the girl's eyes. "Tweren't it be better I went 'ome for the day?"

I shook my head. "I think poor Maurice will need every available hand."

As I returned to my rooms, I wondered if I should be more worried. Certainly, Henry would understand once I explained the fragile relationship we had with the people of Whitfield and the goodwill returning the girl to our service had created. I hastened to dress and struggled to brush the mud from my hair as I thought on the details of how I would tell him.

Unfortunately, it started to rain. Not simply a drizzle, but buckets poured from the sky. Supper had been ready for an hour by the time Henry's bedraggled party arrived. I encouraged him to change first, but he threw off his wet mantle and marched toward the supper table. "We're famished and haven't eaten since sunrise."

I counted the men as they entered. "Where is Kelton? I expected him to be with you."

Henry answered, "He chose to take my place in debriefing King David about the state of the castle at Carlisle. It's truly a magnificent structure and important stronghold." Admiration was apparent in his tone.

I could also detect a considerable limp in his gait. "Fare thee well? I was told the horse only stumbled."

St Martin pulled his chin back in half a laugh and then thought better of it and became silent.

From the look on Henry's face, I knew he wouldn't tell me. I approached the knight with hands on my hips. "So how bad was it?"

St Martin looked to Prince Henry and shrugged as if defeated. "We rested after the morning's journey, but as your husband mounted his steed, it was as though the animal went wild. It bucked like an ill-tempered Welsh pony, throwing the prince to the ground and hurting its own leg in the process."

"Was there a burr under the saddle?" I asked, expecting sabotage.

St Martin shook his wet mane. "Nae a burr, but the creature's eyes rolled wild and strange. It pranced about for a good hour afterward."

Henry rubbed his hip. "Whatever got into that animal, it's seen the last of me. I'm finding a new horse tomorrow."

The mood in Eads Hall equaled the grey of the skies outside. The Gaelic word for this sort of gloom was *dreich*, and I felt it all around me.

We all sat to eat. The prince seemed to brood over the events of his morning, and with St Martin and the other guards, I hardly found an opportune time to bring up the subject of Glenore.

I sighed as the salmon was brought to the table with steaming cabbage and onions. Rich stuffing accompanied baked apples. The men dished up their plates and after grace, ate with gusto.

"Is this salmon from the nearby river?" Henry asked.

Somewhat proud, I admitted, "I went fishing on the River Allen today with a friend. We caught this ourselves, and I've got the ruined frock upstairs to prove it."

His face lightened somewhat. "So, you've been busy since I've been away?"

"Aye, very." It felt so good to have this positive discussion with Henry, and I hoped to turn it toward Glenore when the chance arose. "I've been all over the countryside. At St John's, they give bread to the poor every Tuesday, and I assisted. I've met most of the yeomen in the area and visited many of the servants' homes to increase goodwill."

Henry sat back in his chair, almost cheery. "I'm pleased. Truly, this type of charity is what we need to unify Northumbria to Scotland." His smile was naught less than charming.

A few servants cleared the dishes. Carrying two raspberry biscuits piled high with cream, Glenore set them before us with a shy smile.

Seeing her, Henry rose to his feet. "What are you doing here?" he said in a chastising voice. "I dismissed you a sennight past!"

The terrified girl cowered, turned, and ran from the room.

The room quieted around us.

"I was going to tell you." I stood. "The servant and I have come to an understanding, and I invited her to return." I started to follow Glenore but turned to Henry and surprised myself by saying, "Sit down and eat whilst I take care of this!"

He took a step toward me, his hands shaking in anger. "Ada, do you realize by allowing her to return that you directly contradicted my order? I'm the laird here."

I swallowed any reply I was about to make. Henry was tired and sore and anything said would do naught to improve the situation. "We'll discuss this once I return." I left the room and hurried into the kitchen but found the girl nowhere. "Where is Glenore?"

Maurice pointed toward the door leading outside. "*Elle* ran out crying."

I grabbed Maurice's huge mantle and rushed into the rain.

In the distance, the deflated servant headed down the road. "Glenore!" I called.

She turned, hesitating in her step.

I feared she'd keep walking, but she waited whilst I caught up.

Tearfully, she bewailed, "M'lady, ye said wait until he looked pleased. I did just as ye said, and he was still angry with me."

"I'm truly sorry." I realized how unclear my instructions had been. She was right and the blame was solely my own. "Kindly return. I'll make things right."

Glenore bit her lip and shifted foot to foot in the mud. "I cannot, m'lady. I cannot face 'im again."

I took her arm. "Come. Stay in the kitchen and enjoy a warm meal until he's gone to his bedchamber."

The rain had flattened her hair and tears mixed with the rain on her face. Finally, she acquiesced with a nod.

I threw some of voluminous fabric of the mantle over her shoulder and squeezed her close to me. We walked to Eads Hall.

From the kitchen I heard shouting—a man's voice—but I couldn't imagine Henry going on with such volume. Still, it certainly sounded like him.

Glenore stiffened, and I had to pull her on.

When a woman's voice followed just as heated, I knew exactly who was talking. Fenella.

I left Glenore in the kitchen and entered the dining hall in time to see Fenella jab her finger repeatedly into my husband's chest. "Your wife is as much a noble princess with her marriage to you as you are a prince, your high and mightiness. I can't believe those words would come out of your mouth. Do you think bellowing like an old cow makes you more correct? In this case, you should bow on the ground to both those poor women and beg *their* forgiveness. Your wife should never have to endure such treatment, and that little servant you let go is fatherless because of your bloody war!" Fenella paused to take a breath.

Giffard stood beside her completely perplexed, his loyalties clearly divided.

All eyes turned to me as I entered the room.

Henry stared, a look of contrition on his face, but before he could utter a word, I knelt before him. Never again would I allow my behavior to make him seem less in the eyes of those around him. I had handled the situation completely wrong. I should have waited until we had counseled together before allowing Glenore to return.

I hung my head, staring at the floor. "My lord, I know you dismissed the girl with cause, and your concerns are valid. I should never have disregarded your command. I'm truly sorry, my liege lord, my Henry."

He paced.

My heart wrenched for him as he struggled with what seemed frustration and embarrassment.

In the ensuing silence, Fenella stepped between us. "Henry, this should be a time of celebration. We haven't seen one another for two long years. Besides, when your new wife and your best friend see things the same way, how can you think to disagree?" The light laugh that drifted from her lips had an almost musical tone.

Henry looked from one of us to the other and his ill-humor seemed to melt away. He took my hand, helping me up whilst placing his other on Fenella's shoulder. "I must keep the two of you apart or before long you will be running the kingdom without me."

St Martin laughed quietly. "Keep them far from Sybil or she'll be the one wielding the sword."

We sat at the table to enjoy our food. Soon the servants brought warm drink.

"So, Fenella is your best friend?" I asked Henry.

He gave a deep nod. "She's the closest thing I have to a sister. Fenella's father taught me swordsmanship, and Fenella and I were sparring partners until I hit the age of eight."

Fenella offered a dry smile. "More like ten."

He reached his hand out to hers with true joy across his face. "It's so fine to see you again." Then as though he remembered I was there, he pulled away. "You must have been the one to encourage my wife to go fishing and visit the locals."

"Lady Ada is as skilled with her horse as I've ever seen in a woman except myself. She's also fearless. I thought she'd end up at the bottom of the river multiple times, but her tenacity is why we had such a plentiful supper tonight." She lifted her cup to me.

I returned the gesture, suddenly feeling very tired.

As Fenella and Henry talked about their own fishing adventure at Crail in their early years, I got to my feet. "It's been quite a day. If you will excuse me, I'll make sure your rooms are prepared for the night. Stay and enjoy the fire as long as you like."

The echoes of my footfalls leaving the room sounded as empty as my heart. Aye, Glenore could stay, but I felt so little joy in that. Peering over my shoulder, I watched Fenella. She'd become the centerpiece of the room. Giffard stared at her, mesmerized. St Martin appeared taken by her as well. Suddenly, she broke into a laughing duet with Henry.

My fists tightened.

Of course, Henry had friends, and I had to admit I liked Fenella too. So why was I so bothered by her presence? Why had her comments in my defense left me so unsettled?

After telling Mariam to oversee the fires and have the curtains drawn in all the guest quarters, I sat at my vanity with Maggie brushing my hair. When she left, I waited over two hours, but Henry had not come. The rumblings of my heart became clear.

I was jealous.

Chapter Thirteen

Maggie sat at my side, sewing a chemise. "If I may speak, *Domina*?"

"Of course," I said. "You know I will always give ear to what's on your mind."

"Are we still in danger from this man Ranulf?" She pinched her lips together and continued sewing.

"My lord does not think so. I fear I do still hold worry. Do you?"

"Mayhap it's that the last few days have been so quiet." She shrugged one shoulder. "Is not the prince being thrown from his horse an odd thing?" She cleared her throat. "And I wish St Martin had not returned to Carlisle to assist the king. I trust him more than any other to keep the prince safe."

I chewed at the inside of my cheek. I'd said as much to Henry, but he assured me the incident with the horse was common enough. I refused to pester him further, as he convalesced with a foul mood. His limp had worsened over the last few days. A massive bruise ran from his knee to his thigh and across the old hip injury. He had also hit his head again and complained of soreness.

I wished for the herb woman's secret tea that would have taken his pain and caused him to sleep, but none-such was available. I waited on him personally, fearing he'd upset a servant with his grimness.

But on the fourth day, shortly before noon, I retreated to the solar for respite.

Fenella approached. "Here you are. There are things we need to discuss."

"Aye," I answered. Not really wanting to discuss anything with her. "Where is Giffard?"

"I sent him on an errand to the village."

I pictured Giffard obeying like a dog and the thought came with a small smile.

Fenella sat on the bench at my side. "I've been requested by King David to come to Carlisle. He has plans of a celebration for your wedding and asks for my help." Her lips lifted, but I would hardly consider it a smile. "And to show off the castle, I surmise."

"What of Henry's horse? Is he lame?"

She wagged her head. "It's the strangest thing. Old Grey stopped limping the first day he returned. His leg never presented with soreness or injury. Actually . . ." She laughed. "He appeared drunk. Mayhap he grazed on henbane, but the amount would've had to have been small to not cause complete raving madness and death. Curious."

Curious indeed. Did this woman really know horses? "And when do you plan to leave?"

She took my hand. "Are you that anxious to get rid of me?"

I shook my head. "Nae, but why didn't you tell me that you and Henry were such close friends? Had I known . . ."

She thinned her lips. "Then you and I would have never developed a relationship." She studied me with lovely green eyes. "You should know that many thought Henry and I should marry. It was quite a surprise for some when your union was declared, but I'm not of royal lineage. After getting to know you, it's clear you bring to Scotland gifts we need. The way you dealt with Glenore, and even Henry, was as a princess should. I pray your shine rubs off and makes me more refined."

"That is very sweet to say." Were they genuine sentiments or just words?

Fenella laughed as if reading my mind. "Lady Ada, I don't say things I don't mean. Friends?" She extended both her hands.

I took them. "Friends." Mayhap this pain of suspicion would soon leave. "Are you also becoming friends with Giffard?" I tried to hide a smile but failed.

"He's quite the charmer. He offered to ride with me to Carlisle, but I refused him."

"Why?" I asked, hoping the relationship would blossom so I no longer had to worry about Henry having eyes for her.

"Lady Ada," she began then paused. "I'm worried about Henry."

"Nae, his bruise is not that serious. It's only painful. He has no broken bones."

"Not about that," she said. "Giffard told me that since Henry's returned north, he's been kidnapped and had this accident. Both are suspicious."

Was she overreacting? Was Maggie? Would these threats to Henry's life always plague us?

She took a deep breath. "Know this, I am worried and have asked Giffard not to leave Henry's side. I've inspected

Giffard's skills, and though he has the face of an angel, Hugh Giffard knows his way around a sword. Not as well as I do, but what man does?" Her laugh came off feigned. "In these changing times, there is no way to be certain of a Scot's loyalty. But Giffard is an Englishman, and he's loyal to you. And so, he must stay and protect Henry from death and you from widowhood."

Chapter Fourteen

Before the month was out, we left for the marriage celebration King David held for us at his castle in Carlisle, less than a day's ride away. Henry rode his grey horse, who had been naught but docile since his strange episode, and I rode Cooper.

As we approached the castle, a tower came into view that rose to impressive heights. We entered through the main doors to find every brazier lit, bringing warmth and light to the halls. Large sprays of flowers sat atop tables, including azure cornflowers, sweet peas, and daisies. Indeed, we were in for a celebration.

That evening, nobles and other respected guests gathered from around the country to celebrate with us. Henry's relatives brought their children. Seeing little girls in elaborate frocks brought similar happy memories of my childhood in Surrey.

Gentle music from lute, harp, and organ filled the room.

I saw King David for the first time since our wedding day. The Scottish monarch greeted me with open arms, his smile wide and teeth showing. He was shorter than Henry but still carried the stance of a warrior. "Lady Ada, I've heard naught but wonderful things about how you are winning the hearts of the people of Northumbria." He kissed my cheek and shook Henry's hand before they embraced one another.

The king wore royal robes adorned with a magnificent gold belt. To his left stood Kelton, straight-faced and solemn.

Next to Kelton, Fenella winked at me. There was little question where the king's report had come from. Stepping forward, she led us to a reception line to meet our honored guests. "That dress suits you," she whispered in my ear.

"It's my favorite wedding gift from Henry." The silk gown, green like a summer meadow, matched my eyes. Though I adored how the hemline was embroidered in silver with a stunning pattern of birds, her compliment gave me added confidence.

I was curtsied to and had my hand kissed by both gentry and merchants. I complimented them on their fine apparel, and we chatted, finding little things in common. When we had gotten almost halfway through the reception line, Henry leaned close to my ear. "You are so natural at this."

I gazed down the line of dignitaries waiting to meet us. "Thank my mother. All her painful years of training have proven useful after all."

He laughed before turning to our next guest. William Peverel, our host at Westminster, stepped forward flanked by his wife, Avicia, my cousin. Their daughter, Isobel, came from behind. She was a year younger than me, and her coloring and the shape of her brow bore a significant resemblance to my own. Her mouth, however, carried the pouting downturn of her father's.

Peverel bypassed my hand and stepped directly to Henry. "Your Highness." He bowed. With no further greeting he said,

"Isobel would like a formal introduction to Kelton, wouldn't you, my girl?"

Isobel blushed.

I pitied the poor thing.

Henry bowed and took Isobel's hand, kissing it respectfully. "I'm certain he would be honored to make your acquaintance. Why don't your parents stay and visit with Lady Ada whilst we find Kelton?"

Isobel's lips lifted, and she followed him across the floor.

I stepped forward to keep Isobel's parents engaged so she might have a moment to meet Kelton, away from their prying eyes. "Avicia, we so appreciated your hospitality—"

"I think we shall have business to attend to." Peverel interrupted. "Excuse us." He took his wife's hand and nearly dragged her in the direction Henry and Isobel had gone.

Avicia threw me a look of apology.

The guests in the reception line seemed unsure whether to continue introductions without my husband at my side. Before any of us had decided how to proceed, a soldier entered the hall, sword clanking against his mail armor.

The room quieted as he walked directly to King David, pulled from his gauntlet a scroll, and handed it to the king.

King David's brow knit deeper the further he read down the page. He dismissed the messenger but kept the missive, worry covering his face.

Henry left my cousins and Kelton to approach the king. The two briefly discussed the missive's contents in hushed tones.

Whatever could be the matter? What sort of news was so important as to interrupt our celebration?

Distracted, I didn't notice my next guest until he took my hand.

Fierce blue eyes met mine. "Greeting, my lady. I am a cousin to Henry. My name is Madduch, great-grandson of Malcolm the Third, King of Scots." He cleared his throat. "A complex family." He bowed politely. "I see your husband perchance is embroiled in political matters." He lifted a blond eyebrow.

The king raised his hand and demanded everyone's attention. "I've received word that Empress Matilda has again invaded England. If and when her army comes this far north, King Stephen requires our assistance in defending him." He paused a moment and frowned. "Hopefully, that time will not come, and England can fight her own wars."

An affirmative murmur went through the guests.

Madduch kissed my hand, drawing my attention. "May I come to you during one of Henry's lengthy trips away? I presume a beautiful woman such as yourself gets lonely without him."

The sensual tone in his voice took me aback. I withdrew my hand and tried to keep my shock hidden, but my heart thudded in my chest. "I don't think that necessary, but I'm grateful for your concern." I took a step away. "I have plenty of company at Eads Hall to keep me happy." I curtsied and turned to my next guest in line, hoping Madduch would leave my presence.

The man bowed and moved away.

I avoided looking in his direction. Had his unexpected offer been meant with kindness? A gesture of friendliness? I was inexperienced in such things, but the look in his eyes and the inflection of his voice left me wondering. I could hardly imagine him risking such boldness so near the presence of both Henry and the king. Surely, his words were in jest, yet my trembling hands suggested I feared the man's comments were not as innocent as I wanted to believe.

Henry returned to my side to greet yet another couple who wished us well.

After they walked on, he asked, "Whatever is the matter? You're shaking like a leaf."

"The man named Madduch—who is he, and what is he to you?"

Henry briefly glanced Madduch's way. "His kinsmen are bitter against my father, believing they should have inherited the throne. They've made it clear that they intend to take over the kingship if I do not produce an heir."

Despite my valiant efforts not to, I stole a brief glance at the man. Oh nae! He was looking straight at me. I smiled up at Henry, wondering if I should tell him of Madduch's offer to visit me in his absence. "Henry, I am worried—"

"May I again have your attention!" King David raised his hand. "In spite of pending war, we shall carry on in celebration of my son's recent marriage. The musicians will play, and we will dance." He motioned to Henry and me. "And I will ask my son and his new bride to lead the way."

I tried to calm myself, tucking my hands behind my back.

As servants scrambled to move aside tables, Henry gently took my arm and walked us onto what had been cleared as the dance floor.

The music began, and I smiled at Henry. Many watched us, including Madduch. Sharp tingles ran up my spine. I deliberately avoided looking in his direction. He had invaded my peace more than enough for one evening, and my attentions should be upon Henry. Or should they be upon a looming war?

Although King Stephen ruled and King David had pledged peace between England and Scotland, sealing the pledge symbolically by uniting the two countries in the marriage of

Henry and myself, King David was secretly still loyal to Matilda, his niece. If war came, would Henry then have to fight? His loyalty was *supposed* to be with King Stephen. But would he not be required to lead his father's army if it came to that? Worry tied my stomach in knots.

Other couples followed our lead and joined in the dancing.

Henry surprised me when he lifted one of his small girl cousins into his arms and carried her with us as we stepped into rhythm.

The little girl tittered with delight.

His gesture lent a warm feeling and brought me back to my childhood when my parents danced together—particularly the time Father danced with me in his arms. I'd been holding at bay a longing for my mother, my sweet sister, and other members of my family.

As the music ended, I excused myself, hoping my bout of homesickness would quickly pass.

I walked into the hall to find Fenella talking to a kitchen maid who held a tray of food. When she saw me, Fenella dismissed the servant and approached. "Are you enjoying the celebration?"

"Aye, the event is magnificent," I said. "And most of the guests have been very kind, but one was a little too kind, bordering on lascivious."

Concern filled her eyes. "What did he say?"

"It was one of Henry's cousins. He asked if he could come to me when Henry was away."

Her concern faded, and she laughed as if I were a foolish child. "And does that surprise you? You are a princess and quite lovely, married or not."

Her reaction unnerved me further. "Aye, it does surprise me." I stood a little taller. "These are not heathens. Not committing adultery is still one of the ten commandments, is it not?"

Fenella took a deep breath and patted my arm. "Attitudes here are a little more relaxed when it comes to bedfellows. Many royals have illegitimate children who seek power."

Not naïve, I knew this, but I supposed I was looking for Fenella to understand my personal aversion to sharing my bed with anyone but my spouse and hoped in my heart Henry felt the same. "I will be ever faithful to Henry."

"I pray he will be the same to you." Fenella's eyes caught mine with a serious, piercing stare, as though ready to tell me something else.

A ruckus down the hall drew her attention from me to two arguing, drunken guests. "And now I must go and attend to that for which I am hired." Fenella moved toward them. "Enjoy the rest of the evening, my lady."

I returned to the great hall, hardly feeling more settled. As I drew near Henry, he turned from Kelton. They both smiled at my approach. My cousins were nowhere in sight and neither was Madduch.

Kelton said, "I must request your forgiveness, for I'm taking my leave to Eads Hall. I wished to make an appearance at your party but feel it's past time for me to set up residence in my new quarters and become your steward." He took my hand and kissed it. "May you have a blessed evening."

I found his words hard to believe. "Why would you leave in the dark? Certainly, starting at morning light would be sufficient."

He shook his head. "Aye, but I have friends expecting me before I leave the area. May the rest of your stay be without incident."

Henry clasped his cousin's hand. "Safe travels to you."

Kelton left the room, and Henry turned to me. "It has to be hard for him to see our joy when he has so little of his own."

"He has a fine position as steward to a prince. He's a knight. Does he not aspire to generosity and courtesy, as knights are expected to do?"

Henry raised an eyebrow. "You do not like him."

I said naught.

"His father was a king. Although he never says as much, I believe Kelton still feels he deserves something from that fact despite his illegitimacy. It must be hard to go from the hopes of marrying royalty in King Stephens court to being the steward of a prince."

Henry's empathy toward his cousin touched me, leaving no doubt in my mind that he would be a great king.

Light music played.

"Shall we dance, my love?" Henry asked.

He took my hand, and we made our way to the center of the dance floor, joining a large formation already weaving amongst one another. We silently joined the rhythm, moving in and out and around, barely touching hands when we came together. Surrounded by new friends in such a lovely place increased my loyalty to my new kingdom and my new life. Whilst a child in Reigate, I'd never conceived of going so far from home, but now northern England had become the home of my heart. Yet I still longed to see Scotland and be amongst the people there.

Henry tightened his grip on my hand as we passed. He pulled me from the formation and away from the dance floor. "Look what I see." He nodded his head to our left. "Do they not make a handsome couple?"

Fenella and Giffard danced together in another formation. Though she seemed completely at ease, poor Giffard moved stiffly, measuring each step.

"Henry, you should speak to your father about their union. Wouldn't they be perfect together?"

He grew stern. "Not quite yet. Let Giffard earn his place among the Scots first. Then if my father will grant him an earldom, he will be worthy of Fenella. It will also give them time to understand each other before they are wed, as it should be."

His words bothered me. Did he want more for Fenella than he'd had?

Chapter Fifteen

I awoke at sunrise to find Henry moaning in pain. "What's wrong, *mon amour*?" I touched his forehead. "You're burning with fever."

"It's been a hard night." He groaned and turned away from me. "Mayhap it's from too much wine."

"Drink does not cause fever. I'll find help." I pulled down the covers, hoping to cool him, and put on my robe and slippers.

The upper floor was still dark. I hurried down to the kitchen. The fire had been lit, but I saw no one. The kettle still held water, I moved it over the flames then found an assortment of herbs. I picked up several, hoping they'd been labeled.

"My lady, how may I be of help?" A voice echoed from the darkness.

I whirled to see an older female servant, fully dressed and carrying a bucket of water. Relief flooded over me as I recognized her as the one in the hall with Fenella the night before.

"My husband's ill with fever. I'd hoped to find something to relieve him." I attempted to return the herbs to the shelf, but one bottle fell and rolled across the floor.

She set down the bucket and picked up the bottle. "Go to him whilst I make a tea. I have knowledge of healing." She handed back the bottle. "To bring relief, rub this ointment on his chest, shoulders and neck."

I returned to our chamber.

Henry dozed but was still hot to my touch.

I rubbed the mixture on his body as I had seen the herb woman do when Henry was healing from the grappling hook. It didn't have the same powerful aroma as the past ointment. It hardly smelled at all.

Henry stirred and moaned beneath my hands.

The sun had risen above the horizon by the time the tea arrived, brought by the servant who had kindly offered her help. We managed to get Henry sitting upright to drink the liquid. Unlike the foul-smelling concoction that had made him sleep, this tea smelled much like the tea I had each morning.

"How have you learned the ways of medicine?" I asked her.

She seemed reticent to answer but at last confessed, "I served as midwife to the previous Earl of Northumbria." The pitch of her voice lifted, "But I swear, by that which is most holy, that I am loyal to whomever the king chooses." She deeply bowed before me, waiting for what I would choose for her to do.

"Rise," I commanded. "And do what you can for my husband. What is your name?"

"Alba, my lady."

As she administered to Henry, I learned that she'd performed other medical matters at the palace, mostly with the servants. I was grateful she seemed to have more knowledge than I of such matters.

I asked her, "Do you know of a woman near an ancient forest who collects herbs for healing?"

She scrunched up her nose as if she'd smelled something foul. "Many pagan folk think the best medicines come from Galloway Forest. Some alchemists believe the forest carries magical properties, so there are many gatherers there, but I don't hold to those heathen myths."

Days went by, and Henry's room smelled of ointments and herbs, but his health didn't improve. Despite Alba's vigilant care, King David called in a physician. Only he and Alba were allowed in the room whilst the physician examined Henry and performed bloodletting to give him relief.

I listened at the door, but they spoke in low tones that I couldn't discern. More physicians were sent for. Although their reputations proceeded them, each left without making Henry better. Some of their remedies made Henry worse. A sennight past and then another. Nothing helped.

One day, I found Henry pale and limp, the smell of putrefaction upon him. I refused to leave him again, caring for him myself—washing his body and rubbing him with oils.

The midwife and physicians said they had done all they could.

Closing my eyes, I said a feeble prayer, "Dear Father, how can he be saved?" My mind rested upon my vivid dream of the red-headed boy. I brought my mouth to Henry's ear. "*Mon amour*, you are not ready to go. Our son has not yet come. This is not your time." Even as I said it, I wondered if I could be with child and if Henry would die.

He opened his eyes and gazed at me, saying naught, the bright light that attracted me to him dimming.

Oh God, I can't lose him!

A knock on the door startled me.

Giffard stood at the threshold, his head bowed. Such a large and brave knight had as much compassion as the rest of us.

"Aye?" I said, holding tears at bay.

"Lady Ada, I . . . I . . ." he stammered. "Is there anything you wish of me?"

I recalled he was the one who had found the herb lady. "Can you find that woman from near Ludlow again, the one that helped before?"

Giffard shook his head. "Dame Fenella sent me to find her when Henry's horse went lame. There is no sign of her anywhere. But if you wish, I'll ask the locals of their healers."

"Aye," I nodded. "Pray you find someone soon."

"I shall." Giffard left.

Although there was no evidence anything would change, I felt an increase of hope.

Soon after Giffard departed, King David paced Henry's bedchamber with worry. "He must recover. I keep recounting in my mind the joy at his birth. Such hope we had. My beloved Maud was almost forty, of an age most women could no longer bear children. Like Sarah of old, we thought Henry's birth to be a miracle. Where is the miracle now?" His voice broke on the last word.

I had no words to pacify, and instead put my arms around him, hoping my touch would give strength and comfort.

The king pulled away, shaking his head. "We've eaten the same foods, the cup-bearer drank from the same bottle of wine, so none of it accounts for his illness. How is it only he's affected?"

"I know not." The same idea had been plaguing me. Could someone have poisoned him or infected him with illness? Lord

Madduch hadn't gotten close to Henry as far as I'd seen, but I had left the hall on occasion.

Had Henry approached his cousin whilst I was gone? I wish I had thought on these things beforehand when he could have answered me. Now I was left to wonder.

Four days later, Henry was too weak to take drink. I could feel the end was nigh. My heart thudded a slow beat, and I could not perform a task but to sit by Henry's side. I regretted not insisting that Fenella remain with me. Her father had requested her return to Edinburgh. At the time, it seemed right to let her go. I'd even insisted on it. Now I felt guilty that she would not be able to bid her closest childhood friend farewell. Had my motivation for compelling her to leave been selfish? I regretted it as much for her as for me. I could have really used her strength.

That afternoon, Henry's breathing grew shallow. I could do nothing. He would not take the tea, the ointment was gone, and he didn't drift into moments of wakefulness no matter how I called or encouraged.

Fear gripped me like a vise. Henry probably wouldn't last through the night. I called for King David so we could watch vigil together through his final hours. He entered and stood behind me. I assumed so I could not see emotions play on his face.

"King David," I asked in a whisper. "What is to become of me after Henry's passing?" I truly didn't know. With no heir, was I still a Scottish noble? Or would I be returned home? I turned slightly to show him my face in case he didn't know my intent was just.

The monarch looked as if he'd aged ten years in just a few days. He gazed upon me with kind eyes. "Let's not think on that right now." He looked away.

I couldn't accept that answer. I had to know. I bowed my head. "I'm certain you'll be kind, but legally it would be as though we'd never married, wouldn't it? With no heir, I have no claim."

"Lady Ada." King David placed a hand on my shoulder. "We will always be united, I promise you."

Though I believed the king would be more than generous, my situation was tenuous. He grew old and whether his heir was Madduch or any of the other cousins waiting in the wings, would they be as charitable as Henry?

The door open and Giffard stepped in, dust-covered from his travels.

I ran to his side. "What have you brought?"

His chin lowered. "I've searched everywhere from Ludlow to Whitfield. No healer agreed to come or felt they had any more to offer."

I struggled to stay standing.

He gripped my arm.

I shook him off and made my way to Henry, putting my hand on his.

Though the room was warm, his hand felt chilled. His eyes were sunken, his skin almost translucent.

How could this be happening? I couldn't lose him.

Giffard cleared his throat behind me. "I did bring someone. Chaplain Robert asked to come, and he brought an abbot."

"To give last rites? Nae, not yet." I could not accept this was happening.

King David stifled a moan. "His time grows short. You wouldn't want him to pass without the hope of heaven."

I couldn't bring myself to say the words but nodded, holding tightly to Henry's hand.

Chaplain Robert entered. "King David and Lady Ada." He bowed. "I have a special visitor, Abbot Malachy from Ireland."

Malachy's reputation for healing was known throughout all England.

Hope swelled in my chest. I stepped from the bedside and turned to the king and priest. "Did either of you send for him?"

King David shook his head, looking unsure of Malachy's significance.

"Nae," Chaplain Robert said. "He arrived at the chapel Tuesday as we gave bread to the poor. He's on a pilgrimage to Rome and felt he needed to come visit us. Giffard arrived looking for assistance, and now we are here."

Chaplain Robert went into the hall, soon to return with a short, white-haired cleric, dressed in worn and simple brown robes. "Abbot Malachy, this is King David of Scotland and Princess Ada."

He bowed with deepest respect.

The abbot had a holiness about his presence. His blue eyes gazed upon my face and pierced me to my soul.

My own eyes blurred with moisture. "Abbot Malachy, we are so grateful you've come."

Curiosity flickered on Abbot Malachy's face. "How is the prince today? What are his symptoms? How long has he been ill?" He moved to Henry's side and took up the hand that I had just held.

Henry didn't respond to his touch.

A cry caught in my throat.

King David spoke, "The physicians say there is not a hope for him, that he's nigh unto death."

"But you are here now, Father." I blurted. "You can bless Henry, and God will heal him."

Malachy smiled. "My daughter, your faith is strong." He looked as if he was puzzling out a problem. "I will be honored to bless the prince. This explains God's urging that I visit here. Do you have a chapel where I can first pray?"

King David led the holy men to the small chapel within the castle.

I stayed alone by Henry's side.

For the first time in days, Henry opened his eyes. He must have seen my look of despair, for he mustered a faint smile as I knelt beside him.

"My love," he whispered.

I tried to tame my excitement. "Oh, my dear Henry. God has sent Father Malachy to bless you. We must have faith that you will be healed." I smoothed his hair.

His eyes fell shut again, and his ragged breathing returned.

I prayed aloud, "I thank Thee for having sent Father Malachy. I will always believe in Your guidance. I beg of Thee, dear Lord, may there be a miracle performed here this day. As my dreams have declared, I do believe there is to be an heir to Scotland's honorable people—from my own womb." I sobbed. "Even if I am wrong, save Henry this day." I continued praying in the stillness of the room.

King David soon led Abbot Malachy and Chaplain Robert back into the room.

Henry's eyes remained closed whilst Malachy kneeled and prayed. The abbot lifted the crucifix from his belt.

Only then did I notice the base of the cross was made of three cylindrical vials. I sensed its holiness. "How unique," I whispered in reverence.

"This chrism was a gift from the French king. It allows me to bring consecrated oil for Holy sacraments and healing of the sick." He sprinkled a few drops of the oil from the vial, anointing Henry's head. He then gently placed his hands thereon and prayed, invoking God's power. He ended by saying, "Trust me, my son, you shall not die this time. God will make you whole, and you will yet serve in your way. In the name of our Lord, Amen."

Henry's breathing soon quieted. His chest rose and fell at a steady rhythm.

Malachy stood and spoke to King David. "If you need us, we shall be staying at the abbey tonight. May your son continue to be the prudent and brave man he has always been, taking after his father in righteousness." He bowed.

I knelt at the abbot's feet, tears of gratitude edging my lashes.

He bent to meet me and placed the cross in my hands. "This is my gift to you."

I held the beautiful crucifix in my hands, amazed at his kindness, humbled to attain such a holy relic. "Don't you need it?"

"Nae, the Lord will provide another. It's yours to flourish with and maintain your great faith."

He pulled me to my feet and smiled with such kindness that comfort spread throughout my chest. With the comfort came hope. Hope for a future with Henry and a life to serve my God.

The holy men departed. Their humility amazed me. Could such goodness in the world spread to all? My soul rejoiced that they were on God's errand.

Weary and exhausted, I stayed at Henry's bedside through the night and clutched the crucifix, my prayers never ceasing. I must have fallen asleep. When I awoke, morning light filled the room. I gazed upon my love.

Pain had vanished from his face for the first time in weeks.

A servant brought in a tray with fresh bread and tea. As she set it on the table, the maid whispered, "Good morning, my lady. I suppose you could use refreshment."

Henry opened his eyes and sat up slowly in the bed. "I shall join her. That smells delicious." Although his voice had weakened, his clearness of thought took me by surprise.

I dropped to my knees at his bedside. "You've awakened." I put my hand to his brow. "The fever is gone."

"How many days has it been since I've eaten? I'm famished."

"Too, too many." I burst out in unexpected laughter and threw my arms around him.

Henry would live!

He pulled his legs around to leave the bed, but I cautioned, "Go easy, *mon amour*. Take a little nourishment and regain your strength."

The maid interceded, holding a cup for him to take. "My lord, we've worried so. You've been close to death. I'll fetch the king at once." She curtsied and left the room, shouting, "The prince is well! He has recovered!"

King David soon entered still in his nightclothes. He placed his hand to Henry's cheek and exclaimed, "My son! Praise God you are well!"

Shouts of joy echoed throughout the castle, both inside and out. Soon servants peeked in, calling their well-wishes, praising God and rejoicing. One brought a tray of fruits.

Henry ate slowly but heartily whilst King David and I watched and visited, telling him of all we'd done for him and the healing blessing of Father Malachy.

He sat back when finished. "Food never tasted so good."

King David called to his attendant. "Go with haste to the abbey and invite Father Malachy so he may rejoice with us in this miracle. He will be my honored guest as long as he wishes to tarry." He then called to his chatelaine. "Prepare a feast in Malachy's honor. We shall celebrate his miracle."

The messengers returned before noon without the abbot. In much anticipation, King David opened the note Malachy had sent, and read aloud.

I am grateful for the generous invitation to come to your palace, but my brothers and I must continue on our Lord's errands. The miracle is not mine but God's. I am His servant. May He ever bless you.

–Malachy of Armagh

David held the note to his chest in thought. "Malachy is right. We shall give God the glory. Praise the Almighty for His mercy upon us."

In my heart, I loved Malachy for his goodness. He was a true saint, hearing and obeying God's voice that guided him to us in our time of need. A few of his words did leave my heart unsettled. He hadn't said Henry would not "die *at* this time," he'd said he would not "die this time." *This time.* What could he mean?

I put the chrism in my private coffer, hoping not to need it again.

Chapter Sixteen

Within the sennight, we returned to Eads Hall. News of Henry's condition had been underplayed. Most thought the prince had merely suffered a bout of sweating sickness. Only our closest subjects knew the truth.

St Martin greeted us on our return, commenting how well Kelton had kept the manor functioning with efficiency and grace.

I was surprised by his high praise. Henry thanked his cousin for his efforts. Even Glenore commented on how nice the new steward was.

One evening soon after we'd arrived home, a letter came by herald from King Stephen's wife, Queen Matilda of Boulogne. The herald stood in the great hall perspiring, dusty from the road and smelling of horse.

Henry read it to himself, then aloud to me:

Prince Henry,
Ranulf, Earl of Chester and his half-brother William de Roumare,
have captured Lincoln Castle. King Stephen attempted to take it back

without success. Empress Matilda is preparing to be crowned queen. All is in turmoil. I beg you join forces with King Stephen and march on the castle again.

I placed my hand upon Henry's arm, wishing in my heart he didn't have to get involved, but his allegiances had been promised to King Stephen and his wife, Henry's cousin. If Empress Matilda became monarch, Henry could very well lose his holdings.

Henry frowned, his eyes holding deep concern. "Come." He led the herald into the dining hall. "Tell us more of what you know. Glenore, bring this man stew and bread and ale."

The herald smiled in gratitude. "The name's Odo, and I appreciate your generosity."

We settled at the table.

Henry leaned toward the man. "Tell me all you know, Odo."

Glenore brought in mugs and poured the ale. Odo drank long then put his mug down and looked at Glenore expectantly.

Henry nodded approval. "And bring us a bottle of wine."

Odo emptied the mug a second time.

Henry leaned forward. "Go on, tell us of the battle."

Dragging off his cap, Odo scratched his damp curls. "Ranulf, Earl of Chester, and his brother sent their wives to Lincoln Castle under the guise of making a social call upon the wife of the constable."

"Their wives?" I couldn't imagine women visiting with each other could have aught to do with a battle.

"Aye." Odo wagged his head. "After their visit, Ranulf arrived dressed in ordinary clothes with his personal guard—three knights, they were—to take the women home. The men had been invited into the castle to wait for the women, and that's when they pulled hidden weapons from under their tunics and seized more weapons in the castle."

Henry balked. "But four at most against an entire castle could hardly be victorious."

"True." Odo took a sip of wine. "Ranulf didn't have to win the castle on his own, he only had to open the gates. You see, his brother, William, waited outside with his armed knights. The castle fell within an hour."

Henry sat back. "What trickery, that scoundrel. It's exactly what I'd expect of Ranulf."

A trough of roasted chicken was placed before Odo. He rubbed his soiled hands together then broke off a leg and ate it in three bites. "High praise to the cook."

I grew impatient watching him savor the meat. "But what needs to be done now?"

Through a mouthful, Odo mumbled, "Word was sent to King Stephen to come rescue the castle and village." He licked his fingers, picked up the mug, and for a third time drank it to empty. "King Stephen thought quelling Ranulf would be a simple victory and encouraged the earls who supported him to battle at his side."

My breath caught. "Pray tell, which earls?"

"Let me think." Odo pushed his mug toward the wine bottle and watched Henry pour him another drink. "Among them Count Alan, Earl Hugh of East Anglia, and William de Warenne of Surrey. William of Ypres was present, too."

I sank with concern. "William of Surrey is my brother. What of my twin half-brothers, Robert and Waleran de Beaumont?"

"They are unharmed and still close advisors to King Stephen." The herald started into a pudding.

Henry slipped his arm around me. "Are the earls safe?"

"Most of them." Odo snickered. "When they arrived at Lincoln, the king and his earls laid siege to the castle, thinking they had already won. All puffed up in pride, they were. Unbeknownst to them, Ranulf had snuck out the gates and gathered an army that attacked from the surrounding forest."

"Nae." I could hardly bear the thought of Ranulf and his conniving ways. "How could such a thing happen?"

"Oh, God knew it would happen before it did and told the king in so many words." Odo leaned forward and lowered his voice as if telling a secret. "Before King Stephen left on this ill-fated quest, he took mass on the day of the Purification of St Mary. The candle he held suddenly went out and broke in half. Then it mended and relit with him still holding it. You see? He was told."

Henry stroked his beard, clearly confused. "And what did that tell him?"

"The king and those earls sinned because they didn't take the threat seriously. We know the healing of the candle to be a sign that the king will lose the kingdom for a time, but by God's wondrous and glorious favor, he shall get it back again."

Henry stood and started to pace. "Were souls lost in the battle?"

"Aye. Both sides fought fiercely. When King Stephen's knights saw they were losing the fight, they retreated, leaving poor King Stephen with only a few of his most loyal."

"My brother…was he one of those who fought to the end?" I held my breath in hope to hear of his bravery.

"Nae, I'm sorry, my lady. He fought valiantly but was amongst the retreaters. Do not blame him, for it was a wretched battle."

Henry lowered his head. "And what of my half-brother, Simon de Senlis? Did he retreat as well?"

The herald straightened. "Nae, he was one of the few to stand to the end."

"I leave at dawn to speak with my father on how he wants me to proceed."

That night, I followed Henry to our bedchamber as he readied himself for what lay ahead. He drew me against him, his arm firmly around my waist as we took time for a tender moment together.

I could hardly believe he may have to fight in yet another battle. He'd nearly lost his life in war just before we married, and again with the grappling hook, in the kidnapping, and then with his illness. Would it never end?

Although we enjoyed peace throughout Northumbria and Scotland proper, we could no longer ignore what was happening so close—even at the footsteps of the home of my birth.

Henry sighed. "This is a blow to King Stephen's authority. It is not my desire to go, but my duty." His expression was one of confident determination, but just as quickly his face softened, and he tucked a stray hair behind my ear.

"Your father had said at our celebration that Scotland would not intervene when Empress Matilda entered England. Perchance he's still of that mind?" My voice trembled slightly. I was on the brink of tears, fighting not to cry in front of him. My job was to support him as a brave wife, not cause him more concern.

"He may change his mind when he hears that King Stephen has lost Lincoln Castle and my cousin, the queen, has asked specifically for me."

Chapter Seventeen

As worries often are, they'd been for naught. Henry returned a sennight later with the news that his father insisted Scotland would not fight England's war.

The light of the sun finally conquered the darkness. Easter arrived in a cold and quiet event. The following morning, I'd had enough of being inside and bundled into a mantle to enjoy the fresh air outside. I inspected the lone grapevine that climbed the wall, willing it to survive and grow more branches.

I turned to look out over the distant hills and the small huddles of trees which had turned from winter's stark nakedness and began to bud out. Though there was a type of beauty to this barren countryside I was beginning to appreciate, it didn't feel like home.

Henry came up behind me, encircling me with his arms and kissed my neck. His body warmed me, and his breath played across my neck.

"You have a melancholy air about you." He gently turned me to face him. "Are you again missing Reigate?"

I nodded. "I feel like a spoiled child. But, *mon amour*, I look over these bare hills and wonder how you will ever keep the promise you once made—that all I had at Reigate will be mine at Eads Hall."

He kissed my forehead. "I'm sorry it's taken so long to keep my promise. But you'll be happy to learn I've hired stonecutters to make a path through your garden. They will also build a wall to keep out wandering sheep." He chuckled, and his misty breath floated away. "I've retained a carpenter to construct an arbor to hold the many vines that will blossom here and shade you in summer. Tomorrow, the gardeners will plant seeds, bulbs, and trees. Your garden will be glorious. Every time you step outside, you'll see Reigate's splendor."

I brought him close. "Do you truly believe we can fill this bareness with greenery and color?"

"I do. And I shall help divert water from the brook and have a pond dug for you." He gave me a boyish grin. "I want my children to have the delight of watching ducks and swans play as did you when a child."

I laughed with joy and embraced him tightly. My appreciation deepened at his expression of devotion.

True to his word, the next day, despite the still cold weather, stone workers laid a path that wandered through what would one day be my garden. And the following morning they began to build a wall. Gardeners planted all manner of vegetation. Maurice directed them with planting a kitchen garden.

In all fairness, Henry was as new to Eads Hall as me and mayhap excited to fill the courtyard with life. I loved following the path and imagining the flowers and vines that might grow along the wall and over the arbor.

Through the long grey weeks, I wondered if a true spring would ever come. I grew to appreciate the vigor of walks in the cold and being accompanied by Henry when he was available. I especially loved returning to the contrasting warmth of a robust fire, drinking warm ale, and sharing stories together.

Giffard shared humorous dramas from his childhood, and when we could get St Martin to talk, the giant recounted hair-raising battles.

Henry told tales of his experiences in the Scottish court. I shared memories of my mother's charitable work and glorious parties while trying not to miss her so much.

Kelton never joined in.

A warm mantle was still needed to go outdoors, but my breath fogged less and less until one day not at all. Spring arrived as if it had been there all along. In my garden, signs of growth peeked through the soil, and the shamelessly naked branches of distant trees leafed and bloomed in a sure sign they would soon regain their modesty.

I ventured out daily to discover more leaves, budding flowers, and the singing of birds returned from warmer climes. Observing the many rebirths of spring, I reflected that we had been married almost two years with no births of our own. My heart suffered with the emptiness of that void, and my fears grew that I would be unable to please my husband and father-in-law with an heir.

Then there was Kelton. There was something about him. Every time Henry's steward looked at me, I felt his judgments. He probably thought I'd yet to do any act of greatness since I couldn't even produce an heir.

Though he treated Henry with respect, resentment tainted his voice when he spoke to me alone. On each encounter, I could not help but stiffen, waiting for him to accuse me of misdeed.

My patience with his behavior waned, but I daren't tell Henry. My husband had been trying with such fervor to include his cousin. Henry was a better person than I.

As May warmed the earth and finally summer came, to my joy, I was certain I was with child. I wanted to tell Henry in a special way. So, after deliberation, I sewed a tiny newborn gown with a simple embroidery pattern of *fluer de lis* around the hem and placed it in a jeweled box.

I awaited his return from Jedburgh where he and Giffard — who, since the recovery, had not left Henry's side — visited with Henry's vassals on business.

He walked into our bedchamber on the expected day, and my heart fluttered with anticipation. He sat to remove his shoes.

I endeavored to speak calmly whilst announcing, "I have a gift for you, *mon cher*." I handed him the box in joyous anticipation. "It's a token of my devotion."

"A gift?" He opened the box, removed the little gown, and held it at arm's length in puzzled examination. Then realization dawned, and a broad smile filled his face. "Are you . . .?"

"Aye!" I laughed joyfully.

He stood. "When will the blessed event take place?"

"March, I hope."

He laid the gown on the bed, swooped me in his arms and carried me out the door. "Hail to all in the house! I am to become father of an heir to the throne of Scotland!"

I clung to him for safety. The stone stairs loomed ahead. Fearing in his exuberance that he might try to carry me down, I pleaded through a nervous laugh, "Henry, enough, put me down."

He set me on my feet and descended, announcing joyously to the servants as they wandered in, "We shall have a feast and invite all around to join in our celebration. How soon can we do it? Send out our hunters to bring pheasant, duck, geese, roe, all that they can."

Maurice's joy showed in his expression. He clasped his pudgy hands over his ample belly. And Glenore applauded.

With nearly all present, Henry again wrapped me in his arms and swung me around. "Scotland will have its heir, and Northumbria will have a new son to be proud of!"

"But Henry," I whispered in his ear. "What if our baby is a girl?"

Henry stopped as though the thought never occurred to him. His smile returned with a determined gleam in his eye. "Then she will be her father's princess, and we will try again for a son."

Laughter and applause filled our manor.

Henry bent close and whispered, "But we both know it's a red-haired boy."

My body warmed with the knowledge we'd both been given.

With invitations quickly prepared, heralds rode out the following morning.

Excitement hovered everywhere. Maids hummed whilst working. Servants smiled in their chores. And I? I was pampered more than I'd ever been as if already Scotland's queen.

Three evenings later, we had a grand celebration with neighbors from all around, enjoying food, wine, and entertainment. Where Henry found musicians on such short notice, I know not, for Eads Hall was quite secluded in the moors. But find them he did, and the joyous evening was filled with feasting, laughter, dancing and many heartfelt congratulations.

I thought the news would make Kelton happy. That he would accept me now. But as usual, his reaction puzzled me. He stayed glum all evening, standing in the shadows.

A few weeks later, I chose to stay longer in bed than normal. My stomach was not behaving, as I'd been told happens when one is with child. The curtains had been drawn, and my eyes shut in an attempt to avoid a mad dash to the chanty.

Henry had been about most of the morning and burst into the room, startling me.

"I've been talking to St Martin and Sybil and they tell me I'm remiss in my duties."

"How so?" I asked, eyes closed.

"I must find you the best midwife," Henry said and touched me affectionately. "What of that woman who cared for me at Carlisle? Wasn't she a midwife?"

"She was, but nae, not her." I thought on the old woman, Alba, and although she made a great effort, she was too set in her ways and ultimately would have not saved Henry's life. "I'm certain we can find better."

"Aye, aye." He paused to think. "We will scour every burgh from Edinburgh to Glasgow to find the very best midwife in Scotland. Mayhap I can send Kelton to gather names?"

My stomach lurched, and it wasn't caused by the child. "Henry, I grew up thinking my mother would be with me when I gave birth to my first child. Do you think that may be possible?" I ran a hand over my swelling abdomen, marveling at the wonder of it.

"Is that a womanly thing? To long for your mother at childbirth?"

I peeked open an eye. "Well, she has risked her life through the ordeal twelve times, and one of those with twins." I closed my eye, willing what was in my stomach to stay down. "My mother has always had my welfare in mind, and I miss her. Aye, it's a womanly thing, as you call it, to yearn for the wisdom and comfort of one's mother at a time like this."

Henry intertwined his fingers with mine. "Write to her."

I promptly sent a missive asking Mother if she could come for the birth of my first child. To my disappointment, her reply was that with my brother, William, at war in the Holy Land, Reigate needed her.

I understood and tried to put my longing aside.

Maggie and I kept our hands busy embroidering gowns for the coming babe. As summer waned, we'd completed dozens of them, far more than my new child would ever wear.

Autumn came upon us faster than I remember it doing so in Reigate. Was this country always to be frigid? One day in winter, I put down my needle and didn't know how I could continue. The loneliness crept in worse than the cold.

A knock at the door interrupted my boredom. Maggie answered it.

"Lady Ada." Fenella stepped before me and gave a swift curtsy.

"*Bienvenue*, Fenella. How do you fare?"

"By order of King David, I've been freed of all my obligations until your little one has safely made his way into the world. Is that to your liking?"

I attempted to leap to my feet to embrace her but arose considerably slower than I'd hoped. "Praise the heavens. Your company will be a welcome gift."

Giffard was not with us. He'd left months before, asking to be excused from harvest season as his brother in the north had taken ill. In the past, seeing Fenella with Giffard had made her being near Henry much easier. Now, I'd simply have to endure it.

"What is this?" She pointed at the pile of gowns we had embroidered. "You're little one must have a good Scottish *fáilte*. English women may embroider, but a Celt weaves. We will use the wool from local sheep to make blankets to keep your wee one warm. We could dye a few to match your embroidery. That might be nice."

"Aye, is there a craftsman in town where we can purchase the yarn?"

"Lady Ada." Fenella wagged a finger at me. "Proper Scottish women make their own yarn. That's part of the joy."

In the next weeks, Fenella taught me to use a distaff and spinning wheel. She showed me how to stretch the carted wool fiber and feed it through the bobbin as I turned the wheel slowly. She sat at my elbow, encouraging and guiding me as I turned the wheel too quickly, over and over, and lost my yarn in the bobbin only to start over again. Her patience rivaled that of Job.

By the time I finally got the rhythm of it, the weeks felt like days. Then she brought out the loom and I went through the same process of learning a new skill. A month had passed by the time the first blanket was complete. Unlike my beautiful, delicate and tiny embroidered stitches, the blanket was lumpy in places and loose in others. I was excited for a second try and told Henry so that evening.

"Henry, have you seen what Fenella taught me to do?" I handed him the finished blanket.

He examined it and smiled. "I hope she doesn't think she's done with her teaching."

I took my prize. "It may be a little rough, but it's only a first try. Tomorrow I plan on starting again. We are also going to soften the yarn with suet and lye."

"It's wonderful to see you so engaged in this project. I'm glad I invited her to come." Henry grew serious. "Will you have time to do this activity and still prepare for William of Corbridge tomorrow?"

"Of course. The cooks and servants will take care of most of the matters for the evening, and I look forward to enjoying the meal together and being present whilst you discuss your affairs." I sighed and put my hand on my growing belly. "After a good night sleep, that is. This little one sometimes wears me out."

"Mayhap you should retire after the meal. There will be plenty of opportunities in our marriage to share in my dealings." Henry furrowed his brow. "It's the child you must think of. Don't feel you must do too much."

"Eventually, as your queen, I want to be part of all your dealings. I want to be a true partner to you—a helpmeet in every way." I stifled a yawn. "But for now, I get so tired. We shall see how I feel tomorrow."

As I lay in bed that night, I couldn't sleep. When Fenella had first returned to Eads Hall, she told me she came by order of the king, but Henry said that he had requested her.

Chapter Eighteen

On one of Henry's outings, he brought home a cradle carved with the checkered emblem of the Warenne family. I could hardly contain my joy. Gingerly, I knelt to examine it more closely.

Henry knelt beside me. "St Martin had it specially made by a craftsman near Hautwesel. Do you like it?"

"Like? Aye, I *love* it. Our baby will slumber peacefully." I smoothed my hand over my stomach to tame another series of kicks. "Unlike it's doing now," I added with a light chuckle.

Henry placed his hand near mine and waited, but the child didn't move. He frowned with disappointment.

"Do not worry, *mon amour*. Our baby is calmed by your touch." I gave him an affectionate kiss on the cheek. "In a little more than a month, you shall hold our tiny one in your arms."

He returned the kiss. "And then our sweet child will get to see one of your lovely blankets."

I laughed. They had not greatly improved since the first. Blanket making was not one of my gifts. "I made them with love and hopefully that's enough—even for the son of a prince."

"I'm certain it is." He looked at me soberly. "My father has drawn a document that he requests both of us to sign. We must go to Roxburgh Castle to do so."

"He wants me to sign too? You jest? Only men sign documents."

"Father has requested it. Do you think you're able to travel?"

"If I must, but it's so near my confinement, I really should not."

Henry helped me to my feet. "This declaration will renew all the lands held by my father and King Stephen to me as Earl of Northumbria. As my wife and possible dowager, should anything happen to me, he wants you to sign as well. If I die before you, this land would be yours and by rights our children's."

"Isn't that unusual?" I remembered my discussion with King David at Carlisle and thought of the stories I'd heard of widows losing rights to their husband's property after his death or being forced to remarry to retain their land. "Even without you, I could remain here?"

"My father was clear on that fact. He wants you to be supported by the crown."

I shook my head. "But certainly, this consideration can be included without me actually signing the document."

Henry shrugged. "Father insisted on it. I know not why. Remember, unless that document is signed, the point is moot. As it stands now, my right to the land is only Stephen's word. This document will make our position official. The king wants us to come on the morrow."

Pleased by the King of Scots great concern on my behalf, I agreed.

At sunrise, we bundled up and departed. Henry and his guards rode horseback whilst I was buried in blankets in the van. The icy river near home glistened at its shore and icicles hung from trees and eaves, creating beautifully frosted scenery.

The next day, the van stopped after a long climb.

"Come out, Ada." Henry called.

Keeping a blanket wrapped tightly around me, Henry helped me from the van. The wind blew fiercely. Stretched before us was the most marvelous panorama I'd ever seen. "Lovely," I gasped.

"You're looking at Scotland." Much pride was evident in his voice.

My view was carried to distant horizons, snowcapped mountains and rolling hills, a sky halcyon-blue.

"Someday I'll show it to you in a warmer season when the broad valleys are green and fertile and heather stretches as far as the eye can see." He pointed northeast. "That far mountain is Broad Law." He pointed northwest. "And we travel that way to Kelso, where I spent my youth."

Everywhere below us hills broke the view. I felt as if the land called to me, asking to come make my home. I didn't know the future, but my heart told me this was where it laid.

The rest of the journey was cold and uncomfortable, I didn't complain, but I was grateful when we arrived at Roxburgh Castle a day later.

After Henry and his father signed the parchment for which we'd traveled so far, King David dipped the pen in ink and handed me the quill.

Surely, he saw the doubt in my eyes as I hesitated to take it.

"This is the first of many declarations you will sign, Ada. Someday you'll be queen, and I want all the world to respect your power as a member of the royal family."

Was he speaking prophetic? I wanted to believe so.

With a kind look in his eyes, he continued, "You shall see. You're an intelligent, wise and accomplished woman with a good heart. I envision a time when your works shall be recognized as a major contribution to increasing women's privileges. Following your example, women will be able to own property in their own name alone without a husband or man of nobility as overlord."

I flushed at the king's kind words and his vision for women. With greater understanding of why he'd insisted we make the trip at such an inclement time, I bowed my head to the king and stepped forward. Recommitting myself to the good I might do with my station, as my king was doing with his, I signed my name.

Afterward, I felt strange. Like a little girl who sat on her father's throne, comfortable in her imaginations, until she was caught and shooed away.

At the same time, something miraculous had been accomplished from which I would not be shooed away. I began to see the power granted me in association with the great visionary goals of the king and his son. They were grooming me to join them in advancing the cause of freedom for all, even women.

Chapter Nineteen

Over the next month, my time grew closer. The birth had to be soon. How could I get any bigger?

I followed Fenella out the front door. "I'll be in the garden if you need me."

Her eyebrows rose. "Too much walking brings on the birth of a child. You really should go to your chamber."

We'd prepared my chamber for childbirth with clean cloths, bowls, sheets, tapestries to cover the windows, and crucifixes on the walls. "I'll stay close to the house." I told her as she headed to the stables to exercise the horses.

Henry was visiting a number of nearby estates to see how they fared through the long, cold months. He was due home soon, and he'd want to restrict me too. I'd had pains that morning but didn't tell anyone. I needed to venture outside— one last time at least—before my confinement.

All the womenfolk in the manor knew my time was near. I was tired of being watched so closely. I needed freedom.

I meandered along the stone path around the thawing pond, enjoying my solitude. As I passed the arbor, I came upon an old woman in a plain brown mantle, nearly hidden behind the budding vines. Her wild grey-streaked hair looked familiar. When she stepped forward, I realized it was Boudica, a howdie Fenella had hired to be my midwife.

I sensed she'd been waiting for me.

I'd thought either Henry or I would choose who would deliver our little one, but we never felt confident about any of the midwives we'd interviewed. Fenella assured me that, although of a vague blend of druidism and Pictish superstition, Boudica had a widespread reputation for successfully delivering babies. Henry had hired her on Fenella's insistence.

Boudica took up residency in the servants' quarters to be near me when the birthing hour arrived. I still felt unsure but, with no clear alternative in the area, endured the situation.

"Good morning, Boudica." I tried to sound pleasant.

The woman was odd with her very-busy manner, always coming and going and doing. "I 'ope ye be still wearin' the decoction I rubbed on your *brù* this mornin'."

Her demand surprised me. I smoothed my hand over my belly. "Aye, it's still there."

"Fine. The poultice of flaxseed and comfrey will encourage proper position for birthin'." She stepped to me and placed her hands on my abdomen, pushing this way and that.

I tried not to react to her intrusiveness.

"Ye 'ave dropped. 'Tis good. Any time now." She stepped away and shook her bag as if to loosen its contents.

"What are you carrying?" I asked.

"'Tis bird dung—mostly eagle—and cat droppin's, too. If your labor don'na progress, we'll burn the dung. It gives off such an offensive odor that your bairn will 'ave no choice but to be born." She chuckled at her jest and headed away from the garden to reaches unknown.

I grinned at her strange ways and walked on. I knew little of childbirth, being the youngest of my mother's children, and my brother William's wife had returned to her mother's home to birth her daughter.

When Maggie had birthed twins, I'd been hastened from the chamber. Truly, I knew very little about the process.

My middle tightened, then relaxed. Something it had been doing for several days. I thought of it as my body embracing my baby. It hadn't been painful, but now it took my breath away and forced me to sit upon a stone bench.

Soon came the most intense pain yet. It spread across my abdomen and built before peaking. When it finally subsided, I rose to my feet and slowly waddled the way I'd come, both excited and scared. "Fenella! My pains have started." I called toward the stables but heard no reply. As I entered the house, the maids in hearing came running.

Glenore, the kitchen maid, yelled out, "Fetch the howdie." She led me to a chair. "Sit right here, m'lady."

The other maids stared at me, a combination of concern and anticipation on their faces. "Nae need to worry yet," Glenore told them confidently. "These things take time. I've been to many a birthin'." She shooed the maids to their stations. "I'll go fetch Da' Fenella, m'lady." She rushed out the door.

The pain subsided. My breathing returned to normal and I was uncertain what had really happened because I suddenly felt fine.

Minutes went by. I thought to call Glenore back and tell her I'd overreacted. I pushed to stand and my chest suddenly started to pound. Powerful tightening in my belly began again. I tried to endure it, remembering Glenore's instruction to stay seated, but I pushed completely upright just the same. I said aloud to no one, "I can no longer tolerate sitting in this hard chair."

As the pain increased, I doubled over and was in jeopardy of falling when I heard the door open and felt secure hands supporting me. "What do you want me to do?" I'd assumed it was Fenella but was surprised by Henry's low voice instead.

I grasped his arms as the pain tightened. "Wait . . ." I cried out and rested my head against his chest, squeezing his arms as tight as I could. At last the pain subsided. I nodded. "I can move."

"We must get you to your bedchamber." He gently lifted me and cautiously carried me upstairs.

Glenore stepped into the hall and quickly ran ahead of us into our bedchamber.

Maggie rushed in. "What can I do?"

Henry reluctantly left, and the women helped me disrobe to my chemise. I laid against the bed pillows in a brief reprieve for which I was most thankful.

"Breath slow and deep. Try to relax," Glenore ordered, oddly bold compared to the shy girl she'd been when I'd met her. "The more relaxed ye are, the easier the bairn will come."

Sometime later, Boudica burst into the bedchamber carrying a jar and her dingy pouch. "I've brought me apprentice, Jasmine."

A young woman entered, carrying a large bag that concealed most of her face. She moved to the corner of the bedchamber into a shadow.

"Open the window for fresh air but keep out the light." Boudica instructed Maggie. "Nae a one is to wear belts in the birthin' chamber. Nae, not a knot anywheres."

The maids quickly loosened their belts and set them aside.

Glenore sat in the chair to untie a knot in the scarf over her hair.

The apprentice remained in the corner, holding tight to her bag.

"Nae a one is to sit with their legs crossed. We want the bairn to freely find its way into the world." Boudica picked up a looking glass from the table. "Every glass must be turned or covered so the child's soul will remain free." She set the looking glass facedown and pointed at Maggie. "Go. Make sure there be no open glasses in the house. Turn every one of 'em."

She pointed to Glenore. "Open every bottle in the bedchamber."

Boudica looked about. "Start boilin' oats—enough for all to eat."

It sounded so disjointed, but I was not educated in childbirth, and if it would help rid me of this misery, I'd accept all of Boudica's advice.

Another wave of searing pain squeezed my womb. As it passed, my increasing fatigue moved me toward exhaustion.

Glenore wiped my brow as I attempted to normalize my breathing.

The howdie opened the jar she'd brought. "Tis a potion made of rowanberries. It will repel all fairies." She set the open jar at the foot of the bed.

An overly sweet fragrance filled the air, aggravating my nausea. "Could you move it away? I cannot tolerate the smell."

"Nae," Boudica said. "Ye don'na want fairies castin' spells on your *wee yin*. This will keep 'em away."

Another pain spread. There was no use arguing with her as she would have her way. Besides, I was thankful all precautions were being taken, strange as her methods seemed.

I could rest between pains but grimaced with each cramp and did whatever Boudica told me to do to manage things as well as possible.

The day dragged on with little obvious progress.

Maggie took over Glenore's job and wiped moisture from my brow.

My energy was long spent. I caught a glimpse of the apprentice still in the corner. Why was she here? And where was Fenella?

At least I wasn't worrying about Henry. What a gift that he had arrived before the baby. The birthing was women's business—painful and exhausting women's business. Yet, at least he was on the other side of the door, waiting for the joy that would soon be ours. How I longed to see his smile when he held our new infant in his arms

A pain jerked me from those thoughts. *"Maman!"* I called out, wishing so dearly that she were here. She'd gone through this travail many times. I felt bonded to her in a new way, bonded to every woman who had gone through the sacrifice to bring a child into the world.

Hours passed. I didn't understand why Fenella didn't come and wondered if she was queasy about such things. The maids came and went, always being reminded not to cross their arms or legs, not to wear belts, and not to speak in loud tones.

Though my eyes closed often, I heard every word as I braced myself for the next pain and prayed the child would come and that it would soon be over. The sun set and candles were lit.

"It's time to burn the dung." Boudica emptied the contents of the pouch into the fire. Immediately, the offensive odor overtook the bedchamber.

I wanted to hold my breath. I glimpsed at the apprentice in the corner, hovering in the dark.

The howdie came to my bedside, holding a white stone over my head. "Open all roads and doors," she chanted as she circled the stone above me. "In that epiphany by which Christ appeared both human and God and opened the gates of hell. Just so, *wee yin*, may ye come out of this door without dyin', and without the death of ye mother."

Death. I was too exhausted to object to her chants, too spent, and felt I could easily slip into eternal slumber. At this point, I didn't care to live, only for it be over! Sweat stung my eyes, and I could hardly lift my hand to wipe it away. Where was Maggie?

Another wave of pain came. "*Maman*, help me! Help me, dear God." I sobbed, not only for the pain I'd endured for hours but for the ache of my mother's tender touch and loving presence.

Then, a different pain started, bringing an urgency to push out the child. And finally, blessed relief. I sighed, relaxed, and closed my eyes. It was finished. Death was welcome now. I listened for the angels' songs greeting me to heaven.

Instead, I heard the cry of a baby.

Elated voices shouted around me, but I could not move. "He's beautiful!" Glenore exclaimed.

My eyelids fluttered. "He!"

"Aye. Beautiful, with red hair like yours. Open your eyes, noble mother, and behold your prince." Glenore held the infant for me to see.

"He's lovely." I smiled and closed my eyes again. "A son." I must rally. I must live to raise my son. Henry's tiny, beautiful heir.

There was a scurry around me, cleaning up I presumed. The look of the bedchamber had changed. The apprentice was no longer standing in the corner. Fenella stood at the foot of my bed, looking at me without saying a word.

I wanted my friend to know that I was grateful she was here now and that I understood there must be a reason she chose not to be here during the birth. Indeed, if I could have not been here, I may have chosen such. But it was all worth it for my sweet little one. I gave Fenella the kindest smile I could muster. "Did you see him?" my voice was hardly a whisper.

Fenella lifted my boy, and I noticed her eyes glisten with fresh tears. Tears of joy, I assumed.

A joy I shared. I relaxed, and my tired eyes closed again.

"Bring a blanket. he shivers!" It was Boudica's voice. "Bring mead. *Luath*! And the porridge."

Footsteps sounded as someone left the bedchamber. "A drop of mead in the *wee yin's* mouth will ward off evil."

I must have drifted into sleep. The next thing I knew, Glenore awakened me, holding oats to my lips on a spoon, urging me to eat. "It's a Scottish custom," she whispered, "for all the women present to eat three spoonfuls of porridge after the birth of a bairn. It's for good luck."

"Where's my son?"

"He's lyin' beside ye."

I rose on my elbow to admire my child. So beautiful. So sweet. My heart swelled with love.

Glenore shoved the oatmeal closer. "Take a bite. You're Scottish. Ye just gave birth to a li'l Scottish prince." After the first bite of porridge, Glenore encouraged me to eat another. "It'll give ye strength," she insisted.

Boudica sat by the window, circling her hand over the jar of rowanberries and softly chanting.

-162-

The mysterious apprentice had vacated the corner. Fenella was gone too.

I asked Glenore, "Where is Dame Fenella?"

"She begged your pardon but wished to give the news to the king personally."

I laughed at the image of her riding at top speed across the Scottish moors. The king would be pleased.

I turned my attention to my son. "Little one, we made it through in spite of all, and we are alive."

"Aye," Glenore held out the final spoonful of oatmeal. "But ye must take care and rest. Many mothers do not rest and . . . are gone in days. My sister met that fate."

I swallowed the porridge.

Tears gathered in Glenore's eyes. That poor girl had endured so much loss in her life.

I took her hand. "Don't worry, I'll rest and be well. God bless you for helping me."

She smiled with a nod. "Aye. Ye must let me do all your biddin'."

A knock sounded at the door. Henry stepped in and Glenore stepped out, leaving us alone.

"My darling." He knelt and laid his cheek against my breast, wrapping his arms around me. "You're a brave, wonderful woman."

"And you are the father of a beautiful son." I pulled away the blanket so he could have a better look at his heir.

Henry lifted him from the bed. "We saw this little redhead before he was born, didn't we." He tenderly smiled at me and a reverence fell over the room.

My heart expanded and a confirmation bestowed that God was in our lives.

"We shall name him after my grandfather, the great Malcolm, King of Scots." Henry wrapped the child snugly in the blanket and took him to the window that faced northward, pushing open the shutters. Cool air flooded in. "Look, all ye of Scotland!" he shouted. "Your future king is born!" He held up the child for anyone who had strayed to the moors in the dark of night. "Henry, be careful!" I laughed with delight. "Aye, our future king—a child destined by right of birth to someday sit on the throne of his forefathers—but take care not to drop the lad out the window before he can even begin his destiny."

Chapter Twenty

Alone in the nursery, I rocked little Malcolm. "We've placed a great mantle on your shoulders, sweet son. Do you forgive us?" Would there be need of forgiveness? I hoped not. "I suppose these things are not in my hands. God ordains monarchs. For this reason, and many others, you must live."

Malcolm whimpered.

I nuzzled my knuckle into his mouth.

Though a happy child, he seemed to acquire every illness that came into the manor. Having refused the wet nurse, I suckled him myself, hoping it would somehow help him fight the fevers and coughs he had too often.

Glenore came to the nursery threshold. "M'lady, may I speak with ye?" She held concern in her eyes.

To lighten the mood I inquired, "Have the guards been in the kitchen begging more jam and biscuits?"

"Nae, m'lady. It's 'bout gossip I heard in the burgh this day." The worry on her face deepened.

"Sit and tell me what you heard."

She pulled a stool close. "Do ye 'member the howdie's apprentice— Jasmine, I think was her name—who came with Boudica to deliver Malcolm?"

"Aye, I remember her. I thought it odd that she watched from the corner of the room, offered no help of any kind, then disappeared without a word."

"Well." Glenore leaned in closer. "I heard it told, that in the excitement and confusion after Malcolm was born, Jasmine stole the afterbirth." Glenore bit her lip. "She's used it to put a curse on your son." Her eyes watered.

"Witchcraft." I gazed at my son's innocent face. "But why?"

"M'lady, though ye gained favor of many, there's still some who resent the Scottish royals here." She frowned. "'Specially ye bein' English. Ye must know many Scots dislike anyone that's Norman."

Was there any winning the favor of those here? I gazed into the girl's face. "Do you believe in witchcraft, Glenore?"

She looked away, then back, and nodded slowly. "M'lady, I've seen a few of its dark works. Evil things. Never good." Her eyes grew wide. "A man died after a woman cursed him— right in front of his family. One time, a woman drove a dog mad, and it took an arrow to put him out of his mis'ry. And an old hag caused warts to grow on a young girl because the hag be jealous of her beauty."

A tiny foot escaped the warmth of the blanket. I tucked it under again. "But, Glenore, men do die, dogs go mad, and young girls grow warts—all without witch's curses. I cannot believe my son is ill because of an incantation over afterbirth."

Glenore seemed as though she wished to say more but instead stood and curtsied. "I wanted to tell ye what I heard so's ye'd be aware, m'lady."

"*Merci* for your concern. I'll take your words under consideration."

She curtsied again and left the bedchamber.

I pulled my babe close. Did I believe in such things as black magic?

Malcolm coughed, reminding me of just how many illnesses he'd suffered during the first five weeks of his life. I retrieved from memory the image of that dark corner shielding the mysterious woman Jasmine —watching, watching—lurking from the shadows with her large bag. The woman was still lurking in our lives.

My stomach sickened. Babe in arms, I rushed to my bedchamber and retrieved Abbot Malachy's chrism from my coffer. I sank to my knees, crucifix in hand. "I beg of thee, God, heal my son. Protect him. Undo whatever harm this woman might have done."

Weeks passed. Malcolm's health remained fragile and he showed no signs of thriving. During one illness, he couldn't keep his milk down, and I feared he was close to death. I said many prayers on his behalf and cried many tears.

Henry was away, and I had no one to talk to but Maggie. I looked across the chess board at her, almost hating to ask about Jasmine for fear Maggie may well believe in magic also. But I thought not. She'd been chosen from the gentry as my lady-in-waiting by my mother and had come from a bad situation of neglect by a widowed father. My mother and her kind heart brought Maggie to our home as a young girl. It had been my first lesson in charitable kindness.

Maggie thoughtfully considered her next move, fingering her mother's brooch pinned to her surcoat.

"The night Malcolm was born, a woman came with the midwife, do you remember?"

"Aye, she was a queer one." She didn't look up from the game.

"Glenore has told me that her name is Jasmine." I cleared my throat, not knowing if I truly should share this with Maggie. "What I say you must keep in confidence."

She looked up then and drew her brows together. "Aye, I discuss your words with nae a one."

It was true, and I decided to trust her. "Jasmine took my afterbirth to put a curse on Malcolm." Even as I said it, I knew it sounded odd. Yet, the very idea of someone working evil over my son made my heart constrict.

Maggie sputtered for a moment. "*Domina*, nae! This land is wild with its legends, but I cannot believe they have power to destroy a soul. Only God can do such."

She answered as expected. Did magic come from the same power as my dreams? As soon as I thought it, my heart cried *nae*. Never had my dreams led me to do evil. "What Jasmine plays with is harmful to those who we want to have fealty to us."

"That may be so, but truly she cannot harm your child, can she?"

A few days later, Boudica was brought to the nursery, carrying her dingy bag.

I needed to tell the servants that she was no longer welcomed in our home. Malcolm lay asleep in his cradle. I had the impression to stand near him, shielding him from the presence of evil. When she stepped closer, my anger flared. "Why are you here? Haven't you done enough harm by bringing a witch into my home?"

Boudica glanced around the nursery and I knew she understood of what I bespoke.

"I did'na know what Jasmine would do. When she asked if she could come to learn me skills, I thought nothin' of it."

"You said she was your apprentice."

The howdie stared at the floor. "Tis so, but not for child-birthin'. I taught her all I know 'bout herbs, so it was natural to let her come." She raised her face to me with a bolder look in her eye. "But to defend me'self is not me purpose for comin'." She took a step closer. A scent of lavender and oregano came with her. "There's an antidote for this kind of black magic."

Black magic. The words conjured destruction. "What kind of antidote?"

Boudica held up her bag. "I stole this from Jasmine's hovel when she was out."

I didn't need to ask what was in her pouch. I suspected immediately the afterbirth lay within, dried and disintegrating.

"We must take the *wee yin* to the river and sever his ties to her spell." Her eyes darkened. "Then we will throw the contents of this pouch into the current to be carried out to sea, never to return, never to cause your bairn pain again."

"But that is false belief. If my child is healed, it will be from God's doing not from a pagan chant."

Boudica gestured with her hand. "These many weeks ye have prayed, and the *wee yin* is not yet well. It takes action to overcome witchcraft. We must act with haste, and when it's done, ye shall see."

I stepped backward. "Nae. I will not succumb to the ways of witchcraft." I indicated the door with a shaking finger. "Go from me now."

Boudica raised an eyebrow. "I believe your good sense will cause ye to send for me." She curtsied and departed.

My heart raced as she hobbled away. I would not turn to the foolish rituals of superstitious people. God would make Malcolm strong. He had to. The child was a prince, an heir in line to be the future king of the Scots. How could I participate in black magic?

I closed the door to the nursery.

I wished Fenella was here to laugh at such foolish folly. I wished Henry was not away, visiting local merchants. Most of all, I wished my mother here, ever a voice of calm and reason. But I was alone and had to come to my own conclusion.

Chaplain Robert came daily for devotional. He read aloud scripture and shared uplifting insights. I wanted him to bless Malcolm as Father Malachy had blessed Henry, healing him in the instant, but Chaplain Robert never offered a miracle for my son. Mayhap it was simply God's will that my little one should struggle so.

One morning I said to Chaplain Robert, "I have dreams that come true. Is this sorcery?"

His grey eyebrows raised.

"I mean is it a false representation of what God can do?" I asked.

"I don't believe dreams pervert the way of the Lord. Many of our prophets had dreams spiritual in nature that guided them to follow our God."

"I've met people here who speak of curses."

Understanding dawned in his eyes. "Aye, it's the heathen practice of many. In Acts, we read of Paul when he first started his ministry in Athens and found the whole city given in idolatry. He stood on Mars Hill and told them they were too superstitious and that they ignorantly worshiped an unknown God—much as the pagans do here. I believe they want to worship; they just don't know to whom."

"Aye, that may very well be."

"Paul beseeched the people to seek the Lord and told them He was not far from every one of us." And then Chaplain Robert quoted scripture, "*For in Him we live, and move, and have our being; as certain also of your own poets have said, for we are also His offspring.*"

The scripture and Chaplain Robert's words touched me to the soul and gave me a feeling of bright truth, unlike how I felt when Glenore explained the curse to me or Boudica urged me to follow her to the river. "We discount the Lord when we believe there is a higher power."

"That's right, my daughter." Chaplain Robert stood, kissed my hand, and departed.

Days later, Malcolm hadn't improved. I sat and watched his shallow breathing. That bright feeling I'd had with Chaplain Robert once again settled into apprehension. I was brought from my worry by a gentle knock on the door.

It was Mariam. "My lady, Sir Kelton wishes to speak to you."

The news cheered me. That must mean Henry would soon be home. He'd been gone weeks. "Have him come up to the nursery."

Curiously, a frequent visitor had been Kelton. I'd never anticipated this change in our relationship, but he'd become something of a doting kinsman to little Malcolm.

Once, he even complimented me on the way I'd turned Eads Hall into a warm home. Then he took my little one in his arms and sang him a Celtic lullaby. Though I could not understand the words, the tune was haunting and melodic. The experience encouraged me that Kelton was finally accepting me into the family.

Kelton came forward and bowed. "How fares Malcolm?"

"He is no better."

"A shame," he said with his face taut.

"What burdens your heart?"

"I'm leaving for London. King Stephen's forces are struggling. His eldest son has requested my assistance."

I turned away, surprised that the information saddened me. "You would leave Scotland, your home?"

"Scotland was never my home." His voice had a hard edge. "My father is dead and never wanted me. I will become naught more here than a steward."

"You are important to Henry," I said and meant it.

"It's to everyone's advantage that I go. St Martin will be promoted to steward in my place. He's often filling the position in my absence. With an advantageous marriage decided by King Stephen, who knows that I may yet gain the title for which I was born."

His tone had a coldness to it that made me shiver. I wanted to ask whether he bespoke of an earldom or of the throne, but dared not, for fear of the answer. Instead, I remembered a promise I'd made to Henry to support him no matter my personal feelings. "Have you told Henry of your plans?"

He shook his head.

"Speak to him. If he feels he needs you, then stay."

The sound of Henry's voice wafted in from the hall.

"We're here, Henry," he called.

Henry hastened to my side, not glancing at his cousin. "Mariam tells me Malcolm is unwell. Is there to be concern?"

"Aye." I took his hand. "But every physician says they find naught wrong."

Henry nodded. "Kelton and I will try to find help. Someone must know how to cure him."

Should I tell Henry of the curse? I held my tongue. Evil magic had no place in our lives. I also would not tell him of Kelton's sentiments until he felt it time to tell Henry on his own.

The two men, so similar in build and looks, but so different in temperament, walked away side by side. I suspected it would not be that way much longer.

Chapter Twenty-One

Returning Malcolm to the nursery, I cooed in his ear. His crying calmed to little hiccups. I tried to feed him once again, but he fell asleep as soon as he latched onto my breast.

Looking at his translucent skin and thin frame, I knew I needed concrete answers. I needed to pray more and strengthen my faith so I could know the path to save this most precious child.

Reluctantly, I left him with the nursemaid, Mary, and stepped outside.

Spring had finally come.

At the far end of the pond a small grouping of newly planted trees had become a sacred place for me. The young fruit trees were covered in pink blooms. There, secluded beneath a cherry tree, stood a tall statue of Mother Mary. One hand reached out before her as if offering help. In the other, she held a cross.

I dropped to my knees. "Mary, Mother of our Lord," I prayed. "I beg you to strengthen my child so he'll live. I beseech Thee! God healed Henry a year ago in Carlisle. He could heal Malcolm now. Can Father Malachy feel inspired to leave Rome and come to bless my child?" It was possible, wasn't it?

I prayed until my legs stiffened, but I felt empty—as if I was looking in the wrong direction. Still, I refused to consider any other way.

The next sennight, Kelton left Eads Hall for King Stephen's court in London.

King David of Scotland was silent on matters of the English civil war, but Kelton's decision made without his input, solidified his conviction to stay aloof. From that point on, Henry and I rarely spoke of Kelton.

Weeks passed with little improvement in Malcolm's health.

Henry was often gone, acting as joint king with his father. He asked after healers at each passing village but found the same answer. Not a one knew what to do.

With each return, Henry came to the child and knelt with me to pray over him in his cradle.

The curse continued to swirl in my mind. Why would anyone harm an innocent child—no matter who he might be? I seethed at every thought that Jasmine, the howdie's apprentice, would wish my child ill. Each day I held and comforted baby Malcolm, my heart aching.

He often beamed up at me with a beautiful grin that gave me hope. But as time passed and he didn't get well, Boudica's invitation became more tempting. Still, it seemed like a sin even to consider it.

I took to wearing Queen Margaret's silver crucifix, hanging it from my belt. I'd hold it and send up hundreds of prayers daily, besides those at the feet of Mother Mary.

One day, Henry brought home a new physician. After a long examination, the man turned to me. "Your son, I fear, was born with a poor constitution. It's possible he won't survive the year, with even the best of care."

"I will not believe it nor give up hope." Sadness engulfed me.

The physician didn't answer but put a gentle hand on my shoulder as I wept.

In the coming weeks, Malcolm did improve. Mayhap the warmer weather agreed with him. Spring had finally begun to reveal its renewing power. We spent time outside every day, enjoying the garden and the ducks on the pond. He was a great joy to me, but I worried constantly.

I suspected I was with child again and had not yet told anyone.

When Henry was satisfied that Malcolm was getting well, he left to tour his strongholds for fear of war coming north. Empress Matilda tried to gain the crown by bringing her young son—also a Henry—to England from Normandy in hopes the people would accept him as their future king.

Henry wasn't gone a sennight when I entered the nursery and heard Malcolm coughing mercilessly, choking for breath.

Mary looked at me with tears in her eyes.

We all felt so helpless.

I took the babe from her arms. He was paler than any child I'd ever seen, and didn't have the plump cheeks, arms, and legs he should.

I carried him to the kitchen where Maurice boiled water for steam and gave him small sips of warm honey to loosen his chest.

I hardly slept, walking the floor with him most of the night, bouncing and singing, trying to give relief. I cried. I prayed. And, somewhere in the darkness I came to a final decision.

As the morning light peered over the horizon, I called to Glenore, "Go and fetch Boudica."

Boudica arrived before daybreak the next day, carrying a candle in a wooden cup. "Bring the bairn to me." She cradled him with one arm, held the candle close, and peered into his face for far too long.

Could I really trust this woman? Was she a witch too?

"Come." She handed me the babe.

Glenore guarded the door of the empty nursery so the servants might think the child and I rested within. No guard accompanied us so that my actions could be kept secret. I dared not set an example of practicing Pictish myths and witchcraft.

I followed Boudica as if I was the servant. Mayhap I was. "Where are we going?" I asked as we passed the stables shrouded in a heavy mist.

She didn't answer.

Down the lane, in a copse of bushes, she'd hidden her rickety cart and pony.

Although we rode through dense fog, she seemed unaffected by the impediment and urged her old pony as fast as it could pull the cart.

I held Malcolm close and peeked at him occasionally. He slept too soundly. My heart swelled with worry and love. I would not let him die. I prayed God would forgive me for what I was doing. If anyone understood, He knew the love for a son.

As the fog lifted, I smelled musky soil. By the time we reached the banks of the River Allen, the sun had peeked over the hill.

Boudica led me to a bend in the river I'd never seen before.

With Malcolm in my arms, I walked behind her through red poppies. We stopped beside calm waters. Farther downstream, white foam churned before rushing cascades. Nearby, a flock of startled sandpipers took flight, wings fluttering to rise against a mild breeze.

Boudica opened the placenta bag. "Hold *wee yin* aloft," she instructed.

My guilt surged to think that I would involve myself in black magic. I looked into my soul and knew I would try everything possible to save my son. Pushing the guilt aside, I carefully held Malcolm up to the sky.

Still wrapped tightly in the blanket, we both waited for what would happen next.

Boudica extended the pouch over the river, raised her right hand skyward, and chanted, "Sever ties, ye evil powers. Away ye curse, be gone with ye. Leave this child to grow to manhood, a rightful king, God's work to do."

Ceremoniously, she chopped her right hand downward between the pouch and Malcolm, as if slicing the curse that bound him.

"Amen," I said, hoping to lift the incantation to a prayer. After all, Malcolm *would* do God's work if saved.

The midwife opened the bag, inverted it, and aggressively shook out the contents over the river. Small chunks and brownish-red powder fluttered on the breeze, alighting on the surface of the water and floated with the current, then disappeared as though swallowed by the churning white torrents to be driven far out to sea.

Boudica chanted again, "Be ye gone—ye black magic, to the sea, without concern. Leave this innocent behind. Forget your purpose, never to return."

She turned the bag inside out and shook free the last particles of crimson dust.

I pulled Malcolm to my bosom as flecks floated, sparkling in the morning sunlight, before settling on the water.

As the last of the placenta remnants entered the cascades, Boudica repeated in chant, "Be ye gone—ye black magic, to the sea, without concern. Leave this innocent behind. Forget your purpose, never to return."

"It's done." Her shoulders relaxed as if a great burden had been lifted.

Had she felt responsible for Malcolm's ill health?

Gently, she stroked my babe as would a concerned mother. "He's now free. May he live a long, healthy life."

"Amen," I said again.

I kept Malcolm bundled snugly on the cart ride home. Never once did he cry. Peacefully, he slept on.

For days after the peculiar event, I watched Malcolm for any change. To my dismay, he didn't improve significantly. Give it time, give it time, I kept telling myself.

Though I imagine Jasmine's curse was calling forth darkness, Boudica's chants seemed almost prayers addressing God. How could they be bad? Still, I didn't share the details of the experience with anyone.

Even Glenore never asked what had happened at the riverbank.

Chapter Twenty-Two

Henry always came home exhausted from touring his strongholds, his face worn and drawn. With first sight of him, my heart went out.

He took me in his arms. "How is our son? I've worried much over his welfare."

"He's resting but no change." It would be better not to reveal the details to him about the curse. "What have you heard of King Stephen? Is he safe?" I changed the subject to keep from saying more.

"I'll report the whole matter, but first I must see my son." He kissed me, then scaled the stairs two at a time.

I followed, guilt-ridden that I kept such a secret from him.

In our bedchamber, Henry knelt beside the cradle I'd moved there. He gazed upon our boy's beautiful sleeping face and smoothed Malcolm's red hair, but the child didn't wake.

"He's had fever, but he's nonetheless a happy baby." I tried to sound natural, but my voice wavered.

Henry stood, placed hands on my shoulders and studied my face. His brown eyes penetrated to my soul. "What are you not saying? There is more."

Tears stung. I didn't know what to say. It was hard—oh so hard—to keep secrets from my love.

"Tell me, Ada."

He spoke so lovingly and I couldn't hold the secret another minute. "Glenore heard rumors of a curse. I've worried so. Then finally I . . . I . . ."

He took my hand and brought me to the bed.

"I think you should start from the beginning." He stretched out on the bed and patted the space next to him.

For the next while, laying side by side, I told him about Jasmine and the curse, my initial denial of such things, followed by the apparent futility of the physician's efforts, and my fervent prayers.

Henry listened without saying aught.

"Then Boudica came and offered me an alternative," I said. "I resisted for weeks, but as our son continued to suffer, I believed it was my only recourse and felt that God would somehow forgive me. I succumbed." Shame tightened my throat. I buried my face in Henry's neck.

His body was rigid, his muscles tense. "We must find Jasmine and hear her confession. I'll put St Martin on it first thing tomorrow. Cursing the heir of Scotland is not a minor crime."

I bolted up in alarm. "Don't give her a death sentence."

He looked at me grimly.

"We must show her that we can overcome evil with goodness." What was I saying? Did I believe this evil really had power? Another wave of guilt swept over me. "Henry, we don't believe in witchcraft, do we?"

At those words, Malcolm stirred.

Henry left the bed and went to him. "I know our son is not well—be it by devious doings or weak in body. I do believe there is evil that wishes to destroy the royal family. They'll use any means they feel will aid their cause. We must fight it."

He carefully took Malcolm from the crib and sat with him in a chair. "My father has spent his reign establishing Christianity more firmly in Scotland, rooting out superstition."

"He recently initiated St Andrew's Cathedral Priory and other monasteries." I settled against bed pillows. "Scotland must stay unified and never become what has happened to England these last years. They are calling the civil war with Stephen and Matilda the Anarchy."

Henry nodded. "Last June, Empress Matilda went to London for her coronation, but citizens drove her out before she could be crowned. The people want King Stephen on the throne. A trade was made for Empress Matilda's imprisoned brother, Robert, and King Stephen was set free."

"I received a missive from *Maman*. My half-brother Waleran de Beaumont decided to defect, crossing into Normandy to secure his ancestral possessions by allying himself with the Angevins." My mind was so tired of worrying over Malcolm that even talking of politics was a rest. "Henry, isn't there some measure of peace in England?"

He shrugged. "Empress Matilda's Chief General is her brother, Robert, a good and wise man though born of the late king illegitimately. It's he the people love. Empress Matilda is a figurehead. She has never touched the hearts of the people."

I blinked, trying to understand. "I can sympathize with her hopes as a mother. She's the legitimate daughter of King Henry and has three young sons who mayhap should someday rule."

Henry nodded. "It's an unusual war that involves so many women. When Robert and King Stephen were imprisoned, their wives were made prison guards for each side. King Stephen's wife watched Robert of Gloucester whilst Robert's wife watched the king. Each wished exceedingly for the trade and at last acted despite Empress Matilda's order."

"The trade was made behind her back?" I could hardly believe what I was hearing.

"A good woman's faith can move mountains." Henry smiled. "Oh, and with the king's release, Kelton was invited to court. His loyalty throughout the captivity will certainly be rewarded."

"Then the fighting is over?" I asked.

Malcolm fussed again, and I stood to take my turn holding him.

Henry passed the child to my waiting arms and walked toward the bed. He disrobed and prepared for bed. "Nae, the fighting continues, but it's not our fight. We must build peace. That is our mission."

I had to agree. Peace was our mission, even toward Jasmine.

The next day, Malcolm ran a high fever.

The physician was again brought to the Hall. He spoke of bloodletting, of herbs, and pending death. The physician took from his bag a bottle of leeches.

I turned from the sight. Darkness came over my mind. Though I believed it beneficial, I could not watch those blood sucking creatures touch my baby.

Mary gently took me by the arm, leading me from the room to the great hall. "Rest here, my lady. I'll stay with the physician."

Glenore came a few minutes later. "Can I bring you ale?"

I grabbed her hand and pulled her down next to me. "Is it because I took Malcolm to the river that God is punishing me?"

Glenore frowned. "Consent to speak me mind?"

"Aye."

"Heaven's not punishin' ye. You did whatcha thought ye had to. Rest. Mary'll stay with Malcolm."

I heard Malcolm suddenly cry out. Anger lifted me to my feet. "I cannot sit and hear my baby cry whilst those leeches suck his blood!"

"It may save his life."

I ran from Glenore out to the garden. It was as if Mother Mary knew I would come to her. I saw it in her stone face as I fell to my knees. "Mother Mary, Mother of our Lord . . ." When I finished the memorized prayer, through tears I pled to God with all the strength of my heart. "If it's Thy will, bestow mercy on me and save my child. Forgive me for yielding to the lures of witchcraft. I promise to live a faithful life from this day on, always serving Thee. I shall dedicate my life to building up the church here in Northumbria. I will do all I can to help the people abandon witchery and teach them to turn to Thee for their strength if . . . if you save my son. I promise. I promise."

Was it enough? Could I bargain with the Lord? Had He heard me?

As a woman, how much control did I have over God's sanctuaries? In what way could I build churches? Most of my money was controlled by my husband's family. How much power did my promises carry?

I thought I heard a voice and looked up, but no one was there. Then my eyes rested on the object of my prayer. Mary, the mother of Christ—a *woman*. It was through her selfless acts of birthing her son and raising Him that all mankind was given the ability to be saved. I remembered the story of King

-184-

Stephen's capture occurring due to the efforts of two women. And the release of King Stephen and Robert of Gloucester was brought to pass by the love of their wives.

My love for Henry and for my sweet son could give me power to do great things. What had Henry said? The faith of a good woman could move mountains. I could be good too, and do great things.

Feeling a newfound power, I recommitted to my promise. "With all my heart and strength, I will build Thy kingdom among my people. Even so. Amen."

As I stood, I heard a sound far behind me.

"Lady Ada!" Mary called.

I ran from the shrine to her side. "Aye."

"The physician is finished, and Henry has asked for you to come." Her hazel eyes filled with despair.

Uncertain what lay ahead, I followed her into the house and up the stairs. I hurried to Henry's side.

He held Malcolm, and I took him into my own arms.

Tears still on Malcolm's cheeks, his eyes closed as if in sleep.

The physician's face grew quite solemn. "I can do naught more here. I'm sorry to say I do not expect him to live through the night. God give you strength." He replaced his hat and Mary showed him to the door.

Without speaking, I leaned against Henry.

He engulfed the child and me in his arms. "We can now only pray and wait out the night."

We moved the cradle next to our bed where I could rest whilst listening for Malcolm's breathing. With the weight of it all, we succumbed to exhaustion and didn't awaken until the morning light crept through the east window.

I rolled to the edge of the bed, realizing how still and quiet the room was. I feared peering in the cradle beside me. I reached out my hand to gently tip it toward me for a better look.

Malcolm was awake and sucking on his fist. He saw me and babbled.

I sat up, my breath catching in my chest.

Malcolm gazed up at me with his sweet grin.

I scooped him into my arms. "Henry! Look, he lives!" My hand felt his cool, smooth skin. "And the fever is gone."

Henry rolled over in bed and pulled us both into his arms while Malcolm giggled and squirmed.

Joy overflowed my heart.

Henry kissed us both, and we curled up together.

God had granted me the greatest gift I could ask for. In return, there was a price I had promised to pay. I must keep my promise to Him by starting on that journey today.

Chapter Twenty~Three

The next morning, I waited to bid Henry farewell. His father had requested him to Jedburgh to assess the recent events in England.

As soon as Henry was out the gates, I rushed to my room to change into a simple frock. Instead of my fine-spun wimple, I wore a rough scarf and tied it under my chin. That done, I was off to the kitchen with a sturdy basket. I filled it with a loaf of bread and fresh crock of caudle. I tucked in a wooden crucifix and covered it all with a cloth.

I hurried to the nursemaid. "Mary, I'm going out."

Malcolm sat on her lap, pulling at her braid.

She smiled. "Very well."

I passed other servants who glanced up from their work but said naught to them.

I feared Henry might think I was going behind his back, but this was something I had to do. Something that would support him as prince and eventually king, even if he wasn't able to understand it.

Outside, I instructed the stable boy to saddle Cooper and walked to the mounting block to wait.

St Martin strolled over, dressed and ready to ride, holding the reigns of his hefty brown warhorse. He greeted me with a knowing smile. "Lady Ada, I'm here to accompany you by order of Prince Henry."

"To accompany me on what errand?"

The knight bowed. "What 'ere you wish."

I held tight to the basket and closed my eyes, praying for strength. "I wish to go on a mission of peace. Whatever happens, I wish no anger or guile and no recourse." I lifted my chin as my mother had taught.

St Martin smiled genuinely. "I've seen enough war to make such a mission a glad reprieve. Shall we?"

The stable boy led Cooper over, and I mounted.

As we traveled up the road toward the burgh, St Martin said naught more—as was his nature. I appreciated his quiet companionship, for I could not let my courage wane. I *had* to carry out my plan. I'd committed to God and Mother Mary that I'd build His kingdom in Northumbria, and this was my first attempt.

According to Glenore's directions, I arrived at the house. I halted Cooper but remained seated for several moments, swallowing hard and trying to gather courage.

At last St Martin broke the silence. "Shall I accompany you to the door?"

"Nae." I dismounted and handed him Cooper's reins. "I'll go alone, but stay alert in case I need protection."

If Jasmine's curses were real, I doubted there was aught St Martin could do. But I'd learned that there was One who had greater power than curses or sickness or even a wounded, angry heart.

As if outside my body, I watched myself walk to the door of the woman who had wished my child ill and stop before the threshold. "Greeting to you in the house!" I called.

A woman peered through a hole in an oiled parchment-covered window.

"Good morn to ye." Her gaze darted to the guard on the road, then squinted suspiciously toward me.

My fingers tightened around the basket. The house had a wide yard with an overgrown garden and though small, it smelled of mint and lemon.

"I seek the woman, Jasmine." I said a silent prayer that my heart could be filled with Christian love toward her.

The door hinges squeaked. The woman who stood before me was of unusual beauty, with long black hair hanging loose down her back. Several necklaces of beads shrouded her neck. She wore a green cloak that made me think she was about to leave the house. "I be Jasmine."

"I . . . I have come to make a friendly visit. I'm Lady Ada. You attended the birth of my son, Prince Malcolm."

Jasmine squinted one eye. "I know who ye be." She stepped backward. "Ye came to curse me and my house, didna ye! Off with ye!" She raised her arm as if to strike.

I put up a hand in defense.

St Martin galloped forward.

But she didn't strike, whether because of St Martin or another reason, I didn't know.

"Nae! Nae! St Martin." I held my palm toward him.

He reigned in but stayed close and dismounted.

I pulled up my chin and took a deep breath. "I come as a friend to thank you for your loyalty." I handed her the bread, hoping she'd not see my trembling hand.

She stared at the loaf as if it might bite her but took it.

I next gave her the crock of caudle. "And a drink for these chilly nights."

She took the jar with a look of confusion on her face.

Lastly, I held out the crucifix. "And may this symbol of our Lord Jesus give you comfort, peace, and strengthen your faith." I took a breath for courage. "That you may turn to Him in times of trouble and forsake the black magic so prevalent in these parts."

She stared at the cross for an uncomfortable minute before tucking the loaf beneath her arm and accepted the cross. Tears came to her eyes. With a blink, one rolled down her cheek. "Oh, m'lady. Ye are most kind."

I caressed her arm. "May the Spirit of our Lord fill your home with joy and happiness. I bid thee farewell."

I returned quickly to my horse and mounted with St Martin's help, glancing at Jasmine still standing in the doorway.

She smiled and waved tentatively.

By the time it was obvious to others that I carried another child, Malcolm had grown plump and rosy, his pleasant disposition increasing.

Busy with him, the winter passed quickly. Spring came on in glorious colors. In March when Henry was called to Edinburgh for an assembly of nobles and churchmen, we decided to make the visit together. I hadn't yet seen the city. I wasn't concerned about traveling five days. Though my pregnancy was quite advanced, my midsection was still high and I'd never felt so full of life.

Edinburgh was dominated by the castle. Built as if it sprouted from black rock, the magnificent fortress towering over the city. I could see why they called it Castle Rock. The stone fortress was one of King David's first accomplishments at the start of his reign.

The countryside spread before me in swaths of green so unlike Eads Hall. I sighed. "Glorious!"

Henry laughed. "We can live here someday if it suits you."

Most likely we would—when he was king.

Our van climbed the broad esplanade. Just as we came near the drawbridge, four riders on white horses escorted us over the moat to enter the castle gates.

"Look Malcolm. Aren't they powerful horses?" I bounced him on my knee.

He babbled something I'm sure was in answer.

Henry laughed again.

It was so good to see his joy. He seldom was able to spend time with us and was more relaxed since Malcolm's health had improved.

Henry sobered and pointed to a small rock chapel. "Father built the small church to commemorate my grandmother Margaret. She died here at the castle, just days after receiving the news of her eldest son's and husband's deaths in battle.

"Your father has told me the story of King Malcolm's six sons and how he as the youngest never expected to take the throne. Losing both parents at the age of nine must have been tragic."

"Many of those years after were spent in a convent in England and at the English court. It's a wonder my uncles held onto the throne during that time." He huffed. "I wish I'd known my grandmother."

I considered Henry's grandmother Margaret and his mother Maud. Could I ever be as devout as the women in his family? It was no wonder he was such a gentle husband. God praise those women.

I was reminded once again that I had made a deal with the Lord to dedicate my life to building up the church in Northumbria and Scotland, and help the people abandon witchery if He saved Malcolm. And He had. I hugged the child—who had now lived a year—and whispered, "I will keep my promise."

The inside of the castle was the opposite of the rugged outside fortress. Each room was replete with artisan details—the king's crest in gold above a fire hearth, the rich woodwork gracing each wall, and the floors with bright mosaics. Even the ceilings were works of art.

Henry hurried over to a tall man of about his age I'd not previously met. He bowed slightly before grasping the man's forearms in a devoted gesture. "Mormaer Donnchad, it's been too long. How fare ye?"

"Very well." The knight let go of Henry's arms and grasped him in an embrace of obvious affection.

St Martin, always at Henry's side, knelt at Donnchad's feet, one arm across his chest in fealty. "It's a true honor to meet one of such unequaled skill."

I wandered closer, hoping to be invited into the conversation.

"Rise, fellow knight." Donnchad encouraged St Martin to his feet. "Have we met before?"

I'd never seen the serious St Martin so awestruck. "Nae, but years ago I saw you dominate a tournament at King Henry's court. Your swordplay even now inspires my own. It's what made me wish to become a knight."

Donnchad turned sober. "We often had such events during that brief window of peace before the late king's death. How I wish England's throne would settle and end the senseless bloodshed. Then you could dazzle young lads yourself. Perchance whilst you're here you can find time to spar with me?"

The smile on St Martin almost didn't fit his face. "Naught would make me more pleased."

Donnchad's eyes fell on me. "Henry, this must be your beautiful wife. The Countess Ada."

I stepped forward and he took my hand, kissing it lightly.

Henry turned to me. "Mormaer Donnchad is of royal ancestry. The earls of Fife are the highest-ranking nobles in the realm, and they carry with that lineage the right to crown the King of Scots. He's responsible for constitutional powers during the absence of the monarch and pledges to the security of my family."

I nodded remembering Henry telling me Donnchad's parents had all but raised him when his mother had died. Being great warriors, they encouraged Henry's skills to become a knight. "My lord." I bowed. "My husband has shared with me the kindness your family showed upon him in his youth."

"He was as a brother to me." Donnchad slapped Henry on the back.

Later that evening when we stepped into the dining hall for supper, Henry bowed to another large soldier, this one older than the first.

He said to me, "May I introduce Herbert the Lord Chamberlain."

Herbert kissed my hand. "And when do I meet Malcolm, the future king of Scots?" he asked with a gleam in his eye.

So, this was Fenella's father. I liked him instantly. "The nursemaid has taken Malcolm to bed, but we'll arrange a personal meeting for you two." I gave him a smile that I hoped demonstrated my allaying to him.

During supper, the talk was of Henry Plantagenet, Empress Matilda's nine-year-old son, having come to England and what the empresses' next move might be.

Herbert approached me after the meal. "I'd like to talk in private if your husband agrees."

Henry didn't seem as surprised as I by the request.

Herbert took me by the hand and led me to a nearby alcove. "I'm not a man of subtlety so indulge me in a father's concern. You may have noticed Fenella not at supper tonight. Did something happen when she was last at Eads Hall?"

It seemed ages since Fenella and I had raced our horses across open fields. "I don't believe so." I tried to pull to memory anything that could have upset Fenella. "I remembered her crying tears of joy at the birth of Malcolm and wanting to tell the king about the news." Since that time, I'd been so focused on Malcolm's health that I'd not really given her much thought. I assumed she had other responsibilities when she didn't return.

He seemed to contemplate my reply. "If you could speak to her, I'd be most grateful. She appears to be unhappy."

"Certainly," I agreed. "I've always enjoyed her company."

"I'll have a servant show you to her chambers." He called a young man standing nearby.

Having traveled all day, I was weary, but the tone of Herbert's voice and the concern in his eyes made it clear his words were mayhap more command than suggestion.

Up two flights of stairs and down a hallway that seemed the length of a small village, I was brought to a closed door. I took in a deep breath. The weight of my womb winded me.

The marshal rapped twice. "Visitor for you, me' dame."

"Coming." The reply was quick and almost angry.

The marshal retreated the way he'd come.

Fenella threw open the door. With her hair pulled back tightly and brow lowered, her complexion paled. "Lady Ada." she whispered.

"May I come in?" I asked after she hadn't moved to allow me by.

"Of course." Fenella stood to the side as I entered the large, tidy room.

Two chairs and a table sat in front of a small, stone-tracery window. Fading sunlight gleamed off a glazed pitcher and cup on the table.

"Would you care for wine?" she asked.

I sat. "I see there's only one cup. Please continue with your drink."

"Friends share a cup, do they not?"

Was she asking if I considered her a friend? I smiled and reached for the cup, taking a sip before handing it to her.

She watched me intently and took her own swallow.

"I'd like to apologize that I was a poor companion whilst last you stayed at Eads Hall," I said.

Fenella put down the cup. "Did my father talk to you?" She squinted, and I knew she'd detect if I lied.

"Aye," I admitted.

Her face grew red. "It wasn't his place. What did he say?"

Her father was right. She was acting out of sorts. I'd never before seen her lose her composure in such a way. "Your father disclosed no details. He said that you didn't appear to be happy. He worries, as I suppose a father has a right."

"Oh." She reddened deeper and looked toward the window. "When you and Henry first arrived, there was so much to do—vetting the servants at Eads Hall, getting your wedding celebration planned, and keeping you entertained through your confinement. But once that wee bairn was born there wasn't a place for me anymore."

"Why do you speak such nonsense? You're always welcome in our home," I said.

Fenella smiled weakly. "When I returned to court, I asked my father what he would have me do. He said that I wasn't a servant, but nobility, and it was my choice. To tell the truth, I'm better as a servant."

I hesitated to mention what was in my heart but finally said, "Aren't there any young men you find interesting?"

Fenella laughed. "I think that's what my father was referring to by saying I have a choice. Although I'm pleased he'll allow me the choice, and not choose a husband for me, I want to know *why* I must marry. I'm not like you. I don't think I'm the type of woman who can cheerfully care for a man and bairns."

Her comment surprised me. I remembered her dancing with Giffard at our wedding celebration and thought she'd enjoyed his company. Had her heart truly been so set on marrying Henry that she couldn't entertain marrying anyone else? A familiar bite of jealousy tightened my chest. I wouldn't let it take my heart. Perchance she just wanted to be needed.

"We're going to Perth to visit Hugh Giffard and his ailing mother. I know he'd be pleased to see you, and I certainly could use the company.

She didn't take a breath before she said, "When do we leave?"

"After the assembly of nobles and churchmen. Mayhap a sennight?" I got to my feet and felt a flutter in my midsection. I placed my hand on the womb until the baby stilled.

Fenella looked to the floor. "When will this little one make his appearance?"

"Months at least. But you can see why I would like female companionship."

Fenella smiled openly. "And you shall have it."

Chapter Twenty-Four

The journey to Perth was most enjoyable. Henry chose to ride Cooper alongside St Martin. Both seemed pleased to be in the open air on such a fair spring day.

Mary held little Malcolm and Fenella lounged beside me on cushions in the van. We chatted about the many happenings since we'd been apart.

"Kelton left to acquire both an earldom and a wife," I told her. "It seems he's almost achieved both. King Stephen gave him the earldom and Kelton will soon marry my cousin, Isobel, the daughter of Lord Peverel."

Fenella was not surprised to hear of Kelton's choice in a bride. "She's of Norman blood, so I suppose it was bound to be."

"Whatever do you mean?" I asked.

"Although it isn't written, there's a clear rule. In order to keep a title, you must either be Norman or be married to one," Fenella said. "Which is wonderful for women of the gentry who are Norman or wealthy."

Mary, who was chosen as a nursemaid to a future king because of her own lineage, seemed dumbstruck. "But your father is an earl and chamberlain."

Fenella grimaced. "Aye, but I have four older brothers. The only men showing interest in me are those far below my station. I've stopped riding whilst at court because I'm constantly accosted by ambitious peasants."

Was that what she considered Giffard? Was this the reason she didn't want to marry, which had nothing to do with a broken heart over Henry? I remembered what Henry had told me at our wedding celebration. He said to let Giffard go to court and prove worthy to the king to inherit before he pursued Fenella. Suddenly, my midsection felt in knots. Had I told her that we went to Perth to visit Giffard because I thought him a good husband? I couldn't remember. My mind couldn't hold a thought when I was with child.

Malcolm wiggled out of Mary's arms and reached for Fenella. Almost ready to walk, he moved constantly.

Fenella laughed at the child's antics. She took him on her lap and returned his smiles and babbles.

Malcolm grabbed Fenella's finger and tried to put it in his mouth.

She tutted. "Nae, don't bite me. I see those little teeth in there." She turned to me. "I'd heard he was a sickly child. You'd never guess so now."

Under her breath, Mary said, "'Twas a curse."

I'd never told her a thing. Did all the servants know of Jasmine's curse?

"*Oh?*" Fenella's brows lifted. "The dark arts have always lurked in the corners of this land. Do you believe in such things, Lady Ada?"

"I believe Malcolm had a hard start to life." Whether the curse was real or not, my son had been healed by God. "Through prayer we overcame and he thrives."

"Well, whatever you did, keep doing it." Fenella kissed his pudgy cheek. "He's delightful."

We arrived in the prosperous burgh of Perth by early afternoon, and Giffard met us on the front steps of his brother's home.

I'd forgotten how big he was as he took my hand in his massive one, assisting me from the van.

He stepped to help the next female from the van, and his eyes grew large. His face reddened, and he smiled and offered a trembling hand to Fenella. Once she was standing in front of him, he bowed deeply to us both. "*Fáilte* to my brother's estate. I'm pleased with your presence here, as will he be."

Although he seemed to be addressing Fenella more than myself, I answered, "How could we not come? We've missed you and I've come to see when you'll return. How are Richard and your mother?"

"As you can see, Richard has fully recovered." He gestured to his older brother who greeted Henry, then turned to Fenella. "I came to help Richard due to his injuries, but I've stayed on due to my mother's ailing condition. She fears she has not much time to live. Come. She awaits in the great hall and longs to speak with females."

Henry and St Martin stayed behind us as we walked into the large stone structure and the great hall. A blazing fire in the hearth warmed the room on an already warm day.

Giffard's mother sat in a leather padded chair, a thick blanket pulled to her chin. Whatever ailed her obviously kept her cold. Her hair was as white as snow, her mouth pinched tight from lack of teeth. Yet, her blue eyes shown as if she were a young maid.

She tried to rise.

Henry invited her to stay seated and knelt beside her. "How wonderful to see you again. How are you enjoying your new home, Mother Giffard?"

"Quite well." She blushed at Henry's attention. "It was, as you said." She sounded out of breath. "A bounty for each of my children. My second child . . ." She took a deep breath. "William has joined the priesthood and is on his way to give me last rites." She smiled sadly, keeping her withered lips shut tight. "My wish is for sweet Hugh." She closed her eyes for a moment. "It's for him I beg your intercession and why I asked for your presence, your Highness. He will always be your servant, but has neither land nor title."

Henry cast his gaze on Giffard, who reddened at the attention but remained silent.

"Aye," said Henry. "I'm acquainted with his goodness. Do not fear, for I believe good rewards lay in store for him. When he's ready, we'll send him to court." Henry patted her hand and got to his feet.

Her smile deepened her ancient wrinkles. "Thank you, sire." Then she looked my direction. "And much obliged, sweet Lady Ada, for gracing us with your presence."

I stepped forward to accept the compliment but was hit by a pain intense enough to double me over. Fluid splashed at my feet. I closed my eyes, trying to gain control of my body, then felt strong arms supporting me. When the pain subsided, I opened my eyes to find Henry holding me firmly. I sucked in air.

Mother Giffard ordered her son to get a midwife and asked Henry to lay me in her bedchamber.

Mary left with the men, carrying little Malcolm.

Fenella hovered at my feet, wringing her hands.

Henry sat beside me.

Mother Giffard asked, "Please bring me to your wife's side."

Henry helped her walk to me and kept her upright whilst she felt my stomach. "It's in a good position but may be a little small."

Fenella cocked her head. "How do you know so much about child bearing?"

The old woman shrugged. "I'm the oldest of six sisters and have had five of my own. I learned a thing or two."

A wave of pain began at my midsection and spread until I struggled to not call out. Still, a moan escaped my lips.

"The cupboard in the room two doors to the left has fresh linens." Mother Giffard's tone changed to that of a commander as she spoke to Fenella. "I suggest you get as many as you can carry."

Fenella ran out of the room.

Unlike my first labor, this time the pains came one right on top of the other. I feared I wouldn't survive if they continued at this intensity for an entire day. I could do naught but concentrate on enduring the pain.

Fenella returned. "Leave Henry."

He kissed my forehead and whispered, "May God bless you."

Fenella wiped my forehead with a cool rag.

I didn't know where Mother Giffard went.

I lost track of time and tried to rest between pains. "Who will deliver my baby, Fenella?"

"We're working on that." She sounded unsure.

A priest came beside me and took my hand. I could see in his eyes the similarity to his brother. "William Giffard, the priest," I said with weakness.

Another pulsing pain hit, and I moaned.

He prayed aloud.

Though I couldn't communicate it to him, his words to God comforted me, and I found peace in his presence.

Soon his hand and his prayers were gone.

The sun hadn't set before the pain changed to pressure between my legs. "Where is Mother Giffard?" I panicked.

"She's here," Fenella said.

I sensed movement on the bed.

Mother Giffard was propped beside me. I would have laughed if I weren't in such pain.

She said to Fenella, "You will need to do what I tell you."

Fenella's eyes grew big. "I . . . I . . . don't know aught about childbirth. I'm a maid and have never seen a child born."

Strange, the things that strike you in such a situation. I wanted to laugh at strong and able Fenella being brought to her knees, literally, as she knelt at the end of the bed and looked as if she would be sick.

"Push when you're ready, dear." Mother Giffard spoke as if she was telling me to take bread from the oven—an everyday occurrence that was easy to perform.

She guided Fenella with what to do each step of the way, and with a final push, the babe made its way into the world.

Fenella lifted the child with her bloodied hands and placed it on my stomach. Tears ran down her face. "By the grace of God, you've delivered another son." She was so white, I feared she'd faint.

Mother Giffard leaned over and wiped the baby's mouth, then massaged his chest.

-203-

The baby suddenly roared an angry cry, announcing to the world he lived.

I held him close until he calmed. Another redhead. I smiled, pleased. My newborn stared at me with an intensity impressive for one so young.

Mother Giffard directed Fenella in the final steps of cleaning us up.

When done, Fenella staggered out.

Henry soon arrived.

I smiled at his worried face. "All is well, *mon amour*. Come meet your new son."

He kissed each of our heads. "He's so small."

"Aye, but as strong as a lion. Did you hear his roar?" I laughed.

"What shall his name be?"

"As Giffard's brother held my hand and prayed over me, I thought to name him William, also in honor of my father and brother. What say ye?"

"William is a worthy name."

Chapter Twenty-Five

Over the next few days, the child suckled well and—by the grace of God—appeared robust. We moved to the royal castle for the rest of my forty-day confinement, and Father Giffard purified me during my churching ceremony and thanked God for William's safe delivery.

We then traveled to Edinburgh to introduce William to his grandfather and have him baptized.

In the van, Fenella cooed at little William in her arms.

She'd been a faithful friend, never leaving my side as I healed. And not having spent any time with Giffard.

A part of me still hoped for their union, but I supposed their time was yet to come.

Giffard's last words in bidding us farewell were to thank us for bringing life to his mother. She had so longed for death that she'd almost let it in the door but having seen new life in their walls made her hearty again and more willing to enjoy whatever time she had left. "I hope to visit you all at Eads Hall very soon."

We stayed in Edinburgh a sennight then returned to Eads Hall, for I longed to be at home with my new babe. Life soon was filled with naught but caring for two babies and an occasional guest who came to see Henry.

I longed for my mother and hoped she'd be attending Kelton's wedding, since his bride, Isobel, was a kinswoman. I looked forward to her missive explaining the events in detail. Although Henry was going, he wouldn't bother telling me about what her dress was made of or how her hair was styled. I sighed. Would I ever see *Maman* again?

When the time drew near for Kelton's wedding, Henry left. A part of me cried to go with him and cried for Kelton who, being illegitimate and his father dead, had no kinsman but Henry to attend the wedding. That had to cause a deep wound. I sent Kelton a personal note, telling him how sorry I was for not being able to come. With the letter, I sent the beautiful chrism from Abbot Malachy, hoping the healing balm would help.

In the early summer, I discovered I was expecting my third child. I spent much time outdoors with my two little ones, walking and playing. The gardeners had worked tirelessly. Tulip trees lined the entrance and hollyhocks waved their shocking color in the gentle breeze. On the pond, ducks and swans swam lazily to the edge where irises and day lilies grew. Indeed, I was surrounded by great beauty. The trees were not of the same stately size as those in Surrey, but no matter. This place had truly become home.

By the time Henry returned, summer was almost gone. He stayed home as much as possible, but once autumn began, I barely saw him again. Sharing joint responsibilities with his father, he had to visit allies and be included in the business of

Scotland whilst staying near the Scot-English border to carry out King Stephen's bidding.

Although I would have preferred to have Henry at home more often, I counted my blessings and found a great measure of fulfillment in my children. Between Maggie and Fenella, I felt surrounded by support and love.

I'd hoped the colder weather would relinquish Henry from his demanding schedule. Unfortunately, at King Stephen's request and my great disappointment, Henry departed on a lengthy trip to London that would likely keep him away for months.

I became quite melancholy missing my husband.

One afternoon, Fenella had gone off to market, and I felt particularly alone as I sat in the solar weaving.

Glenore approached, enthusiastically humming an off-key tune. With a smile, she announced, "M'lady, your supper will be served shortly in the dinin' hall."

"*Merci.* I'd rather eat in the kitchen. It's much warmer there. With Fenella gone, I can enjoy the company of the servants." I set aside my project.

"Aye. I will set it for ye." She continued around the room, straightening as she resumed humming.

Though her timbre tested the endurance of my ears, I politely listened and managed to recognize her tune. "That song is one of Henry and my favorites."

"I know." She paused at the door before leaving. "I was 'opin' it might cheer ye, m'lady."

I smiled at her. "Cheer me it did. *Merci.*"

She smiled broadly and all but skipped from the room.

Minutes later, I entered the kitchen and was about to sit for supper when a servant hastened in. "Ye 'ave a visitor, m'lady. Shall I bring 'im into the hall?"

I nodded. Before I could ask who, she was off. Who would venture out this far in the cold of winter to see me? Mayhap Giffard had come from Perth, or Kelton realized how I missed family and chose to come with Isobel?

"Sir Madduch," the servant announced, gesturing toward a man draped in a heavy green cloak.

The visitor threw off his outer garment and slung it over his arm, but remained in the hall, obviously waiting for my invitation to advance. His fine clothing bespoke wealth, and he had the air of a nobleman.

There was a familiarity about him for which I searched my memory. Ah, I'd met him years before at my wedding celebration. Henry's cousin—the one Henry had warned me was charming but cunning.

I stepped toward him. "*Monsieur* Madduch, what a surprise. Do come sit by our hearth." If Henry were here to receive him, what would he do?

Upon my approach, Madduch bowed low and swept his hand in an exaggerated greeting, his smile reprehensibly handsome. "I was passing through Whitfield from Carlisle and thought I'd stop for a visit. Your servant tells me Henry is on King Stephen's errand and is not present."

"Of a truth, but our guards are standing by. We are protected from strangers," I said cautiously, wishing St Martin or Giffard were here.

"I'm a cousin, not a stranger. You need never fear me."

"I was not referring to you, *monsieur*."

He glanced around the dining hall, mayhap self-consciously scanning for guards. He was tall and attractive, with blond hair and blue eyes. So different from Henry's dark hair and eyes. "How unfortunate that I arrived on a day when Henry was away."

From the kitchen I heard Fenella's voice. Though I couldn't make out the words, her tone was loud and agitated. She must have just arrived home, and I suddenly craved her advice. "Have you eaten?" I hoped for an excuse to go to the kitchen.

He looked pleased. "I'd be most grateful to sup with you. A meal for two?"

"Mayhap. Why don't you come sit by the fire whilst I check on our meal? I'll return shortly."

I went to the kitchen and explained the situation to Fenella.

"Well, this is a surprise. Madduch obviously has heard of Henry's absence and is making good on his proposition."

I shook my head. "We don't know that. It's as likely that he came to see the beautiful daughter of the royal chamberlain. I'll set the table for three."

"Nae." She held my arm. "It's important you understand his loyalty and his intent. Trust me. Court intrigue is my career. To truly support Henry, you must try to discover why Madduch has come."

"*Bien*," I agreed. "But don't be surprised if his intention is to make your introduction." I hoped I was right.

The servants moved a small table for two close to the fire and set upon it bowls and spoons. Glenore brought in a cauldron of soup, followed by a servant carrying a bottle of ale and a loaf of bread. Glenore dipped the steaming soup into bowls, and they returned to the kitchen.

My chair faced the kitchen. Madduch's back was to it. Though the light was dim, I detected off and on as many as three heads at a time peeking around the door jamb, Fenella at the forefront.

The atmosphere was intimate—too intimate—as we sat at the small table in the warmth of the fire's glow. I picked up a spoon and ate, stealing glances at this handsome man. "You are unmarried, correct?"

"Sadly." Madduch's smile didn't dim. "I've never felt the right connection to make such an important union."

"What are you looking for?" I asked, hoping to turn the conversation to Fenella.

He laughed under his breath. "I'll know." He took another sip of ale and grinned like a cat with a mouse.

His gaze made me uncomfortable, and I was thankful when Fenella came in carrying William in one arm and leading Malcolm by the hand. This I had not anticipated, and I wasn't certain why she was there. Mayhap she wished to meet Madduch after all?

"The boys are ready to say goodnight." Fenella scrutinized the situation, bowed slightly to Madduch, then turned her back to him and gave me a questioning glare.

I kissed my sons and ran my fingers through William's curls. "Sleep well, my darlings."

Malcolm spoke not a word but held up a toy soldier to Madduch, its sword aloft as if ready to spear the man, before being led away by Fenella. Obviously, my son was not impressed by my visitor.

Madduch watched Fenella take the boys with her out the door toward the stairs. Motioning his head in their direction, he said, "Future kings of Scots?"

"That is their father's intent, if God wills." I resumed eating my soup.

He finished his drink and poured another. He hadn't touched his food.

"The young woman with my children was Dame Fenella. Do you know her?"

He showed no interest. "All that I care to. What truly intrigues me is you. Are you happy here in Northumbria, tucked away in this old, cold manor all alone?"

I shivered despite the warm fire. "I'm very happy here," I said, but then remembered Fenella's words, to discern his intent. "Although, it's extremely quiet, unlike my home in Surrey which was the center of commerce and activity."

He gave a deep nod. "You crave more. I believe we are kindred." He reached for my hand but only grazed the skin with his fingers before withdrawing. "Have you considered taking a holiday to Glasgow? It's a glorious place and I could show you such a grand time." His soft, deep voice dripped with innuendo.

I could no longer play his charade. I pushed my food to the side. "Henry and I would love to come. In the spring, we could arrange a time."

His smile broadened, and he drew closer to me. In a whisper, he said, "It would be more amusing without Henry, trust me."

"Why would I trust you?" I responded, wanting to strike him. "I'm a married woman and respect my marriage."

"I understand, but are you certain your husband does the same? He's gone so often, and there are many willing to bear the children of a prince, even illegitimately."

I wanted to run from the table offended, but something inside my heart bid me stay. Whether to repair Henry's reputation or simply stand for the truth. "People of honor do not turn from their vows."

"When under duress, they do." His voice was smooth as silk. "What of your mother? It's said she left her first husband for the great warrior William de Warenne, and still her children inherited their due. You are one of the children of that union."

I squirmed in awkward silence. I'd heard snippets of the tale from our servants in my childhood, although my mother had never confessed the truth of it. "I've heard her first marriage was loveless—that is not the case here. I love Henry."

"I respect that." He sounded sincere. "But if the day comes that you cannot say as much, promise that you'll consider me."

I rose to my feet. "I promise you that Henry is the only husband I'll ever have. No matter what he does, whether he lives or dies, I will stay faithful to him and never marry another." I gestured to the doorkeeper. "Show Lord Madduch to the steward's cottage at the end of the lane."

Madduch scowled.

"St Martin is at court with his family, and I'm certain he'd not mind you staying there. With Henry gone, it would be inappropriate for you to stay in the manor. Or, if you'd rather, the village has a fine inn."

Rain began a steady rhythm on the window and he quickly deduced his options. "I appreciate and accept your offer. It's most kind of you, Lady Ada."

I left him standing in the hall and hurried to the kitchen.

Fenella laughed out loud. "Remind me never to cross you, my lady. There seemed to be fire spewing from your eyes."

I was still huffing. "Can you believe his accusations against Henry? How could he even think that he'd do such a thing?"

Fenella shrugged. "He's a Scotsman. We sleep with our eyes open."

As I lay in bed that night, Fenella's phrase echoed through my mind. What could she have meant?

Chapter Twenty-Six

I worried I was not keeping my promise to increase the kingdom of God on earth. Though I still met with Chaplain Robert for daily devotions with the children and gave to the poor weekly, I wished to do more. It occurred to me that putting on a celebration to honor the birth of Christ might awaken people's love for him. I threw my efforts into the project, and Fenella seemed thrilled to help.

We planned the grand celebration for Christmas Eve. The kitchen brimmed with roasted pork, beef, and goose on spits over the fire. On the anticipated day, a messenger brought news that Henry would most assuredly arrive before the evening meal.

I prayed fervently for his safe return.

The servants bustled about, washing the wood floors with vinegar and oiling them before putting down fresh rushes. Dried herbs, spices, and evergreen branches tied with ribbons hung from ceiling beams, giving the room a festive aroma.

I breathed in deeply, feeling at home with this treasured tradition from Reigate.

After all was prepared, I went to the solar to weave, an activity I found lessened my worries. Henry would come in due time, as would the baby I was expecting. I took a calming breath and soothed my hand over my swollen belly.

Children's voices came from the nursery, and soon Mary brought the boys into the solar. Dressed in their finest, Malcolm was now three and William two.

Mary touched the sleeve of my dress. "You look lovely, my lady. Trimming your dress with white fur was a grand idea."

I was dressed in a dark green silk gown trimmed with gold embroidery and white fur at the collar. Over the silk I wore a surcote the color of apricots. "Your compliment boosts my confidence," I told her.

"Lady Ada!" Fenella called as she came up the stairs. "Several of Henry's company are already in the Great Hall, spent and famished."

"Then we shall go and greet them." A flutter of anticipation went through my stomach. If his men had arrived, then Henry would soon be home.

We hurried together down the stairs.

St Martin's family greeted me.

Lord Madduch sat in the corner with a mug in his hand.

And the musicians set up a makeshift dais in the hall. Minstrels moved about the room between the guests. A thrill ran through me in anticipation of what entertaining antics they might present.

The servants brought in trays of food—laughing and talking to the point of being boisterous.

I didn't mind, for it was good to be merry at Christmas. As I gazed over the tables filled with custards, Maurice's famous French cheeses, pies, Scottish shortbread, and Christmas puddings, my stomach grumbled hungrily .

"Greeting, Lady Ada!" came a call from the entry.

I hurried to find our servants helping the Giffards remove their cloaks.

Mother Giffard looked the picture of health and caressed me mightily before patting my midsection. "Another one. It's a princess."

Richard Giffard, his wife, and two children bowed to me.

"*S'il vous plait*. Make your way to the glorious food," I encouraged.

Then I turned to Hugh Giffard. "You don't know how joyful it is to finally see you at Eads Hall again."

Fenella stepped to my side. "Giffard, the musicians need assistance, and I was hoping you could come and help me."

Giffard winced.

I suspect he was hoping for something more friendly to have come from Fenella's mouth.

"If you could excuse us, my lady."

"*Oui*, gladly!" The two of them walked off with a good foot between them.

Kelton arrived wearing a sable cloak, his new little daughter in his arms. Isobel stood beside him looking tired, her arms laden with gifts.

"What a wonderful sight. Come in from the cold. *Bienvenue*, welcome!" I motioned them over to the hearth.

The servants took their gifts and cloaks.

I kissed Isobel's cheek and gave my hand to Kelton. "It's been too long. How grateful we are for your presence."

Kelton kissed my hand and put his daughter down. "You must come to see us in the South. We've built a new wing and expanded the stables. My goodness" He scanned the room. "Eads Hall is certainly showing its age."

Kelton's daughter, named Isobel after her mother, toddled over to Malcolm.

"This is your cousin," I said to him.

He looked at her in a thoughtful manner and then ran upstairs.

I had a lot to teach him.

"Where is he going?" Kelton looked a bit offended.

I shrugged. I wished Henry stayed home more to show Malcolm a good example of how to show courtesy to others. I suppose it wasn't Malcolm's fault. Visitors had been few this past year.

Soon Malcolm came scampering downstairs with an armful of toy soldiers. Of course. He wanted to share his favorite toys with his cousin. I all but sighed.

Kelton seemed partially mollified and peered about the room. "Where's Henry?"

I bit my lip. "He's not yet arrived, but I've been assured he's on his way."

Kelton turned to his wife. "So, we can travel days to come, but Henry isn't here to greet us. Surprising." Kelton recognized Richard Giffard and hurried toward him, leaving without giving me a sideways glance.

Isobel gave me a wan smile. "Excuse his gruffness. He was duly excited for the invitation, hoping mayhap King David would be here as well. Much obliged for including us."

"You're welcome, dear cousin."

Malcolm squatted on his haunches to set up a play battlefield. St Martin's boys and the Giffard children came to join in the fun. Little Isobel grabbed a figurine in her pudgy fist.

"Your daughter appears right at home." I told her mother.

Mary put William down and allowed him to toddle to the group.

I basked in the warmth of being surrounded by friends and family. The only thing that would make the moment more joyous would be Henry returning home to join our celebration. Where was he? It appeared his entire personal entourage had arrived. What could have gone wrong?

Unexpectedly, Giffard stepped out from behind the curtain on the minstrel's stage and raised his hand to quiet the group. He spoke most boldly, "Ladies and gentlemen, I beseech you to take your seats." Giffard waited for everyone to find a chair. "The laird of the manor has requested that we start the evening festivities with a Christmas play, performed by our minstrels."

Who was the laird of the manor to whom Giffard referred? Henry had not yet arrived. My curiosity deepened when the entertainers came from a partition behind the stage, dressed in colorful costumes.

A player stepped forward. "This tale is about a young girl from England who fell in love with a handsome knight from Scotland." He strummed on his lute.

My cheeks burned as I realized this was my story. I glanced around.

St Martin and Sybil looked at me, grinning.

How did they pull this over on me?

A knight came from behind the partition and stepped onto the stage in a tunic of chain mail armor. He held his shield in front of his face. The shield resembled Henry's, but it couldn't be him. It was not like Henry to be spontaneous or entertaining before a crowd.

The music changed and soon everyone sang a familiar lullaby—one my mother used to sing.

Fenella came out on stage holding a bundle representing a baby, with an older woman beside her dressed in traveling clothes.

When the clear days come,

To be joyful again,

Let us, let us,

Dance together, together

I rose to my feet and took one step, then another, then I was running toward the stage, pregnant belly going before. *"Maman!"* Tears started as that eternal word rose within, the cry that awaits at the base of each human soul.

I leapt onto the stage and into her waiting arms. *"Maman! Maman!"*

I held tight, crying on her shoulder. After years of waiting, she was actually here. I was home again in her scent, the familiar curve of her shoulders, the sound of her voice. Finally, realizing the enormity of the moment, I stepped away and turned to the knight. "Henry?"

He peeked around the shield and smiled.

"My dear Henry." I went into his arms and kissed him. "I'll always remember your generosity, *mon amour*." I turned to Mother and took her hand. "Bringing *Maman* home to me is the best gift ever."

The remainder of the evening was a blur, watching the rest of the play, introducing my mother, eating, and dancing. It was nigh past the twelfth hour of the night before the house settled and everyone was in their assigned rooms. Indeed, Eads Hall was at capacity. Every room, even those previously used for storage, had been arranged for guests.

After bidding my mother goodnight in her bedchamber, I went to mine to find Henry already asleep. Too excited to relax, I headed to the kitchen, hoping a cup of tea would relax me.

As I approached the kitchen, voices gave me pause at the threshold.

"Why not simply agree and let me get Chaplain Robert to wed us this night?" Giffard sounded as though he was in pain. "I love you."

"Nae." Fenella's tone didn't waver. "You say Lady Ada would not treat us differently, but look at the way she treats Sybil. The woman lives within a stone's throw, and Lady Ada never invites her to the manor or travels with her. She considers her one of the common servants. I will not be condemned to a peasant's life. It would make me hate you over time. I'm sorry."

Giffard grunted. "But Prince Henry promised my mother I would be rewarded for my service. Why not live through these years together rather than apart? Have faith."

"For how many more years?" I heard Fenella rise to her feet.

The thought of being found eavesdropping was more than I could bear. Quickly I ducked into a dark recess behind a hutch, hoping the shadows would conceal me.

Fenella rushed from the room without looking back.

Giffard grumbled something into the darkness and huffed off.

I hadn't realized they'd formed an attachment. And truly, I carried no ill will toward Sybil. I barely knew her. It was simply that I never thought on her or had been asked to include her. We lived separate lives. Me with my children, and she with hers. Mayhap she could help me serve the poor on Tuesdays, or I could have her come sit with Maggie and me as we sewed?

But none of that solved the problem of helping Fenella realize she could marry Giffard and still be one of my favored household—not a servant. Overwhelmed, I went to bed. No one woke me the next morning, and by the time I arose, both Fenella and the Giffard had departed.

Chapter Twenty-Seven

"You don't have a midwife?" My mother said, shock apparent on her face. "Is that how the Scots do things?"

"Nae," I said, trying to calm her. "I had a midwife, but she moved away, and I haven't found another." I didn't care to go into the details of how the last time I saw Boudica was at the river lifting a curse from my first born.

My mother sent for a nun that my half-sister in Leeds had used. The midwife was intelligent and clean but seemed distant in her demeanor. Still, I was grateful for her willingness to come.

During the last of winter, as warmth lifted from the cold ground and we waited for my next child to arrive, Mother and I walked daily. To my delight, my boys took to her quickly and often joined us. We talked for hours, recalling memories of Father, my childhood, and antics my brothers played. We looked for herbs that may have survived the cold. It was a pastime we'd enjoyed together since I was small.

On one afternoon, when we walked alone, I broached a topic I'd never had the courage to touch on in my youth.

Remembering Lord Madduch's telling of my parents' beginnings, I felt compelled to hear the truth. "*Maman*, what happened to your first husband?"

For several moments, she stared into the garden pond. "Robert de Beaumont, Count of Meulan." Her voice held no affection when she bespoke his name. "He was forty years older than I."

"And you bore him eight children?"

"Aye. He was considered by others to be a very wise man but treated me as would a stern parent." She walked further up the path.

I shuffled to catch up, bringing my large belly before me. "I thought he died and left you a widow?"

"Ada." Mother's complexion paled. "My marriage to Robert de Beaumont ended in a scandal." Her eyes held great pain.

What she was saying didn't make sense. "How? It's not scandalous to marry another after a spouse passes, even if you met *Père* whilst your husband still lived."

"It didn't happen that way." She sat on the stone bench beneath a small conifer and invited me to sit beside her. "Some say that I was seduced by your *père*. But the truth was, I accepted him willingly and chose to have an affair."

My breath caught. "An affair?"

"I was still married, a young woman of thirty, but to a man more than twice my age. When I met your father, I didn't intend to fall in love."

What was my *maman* saying? My parents had a dubious beginning?

The lines in her face deepened. "William asked Robert to divorce me so we could marry, but Robert refused. So, thinking we could not continue our relationship in secret, William hatched a plot to kidnap me."

I didn't know what to say.

Tears filled Mother's eyes. "Your father came by night. My husband caught us and confronted us, knowing what we attempted. But he was old and couldn't fight or run after us. At the time, I felt it was what I had to do, but I still live with guilt to this day." She sobbed. "So much guilt!"

I placed my hand over hers, hoping to give comfort or support, yet felt as if she'd struck me in the face.

She took a deep breath. "Robert de Beaumont died of shame following my betrayal." She grabbed my hands. "Ada, we didn't poison him as some have accused, I swear to you." She released me and looked away. "I know he died of a broken heart—broken because I betrayed him." She sobbed again, covering her face.

My parents had loved each other. But, for the first time, the idealistic love I'd imagined for so many years became tainted, full of deceit that caused another man's death. My heart ached for her. And for Beaumont.

She sniffled. "Immediately after he died, your father and I married." She turned again and clasped my hands. "Ada, I beg you to forgive me. I could not tell you of this when you were young. I forbade it to be spoken of in our home. I was afraid of breaking my children's hearts."

The shock left me cold. My mother and father were good people, weren't they? They'd been valiant and honorable parents and individuals in society, in spite of their deception years before. I needed to believe people could change for the better. I swallowed down a dry throat. Surely, they had changed? Who could I trust, if not *Maman*?

I took her in my arms. "I'll always love you and Father. I'm grateful you've told me." I said the words, but inside I felt hollow and cold.

My pains began whilst Henry was in Edinburgh. They started hard and relentless. Maggie and Mother stayed with me.

After an hour, the midwife examined me and in an anxious voice exclaimed, "The baby is breech."

"Breech!" I cried out with another pain. Women had died giving birth to breech babies. Feet-first was not a safe way to enter mortality, for babe or for mother.

Maggie knelt beside me and stroked my brow. "One of my sisters came breech, Ada. It's possible to deliver such a child. Keep your faith." She kissed my brow.

I opened my eyes enough to glimpse the cross hanging on the wall. Have mercy, God. Save me. Save my child.

When the midwife looked to my mother, eyes wild with fear, mother pushed her aside and applied pressure to where the baby's feet lay.

"We must work fast. Ada, I'm sorry for the discomfort, but you must do your best to cooperate with my efforts." Gently as she could, she strove to turn the child in my womb.

I screamed at the unbearable pain.

The midwife balked at *Maman's* efforts. "You're like those witchery howdies who use herbs to turn the baby."

Amid the pain, I remembered Boudica did just that. "What herbs did Boudica use, Maggie?"

She drew her brows together in thought then jumped. "It was flaxseed and comfrey. I'll be right back."

Whilst she was gone, I tried to relax and not push when the natural urge came, nor tense up as Mother investigated and probed around the baby.

Maggie returned and rubbed the poultice on my back and abdomen.

Sweat beaded at Mother's brow. She came to my side and took my hand. "You must arise and get on your hands and knees."

I tried but was too exhausted. I required the help of both Maggie and Mother. Maggie remained kneeling beside me, wiping my perspiring brow with a cool, damp cloth.

"Rock back and forth," Mother encouraged. "You can do this, Ada. The baby is almost ready."

I felt like a beast of the field trying to birth her calf. I could feel this position was better for both the babe and myself, but what if it didn't work? Were we in peril? The pains became overwhelming. Instinctively, I called out as I had at this stage in my previous two births, "*Maman*! Help me!"

"I'm here, Ada. Have courage. You can do this." In God's mercy, this time she was here to help me bring my baby into the world.

As Mother continued to work with me, she suddenly exclaimed, "Thank God the child has turned! The head is in place. You and the babe are now ready." Mother and Maggie gently helped me to the bed, propped up with pillows.

I gained strength just by looking into Mother's eyes.

The midwife took her position. "Now, push!"

I squeezed Mother's and Maggie's hands as I allowed the natural urge to overtake me. Strength came like never before.

Finally, the child within me came forth, crying freely as if announcing, "I'm here!"

"It's a girl. A princess." Maggie cried.

The midwife cut the cord and tied it off. She handed the babe to Mother, who wrapped her in one of my woven blankets and held her for me to see.

"As Mother Giffard predicted." I reached for her, but my hands shook too violently to hold her. My body trembled in effort to recover from so much pain.

"She looks like you, Lady Ada." Maggie cooed at the child. "Auburn hair, delicately pointed chin, and a little pout upon her lips." She laughed.

When my tremors stopped, she was placed in my arms. I admired my daughter then smiled up at my dear mother. "*Merci, Maman.* I may not have survived without you here." I reached for her hand.

"*Merci.*" I turned to sweet Maggie, the girl who my mother once saved from an abusive father so many years ago. No person who wasn't kinsman had become so dear to me as my handmaiden, Maggie. "*Merci* more than I can say."

Maggie simply smiled and said, "I'll have Glenore bring the oatmeal."

"With your brother away in the Holy Wars in Jerusalem, I need to help care for his household in Reigate," Mother told me. "You've convinced me to stay longer than I'd planned, but now baby Adaline is three months old, and you're strong and well."

"I'll miss you so. I pray you can come again soon." It had been heaven having her with me and I dreaded the loneliness that would come when she left.

Hearing of Mother's plans, Henry decided to take her as far as London where he'd meet with King Stephen. Although Empress Matilda had not made significant advances, the people were still divided, primarily due to King Stephen's insolent oldest son, Eustace.

On the appointed day of their departure, Henry arose before sunrise, trying not to disturb me and Adaline. Yet, I awoke and came to him, brushing his hair from his brow. "I love you, my darling. I'll pray for you every day whilst you're away."

He held me close. So tight that I sighed. "And I for you," he whispered. He glanced over to the cradle where Adaline slept. "Take care of our princess. I'll be home as soon as I can." He kissed me again.

Whenever he left, I worried I'd never see him again. As soon as I considered it, my mind latched onto the two young lovers I'd overheard at Christmastide. I needed to do something about Fenella and Giffard. It had been a private conversation, and I had no right to share it, but in that moment, not doing something about it would be the greater sin.

Henry sat on the edge of the bed to pull on his boots.

I sat beside him. "Do you remember the promise you made to Giffard's mother in Perth?"

"Certainly. I promised that once his mother had passed, I'd allow him a way to earn an estate." He pulled on a boot. "But Mother Giffard hardly seems on her deathbed now."

"Wouldn't it be a better promise to keep before his mother dies?" I asked.

Henry paused. "I'll consider it in the future, but right now I must go and oversee if my guards and I are properly packed. When I return, we can discuss this further." He kissed me and walked out the door.

The sunrise brightened the room and little Adaline whimpered in her crib. I drew her close, dissatisfied with the discussion.

Minutes later, holding Adaline, I stood at the top of the stairs as my mother emerged from her room to leave.

She kissed the top of the baby's head and held me in her arms. Then placing her hand against my cheek, she said, "Dear Ada, if there is but one thing you remember of this time together, remember to forgive when you can. In positions of power, you may also bring people sorrow. I pray not. Their sorrow may even be caused by their own actions, but show kindness to them and forgive."

I put my hand over hers. "I will, *Maman*." I now understood why she was such a charitable woman. She was paying her penance. Would she ever feel forgiven?

She took a step away and studied me and my child as if cementing us in her memory.

I embraced her one last time. "I love you."

I stood in the courtyard as Henry road out with his men and Mother's van rolled away through wildflowers and heather that flowed with the breeze in a frenzy of color.

Her words of forgiveness echoed in my mind. I also had a trip to make. Not to forgive, but to ask for forgiveness.

The next day I sat beside Maggie, Mary, and the children, headed to Edinburgh in the van.

When we arrived, I asked to see Dame Fenella. Time passed, and I wondered why the delay.

Herbert eventually came to me and knelt before my chair. "Lady Ada, I bring my deepest regrets."

A hand flew to my heart. "Is Fenella ill?"

"Nae. Nae." A brief smile played across his face. "But she refuses to come."

"Oh." I tried to digest what he was saying. That late-night conversation I'd heard between Giffard and her reminded me of how much she must blame me for her situation. "I suppose 'tis her right." I got to my feet unsure what to do next. "How have I offended her?"

Herbert stood as well. "Twas not you. This was done before you came to Scotland. She thought she would marry her childhood companion and anyone else has become a sad substitute. You've been gracious. Forgive her and forgive me. I'm much better at raising sons than daughters."

Could Herbert have been equally disappointed by my appearance here? I hoped not and said, "I wish your family every happiness."

Little Adaline slept most of the way home, as did Mary and Maggie, which left me with two rambunctious boys. Upon arriving, one other task haunted me. Walking alone down the lane beside Eads Hall, I came to a stately cottage and rapped on the door.

Sybil answered whilst laughing at one of the children behind her. She wore a soiled apron, and her disheveled hair hung down her back. I'd only seen her properly made up for a formal visit. This vital mother, playing with her children, was a side of her I'd never seen.

"Lady Ada, is something wrong?" she asked in alarm.

"Aye," I said. "We've not become well acquainted with each other, and it's my fault. Might you come for a midday meal tomorrow afternoon?"

"Well," she paused. "I'll have to find someone to watch the boys. Their nursemaid is off that day."

"Bring them along. Our boys need to play together more."

She nodded with a bright smile. "I look forward to it, my lady. Thank you."

As I returned to the manor, I shook my head. Though painful to admit, Fenella had been right. I'd not considered Sybil as a friend. But I should. She was nearby and shared the same burdens and joys of young motherhood.

Instead of entering at the door of Eads Hall, I turned to the garden and headed to the statue of Mother Mary. I needed to understand why Fenella had refused to see me and ask for forgiveness.

Chapter Twenty-Eight

As soon as Henry returned from London, I asked him if he had any idea how to help improve Giffard's situation.

Henry frowned at the question. "I have it under control. Trust me on this." His voice was firm.

I found it difficult to comply and brought it up twice more over the next months, only for him to say the matter had been taken care of and not to ask again.

Meanwhile, I had much to occupy myself. Another child graced our home the following year — a boy we proudly named David after his grandfather, King David of Scotland.

Tutors were brought in for Malcolm and William, and we included St Martin's sons.

That winter, I received word my mother had passed away unexpectedly after a short illness. It took me some time to rally. I was especially saddened that my children would never see her again and know of her goodness.

As her thirteenth and last child, we were inseparable and sometimes more like friends. By example, she taught me about love for a husband. Watching my parents had been the main source of my desire for affection in my own marriage. I remembered parties at our home in Reigate where they danced in the great hall, their laughter touching all present. My faith held strong that the power of love had reunited them in Heaven.

In my heart, I forgave her for the indiscretion she'd caused when she'd been young. And I forgave myself for judging her.

In the spring of the following year, Margaret was born. We named this daughter after Henry's grandmother, Queen Margaret of Scotland. I told my new baby of her namesake many times, whispering in her tiny ear, "I hope you emulate Queen Margaret, full of goodness, piety, and service to the poor." The name seemed to fit, for my little Margaret was even-tempered and easy to please.

William, David, Adaline, and Margaret appeared healthy— I thanked God for that—but Malcolm still had occasional bouts with illness. He grew tall and slight of build with a calm frame of mind. If he outlived his father, I imagined Malcolm a gentle king.

William was athletic, robust, and of spirited disposition. I feared he'd be an assertive leader, quick to battle if he believed it necessary.

David was dark and handsome like his father and also proved to have talent with the sword. Pretending he was a knight was all he ever wanted to do. William showed him much encouragement with his athletic talents, and the two could often be found following after one of the guardsmen or St Martin when he was about. Seeking yet another lesson with the sword.

Adaline had my hair color, copper with threads of gold, yet her eyes reminded me of her grandfather David's, the softest brown. Content to be at home, cautious and fair-minded, she was a seeker of justice.

Henry took pride in his three sons and found joy in his daughters, but he was gone much of the time helping his father with the burdens of the kingship. I became both annoyed and concerned when he told me time and again of his plans for return and then extended his stay an extra day or two or more.

I struggled with anger when I didn't get enough of his time and constantly had to remind myself of his great responsibilities. The king was getting older, and it was natural for Henry to be required to take on more and more of the burden of insuring Northumbria's safety and overseeing affairs in Scotland.

Spring had come again to Eads Hall, and the heather flowered in deep purple. Henry had been away for weeks and would not see the blooms. There was so much in our lives he missed. Margaret had started to walk, and David loved to sneak outside to the garden to terrorize the ducks.

Whilst the older boys had their lessons and Mary was upstairs with the girls, I went downstairs for food. *"Bonjour,* Maurice. Have you a small sweetmeat?"

He relished in keeping me happy with his treats. *"Pour vous, toujours."*

I took the sweetmeat and sat by the hearth, the house unusually quiet.

Taking a bite, I happened to spy David sneaking down the stairs, toy sword in hand. For the third time that morning, he headed for the front door.

I laughed.

He was a focused child, to be sure.

As he opened the door, to his—and my—surprise, Henry was about to open it himself. Yet he wasn't due for another sennight.

After eight years of marriage, my heart still fluttered when I saw him after a long period apart.

"Father!" David dropped his weapon and wrapped his little arms around his father's legs. He then quickly retreated up the stairs where he knew he belonged.

Henry took me in a tight embrace, laughing at our child's antics.

After kissing me soundly, he asked, "How would you like to leave the children at home and accompany me to Northumbria's seashore? I believe you deserve a holiday."

"Oh, *mon amour*." I sighed. "Naught could be more wonderful."

The next morning, we were on our way. Oddly, St Martin didn't accompany us. Instead, we had two guards I'd never met before. Henry brought with him his hawk, which lately seemed a more constant companion to him than myself. The travel would take us two days. We stayed in an inn the first night and Henry treated me like a new bride. It was exactly what I'd been needing.

On the second day, we resumed our travels on horseback, side by side, through the vivid heather, around oak scrubs and over hillsides. Occasional roe deer eyed us cautiously and scampered among the trees. Field laborers waved as our procession passed through their land. As we rode up a hill and approached our destination, we were favored with a glimpse of ocean blue.

Henry seemed nervous.

From the worried look on his face, I guessed something was amiss. "Whatever are you thinking?"

He put on a mischievous expression. "It's a secret and has been for some time."

"The sort of secret one shares with his wife?"

"Soon. Very soon."

We rode down a hill. Before reaching the crest of the next, Henry confessed, "I have a gift for you."

He held nothing in his hands. Could the gift be in his satchel? I waited for him to say more, but after a few moments, I could no longer control my curiosity. "A gift? Of what kind?"

He chuckled, sent his hawk off to hunt, and drew his horse near mine. He offered his hand. "It's at Warkworth. I've worked on it for several years. You'll see when we arrive."

Years? This was indeed something special if Henry could keep it secret that long. I took his hand. "Is it with a craft-smith, or something you found on your journeys?"

He simply faced ahead, grinning.

I looked to the horizon, hoping to glimpse Warkworth, the next burgh on our journey. It had been settled at a picturesque spot, tucked within a horseshoe bend in the River Coquet. The sun peeked behind a lone cloud. "I see rooftops!" I stood tall as I could in the stirrups.

The closer we drew, the more puzzled I became, for the skyline had changed from what I remembered. "The burgh does not have a castle, yet I think I see one."

One of the guards laughed quietly.

When I turned to him, he quickly looked away.

Henry, too, diverted his gaze but could not conceal his grin.

We rode through a stone gatehouse on our way to the castle bailey. The ornate gates appeared as if they'd just been added. Clearing the gates, I could see better the scaffolding and masonry work in progress. Golden stonewalls and towers reached skyward.

A thrill rippled through me. "Henry, are you building this for *us*?"

He nodded. "Are you pleased?"

I stared breathless. Although Eads Hall had become home, this new adventure in a new place felt tantalizing. "Very," I whispered in disbelief.

"My half-brother, Simon, transferred the property to me. It's conveniently located as a center for governing. And I'm not building it alone." He waved to a man perched on a ladder across the courtyard.

The man descended and came toward us as we dismounted. When he neared, I recognized our good friend.

"Hugh Giffard is my foreman." Henry patted his shoulder. "He worked with the architects to design each room and gathered the carpenters, masons, and artisans on his own. What he has accomplished in three years should have taken ten."

Giffard bowed. "You are most kind, sire."

Henry signaled to the guard at his left, who produced a scroll from his satchel. Henry handed it to Giffard with a suspicious grin. "Last sennight King David came here and eyed your handiwork. I thought you might be interested in his response to that and your years of service to me."

Giffard unrolled the missive and read quietly, grinning. It seemed impossible for his expression to show more pleasure, but then suddenly he whooped. "The deed to Yester Castle? In Haddington?"

Henry laid a hand on his shoulder. "It's not much to look at, I'll warn you. Naught more than a pile of rocks on an old dungeon. But it comes with a good income, and once you're done here, you can use our craftsmen to make the place fit for a bride."

Giffard reddened and bowed. "Thank you, my lord. It's a life's dream come true." He embraced each of us before trotting to the men and showing them the document.

Henry put an arm around my shoulders. "Giffard's advancement wasn't within my power. I had to convince my father. Remember Kelton deserved advancement and was placed as steward. He had to go to the king of England to get a title."

"Aye," I admitted. "But I thought the reason King David placed Kelton beside you was to improve your relationship."

"Mayhap, but it didn't work as well as he'd hoped."

I moved closer to Henry. "Why did you not share your plans for this castle with me?" The joy of the moment was offset by my concern that Henry could be so involved in all this and keep it from me so long. So much of his life stood apart from my own.

Henry brightened. "I wanted it to be a surprise. Now let's tour your new home, my lady."

Stonecutters and carpenters hardly paused in their tasks as we skirted around their work. A lovely kitchen garden already flourished near a finished section of the outer wall. I could imagine Maurice, hands on his hips, telling the servants just what to pick. The soil appeared fertile in a way that the property surrounding our manor at Eads Hall never would.

"The fortress is far from finished, but the palace is yours and awaits your womanly touch." He swept his hand toward the stone and timber structure.

The grandeur of the arched entry, glass paned windows on the upper level, and its painted wood finishes left me speechless. It was all so beautiful.

"Would you care to go inside?" Henry asked.

With overwhelming anticipation, I approached the palace, fully expecting the interior to be empty.

Instead, a doorman greeted us. "*Fáilte*, my lord and lady." He bowed.

Henry swept me into his arms and carried me into our new home like we were newly married.

Both laughing, he put me down and motioned to the expansive entry, which flowed into the great hall. Not only had the walls been plastered and painted, the hearth had been lined with carved pillars that fed into the vaulted ceiling above. A glowing fire burned within. The room was furnished with cushioned leather benches and a vast dining table stood near the wall, fit to serve three dozen at least.

Henry pulled out the chair at the head of the table. "Shall we sit?"

As soon as he sat to my right, servants brought platters of food. Obviously, much planning had gone into his surprise.

I took it all in with wonder. A palace of my very own and near the sea. My heart sored with the imaginings of my children playing on the nearby rolling hills.

Upon completion of a delicious meal, Henry showed me the chapel within our new home. Something we never had at Eads Hall. He led me upstairs. "This will be our chamber."

A large, curtained canopy bed came out from the far wall. He showed me the nursery in the next room. "And here, space for our children."

All the rooms in the solar had been filled with the necessary furniture to make a family feel at home.

He grasped my shoulders. "You have never had a castle of your own. Now you do. Eads Hall is modest compared to this."

Eads Hall was indeed small and ancient compared to this.

"It's wonderful, Henry, but I will miss Eads Hall—it being our first home together, where we decorated with our wedding gifts. The people have come to be my friends, and I love the gardens you built."

"We'll keep both." He laughed and then pulled me toward a stairwell off the hall. "You must see the view from the top."

We climbed into the sunlight and stepped outside. Before us lay a vast view of the houses below, the meandering river, the green farmlands, and the contrasting blues where ocean met horizon. In the shadow of the castle, a grassy meadow held a large elm tree, its branches wide and inviting.

My chest expanded with the possibilities of us living here. "Henry, it's stunning!"

He wrapped his arms around me and leaned his cheek against my head. "You remember the day when I showed you the view of London from the top of Westminster?"

"I do."

"And does this view take your breath away as it did so many years ago?" He kissed my neck.

"Aye, all the more because I'm with you." I could be happy anywhere Henry was.

We stood in an embrace for a long time, taking it all in. How I loved him and my children. I could not imagine life any better.

That night, I slept in my new home and again had the dream of our early marriage. I sat beneath a great canopied-tree with Malcolm and William beside me, speaking soberly. David played in a corner with Adaline, and Margaret and another little girl giggled together, distracted by a passing butterfly. Why did that dream continue to plague me?

Once the morning light lifted the room from darkness, I dressed and hurried downstairs. In the courtyard, I planned to find Giffard and ask if we could wall the field as an area for the children but found him preparing to leave.

I rushed to his side. "Where are you off to?"

He reddened. "There is someone who has been waiting far too long for news of my estate."

"Fenella. Do you see a wedding in your near future?"

Giffard mounted his horse. "Lady Ada, you will be the second to know."

A month later, we brought our entire household to Warkworth. Though Giffard was still away, it was nearly complete. The children played in the courtyard and spent hours watching the workers building the outer fortress.

How I enjoyed making the palace my own. No other castles in the royal family were mine, each of them filled with centuries of tapestries and furniture chosen by generations before. But Warkworth Castle was my home. It wound itself around my heart like the River Coquet wound around the village.

Chapter Twenty-Nine

On a lazy afternoon in late summer, the children and I went to the seashore to refresh ourselves in the cool ocean breeze.

A number of other families from the village had also come for the same purpose. Whilst Mary watched the little ones play in the sand, Glenore took the boys to the tidepools to hunt for treasures. She'd become like one of the family and sometimes acted as a child herself.

I laid on a blanket and closed my eyes to enjoy the sounds of the waves lapping the shore.

Sometime later, a shout aroused me.

"M'lady, M'lady!" Glenore raced toward me across the beach. "Giffard's been given the haunted castle of Yester, he has. Do ye hear me? It's haunted!" By the time she reached me she was breathing so hard she could barely speak. She curtsied belatedly, as if just remembering she spoke in too familiar a fashion to me. "Consent to speak me mind?"

How could I refuse her enthusiasm? Truth be told, I did want to know the details of her gossip. I nodded approval.

"Did ye hear he plans to wed Dame Fenella? Serves her right to be surrounded by ghosties for the way she's treated ye lately, m'lady. That's what I say."

Unlike Giffard promised, I was not the *second* to hear of his impending nuptials. "Now that's hardly fair," I said to Glenore. "She was very kind when I first came to Eads Hall, and it was Dame Fenella that insisted I encourage *you* to come back."

"That doesn't make-up fer her turning her back to ye." Glenore pouted. "Fair weather friends aren't to be trusted. That's what I say."

David wandered up to Glenore's side. "Mama, what's a ghostie?"

I got to my feet. "Naught more than a figment of people's imaginings." I gave the eye to Glenore to try to convey the importance of little listening ears.

She simply folded her arms in front of her. "Then ye don't want to hear when the weddin' will be?"

"Favor me with what you know."

Glenore smiled at my obvious interest. "Christmastide. The cold weather is when the least amount of work will be done on the castle so they can have themselves time."

"And how did you hear such news?" I asked warily.

Glenore cocked her head. "Why, Hugh Giffard just arrived. I saw him on the road yonder." She pointed behind me toward the castle.

"Then I should return and bid him congratulations. Carry on without me," I said to Glenore and Mary.

The craftsmen had gathered around Giffard, bowing to his beautiful bride-to-be. Herbert, Fenella's father, had also accompanied them.

Seeing Fenella again gave my stomach a roll. How would she respond to me? I wished to retreat but had already been spotted by a few of the men.

Marching forward, I extended my arms. "How wonderful to have you all here. Henry is away, but we are very pleased you could come visit."

Giffard took my hand. "Have you heard our news?" He reached for Fenella, who slipped beneath his arm. "We are to be wed."

"Aye," I said. "A Christmas celebration says my kitchen maid." I hoped he heard in my voice how much I didn't approve of hearing the news in such a way. "Congratulations to both of you, and welcome, *Monsieur* Herbert and Dame Fenella." I was afraid to look Fenella in the eyes.

There was an awkward silence whilst I waited for someone to say something.

"We are most pleased to be here." Herbert bowed.

Fenella said naught.

"I'll see to your rooms," I said. "Stroll by the sea, if you'd like. It's a glorious day."

As I walked away, I heard Fenella whisper to Giffard, "I thought you said she wouldn't be here."

The words stung at my heart. I hurried through the main entrance and called to Mariam to prepare for guests.

Throughout supper, Fenella said naught, simply eyeing me from across the table. In all fairness, the conversation was preempted by Malcolm and William. Once they realized that Herbert the Chamberlain had trained knights of Scotland in his younger days, they asked about his adventures and skills from lancing to javelin. When they started detailing fencing techniques, little David became interested.

I remembered how much I liked Herbert. He must have been a good father to his four boys. Mayhap he didn't know how to handle Fenella other than treating her as one of his sons?

After the meal, and by the time the boys had finished begging me to let them take lessons, Fenella had excused herself for the evening.

I left for my room as well, frustrated with the rift between us.

The next morning, I hardly wished to rise. I asked to take breakfast in my room and dressed slowly, considering returning to Eads Hall. The sound of my sons' laughter drifted through my window, and I looked out into the courtyard.

Each of my three boys sat obediently, holding wooden practice swords that Herbert must have brought with him.

Giffard faced the knight, and the two men furiously dueled.

Herbert delayed, as if on purpose to allow Giffard's win.

Giffard moved in to tap his iron breastplate with his sword. The two men began another set, where Herbert attacked with such skill he appeared as young as Giffard.

The boys shouted excitedly.

Pulling them away would break their hearts. Henry had told me it was time for their training, but I held off. Most training began at age seven, and Malcolm was already eight. Henry was right.

I shook my head. I'd send a missive to Donnchad for a knight to be sent to us for their training.

Sighing, I went to the nursery to check on the girls. Mary had dressed for the beach.

"I'll go with you," I said.

Mary gave a wan smile. "With the boys occupied, why not take advantage of the nice weather and go for a ride? How long has it been since you've taken Cooper over the hills?"

"What a magnificent idea." I couldn't remember the last time I'd had an afternoon to myself. Even with a full staff of servants, overseeing my five children's activities and maintaining our home took all my time.

Excited for the freedom of being alone, I hurried to the stables. As I neared, I found Cooper already saddled, her mane braided with blue ribbons.

Fenella led her white horse, Snowball, out of the stable. She paused when she saw me, her face unreadable. "Do you mind company, Lady Ada?"

I wished to say aye, I did mind. I minded very much that she refused to speak to me these last years. Instead, I answered politely, "That would be fine."

We both mounted, and I directed Cooper toward the seashore. Soon the empty beach lay before us, flat and inviting. I was tempted to let Cooper run free but held her back, trotting at a proper pace.

As if reading my thoughts, Fenella shouted, "Let's race." The wind blew at her hair and her freckles appeared darker. "First one to the outcropping yonder." She kicked her horse's sides and accelerated to a full gallop.

Not to be outdone, I did the same, and soon we rode neck and neck, flying on our mounts across the sand. Like her father, I believe she held back slightly and allowed me to win, but by then I was laughing with abandon, and it didn't matter.

Dismounting, we let the horses graze on the nearby grass and sat together, looking out into the bright blue waves stretching as far as the eye could see. "That felt wonderful. *Merci.*"

Fenella touched my hand. "Nae, thank you. I wasn't certain you ever wanted to speak to me again, and I wouldn't blame you."

I shook my head. "I believe you were the one who wasn't doing the talking. I visited so many times, and you refused me."

"I wasn't refusing you, per se." Fenella took a deep breath. "I was refusing to be injured by my own jealousy."

"You? Jealous?" I asked, surprised. "You're beautiful and a much better horsewoman than I. What could you be jealous of?"

"Lady Ada, you have everything I don't. You have Henry and his beautiful children. Whenever I came to visit, I felt empty and alone."

"And if Giffard hadn't gotten his title, I might still be holed up in Edinburgh Castle by myself not speaking to anyone." The pain was evident in her eyes.

"When I came to this new land, you acted a true friend. I wish there had not been jealousy between us."

"You jealous of me?"

Heat moved up my cheeks. "You're lovely, Fenella. And I worried Henry thought so too."

"Henry *never* looked at me as he does you."

We embraced, and the tension between us eased.

Clearly relieved, Fenella leaned back. "Can I ask you something?"

"Certainly," I said.

"Well, you know I have no sisters. And my mother passed away shortly after I was born. So, I was wondering if you could . . ." she paused.

I nodded to encourage her question.

"I'd be honored if you'd act as mother of the bride." She reddened.

I blinked. We were close to the same age. I was barely twenty-four.

"I need someone to guide me on the many stages of planning. I don't want to do anything wrong, and I especially want Giffard to be proud of me. I need someone to make sure I don't make any mistakes." She touched my arm. "You are natural at hosting dignitaries, even ones you don't like. The way you handled Lord Madduch still makes me laugh."

I shook my head at the memory of Madduch's advances. I didn't believe a word of her reasoning of why she needed my help. She'd planned many royal events and had been taught much from her father. I think what she really wanted was a female companion by her side, to share in her joy, but she didn't know how to say it. Her brothers probably teased her whenever she acted female. "I would be happy to act as mother of the bride." I squeezed her hand. I had missed her companionship.

Fenella looked worried. "If you aren't comfortable, my lady, I can—"

"Nae," I said. "I'm honored to be asked."

We mounted and spent the afternoon riding across the surrounding countryside as though the years had melted away and I was a new bride first come to Northumbria.

Upon our return, a missive was waiting from my sister, Gundred.

My dear Ada,

Maman's passing has been hard, but I am sorry to add to your sorrow by sending you the news of our brother's unfortunate death. William had aligned himself with King Louis of France's crusade and was killed in a battle at Mount Cadmus near Laodicea. Adela is beside herself with grief, and their daughter Isobel cries for her father. The young countess is not yet twelve years in age, bless her heart. Bless us all.

Chapter Thirty

Fenella must have spent every moment of the last six years planning her wedding. Held at nearby Carlisle Castle, with her ideas and my connections, it was nothing less than opulent. She had a pair of swans brought from the South of France to float in the garden pond. In the grand hall, green boughs of cypress and holly draped the walls and hearth, trimmed with scarlet bows at each lift. Red velvet covered the gift table, which stretched as broad and wide as the dining table at Warkworth.

Chaplain Robert officiated the ceremony at the nearby chapel.

I stood on the front row, beside Henry, wearing a gown the color of violets, trimmed with sable. Around my neck I wore my favorite necklace, a large green emerald that Henry had given me as a wedding gift.

After the official ceremony, Chaplain Robert added a few personal words. "As the two of you become one, may your bond reach to your very soul. Every day let your love grow stronger so when you pass from this life that bond continues still, even as our love of Christ our Lord. Amen."

I took Henry's hand, feeling as though that was what we strove for—a love that would last forever.

As the procession came into the castle, Henry and I welcomed each guest. Many friends came from Whitfield and Edinburgh. St Martin and Dame Sybil arrived in great spirits, giving a lovely, hand-carved cradle to Fenella, like the one I'd received so many years before. Tapestries, paintings, and furniture accumulated from the country's elite. The connections Herbert had as chamberlain brought many from both north and south.

And Fenella's past responsibilities planning events for King David had introduced her to many influential people. An elderly nobleman from Brittany arrived with his corpulent young daughter, and a baron from France, perchance the one who brought the swans.

English guests were not as plentiful as the Scots. King David had recently knighted the sixteen-year-old Henry Plantagenet, to King Stephen's dismay, striving to keep Scotland from being a vassal kingdom to England.

A finely dressed stranger came forward and bowed to me. His sharp nose and dark eyes gave him the appearance of a hawk. He bowed not low, but civilly.

"Ranulf, the Earl of Chester," Henry whispered in my ear.

My entire body stiffed. It could not be. How did he have the impudence to walk up to Henry and me, as if he would be welcome anywhere near us.

"Lady Ada." He acted as though we'd never met before. "It's my pleasure."

His smooth voice made tingles run up my spine. Taken back to the cold floor of a cave, hands and feet bound, I swayed.

Henry put his arm around my waist.

"How do you know the bride?" Somehow, I spoke.

"I spent time at the Scottish court when I trained under Donnchad. I grew to know Herbert and his daughter very well. I nearly proposed to her." Ranulf laughed. "Do you approve of her new husband?" Ranulf shook Henry's hand.

I couldn't bear to see their skin touch. Henry being propped up by his loyal men, head bleeding and half-unconscious was all I could see.

"Hugh Giffard is a gentleman and a man of honor," Henry stated.

"That has yet to be determined." Ranulf removed his hat and sauntered passed us.

In the grand hall, St Martin and Giffard stood together as Ranulf passed. With shoulders straightened, they glared at him and then looked to each other in question.

The night progressed with no other incident. After most of the guests arrived, a gilded van pulled in front of the castle entrance. Kelton and my cousin Isobel, both looking somewhat travel-worn, stepped out. Kelton entered, bowed, and said very little to us before he continued into the grand hall.

Henry followed him, but I knew not why.

Isobel lingered to talk. In her hands, she held two wrapped gifts. "Sweet cousin Ada, here is the wedding gift." She handed the larger package for me to place on the overflowing table. "And this, I would like to return to you."

She gave me a package about as large as a loaf of bread but much heavier. I had an idea what it was and was surprised the precious relic was being returned.

Isobel must have seen my questioning gaze. "Father Malachy's chrism has not worked. When I had Isobel, there were complications. The physician expressed concern that I wouldn't be able to have another child, and then you sent this. It seemed a miracle. Kelton prayed over it each day, but still the gift of another child has never been realized." She bowed her head.

"Oh, Isobel." I embraced her. "I'll pray as well, but your little girl is a wonderful gift. I'm certain there will be many strong Englishmen who will fight for her hand."

Isobel smiled. "She's a sweet child, and we are blessed. But Kelton is not convinced. He yearns for a son. You wouldn't understand." She turned and entered the hall, her shoulders drooping slightly. Instead of joining her husband, she went to a corner and sat in a chair away from the other guests.

"A gentle spirit," I said aloud.

"That's what I've thought of you." A voice behind me said.

I jumped. Turning toward the man who spoke, I came face to face with the handsome Lord Madduch in a dramatic green cloak, the smell of wine on his breath. He smiled wistfully. "Someday you'll reconsider my offer."

Ignoring his words, I gave my rote presentation. "Welcome to Sir Hugh Giffard and Dame Fenella's wedding. How pleased they are for your kind attendance." I directed him to place the lovely decanter his servant carried on the table and showed him to the grand hall.

"Have you naught more to tell me?" He pouted as would a child.

"Nae." I turned away to greet another guest.

The music and drinking continued late into the night, long after the newlyweds excused themselves. Some of the knights talked of kidnapping the bride and groom in jest, but whether it was fear of retribution from Giffard's new father-in-law or of Fenella herself, the idea was quickly abandoned, and the night calmed.

Early the next morning, we prepared to return to Eads Hall when a servant delivered a package to me. "Dame Fenella wishes to thank ye for all you've done for her, my lady." The young maid curtsied.

Inside the box, small pink crystals nestled on cloth. "How unusual. What are these?"

"Tis salt from caves in the Orient. Very precious."

I dipped my little finger in the crystals and touched a few to my tongue. The salt flavor was strong and true. "Tell Lady Fenella I wish her every happiness."

When I got to the van, Henry reached in his pocket. "I must have mislaid my gloves. I'll return shortly."

He returned in minutes. "Apparently, Giffard mistook them for his own. He left them on the table with a note."

I laughed. "That was thoughtful to do the day after his wedding. Any man so able to take care of details would make a great foreman."

Henry smiled at the even script of the letter. "He says to thank you for your matchmaking skills. They proved most successful." We both laughed as the van pulled away.

When we arrived at Eads Hall, Henry and I were both exhausted. Before running up to kiss the children after our absence, I hastened to the kitchen and delivered Fenella's gift to Maurice.

His face beamed. He loved trying new flavors. "I'll use it on the lamb tomorrow."

I went to my bedchamber and placed Father Malachy's chrism on the bedside table, so it would be the last thing I'd see every night and the first thing I'd face in the morning.

I wrote a prayer list that evening and at the top I wrote Isobel's name. It was as though her heart needed to be healed more than her womb, for she seemed so low in spirit.

Chapter Thirty-One

I stood at the window of an empty bedchamber, watching Donnchad in the courtyard below teach Malcolm and William the art of swordplay. I winced with each thrust from their child-sized wooden weapons.

"I've been looking for you." Henry came up behind me.

"This is my favorite place to watch the boys—where they can't see me grimace or hear me tell Donnchad to lay easy." I laughed but felt no humor.

"You must get used to raising boys to become soldiers who will someday serve the people. It's a brave and honorable thing they are learning." He wrapped his arms around my waist. "I'll start taking Malcolm with me when I need make negotiations or deal with legal matters. It's time he met his people in Scotland as well."

I leaned back into his chest. "I was surprised when Donnchad himself came to train our sons instead of sending another."

"Mormaer Donnchad pledges to the security of my family. It's his honor and privilege to train future kings. His father trained me. The Earls of Fife are the highest-ranking nobles in the realm." He stiffened. "If ever I'm to die, he is the man you can trust with our children."

I shivered. "Please don't speak of death as I watch my children learn to violently stab another." A movement caught my eye. I leaned closer to the window and caught a glimpse of David by the rack of swords. "Look at him," I said to Henry.

Henry released me and came closer to the window. "Ha! He'll be a fine knight. He's trying to heft the biggest sword."

"He still has another two years before he can become a page in his training for knighthood. What will we do with him in the mean-time?" I asked.

"Keep the weapons hidden, I think." Henry chuckled then drew a hand to his head.

"Are you still experiencing headaches?"

"Aye. And fatigue."

"We must discover the cause, *mon amour*." I touched his arm. "Although, I must admit, I enjoy having you with us more often."

Turning back toward the window, he laughed at David's antics as he inspected and hid behind large shields displaying the mac David ensign.

Henry seldom complained and often changed the subject whenever I discussed his ailments. I think it was hard for him to accept weakness.

I sighed and brought my thoughts back to the boys. "I don't want to think of my children at war, killing others. How have mothers before me come to understand the nature of boys who grow into men?"

"It's an honor to be a valiant soldier. Honor is sometimes all we have. But don't fear, I'll teach them to aspire to the ideals of generosity and courtesy. You'll one day be proud of your sons."

"As I am of you, for you're the best man to teach them chivalry. No one learns better than by example."

He shrugged at the compliment. "At fourteen, they'll become squires and begin fighting on horseback."

I shuddered.

He put his arm around my shoulders. "The people expect a strong king who cannot be defeated by his enemies. We must teach our boys of their ordained destiny."

"You're right, I know. How blessed they are to have you."

He kissed my cheek. "And how blessed we all are to have a woman of faith whose nature is gentle and kind. Just the timber of your pleasant voice makes one know that God exists. There's been no greater joy in my life than to have you beside me."

I jabbed him with my elbow, both embarrassed and pleased.

Henry stood taller. "I forgot why I came to find you. Father's asked us to divide our time in the coming years between our southern homes and his court in Edinburgh. He specifically asked that you sign charters and act as a witness on them as well."

"Your father's desire for me to serve in court is an honor. My father trained me somewhat in governance, which I know is unlikely for a girl. The morning of our wedding, as we strolled through the beautiful gardens of Westminster Palace, you spoke passionately of your love for Scotland and its people. My hopeful heart awakened to the belief that you were a man with whom I could build true love and serve Scotland."

"And do you love the Scots?"

"Aye. Mayhap one more than the others." I wrapped my arm around his waist. "My mother once taught me a parable. She compared a crescent moon to a full moon. Then she described two kings. One saw the power and wealth of his position. The other envisioned ways to help the poor, remove the oppression of tyrants in his land, and bring new freedoms and opportunities to his people, including women. *Maman* then asked, 'Ada, which king saw the crescent moon and which saw the full moon?' You Henry, have always seen the fullness and have taught me likewise."

He kissed the top of my head. "I've been favored to be the son of a noble king who taught me to see the fullness. We'll leave in a sennight for Edinburgh."

Chapter Thirty-Two

As if providence tested my happiness after the joys of Warkworth and time at court, Henry became ill enough to cease venturing out. When I embraced him, I couldn't help but notice the weight he'd lost and waited for his strength to return.

In the winter months, we stayed at Eads Hall away from the damp cold of the coast. Though I loved the manor, I missed our frequent visits to Warkworth. I longed for the peaceful majesty of the nearby ocean and the newness of the castle as if it offered us a renewal of life.

"May I entreat you to rub my back?" Henry requested as we retired to our bedchamber one evening.

"Certainly." I sat behind him on the bed and massaged his neck, working my way down his back. I wished my hands possessed the healing touch that took his pain away. I remembered the chrism and dropped some of the vial's oil into my palm, massaging it into his skin, praying that the healing powers would restore him.

"The physician's visit today was worthless." His words dragged. "They know no more than I about my illness. The herbs they've suggested have been for naught."

Fearing his negativity would impede healing, I said, "We'll keep trying to find answers. Don't give up, *mon amour*. We'll get you well." My hands moved further down his back. As I worked, his muscles relaxed. I would have continued, but soon he could no longer sit up and had to recline against his pillows. I pulled the blankets around him and kissed his forehead. "Try to get a good night's rest."

He sighed, looking up at me with a question in his eyes, then closed his lids.

My love swelled for him. Father Malachy's words of eleven years previous flashed in my memory. 'You shall not die *this time*.' Nae! Nae! Not this time, not ever! I cried in my heart to God. *I beseech Thee to heal him.*

Before sunrise, I awakened to find Henry's place on the bed empty. Alarmed, I slipped on shoes and robe and began my search through the rooms.

When I did not find him inside, I donned my mantle and ran outside, searching the courtyard and stables. I finally found him sitting on a bench near the frozen rosebushes, the branches looking like thorny pokers. "Did you not sleep well, *mon amour*?"

He shook his head and held his hand out in invitation. "Come sit with me for a while."

I sat close to him, hoping to warm us both. I smiled when he ran his hand over my growing middle. I was expecting our sixth child, and my ample night smock could not hide it.

He smiled then became serious. A shadow crossed his brow. "I think someone is trying to kill me. I think I'm being poisoned."

My throat went dry. "Nae." I took his hand in both mine. It was cold. So cold and rough in a way I hadn't noticed before. He'd taken to wearing his riding gloves more often. Now I guessed why. The disease must be attacking his hands as well. "How can this be? St Martin watches over you and a servant tastes all your food before you eat even when you travel. He's not sick. You and I share the same dishes, and I am well."

"Mayhap then it's something else—but it's something." He put his arm around my shoulders and pulled me closer. "Remember a few days ago when we went walking with the children?" He gazed up to the glow of dawn on the horizon. "I was too weak to play the simplest games with them. I could only watch." Tears glistened in his eyes, reflecting the rising sun.

I laid my head on his shoulder. How could I pull him from this melancholy? I'd never heard such discouragement from him before. Surely, he'd be well soon. "Nonetheless, it was a lovely day," I said trying to cheer him with the memory. "Maurice brought us pastries and warm ale, and we sat huddled together to eat. I treasure our times together as a family."

"I hope it wasn't our last outing." He kissed my head.

"Of course, it wasn't. You must stop speaking such." He could not leave me or the children. I'd be unable to carry on. I reached my arms around him and held him close. "I love you too much to let you go."

We sat in the silence of our individual thoughts as the sun rose above the horizon and warmed us.

I wasn't certain what to do. Should I notify Maurice that Henry's food might be poisoned? But what could he do differently? No one else was sick. I suspected that if Henry were being poisoned, it had happened months before, and now he was coping with the effects. But what if it *was* ongoing? Who would want to kill my husband?

Finally, we stood — Henry shaking — and headed toward the house. Slowly, he led me the long way around the pond, stopping to touch a new bud now and then or talk of what might bloom first in the garden. Was he trying to hold on to life, or was he telling the land goodbye?

I blinked away tears and looked to my precious statue of Mother Mary. In my heart, I said a brief prayer, *God, help us know what to do.*

Henry jerked slightly, wincing in pain.

I held to his arm, not knowing how to help.

As the pain lessened, he breathed deeply. "I need to lay down again."

By May we still hadn't left for the coast. One night in bed, after Henry's health had declined for weeks, I listened to his ragged breathing.

He rolled toward me with great effort. "We need to leave Eads Hall. I fear my life may be short. For our safety, we shall leave by night and go to Scotland. Father is staying at his country manor at Peebles."

I gasped and laid my hand on his cheek.

He was so cold even with the covers heaped on. What was happening to my Henry?

"If anything should happen to me, I want you to be with my father and those he trusts. That way I can be assured our children will be safe."

Great sorrow and dread overcame me. Could my sons and daughters be in danger too? I dared not speak and held him in my arms, praying for wisdom and strength to accomplish what I had to do to protect Henry and our children from any unforeseen danger. "By night? Are you sure we need take such measures?" Did he know things I was not aware of? Or was he becoming too cautious or even delirious?

"Aye, we must take all precautions. I've lived my life looking over my shoulder, and still I must. You recall I warned you before we married that there would be those plotting against us." He cleared his throat. "We'll hide at Peebles until I'm well. The abbey has an infirmary where they can help me. We'll start our journey as soon as we can be ready." He cleared his throat again, obviously in pain from just talking. "Notify the servants to prepare our things, but do not tell them our destination. Not even guards will accompany us."

Was this illness driving Henry mad—to the point of being unable to reason? If I believed Henry knew best and we were truly in danger, then I must also believe Henry was being poisoned. I released him and wiped tears from my eyes. I needed to be stronger.

"My father has enough servants to attend to us."

"But…"

He pulled me close again, hands trembling. "I know not who to trust, Ada. We will go in secret."

"As you say. We'll start our journey tomorrow," I said with trepidation.

"You're a brilliant horsewoman and can ride the horse that pulls our van. I've thought about all this for days. We can do it."

We left the next night for Peebles. Henry rode a horse for the first hour but had to rest in the van after that. As the sun rose and the children awoke, Malcolm and William attended to their father as best they could.

David had been given a wooden practice sword by Donnchad, which he held at ready as if to protect our little band.

Each time I glanced back, I saw the worry on their faces. Adaline and Margaret were gentle little girls who either sat silently staring at their ill father or played quiet games together.

We looked like refugees, not the royal family next in line for the throne of Scotland. I shifted on the saddle, praying the little one in my womb would not come early, as William had.

Before darkness came upon us the next day, I pulled the van into the forest and slid off the horse. My body hurt everywhere and my hips burned with fatigue. I needed to close my eyes and find a place to lie flat.

When I came to the opening of van, Henry sat leaning against the canvas canopy with Margaret on his lap. Adaline sat beside him, her head against his shoulder. Henry was talking in low tones to his children and they intently listened to what he said.

"Malcolm, help your mother into the van."

"Aye, Father."

Malcolm gave me a hand and William arranged cushions for me to lie on.

Henry handed me a chunk of bread from under a cloth. "If I don't get well, I expect you all to help your mother."

The mood in the van was somber—the children too young to comprehend the full import of what was happening or what changes lay ahead.

I reached my hand to him.

He took it but his grasp was weak. The fervor for life he'd always had no longer shone in his eyes. He turned to Malcolm. "As the eldest, you'll have responsibilities to your country one day, but it's your family that I want you to think of now."

How unusual for our family to be completely alone with no servitors listening and watching our every move. Although

-264-

Henry's words were dismal there was a feeling of true unity in our cramped little space.

"How much I want to say to all of you—so many words that have never been said. My entire life I was trained to serve my country with the expectation that I would one day be king. I have always been looking forward and forgetting what trailed in my wake." He pulled Margaret closer to him and looked intently in each child's face. "If I leave this life, know that it's not the end. If God graciously grants me Heaven, I will wait for all of you there. We may be separated on earth, but we will always be a family that belongs to each other."

Tears wet my face and fell to the cushions. "May God grant you many more years with us."

It was late in the evening on the third night when we spotted the castle near Peebles, a smaller structure than King David's other abodes. It was built of lumber and stood on a ridge between the River Tweed and Eddleston Water. Would this be a place of healing for Henry?

As I pulled the van into the courtyard, guards surrounded us, and Henry called out to let them know who we were. After disembarking, our dusty band filed into the hall.

King David came immediately to greet us. "I had no idea you were coming." The moment he saw Henry leaning against the wall, his knees nearly buckled. He rushed forward and took Henry in his arms.

"Take him to a bedchamber," King David said to the servant beside him.

The man had to support Henry in order to help him walk upstairs. A footman hastened forward to assist.

I whispered to the king all that I knew but didn't want my children hearing the details.

He nodded and said, "He'll recover in my care." But his words were more a question than a statement. "Get rest, and we'll talk in the morning."

I took the children upstairs. The bedchamber was a suite with a nursery and beds for all. The servants undressed Henry, whilst I stood helpless, looking on.

The attendants made him comfortable and attempted to give him water then prepared to leave.

I spoke up. "Is there a suitable woman who could act as nursemaid to the royal children whilst we are in residence?"

Their shock at my request was clear enough, but I didn't want to explain that Henry trusted no one at Eads Hall and no servants would be arriving. Was it really possible Maurice, Glenore, Mary, or Maggie could have poisoned Henry for spite? Nae, I didn't believe it. It had been foolish to come without them.

King David's servants left.

I turned to my exhausted children. "Shall we get ready for bed?" They needed almost no help at all to prepare.

Soon, an old woman with kind eyes and in a nightcap, curtsied at the threshold. "I come to help with the bairns."

I thanked her and, once all was settled, closed the door between the nursery and where Henry slept. I quietly approached. He rested peacefully. I dared not disturb him and sat in a chair by the window.

Rain fell, drumming steadily upon the slate roof of the manor. I closed the shutters and moved the chair beside the bed to be near Henry. He looked as ill as he had after our wedding celebration when I feared him on the verge of death.

Where was Giffard to find help? Where was the healing woman who provided healing herbs after the grappling hook accident? Or Father Malachy to bring the power of God to restore Henry's health? The chrism lay still upon my nightstand at home.

I was powerless and alone. So alone.

The door adjoining our chamber to the nursery opened, and Adaline whispered, "Mama, is Father alright?"

I knelt in front of her, putting a hand on her soft cheek and wiping away her worried expression. "Your father is sleeping. Pray for him and remember, whatever happens, it's God's will."

I peered into the nursery and was a little surprised to see the only one asleep was the nursemaid in the corner.

The children had discovered a toy chest and each had found a treasure to play with.

The old woman at last awoke and whispered her apologies.

I raised my hand. "Let them have their amusement. They need not sleep quite yet."

Malcolm approached his brothers and dug through the items, pulling out a small knight, exquisite in its detail. David leapt toward him wanting to see it. His older brother handed it to him graciously. "Mayhap I could find another." Then he dug into the chest, enjoying his search.

I closed the door and returned to my chair, listening to the children laughing and playing behind me. Tears of gratitude came. I let the tears roll freely down my cheeks. God had been with me through all these years. He protected Henry until they could come to earth. My sweet little angels were the proof of His mercy.

Chapter Thirty-Three

Could my faith restore Henry to good health as it had when Malcolm was an infant? The answer came so quickly and powerfully that I knew it to be true. Henry was dying. Did I have enough faith to *let* him die this time?

This time.

The words of Malachy's prayer echoed through my mind. I dried my face and watched Henry's chest rise and fall in shallow breaths.

Peace filled my soul. The peace that only God can give.

Above Henry's bedstead hung a tapestry portraying a bouquet of flowers. In the corner, an intricate wooden cupboard reflected the same motif. It suddenly occurred to me—this was Henry's mother's bedchamber—Maud's room. That's why it was connected to the nursery.

I would not follow her or Queen Margaret—two devout and saintly women—loved by the people. I would not be queen as Margaret and Maud had been. Could I still help the poor and offer God's gospel to the people of Scotland? The Lord's hand had been in the lives of *those* women, I was sure. He guided those who were born to take the throne as He did their mothers. I grasped Margaret's silver crucifix hanging from my belt.

If this chamber was Maud's, was it the chamber in which Henry was born? How appropriate, then, that he would come here to die.

Nae, I mustn't think this way. He must get well. I was not ready to let him go.

I needed to wake him, get him to interact, so he wouldn't leave me just yet. I touched his hand. "Henry."

He opened his eyes a little.

"Did you hear the news?" I tried to sound cheerful. "Empress Matilda's son, Henry Plantagenet, is to marry King Louis of France's daughter, Eleanor."

"Wait." Henry sounded groggy. "Isn't she already married?"

I nodded, enjoying the feeling of normalcy in the conversation. "King Louis is annulling her first marriage in the hopes that they'll finally rule England together and the kingdom will be at peace."

"Annul their marriage?" He fell silent, and I listened to his labored breathing. I thought he'd fallen asleep, but he surprised me and said. "I remember the day we wed. You so young, innocent—so beautiful. You still are." Speaking sent him into a cough.

I grasped his hand. "I believe I got the best part of the king's bargain, *mon amour*."

His eyes closed. "I made you a promise those many years ago that I would be faithful to you, and I want you to know I have kept my word." A tear slid down his temple.

I wiped it away.

"You've been the best, the dearest wife, and I love you."

I fell to my knees beside the bed and put my hand on his chest. "I love you too, Henry."

"I beg of you, come . . ." He stopped to breathe. "Lie next to me."

I couldn't fight the tears any longer. He opened his arms, and I nestled into him like I had through the years. Once settled, I didn't move again, wanting to keep this moment forever.

We both fell asleep—tears in our eyes—to the voices and laughter of our children playing nearby.

The pain in Henry's stomach didn't improve. He managed to get out of bed each day, which gave me hope. He walked slowly and used a cane, but I heard him moan often.

One day, I found him in the kitchen speaking to the cook. "I beg your consideration to cook only mild foods."

"Of course." The cook's features softened into pity. "I'll make every dish as bland as you ask."

"And could you have my meals sent to my bedchamber. I'll no longer come to the dining hall."

The cook pursed his lips and nodded.

We took the stairs one at a time to return to our bedchamber. About every third step, Henry stopped to rest.

I waited as he winced in pain and gave him an encouraging smile. "Don't overdo." I mopped his sweating brow and helped him into bed. "You tossed restlessly throughout last night."

He let out a long breath. "The pain is becoming too severe."

"Here." I lifted a wooden cup of tea from the table. "Drink this. It gave you relief yesterday."

"Relief from pain—aye—but it made me sick to my stomach. Nae, naught will help. The physicians cannot even help. Their concoctions are worthless."

I set the cup on the table and knelt beside the bed. "If you can sleep for a few days, mayhap you'd make a turn for the better?"

Henry's dry hand cupped my face. "Forgive me for not having enough faith to live." His voice sounded weak. "The pain is almost . . . unbearable. I'm most grieved to leave you with child—to leave you and the children alone without me to watch over you. My father will help you."

"Henry, hold on a little longer. I cannot bear to let you go."

"I cannot." He groaned and paused as if letting pain pass. "I will love you for all eternity."

"I will love you forever too."

His brown eyes looked at me with such love. "I've never understood 'til death do you part.'" He grimaced and swallowed. "My love will not end with death. I'll love you . . . for all eternity, Ada. We will never say good-bye."

My heavy heart thudded. My soul cried out in a pain I didn't know how to ease.

The next morning, Henry didn't awaken fully. His moans had stopped, and his breathing remained labored. He grimaced from time to time.

King David came quietly into the room. "I've asked that perpetual masses be said."

The tightness in my throat kept me from responding.

"I've brought something I hope will help Henry revive." He held out a narrow gold chest of magnificent workmanship about as long as his arm from the elbow to the tip of his fingers. He opened the lid to display wooden fragments of some kind.

For such an ornate box, the contents inside were simple and unadorned.

"It belonged to my mother, originating from the Holy Land. She believed it was pieces of our Lord's Cross."

Goosebumps rose on my arms. I instantly thought of the chrism from Father Malachy and how it had healed Henry. But I was too afraid to hope. "*Merci*. It may give him peace."

The king attached the cross fragments to the bedstead. "It was kept in the Holyrood Abbey which I built in Edinburgh when Henry was a lad, but I had it brought here on Henry's behalf." He gazed upon it again and made the sign of the cross. "Pray, for only God can save our Henry now."

I crossed myself and said a silent prayer, feeling sheltered in God's love with the holyrood relic hanging above Henry's head. But I knew God's answer *this time*. I prayed that King David might also find the peace that was given to me.

Before the next dawn, Henry's breathing became more distressed. Several were called to the room—a priest I didn't know who didn't speak peace as Chaplain Robert often did, a physician who had never met Henry, and a knight who stood guard at the foot of the bed. If only it were St Martin, who had spent the last thirteen years in loyal service. It was all so wrong.

Through the dark hours of the night, we all kept vigil. At last, as the sun peeked over the horizon, and Henry's father stepped forward to give final words to his child. He knelt beside him and wept. "My son, I have been so proud of you and had high hopes for when you would become a just and honored king. But alas, it will never be. Go now into God's hands."

His words were balm to my already-wrenched heart as I knelt beside him, and we wept together. In spite of my sorrow, an overwhelming peace came over me. I stood and looked around, feeling a presence of unseen others—angels, I presumed. I turned to see if King David had felt their presence.

He kept his head down and continued weeping.

In a way I didn't understand, the presence of a woman appeared at the bedside. I knew in my soul it was Henry's mother. She reached toward him—the son she left in his youth—and took his hand. Then as silently as the vision came, it left, and Henry's chest stilled.

I cried, "Henry, *mon amour!*"

David put his hand over Henry's heart for several moments. He slowly stood and took me in his arms.

The physician examined Henry's body and then faced us. "Let it be known and recorded that on the Twelfth day of June, in the year of our Lord 1152, Prince Henry of Scotland, the son of King David mac Malcolm, Earl of Huntingdon, Prince of Strathclyde has passed from this world."

The priest made the sign of the cross and bowed his head reverently. "Thirty-seven years of age. He lived a life worthy of an eternal reward."

Henry's face was as calm and beautiful in death as it had been in life.

I pray dear Lord, that You will take care of Henry and give me strength for what I must endure for the rest of my life. Give King David the comfort he deserves.

My thoughts went to my sleeping children, now fatherless. Tears fell, not only for Henry, but for our children, and their future without their father. I smoothed my hand over my unborn child and wondered what lay ahead. A widow at not yet thirty years of age, I had to be strong and go forward with only *a memory* of my sweet Henry.

King David said, "I pray this illness that took my son touches no one else in your household."

"Henry didn't think it was an illness," I said, knowing he had told his father as much. "He thought it poison."

King David shook his head. "That would be hard to believe. According to the physicians, poison usually cuts a soul down in his prime. It doesn't eke the life out of a person over many months. Nae, I believe it was an illness."

"Aye," I said, not wanting to argue. The king could be right.

If my husband was killed for the throne, the person responsible would have killed others—the king for one, who showed no signs of poison or illness. Mayhap Henry had died of natural causes.

But if not, I had to be vigilant or my entire family could be at risk. That meant I needed to know whom to trust.

Chapter Thirty-Four

King David sent a missive that Henry's funeral would be held in a sennight. Based on the advice of his physicians, he felt more certain his son's death was from illness.

The more I thought on it, the less certain I became that he'd been poisoned. But I still wondered who I could confide in and trust. I was so exhausted I could hardly stand.

I found comfort in the movements of the child in my womb and remembered a phrase from one of Chaplain Robert's devotions: *One life enters, another life leaves. That is the way of this earth.*

I sent for him.

He entered the room with his head bowed and sat across from me, a look of empathy and understanding on his gentle brow. "Dear Lady Ada, how may I be of service to you at this time of loss and sorrow?"

I would not mince words. "Chaplain Robert, Henry thought somebody was poisoning him but had no idea whom."

He nodded deeply. "Thus, you took flight, but too late."

"And now I know not whom to trust. Glenore's father was killed in a war begun by Henry's father. St Martin fought against my husband in a battle over a dozen years ago, but since then has been his closest associate and guard. We made our household with enemies whom we thought became friends." Finding a listening ear, my concerns poured from me. "His steward and cousin, Kelton, has often been unkind to me, and then there was an earl, Ranulf, who thought Henry acquired his land unfairly. With whom can I be certain my children and I will be safe?"

Chaplain Robert closed his eyes as if arranging his thoughts. When he opened them, he looked at me with a calm that quieted my flustered mind. "Nae. Not a one of your servants has confessed, which is good, for if they had I could not share it. But what I can tell you is what I have observed at the church and at Eads Hall."

"Do tell." I sat forward, hoping it would be enough.

"Glenore has taken to lighting candles since the day you left. She comes to the church at dawn and says a prayer for each one of the children by name with each flame. Then she lights ten more for Prince Henry. At least until she heard the news." He paused. "For you, sweet lady, she lights more than that."

Tears glistened at the corners of my eyes. "How many more?"

"As many as there are. She not only just prays for you, she asks everyone she meets to pray as well. At first, it was just to heal the prince, but then it was to strengthen you and help the children sleep at night, and for the wee ones not to be scared without their Glenore."

I envisioned the poor girl, abandoned and alone. We had grown close these many years. Surely, she was true to us. "Oh, how I wish we had not left her and the others."

Chaplain Robert seemed to grow uncomfortable.

"What is it, Father?"

He bowed his head. "Your kitchen maid is quite persuasive and asked to accompany me here. She has agreed to wait outside the gates until someone fetches her. I hope I did the right thing. Do you suspect her of evil doing?"

"Nae! Let us have her called." I rose to my feet and summoned a servant to bring Glenore to the manor then returned to the cleric for there was more I had to know. "Has anyone else's behavior been unusual?"

"Aye." He didn't blink. "St Martin."

"In what way?"

"He guarded the manor, not allowing anything to be touched or moved of your personal property. As far as I'm aware, the chambers have not been entered since you left them."

"Why would he do such a thing?"

"He guessed as we all did that you suspected treachery when you departed," Chaplain Robert said. "He felt sealing the rooms would allow one to look for the enemy, if there is one to be found."

"And if he is the enemy?"

Chaplain Robert shook his head. "He thought on such. Two guards stand watch even against him. The rooms are secure for when you want to search them, if that is your desire."

I bit my lip. "Tell me, is this for a show or should I trust him?"

"If it is for show, then he has fooled his wife for she sat at the chapel with Glenore, crying over your plight. How you are loved." Chaplain Robert swallowed; his Adam's apple bobbed. "Certainly, your family has enemies, but I believe St Martin is loyal."

I could see truth in his eyes. "Does he wait outside the gates with Glenore?"

Chaplain Robert lifted his hands. "Only if you wish to call for him."

The comfort of their support lifted my weary soul. *"Merci,* Father."

He patted my hand. "I'm here for your spiritual needs—for anything you or your children need."

In the hall, I heard a commotion and hurried to see what it was. The children must have seen Glenore enter and escaped their elderly nanny to rush down the stairs and into the young maid's arms. She knelt, surrounded by my children so completely, I could see only her cap.

Malcolm stood straight and tall as he told Glenore, "We had to say farewell to Father. He has gone to heaven."

William tugged on her sleeve. "Will he become a ghostie now?"

"Nae." Her voice was sincere. "Your father is now an angel and he's watchin' over all of ye. 'Member that and be brave."

I approached. "I promise, I will try to be brave as well." I thought to convey my contrition over leaving her but saw naught but love for my family in her face.

She smiled at me and then turned to the children. "Now, embrace your mama quickly. I want to see this fancy new castle. Where are your rooms?"

"Upstairs," said David. "And there is a huge toy chest filled with treasures."

"And toys," added little Margaret.

They hurried off as the front door opened again. St Martin entered and bowed at my feet. "Lady Ada, know that I pledge my life to you and your family's safety."

"Rise," I bid him. Upon seeing the curious expressions of nearby servants, I led him to the solar where Chaplain Robert still waited.

I asked, "Do you believe my husband was poisoned?"

St Martin was not quick to answer. "It's a possibility that should be considered, until we know you are all safe."

My chest grew tight. "Do I need to worry for my children during the funeral tomorrow? How can we protect them?" My hand fell over my midsection.

St Martin placed his palms on the table. "If someone intends to do your family harm, they would be fools to do aught during the funeral when the eyes of the kingdom are looking at you and your children. Nae, it's far more likely that you will notice a detail out of place."

"I have not seen anything questionable in the past, but I'll be alert."

Chaplain Robert stood. "*If* he was poisoned. Remember, Prince Henry could have fallen ill. It may have been God's will and simply his time."

His time. This time. Nae, I would find the one responsible. I would make this right.

Chapter Thirty-Five

In the solar, I gazed upon a tapestry of a soldier being knighted. The castle at Peebles was ancient and had many interesting artifacts.

The king walked up behind me. "That's a representation of my father, Malcolm. He began training at age five and was knighted at the age of sixteen, young by any standard."

Not much younger than little David. Would that I could keep my children from violence. And poison was as strong a violence as the sword. I took a deep breath to lift the heaviness from my heart. "I haven't buried my husband yet." I looked at him. "But I've heard talk. Are you already planning to take my children from me?"

King David met my gaze. "Not yet, but I don't expect my time to be long on this land—at least not as a man who can walk upright without a cane. Your sons must be ready to take the throne."

"I've lost my life's love. I'm a widow." I lowered my head. "Let me grieve."

"You are more than that." King David's tone grew intense. "You're both Count and Countess of Northumbria as promised on your wedding day. You must rule despite the pain in your heart, and that means you must make hard decisions."

I'd nearly forgotten that winter ride days before my oldest son was born when I had signed the documents for my dowager rights. "Aye, I hold Haddington, as well Crail." Odd that the king had made provisions for the death of his only son so close to my marriage. Had he known this day would come? Tears rolled from my eyes. "Is there not time to simply grieve?"

"I grieve for you and for me. I grieve for your children, one of whom will never know their father. But I must take care of all of you. I'm old, and there may be no repose for me."

I lifted my head. "What do you mean?"

He placed his hand over his heart. "When my beloved Maud died, I wondered if I would grieve forever. But I learned we just keep breathing until we feel alive again. My heart was broken, yet I found hope through my son, Henry. Now my hope is gone."

This man knew my pain and more of his own.

"Malcolm is but ten and a sober child," I said. "Someday he will make a fine king with your help. Let him be your hope."

King David walked to the window. "I pray I can live at least ten more years to train him. Malcolm and I should travel the kingdom after the funeral to assure the country of their future. It would also let me get to know the boy better." He paused. "And Donnchad has already agreed to take William and David to finish their training as knights once you are ready to allow it."

"I pray you will live far more than ten years. For my children's sakes, as well as yours."

King David took a step toward me. "Ada, I need you to understand how serious this is. With Henry gone, when I die, you and your children will become targets. There are those who have a hunger for power, waiting in the shadows, seeking opportunities to eliminate you and your family, hoping to assume your royal positions. You cannot be too careful. Do not be caught alone without your guards."

"Aye, I will be careful."

"As soon as I die—"

"You must stop saying that!"

"*You* must listen." He took hold of my shoulders and looked at me with brown eyes so much like Henry's. "As soon as I'm gone, take your family to Crail. You must go in secret. You'll be safer there. My servants and guards at Crail know to expect your arrival after my death." His grip tightened. "My greatest desires for you and my grandchildren are to be safe and to protect the throne of Scotland."

I studied David's earnest eyes. Did I want to live in Crail? "I'll take my family," I committed. "But Father David, I will pray for your health."

He relaxed his grip and sighed with relief. "Your promise and prayers are much appreciated."

"How long should we stay in Crail?"

"Until Malcolm is settled into his position as king. He will send for you when he's ready. Donnchad will advise him."

"Consider it done," I stated with dignity. "You have my solemn word."

At that moment, I knew my beautiful sons' childhoods were over. The demands of nobility were about to descend upon all of us.

Henry was to be buried at Kelso Abbey in Roxburgh—a new sanctuary built by his father. As I arrived at the church near the confluence of the Tweed and Teviot waters, I was not expecting the reception I received. King David told me Fenella insisted on filling the church with white tulips. But she also included white wood anemone trimmed with ferns and lace bows.

When she didn't approach me, I refused to judge her. Giffard sat by her side and although her eyes were dry, they were bloodshot. The loss of Prince Henry, her dearest friend, had shaken her.

Kelton was one of the first to seek me out before the service.

With tears in his eyes he embraced me. "Dear Sister—for that is how I've come to think of you—I share your grief over this momentous loss."

His estate was almost a sennights journey, and I couldn't fathom how he could arrive so quickly. "How is it you are here?"

He gave me a half smile. "I was visiting in Edinburgh when word came. It was a blessing to be so close."

I appreciated his support. When we first met, I would not have thought him loyal to Henry. But since his marriage to my cousin and becoming an earl in his own right, Kelton had grown to become more compassionate.

Many of the villagers from Whitfield had come despite their poverty.

When we all sat, Chaplain Robert began the service. As the choir sang a psalm, the door opened. Lord Madduch entered and sat on the other side of the full nave. How often had he asked me to consider him if my husband died? Could he have killed Henry?

My gaze lit on his green cloak. I'd seen that garment before. Aye, it finally registered. After I had Malcolm, Jasmine had that same green cloak. Was there a connection between the two? Could he have bought poison from her? I sighed. My tired mind was inventing plots that made no sense. I shook my head and listened more intently to the solemn tones of the music.

After the service, we all stood to retire to the abbey house.

St Martin placed a hand on my shoulder. "What is it?" He invited me to step to a corner.

"I'm weary, that is all. I'm having fancies of Lord Madduch's cape," I whispered. "It's identical to a woman who cursed my son." My throat grew tight.

"His mantle is common among Highlanders." St Martin looked at me with deep concern, but kept his tone even. "You will see four in this room alone."

He was right. A few of the wealthier landowners had similar cloaks. "He's also said multiple times that he had dreamed of us being married after Henry's death."

"I'll look into it. For now, focus on your family and trust me. I'll find what can be found. That is my promise." St Martin left.

I felt comforted and then foolish. The cloak was common. Jasmine's father could have been a highlander. It was easier to blame outside forces than to accept my husband died of a disease.

The child in my womb kicked as if to remind me she was still there and coming soon. How could I be ready for her? How could my heart be ready to rejoice in a new life when it was so filled with sorrow? Nae, I must leave this witch hunt and focus on my children. Every minute I could spend with Malcolm before he left with King David was precious.

I moved further into the room to be with my family. A hollow numbness lived where my heart should be. I leaned on Malcolm for support, and he clung to me, turning his head into my veil so others wouldn't see him cry.

Henry's final resting place was below the alter in an underground vault that suddenly became more sacred by holding his body there. I stood beside his grave—empty, numb—my children huddled at my side. I didn't want to leave him and return to Eads Hall. I wished to lie down on his grave and die. But I had to keep living for the children.

Chapter Thirty-Six

Alexander St Martin escorted us to Whitfield. The journey seemed an eternity. Our rooms were opened, and I was surprised to see Abbot Malachy's chrism on the bedside table, untouched. I attached it to the bedstead as King David did with the holyrood relic of Christ's cross. That night, I prayed beneath it that I might feel peace and focus on what was most important. For now, that was this new child who could arrive any day.

Chaplain Robert attended to us, leading us in prayers morning and night. I came to depend on his visits giving me encouragement and bringing God's comfort into my home.

The world around me continued to go on. The sun should stop shining. The trees should weep silent tears for my losses. But naught changed. Naught but my pregnant belly, which grew larger, making my daily tasks more arduous.

Were it not for my children, I would have lived in continuous sorrow. But they played again. They ran, they giggled, and their questions about their father grew fewer. My daily routine with them was my very meaning. In spite of my efforts to be strong for them, they sometimes detected hints of the wound in my heart and came to me, one by one. We embraced. We cried. The pain healed for a moment or a day.

We were all together for a short time longer. King David was expected to take Malcolm with him soon. So strange how suddenly a young boy, not yet eleven, lost his father and his childhood.

People came by with gifts of condolence, entire families—families with fathers—reminding me of what I once had. They wanted to talk to me, take my hand, and bow to me. "Dear Countess Ada, we are so sorry for your loss."

I saw the sorrow in their hearts, and strived to smile. I took their hands and reassured them as best I could. They thanked me and left comforted.

I felt like property owned by the dynasty to be used as a symbol of sadness over Henry's death. The young and handsome prince. The future hope of Scotland. Not only was he lost to me, he was lost to all of Scotland.

On day, Maggie asked, "*Domina*, what should we do with the princes' clothes? Many of them are so ornate, so much like a king in the making."

I touched the clothes she'd laid on our bed. Each cloak, each hat, each tunic held a memory. William had fallen our last time at Warkworth. Henry had rescued the boy, picking him up. His scrapped knee left a spot of blood on Henry's cloak somehow missed by the washers. I touched it, remembering the way he held William close and assured him all would be well.

"Oh Henry!" I buried my face in the cloak. "You taught our sons to be great men—men who have not only courage but also compassion for others."

Maggie laid her hand on my back until I was done crying.

I took a deep breath. "Let's save the fine clothes for our sons—yours and mine—and some for Chadwick. You choose." I turned from her. "I must rest. This baby is so active." I took the cloak with me into the solar and curled up with it, smelling my husband.

Chaplain Robert left after leading our evening devotional.

I often found solace in prayer, but once I rose, gloom set in again.

I went to my room and sat at the dressing table, waiting for Maggie.

When she came, she brought a smile that somehow found a home in my heart. "*Merci*, Maggie.

"For what?" She smiled again.

"For that lovely smile of yours. It's good to know some things never change."

She placed her hands on my shoulders. "Let me help you, *domina*."

As she brushed my hair, I picked up the looking glass and peered at my reflection, too tired, too discouraged to do aught more. My childhood maid, Clare, used to scold me not to be vain. But I was not admiring my beauty—not when I appeared so worn and aged.

Maggie stroked my auburn hair—the hair Henry loved so much, but never again would entwine in his fingers.

"A pence for your thoughts." She waited for my reply.

I put down the looking glass. I couldn't keep my throat from tightening as I spoke that which had been turning in my head for days. "Here I am, twenty-nine years old and expecting my sixth child." My hand instinctively caressed my large belly. "My husband was buried a sennight ago." I looked at Maggie. "How can I go on without him?"

"You must—and you will," she said kindly. She set the brush on the dressing table. "Let me help you into bed."

I pushed myself up to standing. "I feel so weak."

"In a few days, you'll feel better. You've been through a lot." She put her arm around my shoulders. "I remember hardly being able to stand before I had the twins."

I recalled the day my mother rescued Maggie and made her part of our family. "Now Turstin and Alric have grown into fine young men. They valiantly escorted us home a few days ago, so handsome and alert on horseback."

"Aye." Motherly pride filled her face as she helped me into bed.

I relaxed onto the feather mattress. "You're so good to me, Maggie." I took her hand. "I don't know what I'd do without you."

She returned my squeeze then straightened my blankets. "Tomorrow the sun will rise and bring renewed hope." She blew out the candle. "Will you be all right if I leave? I can stay through the night if you wish." Maggie's offer sounded like something my mother would say.

"Nae, I'll be fine."

Alone in the dark, I was unable to resist reaching to the empty side of the bed. My heart ached and tears flowed—tears I thought had been dried up but now seemed to come from a never-ending source. How could I live never again feeling Henry's strong arms around me?

Retrieving the crucifix from the bedstead, I slipped from the bed onto my knees. "Mary, Mother of our Lord." I pronounced the words carefully, trying to summon heaven's aid. "I thank

Thee for the time I had with Henry, and for the good man he was. I could not have endured what my mother did in her first marriage. Strengthen me with a belief that I shall be with my Henry again." I prayed my energy would return, for I must arise in the morning and be a mother to my children. Their hearts hurt too. I would teach them the best I could that their father had gone to rest in God's heaven. And that someday, we would be with him again.

After a restless night, I entered the girls' nursery.

Little Margaret still slept soundly, but seven-year-old Adaline had awakened.

"Mama, I miss Father."

"As do I, my sweet." I sat beside her on the bed, placing my hand to her cheek, willing my tears not to start. I pushed a lock of wavy red hair behind her ear. As Malcolm would fill his duties, ours were to move forward with good cheer as the first family of Scotland and not wallow in our sorrow.

I picked up Adaline's poppet from the pillow and studied the painted face, turning it for her to see. "You have Lady Smiles. She has been a loyal friend." I did my best to muster a smile as encouraging as that of the wooden poppet—a pretense to mask my aching heart.

Adaline prolonged her scowl. She missed her father, and a smiling poppet was not going to change that.

I tickled her face and neck, hoping to break her frown.

It didn't work.

I teased, "A big, ugly spider is crawling on your forehead."

There came a brief giggle, followed by tears. This morn, there was no escaping the reality that Father was not coming home. She sat on what little lap I had left, and we cried together.

Minutes later, Mary entered. "Come break your fast, little ones—oatmeal, cream, berries, and sweet bread—all your favorites. But you must be dressed before you eat."

The others awakened, slid from their beds, and met the maid at the cupboard.

Adaline, apparently recovered and joined in dressing for the day.

Being weak of body and heavy with child, I could do naught but watch. The scene confirmed how much my children blessed my life.

Chapter Thirty-Seven

King David came to Eads Hall a sennight after we'd arrived home. I spent much time taking counsel from him, but what he'd really come for was Malcolm.

On the night before they departed, he asked for a private counsel.

He paced the floor of the solar. "I want you and the children to make the palace in Haddington your permanent residence so as to be nearer to me in Edinburgh. I would be more comfortable knowing you were surrounded by the fortresses of Hailes, Dirleton, and Yester. Donnchad shall see you're well settled."

Unprepared for this request, I didn't answer promptly. Bleak as Eads Hall had initially seemed in comparison to my childhood home of Reigate, it now held many happy memories as did Warkworth. It would be hard to leave the places Henry and I had lived together. And what of the children? Could they handle another change?

Yet King David's request had merit. Henry had warned that our marriage would place us in constant threat of danger from other aspirants to the throne. And one of Henry's dying wishes was that I work closely with his father. Haddington was much closer to the king than Eads Hall. Also, as the children's grandfather, King David would be a positive influence in raising them.

"You are as a father to me and my children. Although a move will have its challenges, we love your palace in Haddington and I envision many benefits to living there. When my child is born, after my confinement, we shall honor your request and come." As if endorsing my decision, my unborn child kicked.

He nodded. "I applaud your decision and will send an armed escort when you're ready. But," he paused, "it's no longer my palace, but yours."

"*Merci*, my lord—Father."

"I shall be honored to be so addressed by you, my dear. It's almost as gratifying as hearing the children call me grandfather."

"May I express my concerns regarding Malcolm?"

"Aye."

"I worry for him being so young and of a somewhat fragile nature. Ten years of age and away from home."

King David eased into a chair, the leather creaking softly. "I understand your concerns, but you have my word we will be heavily guarded as we travel. We need to assure the kingdom of their safe future. I have much to teach the boy. Were circumstances different, I would leave Malcolm with you, but I'm aging and feel we can waste no time with his training."

"Malcolm was not much interested in Donnchad's training. He's more thoughtful and somber. He studies the *behavior* of the knights—their valiance and service. I fear my son is too gentle for the demands of being a king."

-293-

David stood and took my hand. "Dear Ada, there is no way out for him. He was born the eldest, making him destined to become king. He'll grow out of his timidity. Mormaer Donnchad will see to it. We'll make a man of Malcolm yet. There are many aspects to being king, and his observance of others will be as helpful to him as learning to be a warrior. He'll be a good king."

"May your assessment be correct. I'm weary of worrying over the matter."

"To ease your mind in another area, I've made peace with Ranulf. Hopefully, he'll give us no more trouble." He chuckled. "The man was present when I knighted young Henry Plantagenet. Ranulf offered to make a marriage alliance for his son with one of your daughters with the promise to drop his claim on Carlisle."

I almost choked. "Father David! I hope you said nae."

"Aye, I refused him. Ranulf is an angry man who lets politics run his life. Your daughters, when they are of age, can do much better."

He led me to a chair, and left to pour himself a glass of ale. "All is ready for my departure. I have already declared Malcolm Prince of Strathclyde and Cumbria and my successor as king—with Donnchad as his mentor-regent if I die when Malcolm's still a minor. William will take his father's place as Earl of Northumbria, and little David is now titular Earl of Huntingdon. Gifford and St Martin will be their mentors." He drained his goblet and set it on the table. "I'll be able to rest in peace."

"Do not speak of dying. It's too tender a subject."

"I apologize, but we must face facts. I'm getting old and my heart has taken a blow." He cleared his throat and sat again, facing me. "I look forward to seeing Henry again, and my wife, when I pass over to the land of the dead." He lowered his voice. "I pray God has forgiven the foibles of my youth and will grant me that blessing."

"Of course, He will grant it. You are the king of Scots and have done much good."

"And also much vice." He shook his head. "Royals are not exempt from the commandments. Remember that, Ada. I carry so much guilt from looking the other way as my men carried out overly cruel acts in battle, thinking victory was all that mattered. Unfortunately, not always did I put first the welfare of mankind as the scriptures teach."

"But why confess this to me?"

He looked at me with tired eyes. "Because I feel I'm waxing old." He sighed long. "With Henry's death, my thoughts have turned more heavenward. I believe we shall have a great gathering with our loved ones in heaven. Do you believe that too?"

I wanted to believe. "I must hold to that hope or life's tests become unbearable." I remembered the vision of Henry's mother at his death bed. I dared not tell David, for he might want to leave this world this very night.

David leaned into his chair and placed hands behind his head in contemplation. After a few moments he said, "My saintly mother raised me to believe in God. She maintained her faith until the day she died. She never wavered." He looked into my eyes. "Mother knew the day and hour my father and brother had been killed in battle, even though they fought far away at Alnwick. She could sense their spirits with her — perhaps because she was near death herself at the time."

"She was extraordinary. I wish I'd known her."

He nodded. "Perhaps at times you will feel Henry with you. I hope so. I don't know anywhere else, even heaven itself, where Henry would want to be but with you and the children. I never thought Henry's life would end this way. I was sure my mother's holyrood relic would heal him. But, for reasons known only to God, He has called him Home."

For reasons known only to God? God's wisdom must be greater than mine, for I could think of no reason Henry should leave me, his family, and his country.

David knelt right there and bowed his head, praying for comfort and for the safety of my family.

Touched at his humble appeal, I knelt too, as David spoke to God as if He was an old friend.

After the prayer, David sat in a chair and watched the flames of the fire.

I didn't disturb him, knowing his pain, for it was also mine.

At length he spoke. "As for your estates, I've asked Hugh Giffard to take the responsibilities of your dower burghs in Haddington and Crail whilst they are not your residences. You need not worry for funds. You're a wealthy woman, and your holdings are in good hands for the protection of you and the children."

"Giffard and Fenella are dear friends. Your assigning those duties to Giffard gives me peace of mind."

"The revenue from those lands will allow you to live as you have been."

Tears welled and I swallowed them down. "I'd have much preferred to have Henry with me and live a simple peasant's life than to . . ." I lowered my head in attempt to hide my trembling lip. Why was I saying such things to the king?

"I will do, and have done, all in my power to care for you all."

With Henry gone, I could feel that the powerful patriarchal mantle of our family now rested even more on King David—he would be our guiding beacon.

The next morning, the children and I gathered outside around the king and Malcolm, wishing them a heartfelt farewell.

Malcolm still had moments of grieving, and I worried he would not be able to express those traveling with his grandfather. It pained me greatly that I would not be able to take my eldest son into my arms and comfort him, that he had to suffer his losses alone as he dutifully was trained for his role as Scotland's next king. Once again, the demands of nobility loomed ominously in our lives and there was naught I could do to change it.

"Fare thee well, my son." I embraced him. "We will see each other again soon."

He looked at me through green eyes, that were my own. "All will be well, Mother," he said, sounding brave.

I admired his intentions to comfort me.

Although King David had somewhat eased my mind with his endorsement of Mormaer Donnchad as mentor and protector to Malcolm, I still worried for him leaving at such a young age. He'd never been away from us before.

From this day on, I would pray ever more earnestly for King David's good health. Surely God would not take him from us so soon after taking Henry.

Chapter Thirty-Eight

After Malcolm left, the children settled in play.

I dozed off briefly but awakened with a jolt of pain that quickly went away. I gazed out the window at the dark, rainy autumn day and prayed that blessed sleep would come. Closing my eyes again, I smoothed my hand over my round stomach.

Be strong, continue on—for me and for the children—and for Scotland. Thoughts came as if Henry had spoken.

My abdomen tightened again. I took in a deep breath, bracing for the pain. I knew what was coming. I'd done this many times before. But this time, Henry would not be there waiting to see his child.

"Maggie! It's time!" Where was my trustworthy friend?

I had become skilled at the business of birthing, for little Matilda was born fairly quickly with no unexpected problems. A shame I would not use that skill again.

From the first moment Matilda was put in my arms, she seemed at peace. A balm to my heart and Henry's final gift to me. She looked in my eyes, as if to tell me everything was all right and as it should be.

I missed Malcolm and wished he could see his new sister.

Our new home in Haddington would be ready by Christmastide. Only a few hours ride to Edinburgh, the palace was a more secure location at a time when the fate of Northumbria was unknown. We planned to take only our personal belongings and the most sentimentally precious gifts bestowed on us.

Two days before our departure, I was awakened by Matilda coughing. Only two months old, I had taken to allowing her to sleep with me. We sent word to King David to postpone our journey.

A sennight later, Matilda had fever and a hard time keeping food down.

Maggie reached for her. "I'll sit with her tonight whilst you rest."

I stepped away. "But you stayed up with her last night."

"And still you didn't rest. I fear you're wearing yourself to death. What will six children do without their mother?"

I surrendered Matilda and sat on the bed. "I've asked Chaplain Robert to baptize her tomorrow. I know King David wished the rite done in Edinburgh, but her salvation is at stake." I anticipated Maggie would scold me for speaking as if Matilda would die, but she said naught.

With a somber face, she took the child from the room. My dear friend feared, as did I, that my child would not live much longer.

I ran my hand over the chrism on my bedstead. Last rites. Permission to die. I'd assure that she'd die in Christ. The next day, I rubbed the healing oils from the chrism on her head.

It was on the eve of Christ's Mass when my precious baby girl passed away just minutes before sunset. Another part of Henry gone.

Glenore hurried off to retrieve supplies to wrap the body.

I stood at the chamber window, tears blurring my vision of the falling snow. Despite the blazing fire in the hearth, I was cold.

I glanced at the stiff body of my wee babe with her tuffs of dark brown hair and lids closed over dark eyes. She'd been like her father in both appearance and virtuous countenance. God had taken another whom I loved. There had been too many deaths too close together.

We would remove to Haddington as soon as . . . as soon as what? As soon as Henry and Matilda returned to me? That could never happen. Although I wanted to be near King David, I dreaded leaving the memories of Eads Hall. It held a part of my Henry and now Matilda.

Glenore returned and washed and wrapped the tiny body before the children came to say goodbye. Their teary, confused faces tore at my already broken heart. St Martin and Sybil came to pay their respects. We said prayers and kept candles lit around the cradle. Then it was time.

A guard carried in a new wooden casket and set it on the floor. I took the bundled child in my arms and placed her gently in the cushioned box, kneeling beside it. "You gave me comfort after your father died."

Love flowed with my words and I touched Matilda's dark-brown brow. "You gave me reason to live, to keep going. Your short life brought me joy and hope when I was at my weakest."

Suddenly my dream came to my mind.

I caught my breath at the realization. This was what it meant. Tingles ran along my arms. This was the child who hugged her father around the neck and told me she didn't want me to be sad because she would join her father so he would not be lonely.

Maggie and Sybil lifted me to my feet. Though surrounded by friends, I was alone in my grief. Matilda had gone to be with Henry so he would not be lonely, but what about me? It was as though a part of my heart had torn and would never heal.

St Martin carried the casket from the room.

My yearnings for Matilda signaled my milk to come in. It seeped through my surcoat. I covered myself in a mantle and stepped outside.

The snow had stopped falling, and the skies cleared to a crisp blue. We walked behind the tiny casket to the church, my children beside me, their feet kicking up snow. Their heads hung in sorrow—more sorrow than young children should ever know.

When we arrived at the cemetery, Chaplain Robert took my daughters' hands. My sons with St Martin assisting, took the casket to the grave and lowered it on ropes into the shallow tomb.

We all bowed our heads as Chaplain Robert provided a prayer of dedication. He quoted a scripture from Ecclesiastes. "To everything there is a season and a time for every purpose under heaven. A time to be born. A time to die."

I looked at the grave, wondering why Matilda had to die. And then I again remembered the dream. God had been preparing me for this all along. I was not alone.

The gravediggers shoveled the dirt over the tiny box, and the burial was over too soon.

The day after, I slipped from the house quietly without calling for a guard, my aching heart drawing me to the cemetery.

A woman knelt over Matilda's grave, chanting, "May the servants of the Gods escort ye with honor to their own land of light, of beauty, and of joy. Blessed be ye!" Her ragged, brown cloak flapped in the wind.

I paused behind her. "Your words are beautiful, but why are you here?"

Startled, she jumped to her feet. She looked at me with clear-blue eyes, but her skin was dull and flabby. "Tis an ancient Gaelic chant. I'm wishing this child well."

I took the evergreen bow from her hand. "But this is a Christian burial at a Christian church." My lips trembled, remembering when Malcolm was cursed. I would not allow myself to be pulled into that darkness again.

I squinted at her. "My child was baptized in Christ, so has died in Christ and has no need of your ancient chants."

"I'm blessing her. So she's not claimed by hell." She turned and hurried away.

I called after her, "My daughter was pure and innocent . . . my Matilda will never go to hell!"

I fell to my knees and wept. Life here on earth was hell. Matilda and Henry resided in a better place.

"God, dear God, I implore Thee to fill me with Thy love and Thy Spirit. Somehow, fill my empty arms." I wiped my eyes and took a deep breath.

The aroma of the plant the woman had left on the mound caused me to pick up the sprig. Rosemary—the herb that symbolized remembrance.

"My sweet Matilda, I will always remember you." But there was so little to remember. Her life was so short, so fragile.

But Chaplain Robert's words had confirmed it was her time. I saw the dream again—little Matilda staring into my eyes, conveying peace.

Our household resumed preparations to move. A few days before we were to leave, I decided to make one last pass through my bedchamber for aught I may have missed.

Sadness pricked at my heart as I walked through the corridors of my beloved Eads Hall, the never-to-be-forgotten site where each of my children had been conceived in love. I knew not when I'd return—if ever.

In my bedchamber, my eyes lit upon the chrism hanging over the bed where my husband and Matilda had grown so ill. For a time, I had sent the relic to Kelton. According to his wife, he felt it didn't help. Could Kelton have done something to it? My stomach flopped. Mayhap he put poison in the vials that were to be healing oils?

Chapter Thirty-Nine

All three of my sons were in line for the throne before Kelton. He was the illegitimate son of a king—David's deceased brother. Did Kelton really think others would honor his paternity? He couldn't think he could get rid of us all, could he?

I called for St Martin.

He came immediately. "What is it, my lady?"

I pointed to the cross. "I fear . . ." I had to catch my breath. "It may be . . ."

St Martin took his leather riding gloves from his belt and donned them before lifting the chrism and examining it closer. "You think this may have caused Henry's death?"

I nodded. "And mayhap the baby's life, too. There are vials in the base, what if . . ."

He smelled the metal and smoothed his hand across the surface to check for residue. Then he opened the lids of each vial and smelled those. He placed a drop of the oil on his arm and rubbed it in. He shook his head. "I believe it's just oil. But if you have any other concerns, share them. Simply because we have not found the source does not mean Prince Henry's death was without blame."

He bowed and left me alone.

Though the chrism was precious, I now didn't want to bring it with us. I'd give it to Chaplain Robert in hopes it would bring healing to another. If I kept it, I feared it would remind me of great sorrow and no longer bring comfort.

Nothing could bring me comfort.

I asked Glenore and Mary to take the children out so I could face the nursery alone. I glanced over the room where my babies had slept for the past eleven years. Our lives would change forever once we climbed aboard the carts facing north. As I walked around the room touching the furniture and toys they'd grown out of—the bonnet each child wore, a rattle they'd held tight in a little fist, a well-loved blanket—memories that I wanted to treasure.

A servant came to the door. "You're wanted at the entry, m'lady. A peasant awaits to speak with ye."

"Whatever for?" I was mildly annoyed that a peasant would interrupt my work, but then I remembered my mother's and Henry's attitudes of charity. I had done little charity since Henry grew sick. There had been so little time—at least that was my excuse. I stood, determined to do better.

"Tell her I'll be down in a moment."

"Very good, m'lady, but it's a man." She curtsied and left.

I sighed heavy and long and tucked the last of Matilda's gowns into the empty cradle.

In the entry, a ragged man stood before the closed door. He held a young girl in his arms, probably just over a year in age.

"I'm Lady Ada," I greeted him. "What is your name?"

St Martin moved close by with a perplexed look on his face.

"Domhnall, my lady." He bowed slightly, balancing the child in his arms. She was a beautiful girl with dark curly hair and brown eyes who badly needed a wash. "And this bairn be Sophia."

"Well, Domhnall, what can I do for you?" Did he need money or food?

"Tis dis *wee yin*." His strong northern accent caused me a struggle to understand. He turned the girl so I could see her dirty, dimpled face more clearly. "Her ma done claimed it be Prince Henry's bairn."

The food in my stomach almost left. I swayed and stepped away.

Henry had sworn of his faithfulness upon his deathbed. He would not have lied. "My Henry? That cannot be. Return the child and tell the mother she's mistaken."

"Can'na be takin' her. The ma be dead." The man shoved the girl into my arms, promptly turned and opened the door.

"Stop there," St Martin yelled.

The man ran, and St Martin chased after him.

Stunned, I stood speechless.

The child whimpered and looked up at me with soft brown eyes so much like Henry's. Could this child be his?

Nae. I shook my head. Henry would not have lied to me.

What was I to do?

The reality of the situation sank in. This child's future was likely in my hands.

St Martin returned, winded, and knelt before me. "He jumped on a horse and rode away. I sent two guards after him. Don't fear. We'll discover his identity." He stood. "What is your desire? Chaplain Robert could take the child to a monastery, or mayhap Sybil would care for her until you've come to a decision."

In a daze, I stared at the child. She smiled at me. "Sophia is her name." Her coloring was so like Henry's, even like Margaret's.

St Martin came forward. "The little one must be hungry. I'll call a servant to have her fed and you can consider—"

"Nae." The reason I broke from my work was to do charity. How better to serve than to clean and feed this little one. "I'll bathe and dress her myself."

I embraced her as I walked to the kitchen, feeling her warmth against me. My heart swelled at her lovely face, but my mind stayed in confusion.

Who was this child? Henry would not lie to me—especially not on his death bed. I had not prompted him to confess his fidelity. He volunteered it. Though mistresses were a common practice, I believed we were faithful to each other. I still believed it.

Yet why would someone—this child's mother or the peasant—lie? Who wouldn't want their child raised in a royal family? Was her mother truly dead and her father unnamed? Or was Sophia a part of Henry?

Someone was lying, but who?

"Lady Ada, let me take the child."

So focused on the child, I started at St Martin's voice behind me.

"Nae." I turned around, holding Sophia closer.

She snuggled onto my shoulder.

"But you can find out the truth," I said. "Where has she come from? Who are her real parents?"

Bowing, St Martin left the house.

I prayed his search would bring answers. I didn't need more pain.

Chapter Forty

A few hours later, I sat in the nursery rocking little Sophia, now clean, fed, and dressed in a white linen gown I'd embroidered for Margaret years before. At three, Margaret would never let me hold her like this. Nae, she would wiggle free to run or explore or simply dance in circles.

It felt so good to snuggle with a little one so plump with life. I hummed a familiar melody to the rhythm of the rocking chair, and Sophia sat contently as she drifted to sleep.

A soft rap came to my door.

Sybil stood at the threshold. She entered and knelt beside me. "Oh, she's a beauty with her dark curls and thick lashes." She waited until I looked at her. "Have you considered what you'll say to your children about her?"

Doubt swirled through my mind as I tried to figure out how to explain the child's similar coloring and disposition to my own children.

I thought of the whispered rumors from servants in my childhood home and of my parents' dubious beginning.

Sophia was such a pleasant child, though she most probably wasn't Henry's. Was it more important for me to have a child to fill my empty arms and give me solace than it was to guard my late husband's reputation?

I could love her. I could care for her. I wanted to keep her.

Suddenly weary, I asked, "Sybil, what should I do?"

"You need not decide just yet." Her voice was soft. "I'll take her home and bring her when we move north. You can come and hold her or care for her without anyone's knowledge. Does that sound acceptable?"

I nodded.

"Then when Alexander has a better understanding of the truth, you can choose what best to do."

Dame Sybil spoke wisely.

Willing to wait for what St Martin would find, I held the sleeping babe fast, whispering to her, "Oh, sweet child, everything will be all right." I wasn't certain if the words were for me or her as I passed the sleeping babe to Sybil, blinking away unshed tears.

She gently held the child without waking her. "Alexander is in the great hall waiting for you, my lady. I believe he already has information."

"So soon?" I stood. "How can that be?"

Sybil adjusted the little girl so that her head rested on Sybil's shoulder. "Simple. He knew who was the most likely to have knowledge of happenings among those folks."

"Do you mean the biggest gossip?" I asked, not willing to equivocate.

"Exactly." She chuckled. "Everyone knows it's Rowena the candlemaker. They say everything she hears goes in her ear and out her mouth." Sybil swayed with the child in a way that comforted me.

"Love her as if she were your own."

Hurrying downstairs, I met St Martin. He wore a homespun tunic unlike the fine uniform reflecting his station. "Many vendors have set up by the tavern at the crossroads where I found Rowena. She sells candles and should be there still. She answered very few of my questions but wished to speak to you directly."

I needed no further explanation and grabbed my grey cloak, went out to the stable, and ordered my horse saddled.

Two guardsmen prepared to accompany us.

St Martin seemed worried. "Should we bring more guards? With Prince Henry's death and you preparing to leave, the tide of sentiment may not be as positive as it has been in the past."

I shook my head. "The fewer people that know about Sophia the better. At least until we find the truth."

St Martin spoke to the guards briefly before we headed out.

I saw the vendors at a distance and I eased Cooper over to St Martin's side. "Let us not approach together but stay close. I'm hoping no one will recognize me." I pulled the hood of my cloak over my head, dismounted, and gave my reins to him.

The first table I approached displayed tableware, the second vegetables, but nae a candle. I approached a woman selling brooms. "Do you know where I might buy candles?"

She pointed to the end of a row.

"I'm grateful for your help," I said.

The woman behind the last table was older than I'd expected with graying dark hair peeking from under her veil. She wore a tattered shawl that looked as if it once had many bright colors.

I stepped before her table. "Are you the woman known as Rowena?"

She opened one curious eye. "I be. Who asks?"

"I'm Lady Ada."

She jumped to her feet. "My lady!" She curtsied. "My sympathies for your loss."

I swallowed hard. "*Merci.*"

The woman clicked her tongue. "Me heart aches for ye and Prince Henry. Ye have me condolences. I be very sorry for ye." She wagged her head and clicked her tongue.

I looked around, hoping no one heard our conversation or recognized me. "Rowena, will you speak truth to me?" Realizing I sounded desperate, I took a calming breath.

She was quiet a moment, as if choosing her words carefully. "Aye, be this 'bout the bairn that Domhnall took to the manor this morn?" She rearranged a few candles. "The young mother died yesterdee. Such a beautiful and enticing wench. Sadly, her beauty 'twas her demise."

"Yesterday?" Another stab went through my heart.

"Aye. She had great knowledge 'bout herbs, learned from Boudica."

I placed a hand over the lurch in my stomach. "Boudica's apprentice? Jasmine?"

"Aye." Rowena appeared surprised that I didn't know. "Is not Boudica your howdie?"

"She was . . . once."

"Boudica abandoned Jasmine because of the girl's riotous livin' . . . and her treachery."

"What do you mean?" I hoped the entire burgh wasn't aware of the rumored curse so many years ago.

"Jasmine sought to entice many men of means. She used her beauty, herbs, potions, even witchcraft to lure men and gain favor, takin' their money. She was untrustworthy, even in death."

What I dreaded to ask, I did so with a whisper. "Did you ever see Jasmine with Prince Henry?"

Rowena raised an eyebrow. "Aye." She squinted one eye, watching me.

I tried not to react.

She shrugged a shoulder. "I assumed he be seekin' a remedy for his health. The dear man, sick for such a long time before he died." She clicked her tongue again. "Me thinks he was desperate by the time he went to her. I know he did come. I saw him enter her home on more than one occasion. I often travel the burgh whilst sellin' me candles."

"I hope you've kept that to yourself."

She chuckled. "Others saw him at her hovel. I need not say a word, for all know."

All? I pushed on my chest where a pain throbbed. I had to defend Henry's integrity. "He often brought different herbs home to brew and drank them faithfully. To our sorrow, they didn't improve his health. Surely that is all he wanted from her."

Rowena raised an eyebrow. "Not a man is immune to the wiles of an enticing wench, even a man who has a treasure fer a wife such as ye."

Anger prickled. "You need not patronize me."

A calming hand embraced my shoulder and St Martin stood at my side.

I wasn't certain for how long or what he'd heard.

I lifted a hand, gesturing for him to back away toward the two guardsmen standing at a distance with the horses, then took a deep breath. "What of the child?"

Rowena smiled and shuffled through her tapers. She handed me a yellow hog fat candle. A peace offering? "Truth is, the wench insisted the bairn to be Prince Henry's."

Her words deepened the sick feeling in my stomach. "She lied." I raised my chin.

Rowena huffed. "I would not have put it past her. She bespoken lies afore. But on her deathbed?" Rowena grunted. "No doubt her evil doing was to secure care for the child."

Sophia's dark, beautiful wide eyes could be Henry's, but they could also be Jasmine's. I spoke my thoughts aloud. "Another man could have fathered her."

"Of course, my dear." She folded her arms as if finished offering free information.

No way would I allow the village gossip to clam up on me now. "Who do *you* think fathered Jasmine's baby?" I returned her candle to the table with a plop.

She rearranged her display. "Would ye care to buy candles, m'lady?"

With trembling hands, I opened my bag and pulled out a handful of coins, slapping them before her.

Rowena slid the coins into her lap and whispered, "Jasmine had many lovers, even one from Spain, dark eyes and hair as black as crow's wings."

Hope entered my soul. "So, she didn't know who the father was but found it convenient to blame my husband?"

Rowena shrugged and gathered five candles together and wrapped them in a cloth, tying them with string. She handed them to me and patted my hand. "Worry your head no longer. What be done be done. It be not the child's fault. The child be fortunate to live in your household. I pray ye to love her."

Love her? Sure to God, I wished she was not connected to Henry. I stepped away to leave.

Rowena leaned forward and pointed west. "Her hovel stands near the road to the mill. Over the hill nestled in the dell. It has a battered oak door bedecked with dried herbs."

I'd been there before with St Martin. All those years ago, I'd brought her a forgiving heart, a cross, and a loaf of bread, but could I forgive her now?

I turned numbly, walking away—my knees hardly able to support me.

I rode quietly beside St Martin, followed by the two guardsmen. After a short distance, we approached the unkempt cottage. Other than a dog lying in the shade of a tree, it appeared lifeless.

The animal looked up as we approached.

I slowed Cooper to a stop. "Have you been to this cottage before, St Martin?"

He replied, "Aye, my lady, both with you and your husband. Prince Henry hoped Jasmine could heal him."

My heart sank heavily to my stomach. So, it was true that Henry had come without my knowledge. I forced the next words. "What if she poisoned him? What if she drugged him and this nightmare is true?"

His hands clenched his horse's reins. "We were careful. He never partook of her teas until he was home with you."

"You weren't careful enough. The entire burgh knows he was here." I clenched my teeth. "Tell me all you know."

St Martin swallowed hard, causing his jaw to flex. "After trying various physicians, Prince Henry came here. Jasmine burnt herbs by the firepit over there."

"Did he ever go into the house?"

"For massages. Sometimes she would use a salve that she rubbed into his neck and shoulders, and . . ." His tan turned a deep red. "That's why he stayed so long."

"How long?"

"Several minutes. Sometimes an hour, I would venture. I didn't go in but waited outside. He left the door open."

-314-

My body sagged as I tried to push from my mind visions of her hands working their way around Henry's body as I had also done, attempting to give him relief. Had all her doings been for relief only? I wanted to lash out at Henry and ask why he didn't tell me. But then I remembered, he'd been to so many physicians that I had stopped accompanying him. And we'd both been willing to try anything.

St Martin cleared his throat. "Prince Henry would not have slept with the wench. He had moral integrity and conducted himself respectably. He loved you only. If anyone knows this, it's I. I've been at his side for years. The months he was away from you, never did he give his attentions to another woman." He looked me in the eye, and I knew he believed what he said. "She was good at her herbal craft—and at the craft of seduction—but the prince was above succumbing. When the weather permitted, he insisted the door of her home remain open when he was inside. I saw or heard naught that would give you concern, my lady."

Tears smarted—his words balm to my aching soul. 'Moral integrity . . . above succumbing.' I had to have faith that Henry told me the truth.

As we dismounted and approached the house, the dog loped away. St Martin at the lead, we entered the cottage. The two guardsmen waited by the door.

I expected it to be crowded with bird feathers, bundles of herbs, piles of crockery, and cats mulling about and full of exotic smells of incense, scarves hanging from the ceiling, and large inviting cushions on the floor. But as my eyes adjusted to the dim light, my heart sank. "Empty?"

The shelves wiped clean, one tilted precariously. The simple furnishings had been turned over. "This tells us naught."

St Martin put a hand to his chin. "It tells us someone knew more about her than we do."

Chapter Forty-One

At Eads Hall, I took the package of candles into the kitchen.

Maurice's brow creased with concern. "Have you had something to eat today, *ma dame*? They told me you went out."

"*S'il vous plait*. I *am* hungry." I sat at the table in the dining hall, and Maurice brought a large bowl of steaming stew. Although it smelled heavenly, it had been weeks since anything tasted good. My body no longer seemed to enjoy the simple things in life.

Lingering, Maurice watched me as he dried his hands on his white apron. "Will the child be staying here or with Dame Sybil? She is a pretty little thing."

I didn't reply. I couldn't. Were the servants already aware of the accusations? I felt as a child at Reigate again, servants whispering until they saw me nearby. "*Merci* for the meal." I stood. "But I'm no longer hungry."

He sputtered as I walked off.

I went to the nursery to check on the children. They'd not noticed my absence and played hoops and skittles with Mary.

I went to my bedchamber and sat down.

Glenore approached. "Is all well, m'lady?" She held a tray with the bowl of stew on it. "Maurice and I be worried. You'll feel better once ye eat somethin'. The stew be special delicious todee."

I rubbed my face. "It's been a trying day. Please put the tray on the table." I watched her and suddenly wondered if she could be of help. "Do you remember Boudica?"

"Aye, her apprentice was killed yesterdee."

"Jasmine was *killed*? I assumed she died of natural causes."

"Well, if ye call her potions natural." Glenore cheered-up at reporting what little gossip she'd gathered. "It be the talk on the square. Jasmine gave her daughter to the miller right before passin' away at his feet. Poison they think. Either from her own hand or from a scorned lover."

"And do you know where that little girl is now?" I tried not to be angry at her penchant for gossip.

She lowered her head, as if in contrition. "Aye, m'lady. Dame Sybil cares for her. And what an angelic lil' one she is."

"*Merci*, that is all." I needed to be alone.

She eyed me and left.

Exhausted, I collapsed forward with my face in my hands. If Glenore had not already heard the accusation against Henry, she soon would. I had to keep such gossip from the children. And what was my obligation to little Sophia? I had an idea where to turn next.

Hoping for solace and direction, I went downstairs and outside to pray to Mother Mary.

A ragged cart pulled by a swayback nag approached. The driver was an older woman I recognized. Indeed, an answer to the prayer I had yet to utter.

Boudica waved and drew close. She dismounted and stood before me somber and anxious.

Why did I still feel fear in this woman's presence? She carried no bag of black magic. I straightened, trying to show who was in charge. "Have you heard of Jasmine's fate?"

"Tis why I be here." Boudica took a step away. "Whatever that girl did, I'm not to blame."

"I accused you of naught." I wanted to garner whatever information I could from Boudica. I thought to invite her in the house, but between the kitchen staff and Glenore, I hated the thought of listening ears making matters worse.

I led her to the garden instead. We sat on a bench. "Jasmine claimed Prince Henry fathered her daughter. I need to know the truth."

The howdie gazed toward the pond. "I've had no dealins with her since she performed the worse black magic. Worse than cursin' your bairn. Worse than bearin' the prince's child — if it be his."

"What . . . what did she do?"

Boudica wrung her hands. "Jasmine poisoned a man with fatal herbs."

I took in a startled breath. "Murder?"

Boudica nodded. "Nae a one knew it but her and I, and I've not bespoken it 'til now." She looked to the ground. "I feared she kill me too, so I ran. She deserved to die, and I glad of it." Boudica wiped at a tear, not appearing glad at all. "I loved her like a daughter once. Taught her all I knew 'bout herbs and such. But she centered her work on harmin not healin' and gettin' gain through wicked ways. That's why I'm takin' all her parchments and herbs with me." She gestured to her loaded cart. "They'll never harm another, only heal."

"So that's why her home was empty?" I asked.

She shuddered. "Nae. When me left there, a hedgehog ran in front of me, representin' the devil that carries men's souls to hell. Her hovels a place I daren't not enter again. But someone was there before me. I'll never know what they took, but many vials were missin'."

"Don't you have an idea who would have done such a thing?"

"Nae, I had'na seen her for years 'til last spring, and then for a day. She summoned me to be a howdie. I could'na turn me back on her then, could I?" She shrugged. "But she said nothin' at the time 'bout the father, and I did'na ask. Hardly thanked me for comin' neither. Never saw the bairn again, for Jasmine refused me once she was done birthin'. She was a hard-hearted girl, she was." Boudica's eyes held sadness. "But she's gone from this world and can'na do no further harm."

When Boudica left, I gave a sigh of relief as she disappeared down the lane, hopefully gone from my life forever.

Chapter Forty-Two

Mormaer Donnchad graciously welcomed us to the palace in Haddington. Proudly, he showed us the many improvements the king had made to our new home. As we walked in the gardens on our first morning, he explained, "I'm here not only to train your sons to be knights but to attend to any other needs you may have."

"You are most gracious. I admit, I've yet to see the honor in fighting, but Henry often explained to me the importance of honor and letting your opponent's realize strength."

Donnchad nodded. "I'll also teach your children to respect their people and be decisive."

He pointed. "See the River Tyne in the distance?"

"Aye. The river reminds me of the part of the Thames that passed by Reigate in Surrey." We walked toward it. Mayhap, on other days, strolling along the lazy river whilst tossing bread crumbs to the ducks would remind me of my childhood home and help heal my wounded heart.

"It appears tranquil now but be warned that it can rise as much as eight feet, sending water along Crocegait and into the marketplace."

"It must be what makes this land so lush." Indeed, the gardens grew more beautiful than anything at Eads Hall, and the pond was twice the size.

"You are generous to us," I said, watching the children run through higher grasses to the pond where several alarmed ducks hurriedly swam from the shore.

David, in his attempt to catch a swan that had come close to the bank, slipped knee deep into the water. The children giggled and tried to pull him out.

Donnchad chuckled. "I feel it my calling to keep the royal children safe. I might need to go save one from the pond."

That next afternoon, William and David met with Donnchad in the courtyard eager to begin what I had come to think of as their military training. I found just the window from which to watch their sword-play.

Donnchad had them up on horses, teaching them to strike with a sword from the saddle.

I was grateful they seemed oblivious to sorrow and thrilled at their future.

Days later, I rose at dawn and gazed out my window at the lush gardens. Flowers and trees glimmered like jewels in the sunrise.

"Good morn!" Glenore entered the room and placed a tray on the bedside table then took a folded blanket from an open chest and threw it over her arm.

"What's that for?"

She smiled. "The girls want to go on a picnic. Would ye care to join us?"

I gazed again out the window. The countryside certainly was inviting. "Nae, not this time. But there are many acres I look forward to exploring soon."

"Now that ye hold Haddington and Crail, ye may roam all the way to Kirkcaldy if ye wish."

"You're right. I'd not thought of it that way." I tried to sound cheerful, but I didn't. I missed Eads Hall and little Sophia who was still in Sybil's care. St Martin had stayed to act as steward while we weren't in residence. It was odd not having him close. I considered suggesting to the king that the St Martins dwell there permanently, yet something held me back.

Uncertain whether King David had heard the rumors about Sophia, I felt it prudent not to distress him further with the little one's presence and accepted that St Martin and his family would not be with me for a time. Thinking of King David brought Malcolm to mind. I missed him dearly. A sigh escaped my lips.

"Give yourself time, m'lady." Glenore curtsied and left.

Time. I had so much time now—the rest of my life without Henry. I made no attempt to hold back my pent-up emotions and simply let the tears flow. "No more changes in my life," I whispered the plea heavenward, dragging my nightdress over my head. "I've had enough."

Shortly after nibbling at a few things on the tray Glenore left, I made myself go find her and the girls.

I saw them at a distance, Glenore holding to each of their hands. "I'm coming," I called.

They stopped, and both my sweet little girls smiled wide and jumped up and down, waiting for me to join them.

We climbed into an open cart pulled by a workhorse. What should have been a family of eight, through death and obligation, had whittled down to three. Two new guards followed us as we headed toward the countryside. The girls played merrily and boisterously on the ride, chasing away my melancholy. Glenore was as a child herself still innocent in her affections.

We arrived at a beautiful meadow near the Lammermuir Hills. The girls eagerly tumbled out of the cart to play.

We ate bread, still warm from the morning baking, and cheese and fruit, after which the girls rolled a hoop back and forth until they became distracted by a butterfly. The guards sat beneath a nearby tree, watching my daughters.

Glenore stayed by my side me. "Do I call ye countess now or still Lady Ada?

"Lady Ada will do." I laughed. "I've been a countess since before you met me."

She seemed confused. "So how have your responsibilities changed?"

I took a deep breath. "I suppose I have more freedom to make changes and improvements to the area."

She nodded, but I could tell she didn't understand.

"Henry had spoken several times about monastic charters and gifts, but his health prevented him from carrying them out. Mayhap I can make his dream a reality? What do you think?"

"Ye certainly have the power and the means. Why not?"

"Aye, why not." I laughed blithely and picked a blade of grass. "Because women do not write charters and give charitable donations without a man. It's not done."

"You're the daughter-in-law of the king. Is he not a man who would allow that to happen?" Glenore asked.

"I so want to do this without King David's help." I picked another blade of grass. "One of Henry's favorite abbeys was Dunfermline. It's where his grandfather, King Malcolm, and

King David's older brother, Alexander, are buried. Perchance I'll start there. Hugh Giffard's brother, William, is a priest and an excellent scribe. Mayhap he could write up the charter?"

Glenore smiled. "It's good to see ye with hope in your eyes."

"Merely thinking about the possibilities does give me a lift of spirits," I admitted, studying the new countryside. "I'd like to walk to the top of the rise over yonder. I believe it would allow me to ponder the details. Do you mind keeping an eye on the girls?"

Glenore knit her brows. "Do ye think ye should be wanderin' off alone? Eoan could accompany ye."

"And who is Eoan?"

Glenore pointed to the taller of the two guards, a handsome knight. She reddened simply looking at him.

I smiled and shook my head at both the guards who relaxed in the shade of a very large oak. Then I gazed at the hill behind me. "I promise to not go far. You and the guards will still be in hearing."

"Then go, m'lady, and take all the time ye need. When ye return, we'll bring out the cakes and cider."

"Why not share the cakes now?" I motioned my head to the guards. "It will give you an opportunity to get to know them better."

Glenore's broad smile was enough to let her feelings be known about the handsome young Eoan.

Walking across the countryside, cleared my mind and lifted my heart. The path skirted past an apple orchard. My favorite Scottish daisies bloomed, including the beloved heather, so symbolic to the people for its healing qualities.

Blackface sheep grazed in green meadow grass. How I looked forward to telling Henry about this lovely new land.

I stopped in my tracks.

Like a sudden dark cloud masking the sun, the fact that my husband was gone wounded me afresh. I looked heavenward and called out, "Oh, dearest Lord, my thoughts always return to Henry. Why is there nothing to quench the pain of losing our loved ones in death?" Was there no permanent reprieve?

I listened to the whistling breeze as it cooled my tears, but heard no answer.

My headdress was yanked out of place by the increasing wind. Surrendering to nature, I let it go, allowing the wimple to unwrap and flutter down my back. I loosened my braids so that my hair also blew freely in the wind, as a child's might.

Would I stay in pain or accept my trials, treasure the blessings that were mine, and move forward in good cheer? "Lord, Thou dost know my loneliness, my grief, my weaknesses. I am in need of Thy comfort. Take from me my despair and give me hope."

Suddenly, I was jarred from my heavenly pleas by horse's hooves coming from the path. A man rode toward me. Quickly, I moved toward a cluster of young trees hoping to not be noticed. How foolish that I came without a guard.

"Lady Ada." He halted his horse. "Why are you out walking alone? Where are your guards?"

The man's strong brow furrowed and his golden hair curled at his shoulders. But he was without his green cloak.

"*Monsieur* Madduch, greeting." I stood tall and glanced around. I'd ventured too far. "My family is just over the rise in the meadow . . . within shouting distance."

He dismounted. "How fortunate for us to meet. I'd heard you'd come to Haddington. I intended to come and convey my condolences on your child's passing."

He reached for my hand.

I avoided his touch and clutched my hands behind my back.

"You are kind." I took a deep breath. I couldn't cry in this man's presence. But tears came nonetheless. "Forgive me." I wiped the moisture from my face. "Both Matilda's and Henry's passing has been difficult."

He grasped my wet hand and stepped closer. "My dear Ada. A heart that is broken is a heart that has been loved."

"What a beautiful sentiment." My mind furiously tried to think on how to politely refuse his attentions. "I've loved the best of men. Few women have experienced that."

"I too lost my wife years ago so I know the pain you're experiencing."

"And you've not remarried?"

He still held my hand. "Nae. Not another noblewoman has captured my heart." His eyes dropped to my lips then moved to my eyes. "It seems such a short time since your wedding party at Carlisle where first I met you."

Aye. Too short a time.

"And Eads Hall, when we shared a warm stew on a rainy evening, the two of us, before your blazing fire. Henry was away, if I recall."

"Aye." I'd first assumed he was there to court Fenella. To think he wanted to seek my favor whilst I was married and start the sort of scandal I was dealing with in Whitfield. I pulled my hand from his grasp—perhaps too roughly. "I'm grateful to have had Henry with me, if only for a few short years. Even with him gone, my love for him grows." Hopefully, Madduch heard my meaning. To emphasize it, I took a step away from him.

"In their absence, good men become greater in the eyes of their grievers."

Was that an insult? Henry had warned me about cunning men—Madduch specifically. Even though he was handsome and personable, he presumed intimacy. I should not entertain him. "I believe I'll return to my family."

He stepped in front of me and reached for my hand again. "You know, you need not endure alone—a beautiful woman like you. I could come to you, and we could talk. Talking eases pain." He kissed my fingers.

Feeling disgust, I withdrew my hand. "I thank you for your kind offer, but I fare well."

Madduch smiled, amusement dancing in his alluring blue eyes. "Your sons will need a mentor. I shall come and teach them the art of sword fighting, if you permit."

"That will not be necessary. They're with Donnchad in training. King David has provided for them. Excuse me, *monsieur*." I gathered my skirts and hurried up the hill.

Was Madduch really a widower? He might be kind and attractive, but he was too overbearing for my taste. Is this the sort of man who is an answer to my prayer of loneliness?

Yet, his attentions flattered. Mayhap I should not say nae too quickly. I was a young woman with many years ahead of me to spend alone. *Ada!* I scolded myself. I had no intentions of remarrying unless King David ordered it, and I doubted God would send a rival to the throne to be the one who comforted me.

Reaching the hilltop, I looked out to the meadow. The children and guards sat on the blanket with Glenore, probably enjoying the cakes. The pink sky promised a nice sunset.

The guards stood at my approach.

The taller one took charge. "We must be heading home before the sunlight is gone." His voice owned a touch of scolding.

I frowned.

Remembering his station, his cheeks reddened slightly, and he gave me a modest bow.

We gathered the picnic remains, folded the blanket, and climbed into the cart. I watched over my shoulder in case Madduch followed. He hadn't.

On the ride home, the setting sun glowed through deep reds and golden rays formed the shape of a cross over our new palace. The sight soothed my troubled mind.

The girls fell asleep before we reached the palace doors. In spite of the unexpected intrusion by Henry's mysterious cousin, whom I'd decided intended no real harm, it had been the best day in a long time.

Maggie came into my room that evening carrying a washbowl for my bedtime routine.

"When I went for my walk this afternoon, you'll never believe who I met. Madduch. Do you remember him?" I pulled on my nightdress.

"Aye, I remember him." She handed me a cloth with which to wash my face and hands. "You must be careful, *domina*."

"He meant no harm, although he did make minor advances toward me." I rubbed the warm damp cloth over my face. "Strange, but I liked having a man's attention. I've missed Henry so much."

Maggie pulled the covers back on the bed. "Your loneliness makes you vulnerable to a handsome man's attention." She directed me to the stool and brushed my hair. "You're beautiful and will undoubtedly have suitors. Lossing Henry has hurt you, but you must take care not to be drawn into an unworthy match."

She was right, but compared to my prince, wasn't everyone unworthy?

Chapter Forty-Three

I learned time, indeed, contributed to healing. I still missed Henry and Matilda both, but gradually, almost imperceptibly, the intensity of that longing lessened. It was my boys I now missed as their grandfather took all three on a grand tour of the country, showing them off as future rulers of Scotland.

I smiled thinking of little David, barely age six, standing straight and tall before noblemen. He made the most adorable faces when embarrassed by people staring at him. And in York, William, at the age of ten, was made Earl of Northumbria by King David.

When the tour was over, King David would bring all three boys back to Haddington whilst he went to Carlisle for a time. Malcolm and the boys would continue their royal training under Donnchad's tutelage.

I relished having my family together, if only for a short while, resigning myself to the knowledge that Malcolm would never be my little boy again.

Meanwhile, I granted Dunfermline Abbey a toft in the burgh. William Giffard wrote a beautiful charter, which I presented to the abbey. All went well. Interesting, how the breaking of tradition can be so quiet—for a woman to do something only men did. Yet, I believed it would have a loud and lasting effect in the future.

Before I started home, I took solitude in the chapel. Bowing in prayer, the voices of two priests in the adjoining hallway floated within range of my hearing. "Aye, tis a blessing to receive an additional toft for our sustenance, but what think ye of a gift given by a woman with no man's name as support? Is such acceptable in God's eyes? Tis a generous gift, but I find it an embarrassment."

I could hardly believe my ears. Had I been wrong to think I, a solitary woman, could give a gift to a house of God without linking my name to a man? Was that really God's desire?

"I agree," echoed the second voice. "I had to hold my tongue and force myself to look pleasant as she signed the charter, legalizing the gift."

Their approaching footsteps drew nearer.

Panicked, I gathered my skirts and whirled to escape out the back of the chapel and found myself face to face with my critics.

"Countess!" The man tried to mask his surprise with a bow.

The other man did likewise. Their guilty expressions told me they knew I had overheard them.

I prayed for words of wisdom. "Greeting. Is not it glorious, my good men, that you have witnessed history this day?"

The priests looked askance at one another. "History, my lady?"

I checked the anger in my voice and clapped together my hands in celebratory salutation. "Aye. You witnessed today that a woman can stand on her own accord in doing good works. No husband nor brother validated her, only God Himself stood at her side in the gallant deed."

Shoulders squared, I took a few steps to leave, but found the courage to turn back. "And remember this, it will not be the last." I stifled a laugh at their astonished faces and walked out into the sunlight.

My whole body trembled in exhilaration as I headed toward my guards who waited to escort me to Queensferry, across the Firth of Forth and on to Haddington.

In late May, almost a year after Henry's death, William and David returned. I could hardly believe how they'd changed. Though they balked at my motherly attentions in front of their mentor, Donnchad, I hugged each of my sons soundly.

Donnchad left for Edinburgh by the next morning to continue his work with Malcolm, who I was assured was progressing nicely. He was to spend the next season at Donnchad's castle in Fife.

The following night in the nursery with the girls, I rehearsed the tales of the fine deeds of their father and of his goodness as I often did before they retired for the night.

In the middle of my tale, Maggie appeared at the door. "*Domina*, a herald awaits downstairs. He appears to have come in haste and says it's urgent."

I left the girls and hurried to him.

The uniformed herald stood at attention. When he saw me, he stepped forward with the utmost solemnity.

"Oh nae, what now?" I asked.

"Countess, I am the bearer of sorrow. King David of Scotland died two days past in Carlisle."

I swayed and grabbed at his arm. "King David is dead?" My mind couldn't fathom it. "How did it happen? Was treachery involved?"

"Nae, we think not." The herald's voice was calm. "His chaplain found him kneeling in prayer at his bedside. The priest believes King David died of a broken heart. Since Prince Henry's death, he has not been himself."

I remembered King David struggling with grief. It seemed fitting for him to die in prayer. "This is shocking news, indeed." My mind suddenly awoke with a frenzy. "Nae, oh nae!" I called out.

The herald took me to a chair.

"Has word been sent to my son?" For now, Malcolm was king! King! *Oh God*, I prayed. *Help us!*

"Dispatchers have gone to Fife and Scone and to several of the nobles. With the king's body, a regiment marches toward Dunfermline Abbey where he'll be put to rest. The service is planned in a sennights' time."

Dazed, I nodded. "*Merci, monsieur.*" I called for a servant to care for the herald and staggered up the stairs to find Maggie.

This was the day I'd dreaded. Why did it come so soon?

Since Henry's passing, King David had been my strength, my protector, my very father. How could he be gone? I could not stop the tears from falling.

By the time I found Maggie with Mary in the nursery, I could hardly speak.

"What is it? What has happened?" Maggie held me firm.

"King David has died!" I all but screamed.

Maggie dropped her arms and stared with an open mouth.

I paced. "He wasn't feeling well, but I had no idea he was so ill. What are we to do without him? And . . . and . . ." Could I say it? "Malcolm is now *king!*"

Little Adaline stared up at me from her child-sized chair. "Grandfather is dead?" Her face crumpled and tears formed in her brown eyes, then Margaret started to cry as well.

I hadn't guarded my words in front of the children.

Mary went to Adaline and Margaret. "There, there little ladies."

Maggie paced with me. "Let us remember, *domina*, the king gave instructions for such an occurrence. He knew this would be a time not only of sadness but also of danger."

I stopped and stared at her. "Aye, but what did he mean? Was he not taken in peace—naturally in his old age—so we need not be foolish with fear?"

I went to the children to comfort them further. "Your grandfather, good, wise king that he was, prepared well for his death. He arranged for Malcolm to be well guarded by Donnchad. Soon, we'll go north to his funeral where kind priests will attend us. All will be well."

William and David rushed into the room.

"The king is dead, Mother!" William shouted.

I nodded, choking with emotion, trying to be brave.

Little Adaline, striving to grasp all that was happening, said, "If Grandpa's dead, is he with Father?"

I knelt beside her and took her in my arms. "Aye, sweetheart, Father and Grandpa are together now, and little sister is with them both."

I motioned for Margaret to join our embrace. "We must be brave, and we must leave here soon for a safer place."

David grabbed a wooden sword from the toy box. "I'll protect us whilst we travel." He held his chin high, brave and willing, his father's son.

"*Monsieur* Eoan and his guardsmen will do that," I said. "But you can help by getting ready. We'll not return to Haddington for some time." I hoped we would only need to utilize Crail Castle for a year or so, but there was no way of knowing. England's dispute over the throne had lasted over twenty years and still wasn't resolved.

William turned and wiped at his tears, not wanting us to see him cry. He straightened. "How soon shall we go?" He'd grown so much in the last year that he seemed now a young man.

I wasn't certain how quickly to leave. If King David had been murdered, we would have fled that very night to Crail Castle as he'd asked me to do. Two things stopped me from moving forward with that plan. First, I longed to bid farewell to King David, whose funeral would be in a sennight.

Second, in Dunfermline, I could embrace Malcolm and give the young new king my blessing. My heart yearned to touch his gentle face and whisper words of support. If we left directly from the funeral, we could be in Crail that evening, or the next morning by the latest. I could send for the knights from Crail to prepare the passage for our journey. Aye, it seemed the wisest plan.

"We will leave the day after tomorrow," I said. "Now, come close to your mother and let us pray." I put an arm around each of the girls and the boys nestled in. "Dear Lord, bless our loved ones in Your heaven and protect my family here on earth that we may be prepared to do Thy will. Amen."

After the children went to bed, I went to my bedchamber.

Maggie came in. "*Domina*." The concern across her brow was clear. "Didn't the king warn of rival targets and insist we act swiftly?" Then as if pleading, she said, "Let us comply."

"I believe we are," I answered calmly. "King David forewarned that we must leave Haddington upon his death and be off to Crail. But with no immediate threat, it would seem that two days to move an entire household *is* swiftly. Dunfermline Abbey should be safe enough."

Maggie curtsied. "What would you have me do to prepare?"

I'd thought to start in the morning, yet, as she offered, I supposed much could be done tonight. "Very well, could you alert the staff to begin packing our household for the journey, but do not tell them our objective." On King David's advice, we were not to mention our plans ahead of time to the staff lest word leak out to our enemies. Mayhap it best we travel by night.

The king cautioned me thus thinking his death would be from foul play, but still I wished to comply as much as possible. "We could keep the van hidden in the stables whilst we pack so that anyone looking on would not be alerted to our eminent departure."

"I will begin immediately, *domina*." Maggie hurried from the room.

My handmaiden's haste seemed unnecessary.

Although I must inform the guards from Crail of what I required, it could wait until morning. I was exhausted, and I wanted time alone to weep for the kind father-in-law who had been my strength and support as I healed from the loss of Henry.

Chapter Forty-Four

The day after the news of King David's death, I came from the kitchen to find the entry filled with baskets.

"What is all this?"

"Gifts from the people," the doorman replied. "You're now the Queen Mother of the Scots. They brought these by quadriga this morning whilst you worked in the stable."

I picked up a scarf and let the fine silk run through my fingers. "They send me their best?" Gratefulness filled my heart to overflowing. I'd been so focused on the malicious ideas of what could happen to us that I'd nearly forgotten the true goodness of the Scottish people. I picked up a bottle of wine and looked over other items in the pile. "We'll take it with us. Look. Here are honeys, dried herbs, nut oil. May God bless them for their generosity!"

Notes of sympathy arrived. One particular sentiment written by a cleric who'd grown up with King David echoed my feelings by describing the king as "a man gentle and devout, a person of sweet spirit and cheerful heart."

That same afternoon, as if in answer to prayer, Hugh Giffard arrived. His familiar happy countenance was both a surprise and a comfort.

"I came to offer my help in any way you desire."

I invited him into the solar to confidentially inform him of our immediate plans. I didn't disclose that we prepared to leave. Still concerned about the details and uncertain whom to trust, I wished to keep our possible departure to Crail a secret.

Giffard seemed greatly concerned. "You face a serious menace. For your safety, bring your children and come with me to Yester. Lady Fenella will happily receive you. I have ample guards and no one will suspect you to be there. In a few days, we can travel together to the funeral services, ensuring no harm will come to you and yours."

Haddington Palace was well known and possibly a target. Yester, hidden in the south woods and but an hour's ride, appeared the best temporary solution until we could journey to Dunfermline Abbey.

With Giffard at the lead, the children and I left within the hour with Maggie, Mary, Glenore, and a few loyal guards. Eoan and another regiment of guards would take our loaded carts to Queensferry crossing, where we would meet before the funeral, and escort us across the Firth of Forth. The plan was laid, and it was the best choice given the information we had.

We came through the forest and arrived at Yester Castle near sunset. The beauty of the new manor took my breath away. I'd heard of the extensive ancient chambers below ground and could hardly tell where the ruins ended and the new stonewalls began.

In contrast, the top floors were half-timber construction, brightening up the residence and greatly diminishing the time and cost of the project. No wonder Giffard was able to get the residence ready in a few years. The home had a charm that could not be denied.

The secluded location, hidden on a forest hilltop, was also the perfect place for us to hide.

Fenella greeted us warmly as we entered. It was the first I'd seen her since Henry's funeral, and even then, we hadn't spoken. I tried to not feel hurt that she had never attempted to contact me during those difficult years when he had been ill and or after his death.

She led us to the dining hall for a warm meal. The new oak floors gleamed with fresh oil, but the stone stairway leading down to the kitchens was of ancient sandstone worn smooth with time.

After dining on thick stew and fresh bread, Fenella showed us to our rooms. Once we had the children settled, I left Mary to watch over them and went to find Giffard and Fenella in the solar.

The couple arose at my entry.

Fenella led us to chairs facing a warm and glowing flame. "Come, sit by the fire, and we shall visit before retiring for the night."

"I'm grateful you came for us, Giffard," I said. "Your concern for our safety gives balm to my soul. The death of the king is still a shock to me."

"King David was much loved by his people because he first loved them," Giffard remarked. "Although he fought for our defense when necessary, he was in many ways known as a man of peace and will be missed by all."

His kind sentiments brought warmth to my core. "I know not how we will manage without King David. I've so depended on him since Henry's passing. I believed and hoped he would be with us for years."

Fenella took my hands in hers. "You'll manage well. You've nobility and strength flowing in your blood."

I shrugged. "I do not feel strong. I feel alone and weak. First Henry, then Matilda, and now David—all gone. I just want to hide away with my children and mourn."

Giffard rested his elbows on his knees, leaning closer. "We'll not allow you to go through this alone. We'll stay close."

"Aye," Fenella added. "With our new castle so near to your palace, we should be able to spend many a summer afternoon riding or weaving or swimming in the Tyne."

I'd had the same thoughts before David's death, but now that could not be. At least not for quite a while. I decided to tell them our plans. "As soon as King David is buried, my family and I will leave for Crail. The king suggested it before his demise—for the protection of the royal family—and there we will stay until Malcolm sends word that it's safe for us to return to Haddington."

Fenella reached for my hand. "Surely you will be much safer in Crail. And to make certain of it, we shall go with you and stay until you're well settled. Won't we, Hugh."

Giffard nodded enthusiastically. "Aye, we'll protect you until every danger is passed."

Their offer surprised and cheered me. I wouldn't be alone. "Your generosity is overwhelming. I must thank you both." I turned to Fenella. "Are you certain? You have only recently moved into Yester manor. Are you prepared to leave?"

"For the royal family? For you? Of course." She smiled, with a strange sort of expression that whispered she had a secret.

I wanted to ask what it was.

Fenella changed the subject. "I noticed fine drink in those baskets you brought and thought we might make a toast to young Malcolm, the forthcoming King of Scots. Shall I call a servant?"

"Nae," I was suddenly tired. "Tomorrow will be a full day. I best rest so that I can be useful." I rose to my feet in awe of these great people that put my family above their own comfort. "*Merci* again for all you've done for me. Now and in the past." Turning to Giffard, I added, "If not for your quick action after Henry was hurt by the grappling hook, I'd have never had all those wonderful years with my dear husband. I would have never had my sweet children. God bless you."

"And were it not for you, I'd still be in England, fighting a never-ending war instead of at Yester in our new home with my beautiful wife."

Fenella smiled again. There was merriment in her eyes, and it felt so foreign to my sorrows over the recent deaths.

My only desire was to mourn King David's loss, and I wished to be alone to contemplate and pray. "Feel free to partake of the wine without me. It has been a harrowing day and I shall retire."

In my bedchamber, I tried to rest, but sleep came intermittently. I dreamed that I wandered the fresh halls of Yester manor. Ahead, a young girl with dark curls dressed in white beckoned for me to follow her through the kitchens to an old battered door in the corner. She opened it to a staircase leading down into the ancient dungeons.

At first, I thought the child was Sophia, and wondered if the dream was trying to awaken guilt that I had left her in the care of Sybil and St Martin. But as she turned, I noticed the child's heart-shaped face. It was not Sophia. The girl seemed confident, and my heart tugged at the sweet one's fervent gaze. I increased my pace to follow more closely.

At the base of the staircase, two archways loomed darkly before me. I didn't know which one to take. One was rounded with rough-hewn stone, old and moss-covered. The other had a pointed arch of clean, new granite. The little girl touched my hand and said, "You'll be safe here." Then she was gone.

I recognized her now. "Matilda?" I wanted to hold her. "Matilda?" I cried and woke to the sound of my own voice. Cheeks wet, I sat up. Sleep had fled.

Another sound bid me to my feet. Downstairs, I heard pounding on the large doors and loud voices.

I wrapped my robe tightly around myself and curiously went to the landing overlooking the entry hall.

The doorway stood open, allowing a rush of cold air. "I demand to speak with Lady Ada. I am Eoan, chief guard at Haddington Palace. I have an important message for her."

What could Eoan want in the middle of the night? I started toward the stairs to descend, but halted when Giffard, accompanied by guards, answered, "I will not allow her to be disturbed after the trying day she's had. If you wish to stay the night and speak to her in the morning, you are most welcome. We will gladly give you a place to rest."

"I must speak to her now." Eoan's resolute tone caused me to step into the shadows where I could see him, but he not me.

Suddenly he yanked his sword from its sheath and rushed through the entry with four armed men behind him. "I will see her now!" he snarled, looking up the stairs.

Fear surged through me. There was hate in his eyes. Here, I had thought him to be sweet on Glenore and completely loyal. How could I have been so wrong? I struggled to breathe and hurried to my sleeping children.

Swords clashed below.

What was I to do? Crouching in the dark, I shook my son. "William. Arise! We must hide."

William awakened to the commotion echoing up the stairs. "What is it?"

"I'm not sure, but we must get the children and hide."

Mary must have heard the fighting, for she dashed into the room, eyes large, face white. In nightclothes, she lifted little Margaret from her bed still wrapped in her blanket.

I called to the others, "Adaline! David! Come!"

Maggie and Glenore joined us on the landing and the sounds of fighting continued to rise up from below.

I led everyone down the rear stairwell that emptied into the great hall, dimly lit with a single torch.

The hall held an eerie air. I listened for danger yet heard naught but our footsteps. We crept down the ancient stone stairwell, cold rock beneath our feet. It opened to an underground kitchen. It looked surprisingly familiar. I shuffled to a dark corner and there, behind an old shelf, I found the battered door from my dream. "Quick, in here," I whispered, shuddering at the foreboding darkness.

William bravely led the way into the tunnel.

I took Adaline's hand and we descended together.

Mary carried little Margaret, and Glenore and Maggie followed, closing the door behind them. The tunnel went black.

"Will we be safe here?" William asked, his voice braver than I expected.

"I believe so," I said with more confidence than I felt.

We descended further until the tunnel opened to a wide hallway running parallel to the ground above. I dared not go further with no light. "Let's sit."

A heavy, moldy odor engulfed us as we crouched close together, deep in the earth. Adaline's hand trembled in mine and I wrapped my arms around her.

Maggie and Glenore huddled David between them.

Except for a sliver of light from the base of the door above, we sat in complete darkness. The stones' coldness and the damp air seeped in. Mary adjusted Margaret's blanket to include herself. I opened my robe to take in Adaline.

-343-

"To where do you think this tunnel leads?" William asked, his teeth chattering.

I put my arm around my almost-grown boy. "To the river below is my guess. Hush now," I whispered. "We must be silent. The tunnel echoes."

We waited and listened, afraid to talk, to move, to breathe.

Above the noise of my pounding heart, water *drip, drip, dripped* further down the tunnel amidst the occasional scuttle of mice.

Adaline shivered in my arms.

William moved closer.

My eyes slowly adjusted to the darkness. The tunnel in front of us became somewhat clear. I could see a new masonry arch. To the left stood another archway, rounder, older. Just as in my dream.

"Mama?" Adaline whispered through the darkness. "Are we going to die?"

"Nae, my darling, we will not die." I was certain of it.

The door abruptly flung open. There stood Eoan holding a torch, his shadowy face filled with hate and passion.

William jumped to his feet and reached out. "Eoan! You've saved us!"

I jerked my son down beside me as the guardsman raised his sword and growled. "Come out of there. Now the true king will arise!"

William squeezed behind me. "Mama, what does he mean?"

"He means to do us in," Glenore said in shock.

I stood and took a step forward. "Hush now, Glenore. Be not afraid, children." Whatever our fate, we'd face it with honor.

Unarmed and untrained against one of the king's top guards, we faced death and awaited Eoan's next move.

Suddenly, he grunted and lurched forward.

I stepped back, putting myself in front of the children, awaiting the sword's blow.

But his eyes bulged, and he fell down the tunnel. He tumbled until he rested near our feet, head hanging at an odd angle. Deep red blood oozed from his back onto his chainmail.

The children screamed in horror.

I stood, unable to move. Then quickly gathered them to me, trying to block them from such a horrific sight.

More light filled the tunnel.

With horror, I stared at Eoan, worried he might suddenly move.

I looked up expecting to see Giffard, but nae, Lady Fenella stood in the doorway holding a sword and a torch. "You're free to come out now. The danger has passed." Blood ran from a cut on her cheek.

William pulled Eoan's twisted body out of our way.

Were we safe? I needed to access the situation before moving forward.

Fenella hurried us on. "Come, I believe Hugh is injured."

We rushed up the tunnel and stairs to the landing. I encouraged my servants to usher the children to their bedchamber.

Fenella disappeared.

William didn't follow the children but stared at me with questioning eyes.

I paused to hold my son. "You must be brave," I said, releasing him. "You're the heir apparent, the next in line for the throne. This is the cost of that honor. Do you understand?"

"Aye." He swallowed. "But may I come with you and help?"

I peered over the railing to the entry hall below. He didn't need to grow up so fast and see four dead men on the floor. "William, I would rather you protect your brother and sisters until I return."

He nodded solemnly.

I hurried to the great hall relieved to find Hugh in relatively good spirits, his men-at-arms resting around him, cleaning their wounds, and recounting the assault.

A capable servant bandaged Giffard's shoulder with what looked to be a kitchen linen, and another gave Fenella a cloth to wipe her cheek.

"The guards recognized Eoan from Haddington and simply let him in," Giffard told Fenella. "There were only four with him. How did they expect to succeed?" Giffard quieted when he saw me standing there, then winced as the cook—or whomever he was—lifted his arm to tie the cloth securely.

"I believe they wanted to kill William and David." I shuddered at the thought.

Fenella scowled. "I'm sure Donnchad has his legions guarding young Malcolm, so what is to be gained by . . ." She stopped speaking then said much more kindly, "The young king could not be safer."

I collapsed into a chair. "King David warned me of the danger, but I wanted to wait until after the funeral before going to Crail. How I wish I'd fled immediately. Then this would have never happened."

Fenella put her hand on my shoulder. "On the contrary, if you'd fled immediately, you'd have been with Eoan, and he might have done you all in on the road. Indeed, I believe you coming here forced him to adjust his strategy." She laughed lightly. "Luckily for us, he's a terrible strategist. I believe this calls for a drink." Fenella gestured to her kitchen maid who brought out a large bottle of wine, a gift from the citizens of Haddington and a representation of good people who cared about the royal family.

The serving maid poured the wine into three stone goblets. She was little more than a girl and reminded me of Glenore all those years ago.

As we raised our glasses, we were interrupted by the thunderous sound of a cavalry's charging horses.

Chapter Forty-Five

The men in the room jumped to their feet. Fenella and Giffard put their goblets down and drew their swords—Giffard with his unfavored hand.

"Mayhap that was simply the first show of force?" he said to his wife.

A huge knight in mail armor burst through the door, sword aloft, a dozen knights at his flank. Scanning the room, he sheathed his sword and told his men to do the same. The knight came to kneel at my feet and lifted his visor.

"St Martin!" I let out a breath of relief.

"Forgive me, but are the children well?" Concern touched every part of his voice. "I came as soon as I heard of the king's death, but you were not at Haddington and had left no word of your whereabouts, Queen Mother."

Queen Mother. His use of my new title surprised me. But of course, always the proper knight, he would address me so. "*Merci* for your loyalty. Lady Fenella and Lord Giffard have risked their lives for my family's safety, but we are grateful for your reinforcements." How could I ever repay this good man?

Fenella stepped forward and called for another goblet. "I believe we have this under control, St Martin, but kindly join us."

"If you'll allow me to taste the drink first," he said to me.

He'd done so for Henry and, for reasons unbeknownst to me, seemed grateful to resume the duty.

He lifted my filled glass and sipped. "Delicate, earthy and sweet." He smiled and handed it back.

After we told St Martin about all that had transpired that day, he looked to me and said, "You have the power to rename Malcolm's regent if Donnchad dies. If you died, whomever is proclaimed guardian would have that same right. It would be an avenue to proclaiming his own king."

"Didn't King David secure these lines of power?" I asked.

"Normally he would have, but he did not expect to die, so there is no signed document to that effect." St Martin took a drink of his own wine.

Giffard shook his head. "Could a woman have such a legal right?"

"In the past it might be questioned, but Countess Ada has witnessed her own dowager with the king and written charters in her name." St Martin's face grew solemn. "Her voice would have legal power if a change were made which, mayhap, is one of the reasons the king felt she should make haste to safety after his death."

I was foolish to have delayed. "Then we must leave for Crail at once."

"Your Highness," St Martin said. "Given these attempts on your life, I believe going to Dunfermline and showing your health and lack of fear will do much to stabilize Malcolm's reign. We can leave from here the day before the funeral and from Dunfermline take you to Crail."

Giffard ran a hand through his hair. "Are we certain that plan is best? Whomever Eoan worked with knows the royal family is here. And with you having made inquiries to their whereabouts, won't it be common knowledge the royal family has fled? Mayhap it would be better if the countrymen knew them to be again at Haddington?"

I could see value in his line of thinking. "Aye, that is perchance best."

"With my men and Giffard's, we have fifty at least to guard you at Haddington," St Martin said. "With your permission, I'll station guards and keep watch tonight, and we'll leave for Haddington in the morning?"

I nodded.

"How many men did Eoan have with him?" St Martin asked.

"Only four," Giffard said.

"That probably means the rest of the king's guards are loyal, and there will be more at Haddington to help us."

"But how do we know?" Fenella's brows drew together. "I think it wise we use our own guardsmen."

I agreed. "Should our enemy always know our residence? Shall we return to Haddington after the funeral and stay only a day, leaving in secret the next night for Crail?"

"It's a good plan." St Martin nodded, but I could see in his eyes he wasn't convinced.

Exhausted, I bid farewell to my faithful friends and ascended the stairs to my chamber. On the way, I met William in front of the bedchamber door, sword in hand covered with the blood of another. He must have rescued it from below.

He'd taken my words too seriously. I read the fear in his eyes—a fear that was beginning to haunt my every thought.

"All is well." I put my hand on his arm that held the heavy sword. "St Martin has brought ample guards. After the funeral, we'll be off to Crail, safe at last." Did I believe my own words?

Wouldn't the person pursuing us continue if not caught?

My hands shook as I prepared to retire. How was I to act confident and full of health when I was as fragile as a weeping child?

Sleep didn't come for me that night. It was most disconcerting to think enemies were not just out there waiting but in my own household. I thought on my experiences with Eoan and of our picnic when we first moved to Haddington. How could I have guessed his betrayal? Would I constantly live in fear?

As if in answer, my mind shifted to faithful St Martin and Giffard who had been with me since I left my home of England fourteen years before. A flash of Fenella holding up her sword and saving my family brought a smile to my face, but then I shivered with the memory of Eoan's unnaturally twisted neck.

I rolled over, considering further how I should have done things differently. I'd pulled away from those closest to me when Henry thought he was being poisoned. We left my closest friends, and I doubted them. I would not do that again. Nae, I would allow myself to be surrounded and protected by those whom I trusted and simply pray they would stay true.

At last, I felt sleep coming. With it, I realized I would also be surrounded and protected by those I'd lost from this life. I thanked my sweet Matilda for showing me the passage to the underground caverns in my dream.

St Martin, Giffard, and more than fifty guards accompanied us safely across the Firth of Forth.

I was learning what it meant to "keep watch over my shoulder." I was as jumpy as a wild horse, suspicious of every stranger—even those in the company assigned to watch us.

Dread hovered from the haunting memory of Eoan's grisly death. Who had sent him? I was sure he didn't work alone.

Malcolm, accompanied by Mormaer Donnchad and many guards, greeted us on the north side of Forth at Queensferry. We dismounted speedily, and I held my young son. His shoulders still small, he carried the fate of his country.

After our embrace, Malcolm said, "I heard of the attempted threat on your lives. Are you certain the family is safe?"

I touched his cheek. "We are well cared for by God and loyal men. But be ever aware of who surrounds you."

"I will."

Donnchad approached. "I've brought more men-at-arms. Your family will be well protected."

"I thank you. Be it known that Alexander de St Martin and Hugh de Giffard and his wife are loyal to the crown and have protected our family thus far. May they join your guard?" I gestured to our entourage.

Donnchad bowed his head with acceptance.

I was grateful he recognized my Norman vassals. They now considered themselves as loyal to Scotland as I considered myself. "*Monsieur* Donnchad, Fenella de Giffard is the daughter of Herbert the Lord Chamberlain and wife of Hugh de Giffard and has been of great service to me. She saved my children's lives a few days ago. Without her, I would not be here this morning. I am in her debt."

Donnchad searched my cavalcade of soldiers with an odd look, probably looking for Fenella and wondering how to honor a woman for such a deed. "She will be remembered." He gestured to Malcolm. "Malcolm and his guards—*with yours*—shall lead us to Dunfermline. I shall forever be at his side. The mormaers of Scotland have chosen Malcolm as Ard Righ and High King. On the ninth, he will be crowned at Scone Priory. As you know, I will act as regent until his majority."

I tilted my head to acknowledge and honor Donnchad—the man my husband had told me to trust. But could I? Who *really* cared to protect our lives, and who wanted us dead?

Dressed in new royal robes of blue and red with sable collar and cuffs, an ornate belt, leather riding gloves, and a crown of gold, Malcolm mounted and led the procession on horseback to the abbey, head held high.

Donnchad stayed close at hand as people lined the roads to watch the procession.

I couldn't help but remember a similar experience when Henry and I had left Ludlow after his injury. Amidst the treachery, there had been support. We would survive this.

Some in the crowd cried. Others appeared stunned. Because their wise and beloved king had died with little warning" Or because his replacement was a child? Most of them waved and cheered at the well-nigh king. Their confidence increased my own. Malcolm was capable of his calling. I knew it. I just had to do all in my power to give him the opportunity to succeed.

Chapter Forty-Six

We arrived at Dunfermline by the afternoon and stayed within the palace for the evening. In the morning, I asked if I might be allowed to say my farewells to King David in private.

Donnchad agreed and had a guard check the sanctuary for my safety, telling me only kinsmen were within.

St Martin led me to a small chamber off the nave where the body was kept. He stood watch at the door, and I entered alone.

"You never knew me as you should have." A voice echoed toward me.

I rounded the corner and paused.

Kelton knelt in front of a long wooden box where the king lay wrapped in a burial cloth.

"You let me serve alongside Henry and never really *saw* me. Mayhap you can see me now?"

From this perspective, he looked so much like my sweet Henry. The cousins had favored one another in form and complexion.

A wave of grief for Henry washed over me. I breathed deeply, trying to stem the tears.

Kelton started and turned toward me, rising to his feet.

"I'm so sorry to interrupt," I said. "I wanted to do as you are and give my last respects." I moved beside Kelton and looked to the coffin. "King David was so kind to our family, especially since Henry's death. I don't think he ever healed from that loss."

Kelton nodded. "Some are saying he died of a broken heart."

"That could well be." I remembered when Henry passed. Had it not been for my children, I'd have longed to join him. "Why must death claim so many of our kinsmen?"

Kelton put an arm around me. "Death is the decision of God Himself. Who are we to question it?"

"Still, the loss is almost more than I can bear." Tears fell from my cheeks. "But I know we must embrace the living and move forward. That's what King David would have wanted." I squared my shoulders.

Kelton removed his arm and faced me. Though still in his prime, the effects of age had slightly hardened his features. A scar I'd never seen before ran down his cheek.

"What wound have you endured?"

"King Stephen of England is considering giving the crown to Matilda's son instead of his own." he lowered his voice, though we were the only two in the room. "I've been assisting the rightful heir to keep what he's entitled to. The politics of Scotland hold little sway for me now."

Through my grief, I'd not communicated with Kelton's family. It seemed his politics are far from mine. "Scotland is my home," I said firmly. "And I give it all allegiance."

He said nothing but glanced at the coffin.

It wasn't the time of the place, in front of King David's coffin, to discuss our differences. I smiled and softened my voice. "How are Isobel and your little daughter faring? She's almost three now?"

"Aye, my girls prosper. They stayed at home, as I've business to the south soon after the funeral. Will you be returning to Haddington?"

"Of course." It wasn't a lie. We were returning if only for a day. "Haddington is my home now." That was also true, although we would have to spend a season or more in Crail before I could return. Mayhap I would live the rest of my life at Haddington Palace surrounded by my children, Malcolm not far away.

"Make certain you're well-guarded. I've heard rumors."

"They are not just rumors," I said. "Recently there was a failed attempt on our lives. What have you heard?"

"Nothing specific, I'm sorry to say, but I'll keep trying to discover more." He looked me in the eyes. "I swear it."

How he resembled Henry! I gave him a swift embrace. "*Merci*, Kelton, for your loyalty. It's so good to see you again."

He left the room, and I stayed by the coffin, thanking King David for bringing me to Scotland, for choosing me for his good son, and for believing in my abilities to make charters and give to the Church what was needed. I prayed to God that my family would be kept safe and that the hearts of those who conspired against us would be softened—and that Malcolm could bring peace.

The funeral was well attended. Malcolm stood at the head of his grandfather's coffin. The rest of my children sat with me in the front pew. Amid those in the nave sat many of Scotland's nobles, including some of England's who allied their cause with ours.

In his vestments, Prior Robert started the service. His voice echoed into the expansive abbey, soaring to the arched-stone ceilings. Based on an earlier foundation, King David had built Dunfermline Abbey to honor his mother, Margaret, finishing it only two years ago. Had he known it would become his final resting place too? The Romanesque architecture—arched arcades and pillars decorated with carved chevrons was a truly magnificent burial place for a king.

To begin the service, a choir sang ethereal chants that brought peace to my soul, their voices angelic. Malcolm stood beside the prior who gave a long sermon sending King David's soul to God, then dedicated the grave.

My son's solemn face and dignified stance showed he knew his station.

My eyes met Madduch's and he stared hard at me before grinning an acknowledgment that didn't belong at a funeral.

Searching for St Martin, I found him in the shadows of the room, vigilant and at watch. Had the knight noticed Madduch's flirtatious interplay?

I avoided looking his way again, wishing he didn't stand near Malcolm, for whenever I viewed my son, Madduch stood in my line of vision. Had he planned such?

The prior finished and the mormaers hoisted the coffin draped with the royal standard onto their shoulders. A stone slab on the floor had been removed earlier and they carried the coffin down the stone steps to the underground crypt where King David's mother, father, and many of his brothers laid. There they would put him in a leaden casket. The last to join his family, he'd rest near them until the resurrection.

Malcolm walked unwavering down the stairs but I detected a slight falter in his bearing. He was yet a boy, my son, the forthcoming King of Scots. "Farewell, Grandfather. We shall miss you." I heard him say.

After the men left the vault, Herbert the Lord Chamberlain broke a white stave and tossed it in, symbolizing the end of his service to King David. I'd heard Malcolm would likely have him perform as lord chamberlain to him.

I deliberately didn't look for Madduch but he advanced with other nobles to give their final farewells.

A woman I didn't know stepped forward. "Farewell to a great monarch."

"Enter into your eternal rest." Madduch's voice.

I stood frozen, trying not to acknowledge my husband's enigmatic cousin who insisted on intruding into my life. I didn't want him to take my hand or look at me with his piercing eyes. His footsteps echoed away.

"David." I hoped he might hear. "I will treasure your goodness always." Memories of Henry's death flooded in. King David had been beside me to give comfort, but none stood in his place now. I truly was alone and void of familial support. Grandfather, father, and king, David truly loved us all—his family and his people.

As my children and I exited, guards stepped beside us and I tried to ignore this intrusion on my new life. I gazed upon the enormous crowd, touched that so many would come to honor King David, both in the abbey and out. The reverent quiet bespoke volumes.

The children and I stepped into the sunshine with guards close to our sides. I greeted those nobles allowed to be in my presence. They spoke kind words of the king.

After a time, Mary leaned toward me and whispered, "I'll take the children to the abbey nursery for their meal."

"I'm expected there myself." We headed toward the abbey palace.

"Lady Ada." Madduch stepped beside me. Close. Uncomfortably close.

A guard laid his hand on his sword, but I motioned that it was not necessary while I wondered if maybe it was.

"I wanted to give you my condolences. I'm sure you're feeling a great loss. David was a celebrated leader."

I gave him a quick nod but dared not look into his eyes. I focused on his cloak—his green cloak. "Your sentiments are appreciated."

Madduch took my hand. "May I visit you sometime soon?"

I swallowed. I had no interest in meeting with this man. I felt his stare on me, waiting for an answer. "Aye, mayhap we can become better acquainted," I said, hatching a plan.

He squeezed my hand meaningfully. "I'm pleased."

I lifted my gaze and our eyes met and held. "I'll see you in Haddington then," I said at last, grateful to leave but curious if he'd show up after we'd gone to Crail. I smiled, thinking of him finding an empty castle.

I hurried toward the palace—guards in tow—where I was to eat a meal and then finish final preparations for my journey to Haddington and our escape to Crail.

As I entered, the tapestries on the stone walls muffled my footsteps. Noises and aromas wafted up from the kitchen below. This is where Malcolm spent much of his time with Donnchad. I was glad for its pleasant feel.

Malcolm waited in the hall. "This place feels so empty now that Grandfather is gone. It would seem natural if he stepped out of the solar to greet us at any moment." His mature contemplations surprised me.

"Death plays tricks on us, does it not?" I put my arm around his shoulder. "People die and go away, never to return. Yet often it seems they are still near."

"Come." Malcolm motioned toward the abbey dining hall. "Our guests are here. Eat before your journey. A meal is prepared."

I took his arm and we entered the dining hall where St Martin's son, Arthur, sat at the table with more of my son's personal entourage. I'd forgotten that Arthur had started training about the same time as Malcolm. How pleasant to see them together.

Kelton and other cousins joined our ranks.

I was the only woman.

Donnchad stood and pulled out my chair.

Chaplain Robert stood to offer thanks to our Lord before we partook. Spiritually conscious for a child, Malcolm must have called on this kind and generous priest, his religious leader during the majority of his life. I was grateful to be reminded we were not alone.

After we ate, Chaplain Robert came to me. Concern weighted his normally cheery brow. "I hear you're returning to Haddington. Is that wise?"

He was a man of honor, and if there was anyone I could trust with our plans, it was him. "Aye, we are, but then on to Crail the next day in secret. If I may, I'd like to call on you to come visit me?"

He inclined his head in favor of such a plan.

"I miss Eads Hall and your daily devotionals. Are the people of the burgh well?"

"Many miss you." He met my eyes. "But what of you? I sense you are unsettled."

"Pray for me." My voice quivered. "Pray for my family. Pray for peace."

Chaplain Robert didn't ask more. "Aye, daily. May God bless and protect you."

I bid him farewell.

Kelton came forward.

I didn't realize he stood so close. The nape of my neck prickled.

He smiled kindly. "We may not see each other for many years. Write and keep me informed of the family's good health."

"Aye, I will." He embraced me.

I took Malcolm aside. He looked pale, but it was to be expected with all the recent strain. "I'm sorry to leave. I shall pray for your safety." I took his face in my hands and kissed his forehead, struggling to control my emotions at parting from him again. "Send for us when you feel it's safe to return."

"I will, Mother." His eyes held sorrow, but above all, I could see that he had courage and determination.

Flanked by St Martin and his guardsmen, I hurried to our waiting van where my children had been settled with Mary and my ladies.

In the doorway, Malcolm was equally protected by Donnchad and his knights. How could we not be safe?

Chapter Forty-Seven

We made certain our return to Haddington Palace was well known, anticipating that no one would expect us to remove from our permanent residence to an unknown location the following night.

I stumbled to bed in hopes of a restorative sleep, that I might have energy to make final preparations the next day for our trip to Crail, and awoke rested. So much had transpired since the black night with Eoan, but I hadn't had a single nightmare. Nor had any of the children complained of such. I suppose that was a blessing, but still I had no answers to who wanted us harmed.

Giffard had spent a good deal of time interviewing each staff member, trying to determine if any were aware of Eoan's intentions, and felt convinced that Eoan and his four guards were the only men compromised among our servants and guards.

Had Eoan been an emissary of Lord Madduch? Or mayhap Ranulf was still hoping for his lands back? There were even rumors of MacBeth's descendants trying to recover the throne.

It was hard to feel completely at peace. As I continued seeing to our final preparations, I passed Fenella twice, and each time she avoided speaking to me. I was again impressed that she was hiding something. Mayhap she knew more than I did or at least had a theory she was hesitant to share?

I completed a final pass through the children's rooms and descended the stairs with a small wooden swordsman, a hand-carved toy Malcolm had adored in his youth, that I loathed to leave behind.

Before I reached the last step, St Martin stepped forward, concern on his weary face.

"What is it?" Had he discovered something?

"May I have a word in private?"

Guards stood everywhere, and I couldn't think of a place we could be alone.

He motioned with his head to walk with him outside.

"Rest assured you are well protected." His heavy shoes crunch on the gravel. "We have increased our guard and secured the palace."

"*Merci*. I don't know what I'd do without you. You shall be rewarded."

He stopped and turned, his expression a mixture of anger and surprise. "I don't act out of compensation."

I laid my hand on his arm. "Of course, you don't. I apologize for offending."

He pulled from his tunic a small wooden box and handed it to me.

"What is this?" I opened the box and was surprised to find an ornate dagger in a leather sheath that could fit in my palm. I looked to him for explanation.

"Mayhap you'll never need it. I expect to have men surrounding you at all times. But there could be moments

-363-

when you're alone in your chambers, and I need assurance that you can defend yourself."

I chuckled.

He frowned.

"I doubt *this* will do any good. It's so small, and furthermore, I've never performed violence upon another. I can't imagine striking out to wound."

"Have courage. Though small, the blade is very sharp. Use it in the direst of circumstances and when the enemy is close enough to wound. Strike the face if you're able."

The direst of times? I recalled the moment Eoan stood at the top of the tunnel at Yester, sword drawn. A blade this small would only scratch an adversary. Mayhap if I agreed, St Martin would let me be. "*Oui*." I nodded.

He showed me how the sheath had a small hook. "You can attach it to the inside of the neckline of your gown without it being seen."

I turned the blade over in my hand.

"Be careful!" he warned.

Later that day, I attached the sheath with knife into the collar of my chemise. "Though I doubt I will use it," I said to no one in the room. Yet somehow, I was grateful it was hidden there.

As night fell, we stole to the stables. The escort of knights mounted their horses, except for St Martin, who wore the cloak of a peasant. He would drive the first cart with our belongings.

The women and children crowded into a shabby van, which Giffard and Fenella would command.

Glenore sat beside me with Adaline and Margaret snuggled to my right. The boys, Maggie, and Mary sat within reach. Wrapped in blankets, hopefully we appeared as cargo.

The knights stayed close by, but out of sight, as our small caravan quietly slipped out into a veil of darkness under a sliver of moon that hid behind sparse clouds. By day, the route was well travelled. Tonight, we had the road to ourselves.

The ride to port took a few hours, and we arrived well before sunrise.

With all aboard, the two boats launched northward amidst well wishes of, "God's speed," from the guards left behind to keep watch as we crossed where the Firth of Forth met the North Sea.

Giffard was aboard the first boat with my family and St Martin the second with servants and guards. Because the boys had toured Scotland with their grandfather, they had seafaring experience. For the girls, the gentle rocking of the boat was new to them.

The shore behind us moved quietly away, and I wondered if we would ever return. I'd left my home in Reigate. I'd left Eads Hall. Now I was leaving my home in Haddington. Three distinct periods of my life behind me, I turned toward the open sea. The cold air and salty spray mixed with the warm tears on my face. To the east, the jagged, shadowy Bass Rock protruded above the sea, menacing in the dark.

After several minutes, Maggie caressed my arm. "Come, *domina*. The captain has given us a cabin. Let's try to make ourselves comfortable." She led the children and me into a chamber below.

The room had one berth, and I lifted Margaret onto it. Her soft, dark hair rested in ringlets on the pillow. Adaline curled up beside her, so different in coloring, but so similar in temperament.

Mary handed me a stack of blankets and pillows. Together we made beds on the floor for the boys and I told Maggie to go be with Chadwick. After a minor debate, Mary agreed to squeeze in with the girls. I took a place beside William, who had not yet given over to sleep.

"Mother," he asked. "You talk of Father being near, but do you truly feel him?"

"Aye," I said, closing my eyes and hoping to dream of my late husband. "Fear not, for your father is guarding us and guiding us even now."

Before sleep took me, Giffard rapped on the door and stepped inside. "The captain advises you'll be safer to sail directly to Crail instead of the usual port at Earlsferry. It may be difficult to disembark and then climb the hill to the castle." He looked over the attentive faces peering up from makeshift beds—all the children awake now. He obviously didn't have children.

"Are you up to it?" He asked.

"Aye!" William sat up. "Malcolm and I have climbed that hill before. It's steep, but we can do it."

The girls nodded as if thinking the climb an adventure.

"If this wind keeps up, we'll reach Crail before sunrise," Giffard said. "Try to get rest. I'll stand guard on deck."

"*Merci*, Giffard."

I tried to relax and couldn't, so I climbed to the deck and watched as we moved northward through the night. I could barely make out the silhouette of the other boat. My heart beat a little faster with dread of danger, but as the strong wind blew my loose hair, a calm feeling came over me.

I'd told William his father was with us, and I prayed it to be so. This challenge would pass as all others in life. I put my hand to my heart and felt the lump of the small knife I'd hidden. With God's help, I'd prevail for the sake of my children and country.

The waves slapped against the boat, and I suspected fog rolling in.

Giffard joined me from the bow. His chipped-tooth smile still endeared him to me. "You could not sleep?"

I smiled. "Nae, but my brave little ones are so exhausted I doubt a mighty squall would wake them."

"Don't test fate until we arrive safely in Crail. The last thing we need is a storm," he said.

I glanced across the deck. We stood alone. "Where is Fenella? I'd like to thank her again for her bravery."

"I'm afraid she needs her rest." Giffard said it in a way that made me worry she may have been seriously injured. "Have you considered the events at Yester? Did you learn anything at the funeral that may make you suspect someone?"

This was the first we'd spoken openly since leaving Giffard's castle. "I believe Lord Madduch might be involved."

Giffard tilted his head. "Why would you consider him?"

I thought to Henry's funeral. "There was a time I believed he poisoned Henry, but St Martin dissuaded me of it."

Giffard looked unconvinced.

"He approached me in a most forward manner at the funeral, asking to see me alone. It wasn't the first time."

"You know, your Highness . . ." Giffard tried to keep a smile from his face but was unsuccessful. "There may be an entirely different reason for his request."

"Of course, I know what you're thinking, but there's something more to him than that. I've been told his greed for

-367-

the throne is so overt, he'd do anything to be near it." I chuckled. "I invited him to come visit me at Haddington."

Giffard laughed dryly. "Knowing you would be elsewhere? That was very brave of you."

I shrugged. "I might not meet him face to face, but if he does call at Haddington, I'll be informed, and we can see what he does next. Mayhap then we can find if he's part of a plot."

Giffard wagged his head. "I'm surprised you don't suspect Kelton. He's next in line as guardian for your children, unless you designate another." He cleared his throat. "If I may be so bold, Fenella and I would be honored to care for them if anything happened to you."

"May God bless you and Fenella for your willingness to keep my family safe. We must put it in writing. I doubt Kelton to be entangled in the plot. He's deeply involved in England's war at the moment and swears he has little interest in the goings on in Scotland. I believe him."

"Very well." Giffard suddenly looked tired. "But might I suggest, rather than waiting for Lord Madduch to come to Haddington, we send spies to follow him? The sooner we discover our enemies, the better."

"Agreed." To think the man most probably was responsible for the attacks on my family had kissed my fingertips yesterday. My fist curled.

Giffard leaned on the railing. "Are you ready for this change in your life?"

I glanced at him then at the dark blackness of the sea. "Providence has given me several turns in the road. I hope each brings me to a better place. I pray for rest from our troubles during our time at Crail."

He nodded. "Fenella and I will stay near as long as you need us—St Martin, too. But that was not the change I was speaking of." He stepped closer to me. "You are a young woman but mother of a child king. Any man you marry will be given more power than should be his right."

I blinked at Giffard. "You would condemn me to a life of loneliness?" My tone grew louder than I'd intended.

He bowed at my indignation. "Certainly not. It's yours to decide. But be aware, any match may threaten the throne."

"I appreciate your loyalty, Giffard." I glanced toward the cabin where my children slept. "I think I'll go below and try to rest."

I made my way down the steps and returned to my bed beside William, but I didn't sleep.

Thoughts raced through my mind of spending my future alone and my duty to protect the crown and the royal line. Henry had told me of the dangers and asked me to think carefully about taking on the burden of being his wife.

"Henry," I whispered into the dark. "Did you know that protecting the throne would become my burden—that after you left me, I'd spend my life alone? I have no protector to appoint me a worthy husband. Your father is gone, and so I shall remain solely yours forever."

Before this sennight, I'd not fully understood my power. I'd fought the idea of remarrying because I still grieved for Henry. But would I always feel thus? I wanted to feel love and give it in return. My heart slowed at the realization that was never to be. Because of my status as the mother of the king—and possibly future kings—my duty to protect the royal house of Scotland had to come before my own happiness.

Chapter Forty-Eight

I rolled onto my side and stared at the dim light entering under the door. When Henry had been alive, being his wife was never a burden. I would not have wanted to spend my life any other way. I gazed over the sleeping children around me. "We have noble and bright children, Henry. You'd be proud of them."

"Aye, Ada." I imagined his reply. "We were happy."

My mother had often bespoken of my greatness. I never believed I could become the woman she'd hoped me to be. Oh, how I'd wished I could! On what path had fate now placed me?

After a time, I dozed only to awaken when the sea tossed me against William. I climbed the stairs to assess our situation and he followed.

"You should sleep whilst you can," I advised him.

Giffard stood at the bow, keeping watch.

"But I cannot." Wrapped in his blanket, William went to the ship's railing. "Look beyond." He pointed toward a dark hump of land. "A welcome landmark, Grandfather used to say. It's the Isle of May. We are almost there."

I breathed a sigh of relief.

William asked, "When will I see Malcolm next?"

"The next time I see him, you shall go with me." The two boys shared a fierce love for one another. Ten years old was very young to be separated from such a good friend.

"I shall miss him," he said.

I affectionately tossed his auburn hair. "I shall miss him too."

"We shall never live as brothers again, shall we?" His voice carried much emotion for one so young.

I put my arm around him, pulling him close. "No matter what you each are doing or how far apart you are, you and Malcolm will always be brothers, do you understand? It's more than where you are—it's *who* you are."

The same could be said of me and Henry. No matter where he was or how far away, I was still his wife and would remain faithful until the end of my days.

William hesitated before asking his next question. "Are you disappointed that you will never be queen? You thought you would be before Father died, did you not?"

I realized then how much William had matured since Henry's death. "We all expected your father to become king. Sometimes fate gives us other plans, and we simply must choose to do our best. I never desired the throne but I have always had a great desire to help the people of Scotland."

"And Malcolm? What if fate gives him other plans? What if he dies like Father or Grandfather?"

I looked closely at my son. He was strong, healthy, and quick minded. Naturally, he would ponder such questions. "It's my daily prayer that God gives Malcolm the fortitude to be a great king. You should have the same prayer."

William swallowed hard.

The frustration on his face told me I'd not sufficiently answered his question. "But what if Malcolm dies?"

I hated talking about the possibility. "Then you would become king, and if not you, David. The greatest tutors are training you, and Lord St Martin and Lord Giffard will continue your military education in Crail. Mayhap Regent Donnchad will bring you to him? You will be prepared to do well if you become king."

William's eyes widened and a look came over him as if he, for the first time, truly understood the kingship would likely fall on him someday.

A shout came from a guard. "Look! We have arrived at Crail!"

William echoed him, adding, "We are home!"

I was surprised that William could think of Crail as home. His words gave hope that I too would consider this northern sanctuary in the same manner. I imagined it might take quite a while.

The helmsmen brought the boats to the pier.

Watch fires lit the shore ahead as if a sign of friendly welcome.

"It's so beautiful." William breathed.

The stone edifice loomed dark above the harbor. The steep incline, covered with tufts of grass and weeds, and the stark rock wall reaching the sky made it feel like a prison.

As soon as we arrived at the landing, a few guards ascended the bank to the castle. Minutes later, servants came hurrying down to us. How comforting to recognize smiles on trusted faces and to hold warm hands extended to lift us from the boat.

One young, but muscular man hefted me in his arms. "Hold on, your Highness!" he said, starting up the bank.

"I can walk," I assured him with a startled laugh. "No need to strain yourself."

The children were also carried in strangers' arms.

"It's my honor to carry the Queen Mother of Scots to her castle," my human packhorse said.

His respectful words changed my outlook on this ordeal, and I tried to be gracious at his sacrifice—the servants helping us well before they would normally rise from their beds.

We, as royal vagabonds, entered the castle and were warmly greeted by the servants with kindness and respect. Enticing odors wafted from the kitchen. We were served delicious porridge, eggs, bread, and ale. The maids tended to the children. William led the way for his brothers and sisters, excited to show them their new rooms.

Mary turned to me. "I'll make certain the children are settled. Do not worry about us. Get rest, my lady."

With St Martin getting his company settled, and Giffard looking after Fenella, I was left with a seasoned servant from Crail named Jack.

He led me to my new bedchamber in its own wing.

I didn't like being so far from the children.

Jack bowed his head. "Anything you need simply pull this cord. It's connected to a bell in the servant's quarters, and we will respond promptly."

"That's convenient." I wanted him to think it unique of the castle he seemed so proud of, but I'd seen bell-pulls at the royal palace in London.

"Crail Castle holds many such bewilderments. Built before King David's time, it will be here when we're all but forgotten."

The sentiment didn't comfort me. As the servant walked away, I closed my door. I wanted to do naught but sleep. Still dressed, I pulled the drapes closed and laid on the bed.

My sleep was filled upsetting dreams. I awoke, wondering why light seeped through the slits of the curtains. With blurry eyes I stared into the newness of my strange surroundings and remembered where I was—Crail Castle.

I fell back into a light sleep and awakened with a start when my bed moved.

Chapter Forty-Nine

As quick as I could, I jumped from the bed to my feet.

A man in a green cloak, hood drawn over his head, laughed and then lunged.

I rushed toward the pull-sash to alarm the servants. Before I could reach it, strong arms snaked around my shoulders and waist.

"Lord Madduch," I screamed. "How dare you?"

With my bedchamber suite so far from the main part of the castle, no one would hear my call.

He must have known the same thing, for he didn't try to cover my mouth. "You think me that drunken seducer? You're as foolish as King David who thought Crail would bring you safety. I grew up playing in these walls." Then he simply laughed, and in that laugh, I recognized his voice. "Kelton? *Why?*"

His grip slackened, and he turned me to face him, hands still clamped to my upper arms with a strength that made fleeing impossible. He smiled as though we were simply at another family gathering. "Oh Ada, do you know the trouble you've caused me? Why could you not have fallen by Eoan's hand? It would have made this much easier."

I was surprisingly calm. "Did you kill King David?"

"In a manner of speaking." He smiled. "Considering his broken heart was due to the death of his son."

"Henry!" I stared into Kelton's dark eyes. How could evil flash in eyes so similar to Henry's?

"It was Ranulf who wanted Henry dead. Well, he paid me to do it after he blundered the poison in the drink at Ludlow and the kidnapping." Regret flashed in his eyes. "I had no choice. Had Uncle simply granted me an earldom, it never would have needed to happen. I allowed your boys to grow up strong and tall. You should thank me, for Ranulf wished them dead."

I could barely comprehend what Kelton was saying. "We're family. You married my cousin. You have a child. How could you risk all that?"

"A girl." Disgust filled his expression. "My wife had a daughter and can have no more. I had hope for a son when the jezebel carried my child, alas, she had another girl."

"Sophia!" No wonder the child looked so much like she belonged to our family. "You killed Jasmine?"

"Nae." He shrugged. "She killed herself with a potion meant for me—a good trick I played on her. A shame she is no longer helpful with *her* poisons. But there are others who can help." He sneered. "You'll be pleased to hear that whilst your enemy, Ranulf, was a guest at my father-in-law's house, Peverel attempted to kill him with poisoned wine. Three other men who drank the wine died, but I hear Ranulf still suffers with agonizing pain. I expect he'll die soon."

"You and Ranulf worked together?" What was I to believe? Kelton was mad.

-376-

"Aye, well, better to get rid of those who know your sins. And I've found that my father-in-law would rather I, not Ranulf, garner the earldom of Carlisle."

Although I had no love for Ranulf, the story of his demise still sickened me. "You are an evil man. How could I have not seen the extent of your cowardliness sooner?"

"Cowardliness? I want the kingdom to be at peace."

"Under your rule," I said, pushing against his grasp. "What of my boys?"

He held tighter.

My hands tingled from lack of blood.

"Oh, King Malcolm may become a little sickly, but he shall live for years yet. His mind has been too *poisoned* by Donnchad to be kept in his place long. But William will live as long as it suits me, mayhap for the rest of his days. We shall be as father and son, and you can go to your grave knowing he'll be well cared for."

My chest tightened with the thought of Malcolm having the same fate as his father. "Nae!" I struggled against Kelton's grip.

His hands left my arms and made for my throat.

In that same moment I kicked his shin and then ducked, pulling the blade out of my chemise. I sliced at Kelton's face, just missing his eye.

He backed away, clutching his cheek. "The kitten has claws."

I didn't pause but ran for the sash, grasping the fabric and pulling with all my might. I yanked over and over, expecting Kelton to grab me at any moment. I turned with the blade still in my hand, but no one was in the room.

It was many minutes before the bedchamber door opened and Maggie stepped in. "What's wrong, *domina*?"

I still clung to the sash, my mind in a frenzy. "Get Giffard—St Martin. Someone!"

She ran down the hall.

I stumbled forward, looking throughout the chamber, under the bed, behind the drapes. Where had Kelton gone?

St Martin rushed in with Jack and two guards.

"What's happened, my lady?" St Martin looked me over from toe to head. "Your neck is red."

"It's Kelton. Where did he go?" I said, knowing St Martin wouldn't have the answer.

"Kelton?" He creased his brow in confusion.

Fenella and Giffard hurried into the room, winded from running.

"It was Kelton. It's always been him." I was talking too quickly, but I couldn't slow down. "He killed Henry. He was here just moments ago. He tried to strangle me. He talked of poisoning Malcolm. My son must be warned!" I couldn't control the trembling in my legs as I sat on the bed.

Maggie sat next to me and wrapped me in an embrace.

"It's said the castle is riddled with secret passages," Jack spoke up. "But they're not mapped as far as I know."

St Martin ran his hand along the walls but didn't find any openings.

The guards checked the adjoining rooms.

"He killed Henry." Tears finally fell.

St Martin stepped to the Giffards. "Fenella, stay with the Queen Mother. Your husband and I will take the guards and ensure every road from the castle is covered. If we can't find the rat within the walls, we'll find him as he attempts to flee." He stepped to me and bowed. "I will send a messenger immediately to King Malcolm with warning of Kelton's threat."

The men retreated, leaving two guards at my door.

Fenella sat in a nearby chair, looking pale, her cheek wound swollen.

I wiped my tears but couldn't stop shaking. "How could Kelton have done it? He hasn't lived near us in years."

"Well," Fenella's voice was weak. "Mayhap he has an accomplice?"

I shuddered. "Aye, he said Ranulf and Peverel." I closed my eyes and drew in a deep breath. I could succumb later, but now I needed to be resolute and think clearly. "I cannot endure watching Malcolm go through a slow, painful death like his father."

"How did it happen?" Fenella looked to the ceiling, biting her lip. "Your husband had guarded protection and individuals tasted his food. How did Kelton poison him?"

"Kelton never said, but I must warn my son. I must go and tell him." I rose to my feet and made my way to the door.

"St Martin is sending a messenger," Fenella reminded me.

"Nae," I turned to her. "I must see him for myself—know that there is no poison. Kelton confessed at length, and I worry I've forgotten some of it. What if I left out a crucial word that could save my son's life? I have to go to Dunfermline and speak to Malcolm. I must make certain he's safe."

"I'm going with you, Mother." William stood in the hallway.

"Nae. It's too dangerous."

He lifted his chin. "You gave me your word that I could go when next you visited my brother. I too need to make sure he's safe."

I looked to Fenella for help. She nodded and got to her feet. "Though I think you foolish, I will arrange horses at once for the both of you. I'm sure St Martin will want an escort." She left in a huff.

We traveled due west on the road to Dunfermline with the afternoon sun over our heads. St Martin refused to allow me to ride on horseback, insisting on a covered van so no one saw the Queen Mother away from Haddington. Though slower, it allowed William and me to rest on the way. A messenger had left before us, riding at top speed to warn the king of a threat to his life.

We'd received no word about Kelton, which meant he'd most likely escaped.

Regent Donnchad was greatly concerned at St Martin's arrival. "For what purpose have you come?" He drew his sword, approaching St Martin. Then he saw me and William descend from the van. "Tell me what's happened." He sheathed his weapon, but his concerned expression multiplied.

"Malcolm may already be exposed," I said, hearing the hysteria in my voice.

William put a gentle hand on my arm. "The Queen Mother wishes to see with her own eyes that my brother is well." He addressed Donnchad with great authority for one so young.

St Martin stepped forward to explain. "Kelton attacked her Highness at Crail and admitted to poisoning the prince. We must be certain Malcolm is well." His tone left no room for disagreement.

Instead of being offended, Donnchad lowered his head. "I've been worried of the young king's health. His food is tasted, and we've taken every precaution, but he has complained of frequent headaches and fatigue."

We entered the large manor where I had so recently had supper after the funeral.

Malcolm greeted us with surprise. He had always been thin for his age, and had been pale at the funeral, but now that he was before me, I was certain he didn't look well. I struggled with what to tell him.

Regent Donnchad took that choice from me. "Sire, there is concern for your safety. If it's agreeable with the Queen Mother, I believe you and your brother should spend the day in the abbey whilst we examine the house."

I thought it a wonderful idea and was pleased that Malcolm took the news without any visible signs of worry. Secretly, I believed he was thrilled to spend time with William.

"May I show Prince William our grandfather's gravesite now that they've placed the stone?" he asked, looking to both Donnchad and myself.

In unison we agreed, and the boys ran off, two hefty guards behind.

I described the details of my experience with Kelton to Donnchad.

He asked me to repeat much of it then shook his head. "Since Ranulf and William Peverel are Englishmen, the matter of arrest is out of our hands. The best we can do is send a missive to King Stephen with that information, making certain justice is done, but it's likely Kelton will have clean hands when it comes to Ranulf's poisoning."

"Agreed, and in so doing he likely removes all the evidence of his other heinous activities," I said.

St Martin paced the room, clearly frustrated. "Kelton did a brilliant job of telling the Queen Mother naught that can be verified."

"We shall cover every room, especially King Malcolm's personal effects," Donnchad said. "Anything that would touch the royal mouth or eyes is suspect."

We spread out immediately. I went to Malcolm's bedchamber, smelling and touching every item of clothing, every book, hoping something would stand out. I confiscated his comb and tooth-twig, knowing they could be replaced by ones not infused with poison.

Housecarls did the same through the kitchen, the solar, the library, and even the stables. The day wore on with dozens of us making our best attempt to find something hidden that could not be found. As time for the evening meal approached, I was discouraged with the hopelessness of our quest.

Donnchad walked into the large dining hall where the others had gathered to discuss our options. "We had planned to begin visiting each earldom in turn with the young king to strengthen support and assure the Scottish people of continued peace. We will attempt to secure every castle and stronghold from such an invisible threat, but I would not encourage delaying. The attack on the royal family in Yester has been whispered at nearly every hearth in the kingdom and calming the people's concern must be of our utmost import."

"Couldn't you stay here or go to Edinburgh and call the earls to come to you, thereby maintaining a safe environ for my son? What if the poison lies in wait? Lord Kelton said Malcolm would last for years as though it had begun already. My husband was also ill for years."

St Martin added, "Scotland is not England. The Scot court travels, showing they are servants of the people, unlike the country of our birth which has its head in London. That condition may allow less protection for King Malcolm. To change that may be hard for the Scots to accept, especially with their new king. Another choice is that once Kelton is caught, we can force him to tell us where the threat lies. Guards are combing the countryside. He will be found."

I was not so certain and felt a great weight on my shoulders as I admitted defeat. "Very well. All we can do is be vigilant and pray Kelton is brought to justice. If you'll have the boys summoned, Prince William and I will return to Crail after sustenance."

The meal was more solemn than the one at King David's funeral. The only people talking were the two royal brothers. Malcolm told William of his new stallion and how he was helping train the beast.

He must take after me, I fondly remembered my love of riding Cooper across open fields. As I listened to stories of the animal bucking and Malcolm holding on for dear life, I worried about his physical safety in addition to threats of poison. As king, danger went part and parcel with the calling. I'd have to put my trust in the good people who had dedicated their lives to my son's training and protection. Mayhap Fenella was right, I shouldn't have come.

As we stood to leave, I embraced the yet to be crowned king, my eleven-year-old boy, then kissed his forehead. "Your mother will be ever praying for your welfare and success. Of that, you can be sure. I will see you next in Scone at your coronation."

The sun had begun setting, and it would be dark before I arrived at Crail Castle. How sad that it would be another day before I could see it in the light.

William bid farewell to his brother by punching him in the arm.

Malcolm would not have it. "Come brother, if I must act the part of king then you must be a gentleman. Shake my hand properly."

William stood tall and did as he was told. "Your hand is getting as rough as Father's." He scrunched up his face as their hands unclasped.

Malcolm shook his head. "It's all that riding."

I froze. Before his death, in the garden at Eads Hall, I touched Henry's hand and commented on its roughness. I grasped Malcolm's hands. Could it be the reigns? The feed? Nae. His hands were not simply rough on the palms, but the backs appeared reddened and weathered.

"Mother, what are you doing?" he asked.

"Your riding gloves. Bring them to me."

"Your Highness?" Donnchad intervened. "What do you suspect?"

"I'm not certain, but the gloves may have poison in them," I said. "Send a messenger to Whitfield to fetch Boudica—and have her come to Crail. She's a midwife of note. If you have trouble finding her, Chaplain Robert may be of assistance."

Malcolm had retrieved the gloves and handed them to me.

I smelled them and guessed the pungent odor to be poison, then handed them to St Martin.

"Aye. Poison," he said, relief finally in his eyes.

"Probably something Jasmine had conjured," I told him. Turning to Malcolm, I asked, "Where did you get these?"

"They were a gift from the people of Fife."

"Kelton, more likely," Regent Donnchad said, as if insulted to link his people to the crime.

I drew a steadying breath and tucked the gloves into my satchel, clutching it under my arm, determined to not let them out of my sight until I faced Boudica.

"Can you and the king come to Crail with us?" I asked Donnchad. "I'd like you to hear what Boudica has to say."

He agreed, and we left within the hour, arriving home long after the little ones were in bed.

That night I slept soundly, not worried about my oldest son's safety or someone sneaking into my room. I had the gloves, Kelton had left Crail, and Regent Donnchad would keep harm away from Malcolm. I was so exhausted, I could have slept through anything, and apparently, I did.

Chapter Fifty

I awoke in Crail Castle the next afternoon to the sun high in the heavens, feeling at last a degree of peace. From my window, I saw fishermen come and go with their cogs. The water was so blue it rivaled the cloudless sky.

Casting my gaze over the quaint fishing town, I had to smile. As William had said when we first arrived, it indeed felt like home.

After dressing and hiding my satchel in my room, I descended the stairs and went to the dining hall.

Glenore hastened forward to serve me. "You'll never guess the events of this day." Her face was aflush, the house surprisingly quiet.

"Aye?" I asked.

She set before me fruit and cheese. "They found Kelton! Dead at a roadhouse not far from here. They believe he had been poisoned. It serves that scoundrel right, I say."

Both relief and dread made the breath catch in my throat. "Are you certain?"

"Of course." Glenore gestured to the servant in the corner. "Aren't that so, Jack? Tell her Highness."

He nodded. "'Tis as she says."

Glenore smiled. "Lord St Martin is there right now."

It would be days before Boudica arrived and I could ask her about the poisoned gloves. But Malcolm was safe, as was our household. "Kelton will face the Lord's judgment for his crimes." I sat up straighter, determined to make this a brighter day. "Where are the children?"

The question made Glenore laugh. "Wait 'til ye see. Crail Castle is such a surprise. Though from the outside its dark and rough, the garden be rare."

Done with my late meal, I rose and followed Glenore to a wide door.

She swung it open.

I caught my breath. The nape of my neck prickled.

The grass was as green as I'd ever seen. To the far right, Sybil played with her boys near the pond, but my gaze went to the center of the scene where stood a beautiful oak tree near a tall stonewall. The tree grew as high as a castle turret, its trunk as wide as four men. The generous canopy spread its branches to act as a protection over all my children, little Sophia with them. My heart cried out that she now belonged.

The dream of my youth. The dream I had again when I first wed.

I breathed out a sigh of relief to see such a setting. It was as if a master artist painted the scene with strokes of unity and peace—a picture of God's hand in our lives. He knew before I married Henry that this would be my final joy.

I'd hoped the place of my dream would be at Eads Hall, but the trees never grew tall enough. At Warkworth, the elm trees grew crooked from the wind. I even perused the oak at Haddington, but it had no stone wall behind.

In the distance over the wall, I saw the gentle shore and again had an overwhelming sense of peace and of *home*.

William ran to my side. "Mother, we've prepared a place for you."

I approached a bench adorned with wildflowers.

Adaline smiled. "It's the throne of the Queen of the Fairies, and that is you." She reached toward me with a crown of wildflowers.

I knelt before my children, and Adaline placed the crown on my head.

The sweet smells of the honeysuckle and primrose took me to my own childhood play at Reigate. I laughed at the children's whimsy.

They ran in circles, joyful to be in this enchanting place that would be our home. Odd that I'd feel this way after being here only two days.

Fenella and Giffard stepped out from the home and waved to me. How grateful I was for such kind friends.

Glenore suggested a game of hide and seek, and soon my family scattered to the far reaches of the garden where Sybil and her children played at the pond.

Madduch was only half-right when he'd said, "A heart that is broken is a heart that has been loved." I knew now that a heart that has been well loved is also a heart that can heal.

In the moment of quiet, I thought of Matilda. She used to stare at me with a look that made me feel things were as they should be. I felt that way this day. Of a sudden, I felt Henry and Matilda were with me, holding hands and watching. Love bloomed across my heart in a depth I knew to be eternal.

I would go on and serve my children and country with the duty God had given me.

The End

Acknowledgements

When my friend, Charlene Hobbs, a professional genealogist, delivered to my home the gift of ten notebooks containing my family genealogy, I was stunned. It was a treasure trove of information. As I glanced through the pages, I stopped at the sight of one name—Countess Ada de Warenne. My heart melted and I began to weep like a child.

I felt a strong desire to learn everything I could about my ancestor who lived over nine hundred years ago. But why?

My husband Brent and I began a journey to learn what we could about Ada. During a five-year span of time, we spent sixteen months traveling throughout England and Scotland to search records, visit historical sites, and walk the land Ada de Warenne walked. During that incredible venture, I grew to love my 24th great-grandmother. Her story needed to be told. Not only her love story with her handsome husband, Prince Henry of Scotland, but the story of a spirited and fearless woman—dedicated to serving her family and the people of her adopted Scotland.

This book was written in first person to read more like a memoir—as if Ada were speaking to us in our present day. Writing the book in this manner became a spiritual experience and consequently, it also did so for most everyone involved in the process of creating the manuscript. At times, many of us felt Ada and Henry with us, as if they were peeking over our shoulders and encouraging us to carry on. Their joy became our joy, their sorrow ours, too. I hope many readers feel that same spirit as they immerse themselves in the story.

While writing, I was blessed with the best of helpers, editors, teachers, advocates, and friends who shared their time and talents in unparalleled ways.

I am grateful first and foremost to my husband, Brent. He was forever patient with my intense fascination and deep love for Ada and her family. Brent has been with me each step of the journey. He's read all the books and articles I've read about the royal family, and he's been with me during every venture. He has read each page of this book, sometimes multiple times, and has been honest when it needed something more. I will love and treasure you, sweetheart, throughout all eternity.

Thank you to my family—children and grandchildren—for there are a bunch of you. I appreciate your support with this adventure. I hope I make you proud.

Thank you to my dear friend, Helen Robertson. It was divine intervention when we met in Haddington, Scotland. Helen shared her extraordinary knowledge of medieval events with great generosity, helping to fill in the missing links of Ada's life. Helen is the embodiment of going the extra mile, literally, driving Brent and I to sights from Ada's life throughout Scotland and England.

I am deeply grateful to Joan Sowards for her dedicated contributions to the original framework of the book. Thanks to Christine Thackeray who took my four hundred pages of Ada's life and helped add the fictional drama that was needed. Her imagination was inspiring. Thank you, Janet Moore Clark, for your talented editing, creative contributions to the story line, as well as the beautiful book trailer. Thank you, Lori Freeland, for your fantastic final edit, making the book shine.

Finally, the book would not have been completed without my friend and accomplished writer, Ora Smith. I shouldn't have been surprised when she told me she is also the 24th great granddaughter of Prince Henry and Countess Ada. That is no coincidence. There are no words to describe Ora, except to say (and she will blush) that she is literally an angel without wings. She is a treasure to me and to this project. Her inspirational contributions and her dedication to historical accuracy brought this book to its completion, for which I am deeply and sincerely grateful.

About the Author

Married 48 years to her husband Brent Hinze, Sarah is a dedicated wife and mother. She's been blessed with nine children, thirty-one grandchildren, and several foster children. Sarah reaches out to an even larger family as an avid genealogist in pursuit of family history. She finds it heart-warming to learn of ancestors' lives—many of whom are from the British Isles.

A Pawn for a King is Sarah's first historical fiction novel. She's written nonfiction books for over twenty years. Find her books at www.sarahhinze.com.

Email Sarah at sarahhinze.hinze@gmail.com

Thank You!

I hope you've enjoyed this book. For more information about Ada de Warenne's life, land transactions, and places she lived, go to Sarah Hinze's website at: www.sarahhinze.com. There you will find photos, videos, up-to-date research, and current speaking events.

Coming 2021 – Book Two of the Ada de Warenne series

Queen Mother to the Kings of Scots: Ada de Warenne 1123-1178

Enjoy a Sneak Peek!

Chapter One

Anno Domini 1153
Scone, Scotland

Eleven years, two months and five days—the age of my eldest son—the heir-apparent king of the Scots, Malcolm mac Henry, Prince of Strathclyde and Cumbria is taking the position his father was prepared to acquire. If he had lived.

In front of thousands of Scots, I stood tall next to my second eldest son, ten-year-old William, and looked toward Scone Priory—a small stone building only a few decades old.

Malcolm was within. As a woman, I was not permitted to watch Prior Richard ritually wash Malcolm and dedicate him to the Lord by the laying on of hands.

Had it been only a fortnight since King David died of a broken heart over his son—my beloved husband Henry— poisoned by his own cousin? Though a year had passed since Henry's death, I missed him as if he had been holding my hand this morning, walking with me through the gardens of Crail Castle.

Both pride and fear battled in my heart. It seemed the powerful enemies and evil forces working against my family never rested. Was Malcolm like his late father, to become the next pawn in a game of battling kingdoms?

The crowd remained reverent on this holy land that was once the center of an early Christian cult of Culdees—ancient worshippers of God. As the queen mother, I hoped to continue the work of the two pious Scottish queens before me and build up the church in Scotland, helping the people abandon their ancient superstitions. Although I married a Scot prince, I was a Norman of English birth and had yet to win the hearts of the people.

Malcolm came out of the priory with the clergy. He wore a clean and simple grey tunic, not the robes of a king. He smiled shyly and waved, his dark auburn hair gleaming in the bright sun.

Cheers from the crowd broke the spell of reverence.

Mormaer Donnchad, the Earl of Fife and the forthcoming regent king, walked behind Malcolm. Born the year before my deceased husband, Donnchad grew up with Henry and pledged to the security of my family. His loyalty helped me sleep at night.

Following Celtic tradition, we all gathered at *Caislean Credi*, the Hill of Credulity, a grass-covered mound marked with a stone cross. It was here, under God's canopy of blue summer skies, the remaining rituals would be performed.

Prior Robert stepped forward and spoke to all in attendance. "This mount is built with soil from all of Scotland. Before landowners left their homes to come here, they placed a small amount of soil in their boots to signify they walked on their own land. To pledge their loyalty to the king, they emptied the soil from their boots onto this hill." Prior Robert smiled as he looked over the mound. "So you see, centuries of dirty boots have grown this mound into a hill."

Chuckles rippled through the crowd.

"Unlike most monarchies of the world—where the king owns the land—in Scotland, the people own the land. The King of Scots is their respected protector. Their law-giver."

Laughter turned into an approving murmur. As a young woman, eighteen years before, I had been at the glorious coronation of England's King Stephen in Westminster Chapel, with all its pomp and grandeur. This ceremony was different in comparison—a mixture of Celtic and Roman customs.

"Now we invite Malcolm, our beloved King David's grandson, and son of Prince Henry to stand before the Stone of Scone," the prior said.

Scotland's most prized relic, no bigger than my pillow, the reddish-grey sandstone was believed to have been a headrest for the Israelite patriarch Jacob. Some called it the Stone of Destiny.

Malcolm stepped before the oblong rock that had been laid atop several wooden slabs.

"This stone is the very same that Father Jacob slept on at Bethel and dreamed of angels descending and ascending to

-397-

heaven." Prior Robert bowed to a man near me wearing a woven mantle of bright greens and blues. "The High Seannachaidh will recite the young king's royal ancestry."

The seannachaidh climbed the mound and faced the crowd. "The mormaers of Scotland verify it is Malcolm mac Henry's right to serve as Ard Righ and High King."

Hoping he was right, I again experienced both pride and fear. I'd heard lords of the Hebrides self-governed and gave a nominal allegiance to the crown. Especially Somerlad, who was the lord of the Isles.

"I shall recite both Scot and Pictish royal ancient lines." The sennachaidh chanted in the manner of a Gaelic poem the history of the royal house. I recognized names such as Fergus, MacAlpin, Constantine, Macbeth, and Duncan. At the end, he sang the name of King David in a respectful tone.

I bowed my head, grateful to be part of this noble family.

Prior Robert again stepped forward and announced he would administer the oath binding Malcolm to the obligations of kinghood and instructed Malcolm to repeat the pledge.

Glancing at me for just a moment, Malcolm looked to the crowd, his expression sincere. "I promise to maintain the true worship of God, protect the realm, uphold the laws of Scotland, and do justice without favor."

The prior bowed deeply to him then turned to the throng. "Let it be known and recorded that on the Ninth day of June, in the year of our Lord 1153, Prince Malcolm of Scotland, the grandson of King David mac Malcolm, became King of Scots."

Malcolm smiled widely and raised his hands.

The crowd erupted in thunderous cheers and began chanting, "Malcolm, Malcolm . . ."

I wanted to fall to my knees and sob but instead grasped William's arm to keep myself upright.

"He will be a great king, Mother." William clasped the hand I'd put on his arm.

Next in line for the throne, I worried just as much for William's safety as I did for Malcolm's. Could we find our enemies and stop them before they killed my sons?

A trumpet blast silenced the assembly, and a group of noblemen came forward, one carrying the crown of Scotland atop a cushion.

Regent Donnchad said, "King Malcolm be seated upon the Stone of Scone."

Malcolm sat.

Donnchad picked up the crown and placed it upon Malcolm's head.

A collective breath went through the throng.

"I speak for all of Scotland's people," Donnchad said. "be it landowners, mormaers, thanes, lords, and chiefs. I pledge to support you to the death with my sword, my words, and my all."

"So say I," the other nobles chanted.

Malcolm inclined his head. "I Ard Righ will uphold you as you uphold me."

Three nobles came forward. One laid the traditional sword across Malcolm's thighs, the next placed a scepter in his hand, and a third gave him a large book.

Malcolm was as calm as a true king.

Donnchad pointed to the symbolic relics. "This is the sword of state that protects the Scottish people, the scepter represents the power to govern with justice, the Book of Laws is the word by which we are governed."

William appeared to take in the ritual with wonder.

I sent a silent prayer to God. *May we have Your watchful eye and kind blessings.*

"Scots come forward and meet your new king," Donnchad called out.

Hundreds of landowners came forward one by one, stating their name and shaking Malcolm's hand as a pledge of their fealty.

During the past year, King David had persuaded the Scottish chiefs to recognize Malcolm as his heir to the throne. But with England's Anarchy still raging, shifting alliances, and frequent disputes over the northern lands of England, would they hold true? Would Malcolm maintain Cumbria and Northumbria, the northern English lands that came to us through The Treaty of Durham, the same treaty that used me as a pawn to be Prince Henry's wife?

The people of Scotland I most wanted to love didn't yet know me, and there was much to accomplish before I could continue Henry and King David's work by serving them, especially the women in need of rights of property ownership after their husbands' deaths.

Several in the crowd came to congratulate me after pledging their allegiance to Malcolm. The ceremony went well into the afternoon. When the services were finally completed, we feasted into the night at tables set up by the riverside.

I sat on a dais between my two sons, King Malcolm and Prince William, fatigued beyond comprehension, barely listening to the conversations around me. Bells, the tabor, and pipes played through the evening and helped keep me awake.

In the crowd, I suddenly saw Boudica, the medicine woman and howdie I'd sent for the week before. She had knowledge of ancient Pictish customs and had supposedly lifted a curse from Malcolm as a babe. Most importantly, she may have answers to how my husband was poisoned.

I excused myself and guards followed me, assuming a threat still remained. The people bowed to me as I walked by. I smiled, inclining my head. When I approached Boudica, I took her by the arm, pulling her away from the crowd and closer to the river. "Did you know I called for your presence?"

"Tis why I'm here." Boudica tugged against my grasp. "Whatever that girl did, I'm not to blame."

I'd heard her say those words before of the witch, Jasmine, who I suspected created the poison that killed my husband. I'd found the same inside Malcolm's riding gloves. "I accuse you of naught." I led her to the river's edge where the noise of the current would cover our conversation. I motioned the guards to stand at a distance.

Boudica trembled like a child caught stealing. Some of her bluish-grey hair poked out of her scarf. Over her very ample body, she wore a brown tunic tied with a woven belt of many colors. A wool bag was tied to the belt.

I released my grasp. "Jasmine claimed Prince Henry fathered her daughter, Sophia. I found out the truth. It was Kelton, Henry's cousin." I spoke to her more gently than before. "I need to know if she was part of the scheme to kill my family and if she could create a poison that killed by contact to skin."

The howdie gazed out toward the darkness of the running river and shrugged. "I disowned me daughter after she killed a man usin' black magic—the worse thing anyone could do. Worse than cursin' your son. Worse than bearin' a misbegotten daughter."

My breath caught in my throat. "What . . . what did you say?"

Boudica turned to face me. "I speak freely now—and the truth. I've thought hard this past fortnight since Jasmine's death." Moisture gathered in her eyes. "I want to be in me granddaughter's life." She wrung her hands. "I have no one."

Dread weighted my soul. Sophia was Boudica's granddaughter? I had decided to keep Sophia as my own. "Your granddaughter?"

Boudica nodded. "Nae a one knew Jasmine be me daughter. I not speak it 'til now." She looked to the ground. "I be shamed by her evil doin's and moved alone to Whitfield, but she soon followed. I tol' her I would'na claim her as kin. She begged me to teach her me skills of herbs and such and tol' me she'd keep the secret of her birth if I'd make her me apprentice. I should have suspected, but did'na know she'd harm again. She got much gain by her wicked ways."

I sat speechless, wondering if her words were a lie. Would this change my plans to raise Sophia with my own children?

"I moved away again and had'na seen her for years 'til she summoned me to help her give birth. Ye know some of this." She shrugged. "I did'na know it was Kelton's child. Does that mean ye are keepin' her?" Boudica's eyes held sadness. "I don'na know how to dispute the royal family, but can ye let me have her? I'll take care of her and not let her become evil like her ma." A tear trailed down Boudica's cheek.

I'd grown to love Sophia and didn't want to give her away. Could I let my family have connections with a person like Boudica and invite her into our home?

Boudica's chin trembled. "Nae a one will know her parentage but ye and me."

I bit my lip. She was right. No one could prove Sophia's parentage. My close friends, the St Martins and Giffards, knew her to be Kelton's and Jasmine's daughter, but they did not know Boudica's connection. Would it be fair to Boudica to keep the knowledge hidden?

The howdie looked older than I'd seen her before. How much longer could she live?

She waited while I digested what she asked.

"Can I see her?" she said in a whisper.

I could not deny her. "Aye, but she's not here. She's with my younger children who are hidden in a safe place until the threat to our lives is lessened."

Historical Note

A Freedom Chain

by Brent Hinze, Ph.D.

Several years ago, Sarah discovered her 24th great-grandmother was Ada de Warenne, born some 900 years before in Surrey, England. Ada was not just Countess of Huntingdon, Princess of Scots, Queen Mother of Scots, and other honorable titles. I add to her appellations "Twelfth Century Advocate for Freedom and Women's Rights."

Sarah and I have walked the grounds of Reigate in Surrey, England, where Ada played as a child. While standing high on Haddington's scenic Nungate Bridge, we have delighted in the grace of swans swimming on Scotland's River Tyne. We've hiked the Haddington countryside to locate remnants of foundation stones of a nunnery that Ada contributed to house Cistercian Nuns, who had come to serve in East Lothian. We've often walked the beautiful gardens of St. Mary's Pleasance where some researchers have indicated is the location of the gardens of King David I, Ada's father-in-law, and the location of the Royal Palace of Haddington, a home where Ada resided after her husband, Prince Henry, died so young at about age thirty-seven. We have attended Sunday services in the nearby magnificent cathedral-like St. Mary's Church, where once stood a smaller church built in 1139, where Ada likely worshipped while in Haddington.

In addition to helping us experience the above sites and many more, our friend, historian Helen Robertson, also drove us north to the quaint fishing village of Crail on the northeastern coast of the Firth of Forth where Ada inherited Crail Castle, built by her father-in-law, King David.

As I have learned about Ada and the times in which she lived, I am pleased to share observations of three generations, Ada being the third, that form what may be viewed as links in a Freedom Chain leading to the increase of freedoms we enjoy in our world today.

The Dark Ages

Our story grows out of what has been called the Dark or Medieval Ages, roughly a thousand years from the 5th to the 15th centuries A.D. The first half of this period is heavily marked by wars and oppression. In the second half, we see a quest for greater individual freedoms and enlightenment.

It has been said, "When God wants to bring about a change for the better, He sends a baby into the world." In our story, He sent several babies in succession who, through an improbable series of events, steered the tiny island nations of Scotland and England onto a path that changed our world.

Let us remember that history depends on the information available, its accuracy, and our interpretation. What follows is my interpretation from the historical materials I have found.

Freedom Link One: St. Margaret, Queen of Scots

The first link in our freedom chain is Scottish Queen Margaret, the grandmother of Ada's husband, Prince Henry. In the 11th century, Queen Margaret, although by bloodline an English princess, was born and raised in the royal courts of Hungary. To learn how this came to be, we step back into history two more generations to a most intriguing story of survival.

Twenty-nine years before Queen Margaret's birth, her grandfather, King Edmund Ironside, was defeated by Canute the Great of Denmark who took control of the English crown on Christmas day, 1016. King Canute was described as an exceptionally tall, strong, and vicious Viking who ruled over the North Sea Empire of Denmark, England, Norway, and part of Sweden.

That same year, Margaret's father Edward, heir to the English crown, was born. King Canute manifested the typical paranoia of monarchs who feared potential rivals who might usurp and steal their throne—a throne that, in most cases, they themselves have usurped and stolen. King Canute had months-old Edward and his fledgling brother Edmund sent to the Swedish court of King Olof Scotkonung, a distant relative. The legends are sketchy here, but apparently King Canute directed King Olof to kill the small boys to eliminate any future rivalry.

Now we know that kings are more accustomed to giving commands than taking them, so Olof secretly refused the order of fratricide and sent the infant boys to his daughter, Ingigerd, Queen in Kiev, Ukraine. Thus, young Edward avoided the assassination attempt and grew to adulthood in Hungary where he became known as "Edward the Exile." Eventually Edward married Agatha, a German princess. They had three children. Margaret, the middle child, entered the world in 1045.

Margaret was born and raised in the decorum of the royal courts of Hungary. She was well educated and a very devout Roman Catholic. As her faith grew, so did her concern and sensitivity to the needs of the poor, a trait that would distinguish her all her life.

When Margaret reached age twelve (astonishingly the legal age of marriage for girls in that era), King Edward the Confessor regained the throne of England. Having no heirs, he invited Edward the Exile back to England as his heir to the throne. The invitation was accepted, but Edward the Exile would never be king. Suspiciously, within days of the family's return to England in 1057, he died. Poisoning was not ruled out.

Margaret, with her brother, sister, and now widowed mother, remained in England for the next thirteen years, when—surprise—the monarchy changed again. William the Conqueror, from Normandy, France, invaded and seized rule of England in 1066 by winning the famous Battle of Hastings. William de Warenne, Ada's grandfather, was awarded the Earldom of Surrey for defending William the Conqueror in this battle, thus becoming one of the wealthiest of Englishmen.

Within two years, Margaret, her mother, and younger sister, Cristina, no longer felt safe and moved north near the Scottish border in Northumbria. Younger brother, Edgar, a threat to King William's throne, was exiled to Normandy. Conditions worsened. Margaret, her mother, and her sister determined it was time to return to Hungary for their own safety.

As Margaret's ship attempted to cross the English Channel, a mighty storm arose, driving the ship northward up the Channel all the way to middle Scotland where they were propelled from the North Sea into the Firth of Forth. They reached land at a site on the northern shore that today is known as "Margaret's Hope."

What happened next lead to an unlikely union that would alter the future of Scotland. King Malcolm III showed up on the seashore to greet the survivors in person. One suspects the reputation of Margaret's great beauty may have had something to do with this personal welcome by the king. In spite of the battering survived by the three storm-bedraggled women, Malcolm was instantly attracted to Margaret and offers her, her mother, and sister asylum in his castle. The hungry, exhausted and homeless women see no other options and gratefully accept the king's invitation.

Thus, beautiful Margaret, driven to King Malcolm's very shores by a ferocious tempest, became virtually a captive in his castle.

A version of "opposites attract" appears to have been at play here. Malcolm has been referred to as a warrior king who gained the throne by killing. He was a warrior's warrior who presided over a kingdom of clans of similar rough and tumble nature, whom he personally led into battle on his powerful steed with sword at the ready. It's also said he lacked formal education, could neither read nor write, nor was he particularly refined in royal gentility.

By contrast, Margaret was highly educated, a devout Catholic follower of Christ, a faithful student of the Latin Bible, a daily patron of Mass, one who prayed and fasted often, and faithfully served the poor. She was trained in the etiquette and arts of royalty but had actually considered becoming a nun.

As it turned out, Margaret would never be a nun. Nor, so far as we know, did she ever make it back to Hungary. In spite of their differences, she and Malcolm found love together and married after about two years in Malcolm's castle. Thus, by age twenty-five, Princess Margaret of England became Queen of the Scots. She would reign twenty-three years. So beloved was she for her good works, she was labeled the "Pearl of Scotland."

We are indebted to Margaret's confessor and confidant, Turgot, prior of Durham and later Bishop of St. Andrews, for knowledge of Queen Margaret's life after she arrived in Scotland. Turgot wrote her biography twenty years after Margaret's death.

Margaret brought a degree of sophistication to Malcolm and his realm. It's said that he frequently asked that Margaret read to him from the Bible. He helped her build and support churches and establish Queen's Ferry for the poor and pilgrims to St. Andrews to cross the Firth of Forth. When not out warring, he joined Margaret in distributing food to the needy on the castle steps each morning. Following this tradition, Margaret invited hungry children into the banquet hall for breakfast, some whom, it's said, she literally took upon her lap and fed with her own spoon.

Malcolm once exclaimed, "I could not understand why my shirts kept disappearing. Then I caught my wife giving them to the poor. I should have had her thrown in prison...but how could I?"

In an era when girls of noble birth were often destined to enter arranged (and sadly loveless) marriages, Margaret and Malcolm achieved a great love. Together they had eight children, two daughters and six male heirs to the throne. Daughter Matilda became queen of England through marriage to Henry I. Three of the sons became kings of Scotland, two entered the priesthood, and the second daughter became a countess.

Although Margaret is said to have "tamed" Malcolm in some ways, he never lost his "warriorness." After all, a king has to defend his throne and his people. During the Middle Ages, some border lands passed back and forth between Scotland and England. In an attempt to regain those lands for Scotland, battles were fought and lost. In 1093, King Malcolm, at age sixty-four, raised yet another army and led an attack against northern England in an effort to recapture the lost lands. On the 13th of November, Malcolm and his eldest son Edmund were killed at war. Third son, Edgar, escaped and fled north to report the tragedy to his mother, Margaret.

I admit to being a romantic and find the rest of the story touching. The story goes that earlier Margaret had experienced a foreboding at the time the lethal arrow pierced Malcom's armor and entered his heart. I like to think this very different pair had built such a deep love between them that Margaret, by virtue of her spiritual sensitivity, could sense things happening to her husband even from a distance.

Margaret had been ill and with her foreboding the illness worsened. Within three days of her son, Edgar, returning and confirming Malcolm's death, Margaret's spirit left her body to join her beloved husband in the realms beyond. Margaret was forty-eight.

Prior to Margaret's storm-driven arrival, Scotland was described historically as divided, clannish, barbaric, illiterate, and battle-torn. Margaret tempered King Malcolm's reign. Together, the couple altered the future of Scotland. Joined by similar freedom quests in other nations, human rights and quality of life were evolving out of the Dark Ages.

So famed was Margaret for her kindness, fairness, compassion, charity, and faith that in 1250 A.D., about a century and one-half after her death, she was canonized by Pope Innocent IV. Saint Margaret's name is now seen on churches, hospitals, and schools in various nations of the world. Her memory is celebrated on an annual Feast Day, on the 16th of November, the date of her passing.

Freedom Link Two: David I, King of Scots

Saint Margaret raised exceptional children who emulated her admirable traits. Several sons became Scottish kings. David, the youngest, was the last son to become king. He has been labeled one of Scotland's greatest, known for his wisdom, fairness, and negotiation skills by which he at times resolved differences to avoid war and advance peace.

An interesting twist occurred here in our study of the remarkable people in our Freedom Chain. Nine-hundred-year-old timelines can be hazy, but it appears David was about twenty-eight when he married the older widow Maud. Earlier, at sixteen, Maud, great-niece of William the Conqueror, had been assigned to an arranged marriage with a wealthy forty-six-year-old noble, Earl Simon de Senlis. Maud bore Simon two sons and a daughter. Two generations later, during the Baronial Rebellion, one of their grandsons, Saer de Quincy, was among the twenty-five original signers of the Magna Carta.

After twenty-one years of marriage, Simon died, leaving Maud a wealthy widow; Countess of Huntingdon at thirty-seven. A year later, Maud married David, creating another unusual pair in that she was about ten years his senior. Nonetheless, they enjoyed a happy, loving marriage that produced four children. Their son, Henry, lived to become heir apparent to the Scottish throne following his father, King David I, and husband of Ada de Warrene.

In keeping with the male-favored laws of the era, when David married Maud in 1112, he acquired her lands and holdings and became Earl of Huntingdon, greatly increasing his wealth, influence, and reputation. The couple became king and queen some twelve years later.

King David carried on the good works of his mother, Queen Margaret. With Queen Maud at his side, the pair practiced

Christian values and continued to improve conditions in Scotland. David became known as the "Angel King." David and Maud were champions of freedom, worthy forerunners of the Magna Carta.

Dates are unclear, but it appears Queen Maud passed on before her younger husband, King David. Their son, Henry, was carefully groomed to become king after his father, but fate intervened.

Freedom Link 3: Ada de Warenne, Queen Mother of Scots

A Pawn for a King portrays the life of Ada de Warenne. This story illustrates how Ada represents another miracle in our Freedom Chain. Though she was married off as "a pawn for a king" into a politically arranged marriage, by the grace of God it was a marriage of happily shared love and mutual devotion to service. Ada's marriage to Prince Henry of Scotland in 1139 made her a Scottish princess. After only thirteen years of wedded happiness, Henry died before becoming king. What a shock to Ada, their children, and Henry's aging father, King David. Most Scots lamented Henry's premature passing, for they had looked forward to his reign as a great and just king.

Ada, after losing her beloved husband while still a young and beautiful woman, never remarried. She braved twenty-six years of widowhood during which she served as a mother, a grandmother, and a Queen Mother to her family and to her adopted people of Scotland whom she, like the Biblical Ruth "made her own people" in their march toward improved quality of life through greater rights, greater opportunities, and greater freedoms for all.

Conclusions

We have reviewed the improbable stories of three related couples from the small island nation of Scotland—Margaret and Malcolm, Maud and David, and Ada and Henry. In my judgment, these persons are among those to whom we are indebted for the quality of life we enjoy today. As if guided by the hand of Providence, these couples overcame obstacles to join together in love. In an era when marriages were often arranged among the nobility for political purposes, each of these couples was miraculously blessed with loving companionship. When royal power was often exercised for personal luxuries and pleasures, these couples used their royal influence to advance rights and freedoms for others.

Perhaps Ada's most potent link in the Freedom Chain was her impact on the legal system. Initially invited to witness and sign charters by her father-in-law, King David I, and husband Prince Henry, and later by her sons King Malcolm and King William, Ada de Warrene was one of the first women to be recognized as a legal witness. Previously, legal documents and rights of ownership were male dominated. Once the legal door opened, other women joined Ada, not only being recognized as legal witnesses, but also establishing the right for women to own property independently protected by charters (documents) signed and verified by legal witnesses—both men and women.

Within thirty-seven years of the death of Ada de Warenne, the growing Freedom Chain led to the Magna Carta, that "Great Charter of Liberties" established at Runnymede, England, 15 June 1215 A.D., identified by historians as the cornerstone of the British Constitution, and later the American Constitution. Lord Denning called the Magna Carta, "the greatest constitutional document of all times—the foundation of freedom of the individual against the arbitrary authority of the despot...."

In her 2009 book *Warriors and Wordsmiths of Freedom: The Birth and Growth of Democracy*, Linda McDonald-Lewis, born of a Scottish father, points out that on 6 April 1320 Scotland produced a similar document called the Declaration of Arbroath, sent to the pope as a declaration of Scotland's sovereignty and rights to independence from English rule. 456 years later, English control was again the motivating factor for the U.S. Declaration of Independence of 4 July 1776. Both the Scottish and American Declarations were framed and sealed or signed by representatives of the people.

The 14th century Scots chose Robert the Bruce as their leader, the first European nation to bring someone to power by the voice of the people in a manner representing modern democracy. Both documents supported the rights of the people to establish their own government rather than be controlled by monarchs or dictators.

During the birth of America, Thomas Jefferson and other Founding Fathers studied the ideas of enlightened leaders who advocated freedom and rule by voice of the people. This included the writings of Voltaire, French proponent of civil liberties who said, "We look to Scotland for all our ideas of civilization."

The Scots had a long and storied history of warfare in search of freedom as stated in these famous words in the Declaration of Arbroath: "As long as but a hundred of us remain alive, never will we under any conditions be brought under English rule. It is in truth not for glory, nor for riches, nor honors that we are fighting, but for freedom—for that alone, which no honest man gives up but with life itself."

How similar to U.S. founding father Patrick Henry's famous cry, "Give me liberty or give me death!" Or the (albeit fictional) cry for "FREEDOM!" at the execution of Scottish freedom fighter William Wallace depicted in the movie *Braveheart*.

And in the U.S. Declaration of Independence: "We hold these truths to be self-evident, that all men are created equal, that they are endowed by their Creator with certain unalienable Rights, that among these are Life, Liberty and the pursuit of Happiness."

What are the odds that the tiny island nations of Scotland and England would have such a powerful impact on our world? From both small and great we see our debt to people like Ada de Warrene, along with many others, who have led us to a greater vision for humankind—from monarchies to democracies and from oppressions to freedoms.

May the stories of Ada and her associates inspire in us the wisdom to appreciate and protect our freedoms while teaching our children to do the same. And may we do our part that the Freedom Chain may one day extend to all peoples and all nations around our globe.

Brent's reading list:
- Turgot, Bishop of St. Andrews, *Life of St. Margaret Queen of Scotland* (E-Book).

- "Ada de Warenne, Queen Mother of Scotland" (c.1123-1178) Victoria Chandler The Scottish Historical Review, Vol 60, No.170, Part 2 (Oct.,1981) Edinburgh University Press.

- Oram, David I: The King Who Made Scotland, Tempus, 2004.

- Hammond, Matthew H. (2011)" Women and the adoption of charters in Scotland north of Forth", ca 1100-1286, Innes Review, 62 (1), pp.5-46.

Medieval Palace Revealed

by Helen Robertson
(used with permission)

"The King's Yaird"

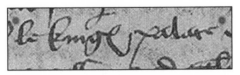

"le Kingis palace"

Introduction

The above image shows a northerly view taken from a drone hovering to the south of St Mary's Parish Church in Sidegate. The area within the [gray] boundary lines was known as the 'King's yaird' in the 1400s, hence the title on the main page.

> It's quite remarkable that this area of land can be traced back 850 years; that it remained within the same boundaries for almost 600 years (particularly after that 100-year break between 1560 and 1670); and that even today (2018), those original boundaries can still be clearly identified.

The name of the site has changed over the centuries, but the site within those boundaries appears to date back to the mid-1100s as a single identifiable unit.

In 1560 it was separated into lots when it fell into the hands of the local burgesses. One hundred years later, around 1670, those separated lots merged, returning it to its single unit status. However, 200 years after that, in 1878, the land was split permanently when an area of around 1¾ acres was sold to St. Mary's Parish Church to extend the graveyard.

The information contained in this paper relates to the piece of land within those yellow boundaries, or at least not too far beyond them.

The focus is on the discovery of early royal charters and primary source records, which indicate a royal presence in Sidegate from the time King David I held Haddington as one of his royal demesnes in the early to mid-12th century, almost 900 years ago.

To set the scene, (very briefly) the principle evidence (charters and primary source records) are shown [on the next page]. Those will be discussed in greater detail later as we move through the research.

Royal lands in Sidegate:

3 royal charters and 3 primary source records (PSR)

1180 – King's garden - referred to in a *royal charter* by **King William the Lion** confirming an earlier charter by the late Countess Ada (*this earlier charter must have been dated between 1152 and 1178, when Ada held Haddington*)

1245 - King's garden – *PSR (primary source record)* – the monks and prioress of Haddington settled their quarrel with the Priory of St. Andrews

1280 - King's garden - *PSR* – gardener received 18s4d for service in the king's garden and for having custody of the food supplies

1337 - King's orchard – *PSR* - no levies received as a result of the 100-years war. (*1337-1453*)

1477 – King's Yaird - referred to in a *royal charter* by **King James III** gifting the 'King's yaird' to Cockburn of Clerkington; Cockburn then gifted those lands to the Franciscan friars in **1478** at which time the King's yaird became known as the 'Freir croft'.

1498 – Kingis Palace – mentioned in a *royal charter* by King James IV

Private ownership of the land after 1478:

1477 to 1478 – Sir James Cockburn of Clerkington - gifted the 'King's yaird' by King James III.

1478 to 1560 – Cockburn gifted the 'King's yaird' to the Franciscan friars in exchange for a regular mass for his soul. It then became known as the 'Friars' croft'.

1560 – at the Reformation the friars handed their lands over to the town.

1560 to 1670 the former 'King's Yaird/Friars' croft' was split into 3 separate lots.

1670, 1673 and 1676 - three separate purchases were made by Alexander Maitland for the ground which later became the garden ground attached to Haddington House.

1878 - land belonging to Haddington House split again, this time permanently - 1¾ acres sold to extend St. Mary's church yard.

2018 - today the reduced area of ground accommodates: Haddington House; St. Mary's Pleasance; the private dwelling known as "Friars' Croft"; and the private car park belonging to the Lamp of Lothian Trust.

The image on [captioned "The King's Yaird"] identifies the sites relating to those early royal charters.

The remains of the early church of St. Marie and St. Michael lie beneath the choir of St. Mary's - its graveyard is beneath the nave.

In **1139**, King David I gifted that early church to the church of St. Andrews;

Between **1152** and **1178** Countess Ada gifted land to the early church (still in the hands of St Andrews); and

in **1225,** St. Andrews agreed the appointment of Haddington's first vicar, David de Bernham. 'de Bernham' was provided with a residence, garden and orchard lying to the west of the early graveyard.

King William's charter of **1180** confirmed an earlier charter by his late mother, Countess Ada. Ada's charter, gifting land to the early church, could only have been made while she held Haddington (between **1152** and **1178**).

The description of the gifted land in King William's charter was that it lay next to the graveyard; the 'king's garden'; and the 'house of Pagani'. The location of the house of 'Pagani' is not known, but there are two firm locations (the graveyard and the king's garden) which allows us to pinpoint the land gifted by Ada. I suspect that land became the vicar's residence and garden in **1225**.

Ada received her dower of Haddington in **1152** when she became a widow. Before that, King David I had control of all the royal lands in this area.

We now move on to explain how, purely by chance, I came across those charters and early records.

Research History

Haddington House – view from rear garden 2011   St. Mary's Pleasance – aerial view 2013

Original Research

In **2014**, my original research into the ownership and occupancy of Haddington House and garden between **1680** and **1970**, revealed that Alexander Maitland, the owner/occupant in the **1680s** did not buy the house and garden as a single unit. He made three separate purchases, each from different individuals, and each transaction referred to the land as formerly known as the 'Friars' croft' and before that the 'King's yaird'. Clearly, Maitland was buying up land which, at one time, had been in single ownership. I was intrigued. It would have been wrong to stop my research at that point. So,

I decided to carry on and see how far back my research would take me and I had some questions to resolve:

- how had that land become separated?
- who were those friars?
- And, what was meant by a king's yaird?

The next step was to study those transactions. I had listed all the transfers of land relating to the Maitlands' purchase to look for further clues (see Appendix ?). The lists revealed was that those transactions were all made by local burgesses, which, again, I found difficult to understand.

Arriving back at **1560** I felt I had reached a full stop. Even although I now knew that the earlier 'Freir croft' or 'King's yaird' had somehow found its way into the hands of the burgesses, I still didn't understand how this could have happened. I needed more information; I was finding it difficult to access information relating to the Franciscan friars; and to learn more, meant taking yet another step back in time – was it worth the effort?

But I didn't to give up, and perseverance paid off. Eventually, I found 'William Moir Bryce' and his two volumes relating to the Scottish Grey Friars. Vol. 1 contains the history, and Vol. II the documents. Those documents were the all-important copy charters, they were invaluable. At last I was able to make progress.

Dr William Moir Bryce was an Edinburgh lawyer and antiquarian. His two volumes were published around 1909 and they tell us a great deal about the grey friars' 300-year presence in Haddington. When those volumes were published, they also brought greater understanding to the writers and historians of that time. At last, the longstanding arguments about the identity of "The Lamp of Lothian" were finally put to rest when it was confirmed that the description 'Lamp of Lothian' referred to the early Franciscan friary and not to St. Mary's Parish Church.

See below scale image showing how Haddington town centre would have looked in the 12th century. http://www.gov.scot/Publications/1997/04/pan52.

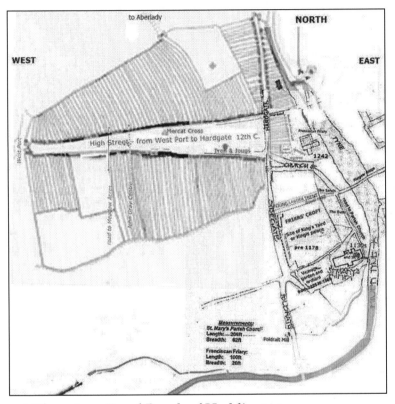

12th century Royal Burgh of Haddington

The image shows the 12th century royal burgh, as well as details relating to the Franciscan friary in the early 13th century. As the early royal burgh, and the Franciscan friary, each have relevance to this story I've included 'just a bit' about both.

The Early Royal Burgh

The image [on previous page] portrays Haddington's town centre in the 12th century. The sketch of the town centre, on the left, is borrowed from the Scottish Government's website, and it appears to have been drawn to scale, as the burgage rigs with their 20ft street frontages, seem to relate to what we can still see on the ground. It's combined with a separate scale drawing (again borrowed) which now includes the friary details and names and locations found in the early charters

But, let's look first at the early burgh.

It's well known that David I, king of Scots, introduced the burgh to Scotland, and conventional thinking dates Haddington's medieval town centre back to his reign between 1124 and 1153, but it must also be borne in mind that David ruled Lothian as 'Prince of Cumbria' from 1113, therefore his connection with Haddington may well have been earlier. The town's narrow street frontages, long narrow rigs, and former market cross, complete with unicorn (as shown on the sketch), mark it out as one of David's earliest royal burghs. Haddington was also a royal demesne in David's time and he would have had a royal residence/royal court in the town for his use when touring his realm.

Haddington's Royal burgh status is confirmed in several charters around 1140, when King David described the town as 'burgo meo'. But we don't need to seek out charters to recognise Haddington's rich heritage. A walk around the town can tell us so much about Haddington in medieval times.

From the West Port, proceed along present-day Court Street, down into the High Street; cross over into Church Street and continue along the route of the old 'common highway' to the site of the early church of SS Marie and Michael. Over the entire length of your journey you will be walking in the footsteps of those who lived-out their lives in the town, almost 900 years ago, and that route would still be recognised by those early residents if they could return today.

Haddington town centre, and its medieval quarter in Sidegate, still speaks volumes about its heritage. Beyond the town, it's no secret that 'Haddington has one of the best-preserved medieval street plans in the country' – but are many people in Haddington aware of this?

John Richardson, a former member of Haddington's History Society certainly was aware. An article in the Scotsman in 2006, provides us with his view: (it's an opinion I share)

"Haddington was one of the first of the Scottish royal burghs to be created. Granted its charter in the 12th century by David I, and with its surviving (just) medieval layout, it is of national, possibly international, historic significance. It is an architectural gem with many extremely fine, listed buildings in a highly attractive townscape".

The very early history of Haddington and its royal connections is sadly neglected, and all but forgotten. Hopefully the emergence of an early royal presence in Sidegate will be followed up, as it has the potential to stimulate a revival of interest in the distant past.

Also by Sarah Hinze

Nonfiction

- *Memoirs of Sarah Hinze, The Memory Catcher: Capturing the Memories of Heaven*
- *Memories of Heaven*
- *The Announcing Dream* (Revised & updated edition of *We Lived In Heaven* and *Coming from the Light*)
- *The Castaways: New Evidence Supporting the Rights of the Unborn Child* (15th Anniversary Edition)
- *Songs of the Morning Stars* (Revised edition of *The Castaways)*
- *We Lived in Heaven* (Revised edition of *Coming from the Light*)
- *The Castaways*
- *Coming from the Light*

Fiction

- *A Pawn for a King: Ada de Warenne 1123-1178*
- *Queen Mother to the Kings of Scots: Ada de Warenne 1123-1178* (coming 2021)

Find all her books at www.sarahhinze.com

Made in the USA
Columbia, SC
23 September 2019